W9-BJQ-805

OCEAN VU, JOG TO BEACH

OCEAN VU, JOG TO BEACH
A Novel

CLEMENT BIDDLE WOOD

A THOMAS DUNNE BOOK

ST. MARTIN'S PRESS—NEW YORK

For Jamie,
present at the creation,
and
for Clem, Cabell, and Connie,
who will know why.

OCEAN VU, JOG TO BEACH.
Copyright © 1988 by Clement Biddle Wood. All rights reserved.
Printed in the United States of America. No part of this book may
be used or reproduced in any manner whatsoever without written
permission except in the case of brief quotations embodied in
critical articles or reviews. For information, address St. Martin's
Press, 175 Fifth Avenue, New York, N.Y. 10010.

Design by DIANE STEVENSON/SNAP•HAUS GRAPHICS

Library of Congress Cataloging-in-Publication Data

Wood, Clement Biddle.
Ocean vu, jog to beach.
I. Title.   II. Title: Ocean vu, jog to beach.
PS3573.0589024   1988   813'.54   88–1983
ISBN 0–312–01830–4

First Edition

10 9 8 7 6 5 4 3 2 1

ACKNOWLEDGMENTS

Jessie deserves a medal for her patience and devotion during the writing of this book. My thanks to Alex, Shana, Leigh, Michael, and Val for pampering me at crucial moments; to Joanne for the title; to my namesake and my brother Bill for advice on law; to Heyward for checking the Russian; to another Bill and to Daniel for counsel on rugby; to Buddy for his knowledge of the track; to a different Michael for consultation on arbitrage; to Bob and Mary Ellin and yet another Bill for reading and advice, heeded or ignored; to Millie for speed and accuracy; to Owen and one more Michael and Tom and Sandy for everything; to Marion, Roger, Sally, Tommy, Wendy, Alexander, Susan, and Lucy for Y-person chatter; and finally, to Caroline and Floyd for a key conversation that made a superannuated preppy rethink his career priorities.

—CBW

CONTENTS

And summer's lease hath all too short a date . . .

> —Shakespeare, Sonnet XVIII

The youth of America is their oldest tradition.
It has been going on now for three hundred years.

> —Wilde, *A Woman of No Importance*

MAY DAY

1

THE GROUPER PHENOMENON: A CAPITALIST EXPERIMENT IN SEASONAL COMMUNAL LIVING

Groupers: *the word—Scope of this study—The Young Urban Professional subcaste—The author's credentials—On language, formal and colloquial— The author's apologia for his methodology—The specimen Y-person C. WHEELWRIGHT described— Summer rental as a career decision*

Groupers!

In the beginning was the word. I fell in love with it.

Say it, roll it on your tongue, taste it, shout it, carol it. The syllables sing. The growl of the GR, the croon of the OU, the pow! of the P, the purr of the ER, the zizz of the soft S. Groupers.

GROUPERS was my original title for this work, a fine and poetic title, but it confused my publishers, who chose another. Publishers, after all, are paid to be commerce-minded clods. It was to me, a poet, a poet making his first voyage of exploration in the many-splendored language of these United States, that "groupers" sang.

In fairness to my prose-packagers, I must admit that most native speakers of American English are unfamiliar with the term in its colloquial sense. When I first heard my young American friends apply it to themselves, I went to the dictionary and was surprised to read that a grouper was "any of several serranoid sea basses, esp. of the genera *Epinephelus* and *Mycteroptera*, found in tropical and subtropical seas," the word being derived from the Portuguese *garupa*.[1] My friends are not fish. Thinking I might have misheard them, I read the entry immediately following: "*groupie,* n., *Slang,* a young girl devotee of rock-'n'-roll musicians, esp. one who follows them to make sexual conquests."[2] Bah.

Here then was I, émigré and immigrant with the ink still moist on my visa, I, poet, word-worshiper, half-trained ethnologist and linguistics scholar, I, face to face with a neologism so recent or so obscure that the lexicographers had overlooked it. "Then felt I like some watcher of the skies / When a new planet swims into his ken."[3]

Listen as I might to the conversation of my new American

---

[1] *Random House College Dictionary* (New York: Random House, 1975) p. 584.

[2] Ibid.

[3] J. Keats, a poet who, although British, is sometimes allowed a guest appearance in the textbooks of my new country.

friends, I could not divine the meaning of the word from context. Much later, after they had learned that I could, in a pitiful way, speak their language, I went to my friend Clive Wheelwright and asked in my comic accent, "What please is grouper?" (When speaking AmerEng, I, like many recently arrived Russians, grandly ignore the definite and the indefinite article.) A specialized term, Clive told me, used in the jargon of residents and realtors in certain resort areas. He himself had never heard it until Mrs. Slocum told him and Moira about local anti-grouper ordinances while showing them her house. Her definition was as follows:

"Groupers are groups of ten or twelve or heaven-knows-how-many young people who rent your house and get drunk and smoke marijuana and throw wild parties and disturb the whole neighborhood and leave the place a perfect wreck."

To which Clive and Moira could reply only with such conventional pieties as "Good Lord" and "How awful."

Certainly the two of them never thought of themselves as groupers. No more did I when I accepted my sweet Cathy's invitation to visit them all in Hastings. No more did any of the others, except for my friend Stu Stuart, incurably gregarious, forever short of funds, who enlarged the group by recruiting Dreda Scott and the brothers Degan; Dreda in turn brought in first Chip Buford and later Baudouin, Vicomte du Boisdormant.

But I digress. This is not to be an account of Mrs. Slocum and her young tenants, nor of the dismaying things that happened in and to her beautiful and historic house.

I propose, rather, to offer an in-depth investigation of the concept "groupers," a prose documentary on the behavior of those who "group," a sociological study of a houseful of persons belonging to the category Young Urban Professional[4] with whom

---

[4]Also called "young upwardly mobile professional," the *m* in "mobile" being ignored in formation of the acronym.

I was privileged to live for an entire summer in cheek-by-jowl contiguity.

They treated me, these groupers, more as a pet than as a person. Clive, as tall as I am tiny, would sometimes pat my gleaming pate while giving me orders; the beguiling Cathy enjoyed combing burrs and snaggles out of my beard; Stu, when he felt the need of company, would whistle for me. Mostly, however, they ignored me, and it was in these times of neglect that I, their cunning little Russian teddy-bear, could study their behavior most closely.

To understand the grouper, one must first understand the Young Urban Professional, the socioeconomic stratum to which virtually all groupers belong. Many readers of this work will doubtless be academics, hence unaware not only of the term "Young Urban Professional," but of the acronym derived from that term and of the diminutive derived from that acronym. The American popular press (*Newsweek, Time, New York, Vanity Fair, Women's Wear, W*, and the like) discovered or invented this new class a few years ago and has written of little else since. In time of economic boom, these young men and women were hailed as a vanguard; when the market crashed, they were pronounced—to the glee of many—extinct. In fact they go marching on, indomitable. They are said to be "upwardly mobile" (a cant term), interested in "fitness" (another), in "cuisine" (their word for cooking or ordering food), in the acquisition of apparel, gadgetry, or anything else that can be described as "designer."

The author of a celebrated comic strip has dubbed them "Y-persons." His satiric instinct is accurate: members of this new caste never in their own conversation use the popular diminutive by which outsiders refer to them. It would be misleading to say they shun "the Y-word" as if it were an obscenity, for obscenity looms large in the speech habits of many Y-persons. My friend Stu Stuart is a prime example.

Countless articles and even a tongue-in-cheek "handbook" have been published concerning these young persons (the word "person" is much in vogue in their milieu), but to my knowledge, no serious study of them has yet been undertaken. Here I shall examine the cases of seven such persons, a point platoon of traditionally materialist and ruggedly individualistic young Americans who have rallied to the battle cry, "I want it all and I want it now." Yet—and this is what fascinates me, born and raised as I was in a socialist society—these children of capitalism chose to live for many months in a commune: not a commune in the Marxist-Leninist sense, nor in the quaint 1960s counterculture sense, but a consumer commune of their own devising.

What, the reader may ask, are my credentials as a social scientist? If the name of V. Y. Ouspenskiy has any renown, it is as a poet; few know of my murky past as a fledgling social scientist. Before I emerged as a cult figure in Moscow's literary bohemia, I was a student. A student must study something. Like many another indolent youth, I opted for the biggest, vaguest subject of them all. Came the day when I found myself flunking sociology; I sought refuge in linguistics. Flunking that, I became a poet. Such was my success that jealous literary *apparatchiks* classified me as a "dissident" poet. So here I am, an apprentice American.

(Ouspenskiy, Ouspenskiy! Look at yourself. Lured back into sociology, and all because you fell in love with an obscure but beautiful American word!)

I choose to write this work in English, a language which for me is a torture to speak. My Russian accent ("Rossian oxsent") is ludicrous—nay, excruciating. Luckily my pen is nimbler than my tongue. When studying linguistics, I concentrated on English and AmerEng, while dabbling in Tatar, Chechen, Uzbek, Doric Greek, Latin, *Mittelhochdeutsch*, and French. My formal English prose is passable. The informal AmerEng in this text reflects the speech patterns of my Y-persons. Those familiar with my verse know of my tumultuous love affair with the Russian colloquialism; they should not be surprised to find me casting a raffish eye upon her American cousin.

As to methodology, I haven't any. The organization of a prose work is beyond me. This could well be why I fled from academe into the all-forgiving embrace of poetry, a field in which the incoherent is often mistaken for the avant-garde. My plan (for I do have one) is to examine the behavior of the specimen Y-persons not over the entire period that I "grouped" with them, but at five carefully selected "points in time" during that summer. (I am being swallowed alive by American culture; native speakers have discarded the handy "now" for the cumbersome "at this point in time.") It is my intention to take my young upwardlies one by one and study the case history of each with socio-scientific detachment. Can I discipline myself to do so? I doubt it.

Yet it must be correct to begin with the model Y-person C. Wheelwright; it was Clive who signed our lease, Clive who became our leader and, when we turned to sport, our captain. (Co-captain, to be exact. Clive was obliged to share that honor with his antithesis, the renegade Y-oid Stu Stuart.) But enough of parenthetical digression. Let us now put our smear of a certain American subculture upon the slide and focus our microscope upon the organism known as

WHEELWRIGHT, CLIVE R. ► *twenty-eight years of age; tall, lean, wiry; blond hair; ruddy complexion; wears glasses. Habitually serious, as befits a young lawyer. Native of Maine. Schooling: Penobscotport Academy, a private school[5] of which his father has long been headmaster; B.A., Dartmouth College; J.D.,*

---

[5]The curious term "private school" is explained in chapter 3, *infra*.

Columbia Law School. Employed at the time I met him as a junior associate at Tucker, Edgway & Masoch, an improbably large New York law firm. Residence at that time, a building on Central Park West: splendid address, minute apartment with view of airshaft, shared with his then fiancée Moira Fairchild, of whom more below. Despite earnest mien, C.W. has mild sense of humor.[6] Is a compulsive sportsman, or "exercise freak." When in city, runs six miles (9.6 km.) a day in Central Park; feels guilty if he doesn't. Skis, plays racquet games, enjoys contact sports, e.g., ice hockey, rugby. Happiest when sailing. Put him in a boat and the grave young lawyer vanishes. Imagine a clean-shaven, bespectacled Viking; you have imagined Clive afloat.

With that information, we are ready, reader, to move on to the first of my points in time,

SATURDAY, MAY 1

On May First of last year, when our study begins, there are no displays of tanks and gymnasts and party leaders in New York, such as one would see on May Day in Moscow. For Clive and Moira, it is simply a fine spring day, a Saturday, a good day to drive out to the country and implement the "career

---

[6]Extremely mild. For example, when I told him what the dictionary had to say about serranoid sea basses, he consulted the encyclopedia and decided I would be amused to learn that a certain grouper, *Epinephelus nigritus*, is known as a warsaw. To a Russian, there is nothing amusing about Warsaw.

decision" they have jointly made. They anticipate heavy expenses in the near future: their wedding reception in October,
for which, since both sets of parents are insufficiently affluent,
they themselves will foot the bill; their honeymoon, which, by
the rules of their caste, must be spent in a place their friends
have never visited (they have chosen Sri Lanka); the purchase
of their apartment, which is about to "go co-op." In spite of
these considerations, they have decided it would be "productive" both "careerwise" and "healthwise" (hereafter I shall dispense with the quotes on such words) for them to get out of the
city on summer weekends. The "must place" (there I go again)
is Hastings (where else?) on the South Fork of Long Island's
East End, halfway between the Shinnecock Canal and Montauk
Point. (I must discipline myself parenthesewise as well.)

Picture them then in Clive's sensible Subaru, leaving Manhattan on that balmy May morning by the 59th Street Bridge
(no toll: they believe in small economies); imagine them (but
do not imagine that I, Ouspenskiy, am imagining; all that I
write is based on notes or tapes of conversations with the persons under study) speeding eastward. They do not think of
themselves as the founding members of a capitalist/consum-
erist summer commune. Yet before this May Day is over, that
is what they will become.

2

LOCUS
DETERMINED

The Long Haul, eastbound—The specimen Y-person M. FAIRCHILD, described—The Slocum House, locus of the communal experiment, found, inspected, coveted—Workings of the legal mind—A unilateral decision

It is, as they would say, an awesome day. Clive notes blueness of sky, greenness of certain trees in new leaf, pinkness of others, goldenness of down on the cheek of the girl beside him, whiteness of gulls as they soar overhead, their woebegone cries drowned out by the roar of the Long Island Expressway. Skillfully (he likes to think he does everything skillfully) he drives through light-to-moderate traffic, enjoying the responses of the Subaru, admiring the high-tech emerald digits on the dashboard, maintaining seventy-five in the clear, easing back to sixty when his radar detector beeps. (Very well then, he did not tell me all this in conversation or interview, but I have driven with him on this very road; I observe; I am a poet; I know things.)

As they drive, they talk about Hastings.[7] It is less than two hours from the city, a high-prestige area, key for networking, with upscale restaurants, country lanes for jogging, the great Atlantic beach. For Moira, there will be the sun to worship and the local artists' colony to scout; for Clive, jogging and Mr. Edgway.

The ninety-one mile (145 km.) stretch from New York to Hastings, which Clive and his fellows, under summer weekend traffic conditions, will come to know and dread as the Long Haul, is today a pleasure jaunt. Not long after crossing the Canal, he swings left off the Highway to follow the back roads to Hastings. Back-roadmanship, they have been told, is essential for survival in summer. Moira holds the county road atlas open upon her rosy knees, but Clive, a navigator born, has done his chartwork before leaving home port. They drive through gently tilted fields, fringed on the north by wooded landswells which the map calls hills. Crops are greening. Huge potato barns, half submerged in the earth, rear up here and there. On glassy ponds Canada geese nibble and doze. Above the flat

---

[7]Sometimes called Hastings-by-the-Sea, to distinguish it from nearby Hastings Haven and the more distant Hastings-on-Hudson, Hastings Center, and plain old Hastings, all of which are in New York State.

landscape hangs what Moira is moved to describe as a Fragonard sky.

And here, reader, I am moved to describe Moira; then back, I promise, to our study of specimen Clive.

FAIRCHILD, MOIRA L. ▸ *Like Clive, twenty-eight; like him, tall, blonde, wears glasses; appears serious, even severe. Yet behind her severity lies mischief. When Moira is amused by one of Stu's outrageous remarks, or by some naïve comment that her sister, my sweet Cathy, has let slip, the cheek muscles in her long, oval face quiver, her fair skin flushes a delicate pink, her lips part in a delightful half smile. (Not a digression, the girl is charming.) What else? Born and raised in a New Jersey exurb (which, I am told, is something better than a suburb), father a middle-level executive for an oil company, mother a busy committeewoman, particularly "big on Bloodmobiles." M.F. works for Art Futures, a trendy (I have resisted putting that in quotes) gallery on Manhattan's Fifty-seventh Street. Education: New Jersey public schools;[8] B.A., Barnard; a year at the Rhode Island School of Design, from which she withdrew after deciding, in her common-sensical way, that she had insufficient talent to paint paintings for a living but enough to peddle them. Has lived with Clive for nearly three years. They consider themselves perfectly matched. (We shall see.)*

At Hastings, a village with colonial frame houses and many a discreet boutique, they cross the Highway at the traffic light and cruise south toward the ocean. They have heard that the summer rental market is off this year, that by avoiding agents and stopping at every FOR RENT sign, bargains can be found.

---

[8]Not to be confounded with the *British* public school. *Vide infra*, chapter 3.

The first house they visit is too "pricey," the second too "down-scale"; the third "the pits"; the fourth, they agree as they turn into the driveway, is "it."

(Oh, those quotation marks!)

Clive parks the Subaru next to a Dodge hatchback in the driveway and walks with Moira toward an old shingled farm-house, to which a cool Victorian veranda has been added. A white-haired woman rises from a flowerbed, pulls off her gardening gloves and introduces herself as Lavinia Slocum.

Let us look at them now, our two young upwardlies, through the eyes of this prospective landlady. Both are fair, clean-cut, handsome, serious. He wears an immaculate gabardine suit, yellow silk tie, blue button-down shirt, running shoes; she is in a cashmere twin-set, tweed skirt, loafers. If you, reader, had a house to rent, you'd beg them to take it.

In effect, Mrs. Slocum does so. Waving her hand toward a privet arch framing a narrow vista of dune and blue horizon, she announces: "Eleven minutes' walk to the ocean."

In the garden Clive feels guilty. There are daffodils, pansies, tulips, forsythia fading, dogwood coming into bloom, and a quorum of other vegetation he can't identify. Somehow he managed to grow up in the wilds of Maine without learning the names of birds, trees, or flowers. When Moira says, "What lovely aqualigia," and kneels to look at them, he thinks for the nth time how perfect she is, how they complement each other. He also makes a mental note: Crash course on natural history urgent. Self-improvement is ever on his mind.

They walk back to the house across a broad lawn, meticulously trimmed, ready and waiting for croquet. As they follow Mrs. Slocum up the steps of the back porch, Moira squeezes Clive's hand and whispers, "I'm in love with it already." Her breath is warm in his ear. He tries not to think about the price. They have agreed that seven thousand for the season is an absolute ceiling for them. This place, he is sure, will rent for far more.

The house is beautiful. The kitchen, gleaming with copper

pots, has a microwave, even an icemaker. In the living room and library, Clive looks first at the clipper ship prints, then at the family portraits and hand-carved mantelpieces, while Moira admires a set of Hepplewhite chairs, a Queen Anne table, an Adam sewing stand, a Chippendale armchair and secretary. He imagines himself seated in that chair, working on some leveraged deal for Mr. Edgway. There is, Clive and Moira notice, no television set. On their way up to the second floor,[9] Mrs. Slocum pauses on the stairs and peers at them sharply.

"You two do know about the anti-grouper laws?"

"What are groupers?" they ask in unison.

You already know her answer. She delivers her definition: "Groupers are groups of ten or twelve or heaven-knows-how-many young people who . . . [et cetera, et cetera, *vide supra*] . . . and leave your house a perfect wreck." You also know the replies of our young couple, "How awful" (Moira) and "Good Lord" (Clive).

Mrs. Slocum goes on up the stairs. "There's been terrible trouble here with groupers. Whole neighborhoods kept awake all night long, people's houses and furniture dreadfully abused. We've had to pass laws to protect ourselves against them. I hear they've done the same in other summer communities—the North Shore here on the Island, the Cape, Nantucket, the Vineyard."

She shows them four bedrooms—three with fourposters, one with twin beds. On every bed is a homemade counterpane. The single bathroom is a museum of the Victorian plumber's art: tub on claw-and-ball feet, toilet with wooden seat and overhead box, brass chain with enameled pull. Moira is entranced.

The mention of anti-grouper ordinances has made Clive think of what his professors at Columbia had to say about unenforceable laws. As they start up to the attic, he asks Mrs. Slocum to give him some examples.

"The most important one," she tells him, "is that there must

---

[9]First floor, European count. Americans have built their country from the ground up!

never be more than five cars in the driveway of a rented house at any time."

"No problem, there are just the two of us and the Subaru. Anyway, I'll be working most weekends. A senior partner in my firm has a place out here. He'll keep me busy."

"You're a lawyer, Mr. Wheelwright?"

"Corporate law. I do LBO's, mostly. Leveraged buyouts."

"My goody, all that still goes on, even now, after the crash?"

"Yes. We're busier than ever."

Moira explores the attic, which is clean and spacious, with one old couch and a few trunks. "I'll be working too, Mrs. Slocum. My boss at the gallery wants me to scope out the art on the local scene."

"You're married?"

Clive chooses his words with lawyerly care. "We're about to be."

He hasn't said when; she doesn't ask. Apparently reassured, Mrs. Slocum leads them back downstairs to the living room, where Moira exclaims over a coromandel screen.

"We call it the Cap'n's screen." Mrs. Slocum nods toward the portrait of a seafaring man over the mantel. "Cap'n Caleb Slocum brought it back from Canton in the 1850s. There've been Slocums in this house for over two hundred years. First time it's ever been rented. Taxes! And my daughter's having a third child, she needs me out in Denver. I'll be gone all summer, might as well rent, much as I hate the thought of strangers living here. I've advertised." She shows them a clipping from the local paper, the *Conquest*. The ad begins with the words OCEAN VU, JOG TO BEACH. Mrs. Slocum goes into the kitchen; they follow. "Frankly, I didn't care for any of those others who came round." She puts the kettle on the gas ring. "Seeing the two of you has made me feel better. No pets, of course."

Moira tells her she is allergic to both dogs and cats; this is news to Clive, who has been thinking of giving her a puppy for her birthday.

"No drugs." They nod. "No wild parties, not that you look to be the type." Mrs. Slocum sets out her Lowestoft tea service. "House guests are all right, in reasonable number. I have no maid and no gardener. You'll promise to weed and water?" Clive assures her that Moira has a green thumb. "Good. Then I'm going to ask you a very modest rent." Moira and Clive exchange glances. Here it comes, they think, the bottom line.

Not yet. Mrs. Slocum pours hot water over the tea in the pot, leaves it to steep, slices a lemon, takes her cinnamon toast out of the toaster oven. (*Vot kak*, you are thinking, this is sociology? May we not be spared this leaf-by-leaf account of the traditional Long Island tea ceremony? To which I reply that everything, the whole ball of wax, is sociology to V. Y. Ouspenskiy. Remember that I came to know C. Wheelwright and M. Fairchild well; I was to meet L. Slocum at the end of summer. My approach is to hear the specimens under study speak, watch them move, tape their accounts when possible, make notes when not, then to reconstruct their behavior as if I had been present. Call it creative sociology if you will, but bear in mind that a poet has vatic powers.)

Just as captains of industry or chiefs of state, before settling down to discuss matters that may cost billions of dollars or lives, will ask each other, "How's your golf game?" or "How are the wife and kids?" Mrs. Slocum chooses to dally over the preparation of tea, rather than name her price. Meanwhile our two Y-persons think about the house. Clive's memory has been stirred by the musty smell of starch and mothballs in the closets and by the dull glow of wax on the random-width oak flooring, which remind him of his childhood in the rambling, turn-of-the-century Headmaster's House at Penobscotport Academy. For Moira, there is a sharp contrast to her family's lakeside custom rancher in northern New Jersey, all machine-hewn beams and plate glass, where her father, a transplanted Californian, comes home from the refinery he manages in Elizabeth to pretend he is living in a hunting lodge on Lake Tahoe. I, Ouspenskiy, have seen Clive and Moira's apartment on Central Park West, which is full of quaint Danish Modern furniture from the early 1950s and huge, inchoate paintings on loan from Art Futures. The Slocum House is another world.

Clive, normally the most prudent of men, is about to behave rashly. Working within him are the appeal of the old farmhouse; a liking for Mrs. Slocum, who so obviously wants them to take it; love for Moira, who has fallen head over heels for house and contents; the quite human and specifically Y-person wish to appear more prosperous than he in fact is; all of these, plus plain old lawyerly cussedness, which has been snarling within him like acid indigestion from the moment he heard about the anti-grouper ordinances. Such regulations, he thinks, may or may not be constitutional, but they exist, and if they exist, his legal training tells him, there is a way to get around them. Such is the legal mind.

The tea tray is ready at last. Mrs. Slocum carries it into the living room and settles herself behind it. On pins and needles to hear what rent she will ask, Clive and Moira watch her pour.

"Now. The terms of the rental. I'm renting for the usual season, from the Friday before Memorial Day to the day after Labor Day. Sugar, dear?"

Moira asks for one lump with lemon.[10]

"Where was I? Oh. Fifteen thousand for the season, five thousand payable now, the rest when you move in." The flush on Moira's face fades. Clive's mind races. "If you'd like to look at the lease, Mr. Wheelwright, it's there on the table beside you."

He picks it up, scans. It is standard boilerplate, with a few lines typed in concerning pets, drugs, and "strict observance of all ordinances of the Town of Hastings prohibiting group rentals."

He pulls out his checkbook and says, "Mrs. Slocum, five thousand now, you said? How would you like it made out?"

Moira looks as though she might fall through the floor.

---

[10]Unusual. Somebody has convinced the majority of Y-persons that sugar is bad for them.

3

NUCLEUS FORMED

W*hat does not concern us—What does—Further workings of the legal mind—Recruitment for the commune—The specimen Y-persons S. STUART and C. FAIRCHILD described—A celebration—Recruitment continues—The specimen D. SCOTT described—C. BUFORD not described, and why—The criminal element?—The journalistic mind—The Long Haul, westbound*

Bear in mind, reader, that you and I are not interested in the Slocum rental *per se*. What does concern us is the manner in which our specimen Y-persons form their seasonal commune, and why. Summer in the Hastings area (they are addicted to the word "area") is important ("key") to them not simply for the beaches, sea, and sun, which they could find in other places equally close to New York, e.g., the Jersey shore. The very name "Hastings" has a resonance for them. In Hastings they can expect to find colleagues and rivals who, like themselves, are trying to claw their way upward in their chosen fields. They can hobnob with these peers, exchange information, conspire with—or against—them in their career climbs. (This process is known as "networking.") Also in Hastings, sequestered in ostentatiously rustic houses close to the beach, many of the city's rich and successful estivate. Y-persons may associate on an informal basis with those who are their present or potential bosses. We shall see an example of the former in C. Wheelwright's relations with the senior partner N. Edgway and of the latter in D. Scott's *démarches* toward C. Herkimer, from whom she hopes to wheedle a job.

Scaling the ladder is a vicious game in all societies. Read Gogol, Dickens, Balzac. In the Soviet Union competition is fierce among career officers, bureaucrats, and members of the Party hierarchy. I, Ouspenskiy, have shamelessly licked the boots of better-known (but worthless) *samizdat* poets and nudged aside, not to say squashed, lesser versifiers in the course of my upward soar in Moscow's literary underworld. But what a complex behavioral code these ambitious young Americans are obliged to observe! Note in particular the fashion in which they form their commune. They seem to find one another by chance; their joining of forces appears casual, even slapdash—"laid back," they would say. Although this is a pose—they speak often of "role-playing"—the pose is chosen by the *poseur* (a bilingual pun!); for the poser, it becomes reality. (Another *jeu de mots*: "poser" may also mean "a question or problem that is puzzling or confusing.")[11] Upwardlies strive at all times to give the impression of "being on the fast track," yet laid back. Self-deception is key in the behavior patterns of these capitalist/consumerist young burghers and indeed in every facet of American life.

Back now (as they say on the "soaps" on the "tube") to Clive and Moira, who have taken leave of their landlady and are settling into the Subaru.

"Five thousand!" Moira cannot contain herself. "And ten later! Clive, you know we can't afford it. There's the wedding, the honeymoon, and the mortgage, with we don't even know yet how many points."

"Not to worry." Clive snaps his seatbelt, looking over at her to make sure she has done the same. He is obsessively careful, or so she always thought until he wrote the five thousand dollar check for Mrs. Slocum. "No sweat. We'll get another couple in to share the rent."

"Groupers!" A tremolo in the first syllable shows that Moira is at this point in time anything but laid back.

He begins talking in his lawyer's voice. She has always preferred his real voice. "Mrs. Slocum said we could have house guests 'in reasonable number.' I propose to invite two house guests to share the rent, two being by any definition a reasonable number. What is more reasonable than to ask one's house guests to chip in on expenses?'"

Clive pulls out of the Slocum driveway into Slocum Lane and turns right, toward the ocean. Moira is silent; he interprets her silence as assent. In three years with him, she has learned one thing thoroughly: rationalization is the handmaiden of the law.

They park in a deserted lot behind the dunes and leave their shoes and socks in the car, which Clive of course remembers

---

[11]*Random House College Dictionary,* op. cit., p. 1034.

to lock. Once he has rolled up his gabardine slacks to the knees, he is ready for the beach.

That beach, reader, is unbelievable. It stretches on and on for a hundred miles more or less from Montauk Point to Brooklyn, with a few gaps, as at Fire Island. Today it lies before them, broad, white, and empty, the ocean sparkling, one sail on the horizon, sandpipers racing along the water's edge, wavelets curling toward shore. Moira thinks of a Fairfield Porter beachscape; Clive thinks, this is it! He throws back his arms and gulps in lungful after lungful of salt air. She loves him for that. A part of him, she knows, is always off sailing on Penobscot Bay. She thinks how right he is: this is what it's all about, why they want to be here.

Clive suddenly grabs her hand and starts running toward the ocean. When she feels its icy coldness on her ankles, she shrieks—then reproaches herself for succumbing to the female stereotype. He kicks water after her as she runs back up on the beach, and goes on kicking, kicking for pure joy, raising little geysers, scooping up handfuls of salt water and rubbing it over his face, his hair. Watching, Moira realizes how hard it must be for him to live boxed in by the gritty concrete of Manhattan. From his office window, he can see a tiny sliver of the East River, the color of Nescafé laced with CoffeeMate.

When Clive rejoins her on the beach, his glasses are covered with beads of water. He methodically cleans them with the treated cloth he carries for that purpose. Then he puts his arm around her waist and they begin to walk along the shore. Moira feels better; she has had an idea.

"About the house. There's my sister. Cath is looking for a quiet place to work on her book. I wouldn't be surprised if she were out here right now."

He looks dubious. "She's still with Stu?"

"What's wrong with Stu?" Moira knows what is wrong. Clive likes Stu—everybody does—but he is thinking that a whole summer with Stu is a whole summer with a whole lot of noise.

A deafening voice behind them bellows, "Yo, Clive!"

Moira starts to say something about an amazing coincidence; Clive turns just in time to catch the football spiraling toward his head. Trotting across the sand to them comes Stu Stuart, a man who never goes anywhere without a football. Behind him is Moira's sister Cathy, a small and (to my mind) bewitching girl.

My file cards on the two Y-persons now coming into focus read as follows:

STUART, STURGIS MacR. ▸ *twenty-nine, known as "Stu." Short, powerful, barrel-chested, a bundle of nervous energy ("hyper," his peers would say). S.S. never speaks; he yells. Is an archetypal "jock," and indeed it is easy to imagine him rushing around some locker room in his jockstrap, snapping wet towels at bare bottoms and whooping for joy. Has a jock's incipient beer belly and a jock's dream job: reporter for* Sports Illustrated. *Professional football is his specialty, the Dallas team his obsession. Is careless, to put it mildly, with money. Father, retired army officer; mother, divorced and remarried. Typical army brat childhood at posts in Texas, West Germany, Belgium, Kentucky, Japan, Maryland. Speech is laced with archaic World War II obscenities. Education: various military and private preparatory schools, including (briefly) Andover; West Point (two months), University of Virginia (slightly longer), other state universities. No degrees. Living, at period under study, with C. Fairchild in rent-controlled shoebox apartment in Brooklyn Heights. Has surprisingly beautiful golden eyes.*

FAIRCHILD, CATHERINE H. ▸ *twenty-five, three years younger than her sister Moira, whom she both*

*admires and deplores as a "straight arrow." Tiny,
pretty, with enormous eyes, speaks in a breathless,
piping voice that makes every man she meets feel she
is desperately in need of his protection. Has a style
all her own. In clothing, favors 1920s flapperwear:
the sleeveless, breastless look. C.F. is a young novelist,
under contract to publisher Duff/Lorenz for her first
book. Her short stories have appeared in obscure literary reviews. Parents: see FAIRCHILD, M. Residence: see STUART, S. Education: Public schools,
New Jersey; B.A., Sarah Lawrence; M.A., Columbia,
in something called "creative writing."[12] What more
to say? I worship the ground she walks on.*

The meeting on the beach is anything but coincidental. Cathy
knew Clive and her sister were in Hastings, and Stu can sniff
out anyone anywhere.

"Saw your heap in the lot!" he shouts at Clive. "What's the
story?" Stu always asks what's new, what's the story. "Find a
house yet?"

Moira smiles; all is going according to plan. "An awesome
house. We were thinking maybe you two—"

"How much?" Cathy asks in her tiny voice.

Clive has not only caught Moira's look; he has seen her point.
If they share the house with her sister and her sister's live-in,
no one can accuse them of grouping. Noise and all, it makes
sense.

"Seventy-five hundred," he says, "for the two of you, for the
season. Twelve-fifty apiece now, the other twenty-five hundred
apiece by Memorial Day."

The air is rent by Stu's whistle. He punches Clive's shoulder
twice; he always converses by physical assault, stands close to
the other person, shouts in his face, keeps nudging, poking,

---

[12]A preposterous phrase. All writing is creative, even writing a check. Ask Stu.

touching. "Okay!" he yells. "I'll spring for half of the seventy-five!" All three of them turn and look at Cathy.

She stands there in the freshening easterly wind, hugging her bare arms. Thirty-seven hundred and fifty dollars is a lot when you are trying to live on an advance from a publisher, especially if the publisher is Duff/Lorenz. She knows they all want her to say yes. While at the moment she has the money, all signs point to Stu being broke. He is sure to end up by borrowing from her. There are times when he seems to have wads of money. Then it is gone, but where? Betting? Drugs? When it comes to Stu, her novelist's imagination fails her.

He is barking at her now. "Come on, Cath. The Hastings area is crawling with writers, wall-to-wall publishers, agents. That'll inspire you."

"How can I say no to you, Stuey?" Her voice is barely audible. Stu punches her arm. "She got to yes!" All at once he is sprinting toward the ocean, yelling at the top of his lungs. "Going out for a pass—he's behind the 'Skins' secondary— Danny White throws—"

Clive realizes he still has the ball. He throws; he overthrows. Stu runs out into the ocean—Italian cords, tasseled loafers, and all—to make a great catch.

"He hauls it in—and Stu Stuart is going all the way! The Dallas stands go wild!"

Stu lives his Dallas Cowboys fantasy. Now he has drawn Clive into it. The sisters watch their two men run shovel passes and line bucks through the wavelets. They are in total contrast, concave Clive and stocky Stu. Moira thinks, antelope and buffalo. Cathy's comparison is literary, Ichabod Crane and Brom Bones.

The nucleus of the commune is forming. We shall soon see other particles drawn into the field.

Before long they are all at The Village Pub, a shadowy place with a long oak bar, tables with red cloths, a mural depicting the memorable amphibious landing at an even more famous Hastings. The dining area is called The William the Bastard Room. Somewhere along the way the sisters have made a shopping stop (for them, reader, there is always a shopping stop), and Cathy has bought several postcards showing HISTORIC SLOCUM HOUSE, C. 1760. These and a copy of the lease lie on the table as the waitress brings them their drinks—a bullshot for Stu, wine for the others.

Clive, to affirm his leadership, makes a toast. "In this overpriced domestic Meursault, I drink to the four of us. To a happy and productive summer."

They clink glasses and drink. Moira raises hers again. "To Cathy's novel."

Cathy feels guilty. At the moment her novel is a very quick read. "This had better be the perfect place to work, guys. If I don't turn in my draft by September First, the publisher gets to rape me or something."

As usual, Stu is restless. He stands up and loudly announces, "Got to piss." The people in suits at the next table, undoubtedly local real estate agents, turn and look at him. Cathy watches him go. Instead of heading straight for the men's room, he makes a tour of The Pub. Today, four weeks before the season begins, the place is all but empty. Beyond the realtors' table sit several seedy-looking men and women in gardening clothes, probably some of the artists and writers who live in Hastings year-round. Cathy sees no famous faces.

Stu is working his way over to a corner table where two thickset men in dark pinstripes are eating in silence. Mafia, Cathy thinks. (All Americans consider themselves infallible in identifying Mafiosi. They can tell by the blue jowls, the double-breasted suits with padded shoulders. For even the most sophisticated, these criminals are vested with a mythic glamour. Is *The Godfather* the American epic?)

The two burly men are completely out of place here. Stu's

journalist's eye has been on them ever since he came in. Now he pads toward them, rolling a little on the balls of his feet, a grizzly on the prowl. One of them, Cathy sees, is unfolding a large sheet of heavy paper, possibly a blueprint or a survey. Stu tries to peer at it over an upholstered shoulder, but has to turn away when both men look up and glare.

At the same moment the back door of The Pub opens and a young couple comes in. The girl gives a cry of joy—"Stu Stuart!" Stu throws wide his arms. "Dreda baby, come suck face!"

They fall into a hug. To Cathy's eye, the girl called Dreda looks cute as a button, smart as a whip, and preppy[13] as a topsider. She is also black. Although black preppies are rare, Cathy knows at a glance that Dreda is the real thing. She is wearing a Madras jacket, pink polo shirt, leg warmers, Bermuda shorts. Behind her hovers a young man, also black, also a preppy, in red flannel shirt, Norwegian fisherman's sweater, yellow slicker, and L. L. Bean boots.[14]

Dreda is happily patting Stu's belly. "Old Stu-pot. I've been reading your stuff in *Sports Illustrated*."

---

[13]*Preppy.* Another socioeconomic classification, used informally to describe persons who have attended "preparatory" (or "prep" or "private") schools. I have heard middle-aged Americans boast of the large sums (tuition) they have paid to send their children to such places. Why? In the USSR all education is of course at state expense; the very term "private school" strikes me as oxymoronic. Graduates (alumni) of these schools are absurdly proud of having attended them. Again, why? To go to a secondary school not open to the general public is surely an antisocial action. In recent years such schools have sought to mask their traditional elitism by accepting a limited number of black or other "ethnic" students, e.g., Dreda Scott. It is clear that these institutions seek to turn suitably intelligent minority children into surrogate Wasps (White Anglo-Saxon Protestants, formerly a majority in the US, now the largest minority, fighting a stubborn rearguard action). By the way, these American private schools are said to be roughly equivalent to what the English call "public schools." On learning this, I despaired.

[14]I am indebted to Cathy for these vestimentary details. Preppies tend to favor certain traditional uniforms. Their "dress code" is strict, conforming to a costume lore handed down from generation to generation.

"You'll see a lot more when football begins. They hardly know what to do with me between Super Bowl and pre-season. So what's new, Dreed, what brings you here? Hey, want some grouper space?"

"Try me."

While Stu leads her over to the table, we shall again refer to my file cards:

> **SCOTT, DREDA** ▸ *twenty-seven, pretty, black, bright. Works for AstroSums, a firm of arbitrageurs in Wall Street. Education: French lycées in Abidjan, Rio, Washington, Rome, Paris; Phillips Academy, Andover; B.A., Yale; M.B.A., Harvard Business School. Father a retired foreign service officer (?); mother a successful decorator; they live in Georgetown, a fashionable quarter of Washington. D.S. rents a high-tech loft in East Village. Is perhaps an unwitting feminist, chooses men she lives with, invariably "under-achievers": dominates them. Is indistinguishable in dress, speech, and manner from Caucasian prep peers. Successful case of assimilation into white mainstream? Conscious of having been co-opted? These are posers.*

> **BUFORD, CHARLES P.** ▸ *twenty-eight, black, answers to "Chip," a "live-in" of Dreda's.*

I got this far on Chip's file card and thought, why bother? The reader will presently see why.

"New input for the house!" Stu yells as they reach the table.

"My old Andover buddy, Dreda Scott . . . Cathy, Moira, Clive."

Dreda tosses her chin toward the black prepster behind her. "And this is Chip."

"Hi."

To the others, Chip seems handsome but listless. Everyone they meet is "on the make," and if a person happens to be black, he or she is expected to be three times as aggressive. Not Chip. There is no chip on Chip's shoulder.[15]

Stu pulls up chairs; the newcomers sit down. Clive can feel Moira's tenseness, knows her mind is on the anti-grouper clause in their lease. They both see what is coming.

"So what's the story, Dreed? Still on the Street?" Stu is proud of her, wants them all to admire her. "Arbitrage—Dreda's an arb. Bottom-line her on the house, Clive."

"Twenty-five hundred for a one-sixth share." Not looking at Moira, Clive pushes the lease and the Slocum House postcards toward Dreda. He and Moira can each afford a quarter share at thirty-seven fifty, but Cathy showed hesitation, and he has heard that Stu is "flaky"[16] about money. In any case, Clive's hand is forced. The two candidate housemates are black. If he were to say that no more shareholders were needed, Dreda and Chip might jump to the wrong conclusion. A further consideration: if these two come in, he and Moira will save twelve fifty apiece.

Dreda studies a postcard for a millisecond and throws it back on the table. "I'll take a one-third share for five thou."

"A third? Why a third?" Stu's usual shout has become a roar. "What's with Chip? Unemployable? Trust fund go bust, or what?"

"Stu-eee! Personal questions!" To Cathy it often seems that Stu's conversation consists entirely of such questions. She could (as she would put it) die.

Dreda smiles. Her eyes crinkle, her dimples ride out into her cheeks. "It's just that Chip and I don't know how we'll correlate."

---

[15]My apologies. The English language is my new toy.

[16]I considered appending a glossary of such expressions, but no, let the reader learn from context.

"Too much." Chip sounds world-weary. "Dreda is too much."

Cathy studies the new majority shareholder. Even in Bermuda shorts, Dreda has a way of crossing her maple-sugary legs that girls with generations of Foxcroft behind them might envy.

Stu whistles for the waitress. "Another round! See what these two want—Miss Arb and Mister Bean."

While they are ordering, Moira leans toward Clive. He gets in the first word. "We'll save twenty-five hundred between us."

"But the clause about group rental . . . "

Clive puts on his legal face. "Mrs. Slocum mentioned 'ten or twelve or heaven-knows-how-many.' We're only five, with Dreda."

"Six. Chip makes six."

"Chip is not taking a share. He is obviously pro tem." Clive looks at Moira over the top of his glasses, a mannerism copied from Mr. Edgway. "You and I don't count; we're the tenants of record. We have three house guests—your sister, her roommate, and said roommate's former classmate. No one could call three a group."

From across the table, Cathy sees Moira's cheeks flush, her mouth set in a spinsterish line. She knows from childhood that these are storm warnings. To her great surprise, Moira controls herself; she even manages a smile.

"You're the lawyer, darling."

She calls him "darling"! Cathy is thrilled. How Victorian, she thinks. Dare she put a "darling" into her novel?

Drinks come. Food is ordered, awaited, eaten. Stu cross-examines Dreda on her work in the city.

"Arbitrage has changed in the three years I've been on the Street, and I'm not talking about the so-called crash. The latest thing is big Koreans."

"You did say 'big Koreans'?"

"Japanese, too, Chinese, even, all over six feet, the women about five-ten, from the B School or MIT. They wear tweeds, mostly."

"What else do they do?"

"Work like crazy, to screw regular Americans like you and me out of our jobs. Haven't you noticed? The Street is swarming with them, the whole city."

The waitress brings the bill. Clive takes it, reaches for his credit card. Watching him sign, Stu thinks, what a great guy. When the great one pulls out his pocket calculator, he springs to his feet.

"This time I really do have to piss."

"Hold it. Your share is $25.96."

Caught, Stu pays. His wallet is wiped clean. He retreats to the men's room, where he can't help begin to wonder how he is going to come up with his twenty-five hundred for the rent. As of now, he owes Clive a third of that; he thinks of it as "eight and change." The only thing to do, he decides, is to write a check and hope it doesn't reach his bank until after payday. Then there is the matter of his overdraft. Borrow, he thinks. Or bet? Or a little dealing?

On his way out, he again swings past the corner table. One of the pinstripes, the larger of the two, folds up the sheet of heavy paper when he sees him coming. Again they glare.

Outside, Stu finds the others saying things like "*Ciao*" and "Till Memorial Day." Four cars are at the curb: Clive's Subaru, Dreda's new BMW, his own battered old Skylark—and a large black Cadillac limousine with tinted windows and Nevada plates. He nudges Cathy. "Big Vegas money for sure. You can bet your sweet ass those two honchos aren't out here for the ladies' doubles."

Stu walks completely around the Cadillac. His notebook is in the Skylark, but since he happens to be carrying Cathy's postcards, he jots down the license number on the face of one of them.

Buckling himself into the Subaru, Clive watches. "My God, he's going around that limo again, snuffling like a basset hound all the way. Next thing you know, he'll raise his leg."

Moira stands up for Stu. "After all, it's his business to be nosy."

There is no way, reader, for them to know that Stu's interest in the Cadillac and its occupants will ultimately lead Moira to make an uncharacteristically selfless gesture at a moment of decision in her professional life, alter forever the course of Clive's career, and bring to Stu himself a taste of fame and a chance of fortune.

They race. Clive's Subaru, Stu's Skylark and Dreda's BMW go roaring down the Highway, the Bypass, the Sunrise, across the Canal, up the Cutoff, then westward into the setting sun, toward the Apple.

Dreda wins. She reaches the Tunnel in eighty-one minutes, a time that none of them, try as they may, will be able to approach when summer comes.

Next day Stu remembers to ask Cathy for the postcard on which he wrote the license number.

"I mailed them all, Stuey."

"*Mailed* them!" He stamps around the tiny apartment. "Mailed them! Just like that! Wrote your little hi there's to your little friends and mailed them, mailed *mine*. Jee-*zus*, women are inconsiderate."

S. Stuart's rage, reader, is of little consequence to us. Our concern is the summer commune.

Locus determined. Nucleus formed.

MEMORIAL DAY WEEKEND

4

NUCLEUS

EXPANDED

I, Ouspenskiy, got the postcard. The numbers scrawled across the façade of the house caused me great anxiety. A code? KGB? FBI? The message on the back posed a poser:

> **Dear Vlady——**
> **Will be in this amazing house with**
> **friends all summer. We move in May 28th.**
> **Come out and see us!**   **Love,**
>   **Cathy**

The poser: Who was Cathy?

Rather, *which* was Cathy? Since arriving in New York three weeks before, I had met a number of American women, but apart from the deputy director and one or two secretaries at the US-Soviet Union Cultural Relations Institute, I knew the names of none. This Institute came into my life at the time I left Moscow. I shall explain how.

Western anthologists of Soviet verse describe me as a "dissident" poet. They are wrong. In my own mind I was never a dissident. Toward the end of my linguistics period, I applied for an exit visa, thinking to delay my dissertation by going to the States for a year or two of study under the vaunted Chomsky. Nothing was heard of this application until some years later, when suddenly out of a clear sky the visa was granted. Since I had by then become a big man in the *samizdat* poetry game, I no longer had the slightest wish to leave the Soviet Union, but the authorities seemed most anxious for me to go. My half-hearted application for an immigration visa at the United States consulate in Moscow was received and expedited with astonishing zeal. Perhaps through computer error, the Americans thought me an important cultural defector, a lyric Solzhenitsyn. Within a week I was New York bound, my ticket having been provided by USSUCRI, the US-Soviet Union Cultural Relations Institute, which I suspected of being a front for KGB, CIA—or both.

Arriving in New York, I discovered to my surprise that US-SUCRI had published a book of my poems the year before; my royalties came to $56.42. To supplement these earnings, the Institute arranged three poetry readings for me, one at a bookstore in SoHo, the other two at USSUCRI itself. After each session, there were invariably a few persons from the audience (and invariably these persons were women) who came up and enthused over me. I hoped that "Cathy" would prove to be neither the large woman in the brown suit who spoke rapid but ungrammatical Russian, nor the plump and earnest Slovene graduate student from NYU. The one I wanted her to be was the small doe-eyed darling who had attended all three readings and apparently spoke no Russian at all.

Who, I wondered, would take it upon herself to address me as "Vlady?" My given name is Vladimir; certain boyhood friends in Novosibirsk used to call me by my patronymic, Yurevich. What American female would be so brash as to sign off with "Love?" (I naively failed to recognize the banality of this complimentary close. In the days when the US still had adequate telegraphic service, "love," I am told, was jocularly defined as "the tenth word in a telegram." It seemed to me that only the delicious doe-eyed one would presume to such familiarity.)

I marked May 28th on my calendar. A Friday. It was worth a chance. Besides, I was hungry.

Do not assume that I refer to sexual hunger; I had met scores of Soviet dissident women in New York. (Does dissidence stimulate the libido? I think yes.) None could cook. (Is there an inverse correlation between dissidence and gastronomy?) The fact is, I was starving. I could afford only the aptly named "junk food." But there is no need to describe here my first weeks in this country. I was in no position to meet Young Urban Professionals, the subject of this study. My readings earned me just enough to pay the shocking rent on a shocking room, with a view of the Queens entrance of the Queens-Midtown Tunnel. Here I sat disconsolate day after day, cheered only by the old comic books left by some earlier tenant in the dark and roach-ridden cupboard. I became fascinated by the dual persona of The Man of Steel/mild-mannered Clark Kent and began an essay demonstrating the authors' debt to Dostoevsky's "The Double," then desisted. Through leads given me by other *émigrés*, I sought to find a position as an instructor or poet-in-residence at various institutions of higher learning in the city. Each time I was turned down. The "Rossian oxsent" did me in. I was one unhappy "dissident."

Picture then this downhearted poet and scholar wandering amid the pre-holiday hordes in the cacophonous caverns of Penn Station on the morning of Friday, May 28th. Although I succeed in finding a timetable, the 11:32 train to Hastings eludes me. (The difficulty proves to be my unfamiliarity with the curious concepts A.M. and P.M.) I am frantic: "Cathy" expects me (does she not?), and hunger gnaws.

Meanwhile, at the far end of Long Island, our Y-persons are flocking in like birds of prey, ready to swoop—and group.

Moira and Clive have both taken the day off from work. Arriving early, although not as early as expected because of the already heavy traffic on the Expressway, they go over the inventory with Mrs. Slocum and help her pack her luggage, mostly gifts for her grandchildren in Denver, inside her Dodge hatchback. Clive then gives her a check for ten thousand dollars, the balance due on the rent.

The history of this check is of interest in our study, as indicative of the differing relationships between our specimen Y's and the *primum mobile* of their society. Stu's check for his one-sixth share of the balance due, $1,666.67, has bounced once, been represented and, to the surprise of all including its maker, cleared on the second try. Dreda's one-third of the ten thousand dollars was in the money market working for her right up to the close of business yesterday, May 27th; her check reached Clive's apartment by courier at eight o'clock this very Friday morning, May 28th. He has noted that it is for $3,333.33; he had billed her, as the largest shareholder, for $3,333.34. On Cathy's contribution there has been no problem: she has decided to defer payment on all her credit cards until the following month, by which time she hopes she will sell a short story or win the state lottery. Moira is borrowing her share from Clive until the following Wednesday, when she has a certificate of deposit coming due. He has gallantly waived interest.

Mrs. Slocum stands beside the Dodge, ready to go. "I must be the luckiest woman in the world. First, to have three months ahead of me with my adorable grandchildren, and second, to have found two such fine young tenants."

The young tenants feel guilty about not being as fine as she thinks them. This guilt arises partly from the awareness of three (not to be described as four) house guests (not to be described as groupers) lurking in the wings, and partly from an irrational shame over not being able to afford such a house on their own.

"If you want to keep the house a little longer in September, that's fine, Mr. Wheelwright, but I'd have to ask two thousand a week."

"Thanks. We'll stick with Labor Day, Mrs. Slocum."

On an impulse, the landlady kisses them both before settling herself behind the wheel. She then removes her shoes. "Always drive barefoot!" A roguish wink. "Good-bye, dears, and have a lovely summer."

They trot down the driveway alongside the car. Moira gives a final wave. "Good-bye, don't worry, we'll take good care of everything."

As soon as the Dodge has turned into Slocum Lane, Clive says, "I'll call them," bounds up the porch steps and hurries into the house.

Stu takes the call at The Village Pub. On this Friday of the first big weekend of the season, the bar and William the Bastard Room are both packed. He has to raise his voice far above its normally high decibel count to make himself heard.

"Yeah? . . . Yeah? The old bag finally blew? . . . Thanks, Clive, we'll be right over." He hangs up, emits a shattering whistle and strides toward the door, followed by Cathy, Dreda, and Chip. Trailing behind them, Cathy notices, come two hulking young men in tee shirts.

Bumper-to-bumper traffic inches through the town. After much backing, filling, hand-signaling, cursing, and honking, Stu and Dreda succeed in wedging their cars into the motorcade. Just behind them, in a small and ancient Volkswagen, are the two hulking youths. When the Skylark and the BMW turn right at the traffic light, the VW turns too.

Cathy is uneasy. "Stuey, I think we're being followed."[17]

For once he says nothing. He maneuvers the Skylark through a gridlocked intersection, leaving the other two cars far behind.

When he reaches the Slocum house, Stu unstraps his trail bike from the roof rack, then begins lugging in a part of his splendid collection of sporting bric-a-brac: tennis, badminton and squash racquets, riding boots, lacrosse stick, English croquet set, golf bag, and more. Cathy follows him, carrying her suitcase, her electric typewriter, and the precious but slender folder containing the typescript of her novel. Dreda and Chip, who have by now caught up, enter the house behind the other two, with her Vuittons, portable computer, and stereo equipment.

The four of them dump everything in the hall and go through the open door of the library to check in with Clive. He is seated, hard at work, in the Chippendale armchair, with yellow legal pads and law books strewn over the Chippendale secretary, the Early American settee, and the floor. His peers are irritated. Clive has appropriated for himself one of the downstairs rooms, and these are supposed to be for the use of them all.

---

[17]Being American, she fears muggers, not the KGB!

"Comfy, Clive?" Dreda says. "Hope that chair is ergonomic."

"Yes, thanks, it's user-friendly."

Stu kicks at the piles of papers. "Place is a pigsty already!"

Clive looks up, just in time to see two hulking persons appear in the doorway. Each is carrying a case of Budweiser. Stu ushers them into the library.

"Group, meet Mort and Rick Degan. Mort is the big mother."

The Degans set down the beer and come forward to crush Clive's hand. He is impressed by their size. Mort looks to be about six-six, 255 pounds, while Rick is only six-four, 240.[18] Both wear dirty white tee shirts marked "B.C.A.A.,"[19] running shorts, soiled white athletic socks, and gym shoes.

Moira comes in from the garden with freshly cut lilacs. She takes one look at the Degans and blurts out, "Where are you two staying?"

The brothers look aggrieved.

"Here," Stu says. "I signed 'em up. Two more bodies, means we pay less than two thou each for the season."

Dreda promptly gives the correct figure. "Eighteen seventy-five apiece."

Cathy crosses to the desk and breathes in Clive's ear. "Please say yes, Clive-o. I'm living beyond my means." She has never called him Clive-o before.

Moira says in a dry voice, "We're full."

"Hey, you said four bedrooms," Stu yells. "They can take the one with the twin beds."

"No way," Dreda says sharply. They all turn to look at her. "Matter of principle. I'm paying double, I'll take the twin beds." Their eyes shift to Chip, who looks at the Bokhara carpet. Dreda pats his head. "Nothing personal, Chipper. Just keeping my options open."

He is silent; Clive feels sorry for him. Dreda has shamed him

---

[18]198 cm., 116 kg. and 192 cm., 111 kg.

[19]Boston College Athletic Association.

before the others, but Chip takes it with the Christian for-
bearance drilled into him in four years at Groton.

Stu pokes Clive's arm with his elbow. "Remember the Degan
brothers, all-time all-timers at right and left tackle for B.C.?
Tried out for the Steelers. Herniated, so now they sell insurance."[20]

"Fine," Dreda says. "They can tackle a double bed."

"Mort and Rick don't give a shit where they sleep; they're
animals, for Christ's sake."

Rick is furious; Clive can understand why. They have all
been talking through their Ivy League adenoids, as if the Degans weren't in the room, about whether they are good enough
to join the club. Probably, Clive guesses, Stu met the brothers
for the first time less than an hour ago at the Pub and all but
fell on his knees to beg them to group with him. Now he is
calling them animals. Rick looks ready to break him in two.

Mort, evidently the more placid Degan, clamps his huge hand
on his brother's shoulder and says, "Yuh, sure, double bed. It's
only weekends, what do we care?"

Rick glares murderously at Mort, who has dishonored them
both; he has as much as admitted they are animals.

"Take a vote!" Stu shouts. "All in favor—"

"It's my decision." It is Clive's first word on the Degans. He
looks at Moira. To his surprise, she nods. He waves his hand
grandly Deganward. "Welcome to the group." Clive turns and
stares sternly at Stu. "That's eight. No more."

Stu is overjoyed. "Now you're talking. Mort, Rick, give the
man a check. Clive, baby, I'm overpaid. Gave you twenty-five
biggies. You owe me . . . seven?"

Again Dreda has an instant answer. "Six twenty-five." She

---

[20]Selling insurance, for reasons I fail to fathom, is considered a somewhat sub-
Y occupation. I shall use this as a pretext for not producing file cards for Rick
and Mort. The true reason is that in the drama of the commune, they are spear
carriers—or, as Stu has aptly put it, "More bodies."

obviously can't believe that other people are incapable of simple mental arithmetic. "And me twelve fifty."

When Clive reaches for his checkbook, Moira says to him in a low voice, "Stu's in over his head. I wanted to be supportive of him." Clive is surprised; he was sure she nodded yes out of concern for Cathy.

Rick sits down to write his check, but the chair squeals in protest. Moira prods him.

"Rick, a house rule. You and Mort keep off the Hepplewhites." He stands up, looking pained.

Dreda, too, looks pained. Clive realizes that he and Moira have been laying down house rules and making decisions without any thought as to who is paying the biggest rent.

"I suppose you and Clive have taken the best room?" Dreda gives Moira an acid smile.

"Of course. We got here first." Moira sweeps out of the room, lilacs and all.

Writing out the refund checks, Clive admits to himself that he is pleased with the Degan decision. For weeks he has been bothered by the thought of the fourth bedroom going begging.

Dreda is at his elbow. "Yes or no—do you intend to preempt this library all summer?"

Clive puts on his fairminded-lawman face. "Good point, Dreda. Sorry. I'll move all this stuff up to my room."

She accepts her check and goes out into the hall. "You've got to hand it to the Wasps," Dreda says to Chip, making sure her voice is loud enough for Clive to hear. "They've perfected the art of turning the other cheek. And when they do, they break wind in your face."

"Stuey, if we want the *second*-best room, we'd better grab it." Cathy rushes into the hall, picks up suitcase, typewriter, typescript and makes it to the stairs before the overburdened Chip and Dreda. "Clive-o," she calls from halfway up, "give Stuey my refund, will you?"

Stu hangs over Clive, watching him write out the checks. Presumably to flaunt his pack-leadership, he has chosen to do so in slow motion. Behind him, Stu can hear Rick grumbling to Mort.

"Hey, I thought there'd be extra quiff. These here are all paired up."

The brothers give Clive their checks and go up to claim the third-best double bed. Stu is now alone with Clive. His jubilation over the $625 refund is gone. Now he is feeling jumpy because his check for $1,666.67 cleared on second presentation yesterday. The fact that it did can mean only one thing: his check to Max, his bookie, had not yet reached the bank. It has been many weeks since Stu brought the stubs in his checkbook up to date, but he can imagine Max's check bouncing like a beachball. Check to Max, nine hundred and change, he thinks. Nine twenty-five? Nine fifty? He leans over Clive's shoulder. Inspiration strikes.

"Hey, not six twenty-five, twelve fifty. You forgot Cathy's share." When Clive lays down his pen and peers at him over his glasses, Stu thinks fast, talks faster. "Didn't you hear her?" He mimics her voice. " 'Clive-o, give Stuey my refund, will you?' " Clive hesitates; Stu touches his arm, speaks confidingly, man-to-man. "Cathy owes me a thou."

He watches Clive write the check. Pay to the order of Sturgis Stuart, one thousand two hundred fifty dollars.

"Say, you couldn't make it cash?"

"You're right. I couldn't."

Tight-ass Yankee bastard, Stu thinks as he leaves, check in hand. Soon they will hold a house meeting: his chance to challenge the ruling oligarchy.

Clive tries to concentrate on the legal document before him. Proofreading, usually a joy to him, has lost its savor. He is alone, but the tensions of the others linger in the room like groundfog.

Moira returns with the lilacs, prettily arranged. She sets the vase on the desk, looks at Clive, ruffles his hair. "Cheer up. Eight is a lot, but you'll see, we're going to have a fun summer."

He picks up the document, hands it to her. "Scope this out, darling. Draft of our prenuptial agreement."

Formation of nucleus completed? Not quite. There is a ninth body still to come—a foreign body.

5

WORKPLAY

T he workplay concept—Workplay of commune members viewed from periphery—A workplay injury—Workplay of a novelist—Work and workplay of two lawyers—Of an art dealer—Of an arbitrageur—A journalist at workplay—No workplay for the author

"Workplay" is an original concept of mine, a key component in Ouspenskiy's sociological matrix. For a while I toyed with the idea of coining a word with a Greek or a Latin root: *ergo-paegnia, laborlude*. *Werkspiel* must exist already; so workplay it is, meaning the intrusion of elements of play into work and of work into play. Examples are everywhere: four tycoons playing golf, a Dallas Cowboy, a movie crew, soldiers on the rifle range, a presidential press conference.

No one practices workplay more strenuously than upwardly mobiles. The slump in the economy has been a spur to them. Gallantly, they workplay—and consume— even more fervently than before. They will tell you they work hard; they will also say they play hard. The phrase "We play hard ball here" belongs more to the office than the ballpark; a "ballpark figure" is a rough estimate in dollars and cents; one "plays the market," et cetera. Y-persons, however, seem unconscious of the fact that they work while playing and play while working.

Once one has accepted that God is dead, [21] once one has looked at the so-called leaders and the nuclear armaments of both my homeland and my adopted country, [22] one is obliged to conclude that there is no future in heaven or earth. This is as true, of course, in the Soviet Union as in the States. Nearly all Soviet citizens of my generation take refuge in cynicism, hedonism, or apathy. The American Y at least believes in a *short-term* future. Whether that future lasts for one year, or for three, or even for another generation, *something* must be done with the time. There being no God and no long-range future, nothing is left but work and play. You may ask, what of love? One has only to glance at the sex manuals found on the bedside tables

---

[21]Most Y's have. The fault lies with their parents, with media philosophers, and with history. They concede, however, that church is not only a convenient place for a wedding, but cheaper than anywhere else.

[22]Everyone on earth under forty has grown up under a mushroom cloud. Could there be a book in this?

of all Y's to know that for them, love is work. They have chosen another form of gratification: dominance. This can be gratifyingly asserted either in work or in play.

No one has yet told them that play is supposed to be fun.

A peripheral view of the commune's workplay was afforded to Judy and Earl Jessup, Mrs. Slocum's next-door neighbors, not long after the expansion of the communal nucleus to include the brothers Degan. The Jessups are anything but Y-persons. Judy is in her mid-fifties, childless, house-proud. Her husband, a retired potato farmer who has sold off his fields to the developers, looks considerably older, but is still (in Stu's words) tough and horny as a bull moose. Both of them are Bonackers,[23] descendants of the original settlers of the South Fork of eastern Long Island. They speak with the flat local accent, which is closer, I am told, to the speech of New England than to that of the megalopolis.

"Oh, Randy, do hush up."

The dog, excited by the cries outdoors, is barking wildly.

"Way to go, Stu!"

"Get rid of it, Rick!"

Judy Jessup goes to the window of her sunroom, which overlooks the Slocum lawn. Three young men are playing with a football; a fourth is waxing a foreign car in the driveway; a fifth appears to be skiing on grass.

"*Four cars* over at Lavinia's, Earl. Looks like groupers to me."

Her husband, reclining in his Barca-lounger, finishes off his beer and sets down the can on a polished tabletop, ignoring the doily she has provided. "Law allows five, Jude."

---

[23]Many Indian place-names in the area end with *-bonac* or *-ponack*. The term *Bonacker*, which rhymes, roughly, with *harmonica*, originally meant the inhabitants, mostly fisherfolk, of one of these hamlets, but has been extended in popular usage to apply to anyone whose family has been on the South Fork for the past three hundred years.

"Groupers for sure. I'm calling the police."

Earl stands up to have a look. "Jesus, a bunch of fruits. Give me that phone."

"You can tell from here?"

His blunt fingers are punching the touch-tone buttons. "*Five* guys in *one* house? Got to be faggots."

"There's a law?"

"Sure there is." He shouts into the phone, "Put Chief Sweeney on the line!"

Outdoors, the young man waxing the BMW turns toward the Jessup house. At the sight of his black face, Earl reacts violently.

"Chief! Houseful of miscegenating free-thinking tutti-fruttis next door, crumbing up the whole neighborhood!"[24]

Just then, Earl notices that two girls in mini-bikinis are spreading their towels for a sunbath. One of them is pink, the other a rich amber.

"We better not be too hasty, Chief. I'll keep 'em under surveillance."

He hangs up and reaches for his field glasses. Judy grabs them first, holds them out of his reach.

"Dirty old voy-oor."

Stu is engaging in workplay. For a sports reporter, tossing a football with two former B.C. greats is a learning opportunity, hence job-related. The Degans are also workplaying. The $1,875 they have each given Clive is more than they can afford, but they count on recouping by selling insurance to their fellow groupers. Since Stu is the one they have known longest (two hours now), they cultivate him first. If he is injured in the game

---

[24]Reading the Soviet and West European press, one gets the impression that the US has gone gay. In fact, homophobia is rampant, not only among the likes of Earl Jessup, but (as we shall see) among certain of our Y's and sub-Y's. Ouspenskiy's view: the more men who lust after men, the more girls for us traditionalists. *Ergo, vive la pédale!*

(perhaps they sense he is accident-prone), they can talk medical insurance.

On his Skee-Trax, cross-country skis on rollers for summer use, Clive appears to be playing, but with Mr. Edgway close by, he knows he'll be talking LBO's before long, and he always works better after a little exercise to start the juices flowing.

Chip's case is simple: if he wishes to play[25] with Dreda later, he must work on the beautification of her BMW now. As he polishes, he remembers a poem he learned in an Afro-Am Lit course at college, something about a shiny brass spittoon on the altar of the Lord. He wonders if he could impress his boss at the ad agency by quoting it next time they discuss the Bronz-O account.

Sunbathing, Cathy rereads the thirty-eight pages of her novel, inserting many a comma. Dreda, lying beside her with the *Wall Street Journal*, compares foreign currency quotations on the New York, London, Zurich, and Tokyo exchanges, seeing them as computer-graphicized curves in her head, and worries about what Kimmie, the weedy, tweedy young Korean girl in her office, is doing at this point in time.

Moira is up in her room, working out on Clive's ExerCycle, which has a lectern rigged on its handlebars. While pedaling, she reads about yesterday's auction of early 1980s graffiti art at Christie's. When the telephone rings, she takes it without dismounting. A few seconds later, still pumping, she shouts out the open window to Clive.

"For you! Mr. Edgway!"

Clive unsnaps his bindings and offers the skis to Chip, who shakes his head. "No thanks, I'd rather wax the Beamers."

Going out for a pass from Mort, Stu runs bang into a copper beech sapling in the middle of the lawn. Down he goes. When

---

[25]*Play* may seem to contradict my remarks about sex being work for Y's. As will presently appear, C. Buford, although prep, is not a true Y.

he gets up, blood is streaming from his nose. He kicks and curses the little tree.

"Goddamn selfish old bitch had to go plant her stupid tree on the fifty-yard line!"

Cathy sits up. "Tem-*per*, Stuey." She sees the blood and goes to pieces. "Oh God, what do I *do?*"

Both Degans come lumbering up to him. "Hey, man, you got major medical?"

Moira, who has seen the accident from the window, hurries down to the lawn, bringing a towel, a bowl of water, cotton. She leads Stu up on the veranda, spreads the towel on the porch swing to protect Mrs. Slocum's canvas cushions, makes him lie down, bathes his nose, pushes a cottonball up a nostril. Cathy is there, all in a flutter, saying "Poor Stuey."

Clive comes out the front door, carrying an attaché case in one hand, tucking his shirttail into his seersucker trousers with the other. He jumps into his Subaru and is off.

Stu smiles up at Moira. He wants to tell her she has gentle hands, but it comes out as, "You're pretty goddamn good at sports medicine."

Cathy, feeling superfluous, notices that she is still holding her typescript. Four drops of Stuart blood have besmirched the cover. Her decision to go up to her room to get a new folder will give us a chance, reader, to observe this literary Y-person *playing at working*.

Stu's athletic gear is all over the floor and bed. For the moment, Cathy's desk is an oasis of order, the order that always eludes her, but which she believes she must achieve in order to create. She takes a red folder from the neat pile of half a dozen waiting for yet-to-be-written chapters and selects a blue Magic Marker to write on the cover *Corinna's Going a-Maying: II*. Then comes a moment of hesitation: the title has begun to pall on her. She flips through the thirty-eight pages, hoping to find a phrase of her own that will serve as title. One thing about her novel, she thinks, is the beautiful typing. Her eye is caught by a love scene: "Bed with Stefan was good, and in the morning it was still good. . . ."

Cathy cringes. Warmed-over Papa Hemingway. How *could* she? She deletes the sentence carefully with White-Out. How would Jane Austen have put it? The idea would never have entered her head. Edith Wharton? "When her tray of *café au lait* and *fraises des bois* was borne in by Suzette in the morning, Corinna was still . . ."

Still what? And is Corinna any kind of name for a contemporary heroine, born in the reign of John F. Kennedy? Cathy is sick of Corinna; Corinna has appeared in too many of her short stories. The names of all her protagonists come straight out of *The Oxford Book of English Verse*—Corinna, Camilla, Cordelia, Cressida, Cynara. Their names always begin with C, as her own does. Usually they have older sisters named Mona or Mavra or Mavourneen. Nearly all grew up in northern New Jersey, but in her novel Cathy is reaching out. The current Corinna comes from Mount Kisco. With sudden resolution, she writes a note to herself on the inside cover of the folder: "Change CORINNA to ALTHAEA throughout."

Althaea's Folly! Conrad got away with something of the sort. A good title, they say, can double or triple sales.[26]

Stu enters, dabbing at his nose. He picks up a tennis racquet, bangs his fist against the strings, throws it down, takes the putter from his golf bag, addresses an imaginary ball. "Got your refund, six twenty-five. Hey, you couldn't lend it to me, just till payday?"

Cathy, wondering whether Althaea would be happier and more saleable without her middle *a*, answers him absentmindedly. "Anything for you, Stuey." Loving is trusting, she tells

---

[26]In the USSR a writer, be he "dissident" or party-liner, must consider the political nuances of every word he sets on paper. Here we see a writer bowing to another tyranny, that of "the magic of the marketplace" in a "free" society!

herself. A title? Noisily, Stu kisses her ear. She takes the Magic
Marker and writes ALTHEA, trying her out with only two *a*'s.
Althea's Loves? Althea Undone? Althean Days, yet? Aha: *Hal-
cyon!* What about Halcyon? Halcyon Faraday. It has a ring, but
does it ring like Anna Karenina? Like Anna Livia Plurabelle?
Like Emma Bovary?

Stu has found a scuffmark on one of his magnificent riding
boots. He hawks loudly, spits on the leather, rubs the spot with
one of Cathy's bras.

The trouble, she tells herself, is not in the name; the real
trouble is that Corinna ("Halcyon") Faraday is exactly like
Catherine H. Fairchild. So were Cordelia Franklyn and Cynara
Frederyx, in her short stories. Are these thirty-eight pages
indeed Part I of a novel or simply a stringing together of two
or three short stories, in which the two or three heroines all
happen to have the same name? Also, are the love scenes romantic, rather than erotic?

She cannot write a dirty scene. The sweat, the fetor, the
blood, the crud, the slip and slop of sex are beyond her reach
as an artist. What if Duff/Lorenz knew?

Cathy thinks of her refund check. She has just thrown away
$625. Stefan—Stu—never pays back. Her deadline is three
months away; no time for writer's block. The contract calls for
"a novel of not less than 100,000 words." She has nearly thirteen thousand now, leaving eighty-seven thousand to go, or
twenty-nine thousand a month, call it a thousand a day. Not
so bad, but when is she going to reread, revise? If she writes
1,200 words a day, she reckons, with the aid of her pocket
calculator, that she can finish her draft in 72.5 days, at noon
on August 8th, provided she does her first 1,200 today. On the
8th at midday, she will have 23.5 days left to rewrite the whole
novel before her September 1st deadline. Rewriting, she sup-
poses, is easier? She'll have to type 4,255 words a day those
last three weeks of August. Cathy rolls a sheet of paper into

her typewriter. She will write her twelve hundred words today; she must. They will be perfect; they have to be.

Stu pulls the wooden trees from his riding boots, throws them clattering on the floor.

"Suit up, pussycat. Got to go equitate."

Come, my Corinna, come, let's go a-Maying.

It is Clive's first visit to the stately pleasure dome of Nicholas Edgway. The house, built of custom-hewn beams bleached the color of driftwood, sits on eight prime beachfront acres, looking out across the green of dune grass toward the blue of ocean.

Edgway, a handsome, florid man in his early sixties, is paddling about his pool naked, expounding on LBO's. Clive perches uncomfortably on the edge of a deck chair, wondering whether it would be all right to take off his seersucker jacket. When Edgway says, "Enough leveraging for now, let's take a break," Clive thinks he may at last be invited in for a swim, but the senior partner simply rolls over on his back and flutterkicks off to the shallow end, looking like a large pink pool toy.

Until recently, Clive lived in awe of the man and in fear of losing his toehold at Tucker, Edgway & Masoch. The name of the game[27] for a junior associate is to find a partner who will take him under his wing. There are over a hundred partners in the firm, each presumably with two wings, but in Clive's first three and a half years there, none offered him so much as a feather.

Then one day a few weeks ago, at a meeting attended by several partners and associates, Edgway suddenly beamed at Clive and addressed his first words to him since "Welcome aboard" forty months before. These were "Well done, Wheelwright," and referred to some routine work on a title search. Next day Edgway invited him to lunch at the Downtown Club. On learning that his young associate came from Maine, he

[27]A workplay phrase!

produced photographs of his beautiful yawl *Equity*, built in Southwest Harbor, and hinted that if Clive could find a way to spend a few summer weekends in the Hastings area, he could look forward to some good sailing, perhaps even a cruise up to Cuttyhunk or the Vineyard. In that moment, Clive's concept of a summer-rental career decision was spawned. Two hours after lunch, while still digesting, he realized he now felt secure enough at Tucker, Edgway to put in a bid on the apartment. That night he and Moira set a date for the wedding and dreamed of Sri Lanka in each other's arms.

Ever since then, the senior partner has piled work on him, but nothing further has been said about the yawl.

Clive considers Nicholas Edgway to be a brilliant lawyer; he has had the career a brilliant lawyer deserves. Coming out of nowhere, downstate Delaware, he took his B.A. at the state university, attended law school at night, practiced briefly in Wilmington, until—almost a miracle—he was invited, because of his skill in setting up dummy Delaware corporations, to join what was then the firm of Tucker & Tucker in New York. Ever since, he has been working his way up the city's legal, financial, and social ladders—his wife was a Vandenhoek[28]—with such success that today he is all but indistinguishable from Francis Tucker, semi-retired son of the founding partner. Tucker is Old New York Money,[29] born to attend the right schools and belong to the right clubs. Edgway himself is a member of the Knick, the Brook, the Racquet, and even, to Clive's awe, the New York Yacht Club.[30] When Clive fantasizes about the future, he sees himself working and talking and living like the man now breaststroking slowly across the pool toward him.

"Next, Clive, an environmental matter. Strictly pro bono, no

---

[28]Means nothing to me, but seems to impress Clive, to whom I am indebted for these details of N. Edgway's career path.

[29]This, too, fails to move me.

[30]As does this.

money in it for the firm. Tract known as Indian Marsh, not far from here, two thousand one hundred and sixty-five acres of shoreland and woods. Present owner, Estate of Ralph Hatch. The Hatch heirs favor immediate sale. Task is to protect tract from development. Getting this down?"

"Yes, Mr. Edgway."

"Call me Nick, we're on vacation." He pushes off from the side of the pool, floats on his back, takes a mouthful of water, squirts it in the air. "Client, the Hemisphere Foundation, intends to purchase tract with a view to turning it over to State of New York as nature preserve. Follow?"

"Yes, sir."

"Nick, Nick. Pending state approval, client intends to set up trust, call it Wetlands Trust, to effect purchase and hold title. Now, Clive, my first question is as to whether you'd be willing to serve—without remuneration, of course—as a trustee of Wetlands Trust."

Clive is overwhelmed. Little as he knows about nature, the word "environment" is sacred to him.[31]

"Sir, I'm honored. And may I say that I am proud that the firm—and you, sir—are so public-spirited."

When he started law school, Clive intended to devote his career to public interest law. He lived one summer with the Penobscot Indians and wrote an article for the *Columbia Law Review* on the suit brought by the Penobscots and Passamaquoddys against the State of Maine. His life, he thought, would be devoted to working to redress the historic wrongs done to Native Americans and other ethnics. In the last year or two of law school, when his classmates talked of nothing but their interviews with big downtown firms, his natural competitiveness was aroused, the public interest forgotten. Now, suddenly, the senior partner is guiding him back into pro bono.

Edgway comes out of the pool naked and hands Clive a beach

---

[31]And to all upwardly mobiles.

towel. "Mind rubbing me down a bit?" He turns his back. Clive rubs. "Harder. Get the blood flowing. How do you like my little beach cottage?"

"It's beautiful."

"Well, young man, just work your ass off for forty years and you too can live in comfort. Follow me?"

Clive continues rubbing the hairy pink back. Is this, he wonders, a test? A joke?

"Yes . . . Nick."

Superb example of workplay provided by N. Edgway. For C. Wheelwright, just work.

In Clive's absence, Moira has borrowed the BMW, complete with chauffeur. She and Chip have done an art tour of the South Fork: the four small galleries in Squaw Harbor, the three in Nowedonah, the sculpture park in the scrub pines between the Hastings Haven shopping mall and the L.I.R.R. Art has been moving slowly since the collapse of the bull market, but certain items still sell. Moira knows what she is looking for. Standing outside the seventh of the eight galleries in Hastings proper, she thinks she may have found it.

The painting in the window is an acrylic on plywood, 28" x 20", apartment size, an abstract work, but with a certain air of reality. A curved line runs down the middle from top to bottom, with an appendage—a penis?—hanging from its lower reaches. The shape is disturbingly familiar. Clots and clusters of color intersect the curve. The acrylics have been applied in such a way as to create a textured surface, an almost topographic relief. The picture is not beautiful; Moira has seen many beautiful paintings in the course of the afternoon; her quest is not for beauty.

Chip, who has had enough of watching her stand spellbound by the window, tries the door of the gallery, finds it locked. Moira points to a poster:

GALERIE NADYA
Acrylics by

ELOWYN

Opening Sunday, May 30th
5–7 PM

"Two women inside," Chip says. "I'll rattle the door, you flash your dealer's card at them. Let's get in, get it over with."

"No, I'll come back Sunday. Better not to come on too strong." Deeply moved, Moira walks to the car. She has found something rarer than beauty: a saleable work.

Dreda comes out of the shower, spanking clean and singing. She rubs down with a towel, throws a plaid bathrobe over her shoulders, crosses the hall to her room. Chip is out chauffeuring Moira, Clive with his boss, the Degans on a grocery run, Stu and Cathy God knows where. All is still, the house hers. From her window she can see the salmon-pink sun dip toward the heat-haze over the ocean. Dreda throws off her bathrobe, sits down naked at her computer, fondles it with both hands. It is a little beauty, shiny and new, with ecru casing, midnight-blue screen, characters the color of candle flame. She has brought it here not because she plans to work over the weekend, but simply because she cannot live without it.

Her hands play idly over the console, summoning graphics to the screen—crazy, lovely graphics signifying nothing. Stylized bar-graphs, elegant intersecting curves arise at her touch, swell, crescendo, sink in a dying fall. She is playing a carillon, choreographing a ballet. Suddenly an abstraction, delicate, intricate, overpowering, is born on her screen, lives for an instant, dies. Ephemeral art. Dreda tries to recreate the beautiful graphic, but it is gone.

A literary memory from childhood: "Seated one day at the organ, / I was weary and ill at ease . . ." *A Lost Chord*. "But I

struck one chord of music, / Like the sound of a great Amen."
The chances of her finding her Lost Graphic by random fingering of the console are infinitesimally small.

A moment later, she is happily computing the probabilities.

For the first time, Cathy feels the placid beauty of the South Fork. She and Stu are in the state park, riding rented horses across a meadow full of wildflowers. The wooded hilltop above them shines in the clear light of late afternoon. Below them are a road, trees in full leaf, dunes, and sea. Stu, too, is beautiful, decked out in his black velvet-covered hunting cap, tweed hacking jacket, britches, and his impressive boots, which he swears he had made to measure in London. She herself is in blue jeans and an old sweater.

"Stuey, if we ride up to the top, I bet we can see Montauk Light."

"What's so great about Montauk Light?"

"It's cool—not the light, the *idea* of Montauk Light—being the easternmost point in New York State and built by order of President Washington and all. Let's go."

"Piss on Montauk Light." Stu canters off downhill, toward a black Cadillac limousine parked at a scenic overlook by the road.

Cathy follows at a walk. She watches him rein in behind the Cadillac and stare at the license number. Nevada plates, she sees as she draws nearer. There they are, the same two men, not in pinstripes this time but in garish Hawaiian shirts, standing in front of the car, looking out at the coastline. She is close enough to hear their voices. One of them points to a headland.

"The perfect spot, Schulzie."

"Yeah, Lou. A dream."

Cathy tries to pull the head of her horse up out of a clump of yellow daisies. It gives a snort. Both men whirl toward them. Stu casually touches his cap with his riding crop, the classic salute of the foxhunting man.

"Ah there, gentlemen. Splendid day for hacking, what?"
He wheels his horse and trots away. The larger of the men,
the one called Lou, shrugs his shoulders and growls to Schulzie,
"Some asshole who thinks he's the Prince of Wales."
When Cathy catches up to him, Stu, once more without his
notepad, is repeating the license number over and over to himself. His emotion is such that his nose has again begun to bleed.

In my first taped interview with S. Stuart, months later, I
asked him how he had intuited that there was a story, a *sports*
story, in the two men called Lou and Schulzie, and whether it
was by pure chance that he found them on his ride in the State
Park. Both questions seemed to flabbergast him. I present his
reply verbatim:
"Gambling *is* sports, the national pastime. Obviously there
was a story—the way those dudes looked, the Nevada limo,
and why were they way out here in the boonies? On the ride,
was it fate? Or did I scope out their map in The Pub sublimi-
nally? Shit, Vladski, I don't know. I wanted to break in those
boots; they set me back four hundred quid at Maxwell's. So I
followed my wounded nose. There are more things in heaven
and earth, Ouspenskiy, than are dreamt of in your half-ass
philosophy."
To pursue a career goal while breaking in custom-made boots
and riding with a charming girl—*that* is workplay! As for
C. Fairchild, she was soon to write a chapter beginning: "Side
by side, Halcyon and Stefan galloped across the meadow. The
sea below them glowed under a westering sun. . . . "

For the poet V.Y. Ouspenskiy, there is no workplay. He es-
chews work; all is play. Writing poetry is glorious play; even
sociology is play, for in Ouspenskiyan sociology, it is Ouspenskiy who sets the rules. One thing, however, *is* work: getting
from New York to Hastings.
While Stu and Cathy ride back to the stable, while Clive

drives home with a head full of pro bono thoughts, while Moira and Dreda dream of two totally different abstractions, I am still on the Long Island Railroad. Somehow I have found a train at Penn Station, changed to another at Jamaica, to yet another at Babylon. (Exotic names for prosaic places!) At a nowhere place called Speonk, the train stops and all passengers disembark. It turns out that while I correctly boarded a train on the Montauk *branch*, my train was not the Montauk *train*. My train, I am told, "terminates" at Speonk. The next train for Hastings, Nowedonah, and Montauk will be along in two hours and nineteen minutes. Sitting disconsolately on a graffiti-besmirched bench in the minimalist Speonk station, I remember a passage in *Oblomov*: " 'Who on earth [the eponymous hero asks] would go to America or Egypt? The English go, but God made them that way; besides, they've no room to live in at home. What Russian would ever dream of going? Some despairing wretch whose life is worth nothing to him.' "

Ilya Ilyich Oblomov, procrastinator, man of leisure, is my role model if indeed I have one (all Y-persons do; none would pick Oblomov). The first hundred and fifty pages of Goncharov's great novel are devoted to the hero's summoning up resolution to get out of bed. Somewhere in nineteenth-century Russian literature there is a country place for every taste. Stu, for example, might choose the Rostovs' estate in *War and Peace*, where there are pretty girls to tease, wolves to hunt, and packs of borzois to chase them. Clive might feel at home on Levin's property in *Anna Karenina*, where he would find plenty of haying in the fields to keep his juices flowing. Cathy sees herself in one of Chekhov's doomed manors, where axes bite into cherry trees and avuncular Vanyas talk themselves into extinction. My own country home is dear, dilapidated Oblomovka, the haven to which Oblomov returns in his languorous dreams, but never in life. "The wheat grows taller at Oblomovka, the geese grow fatter, the cows moo softer, and the frogs croak deeper than anywhere else in the world." If a balcony grows rickety, the family decides to let it fall down rather than repair it; when a section of fencing collapses, it is propped up by two poles, and sure enough, it stands all summer, until the winter snows bring it down.

Perhaps it is the postcard of The Historic Slocum House, c. 1760, that has induced my Speonkian reverie of Oblomovka. Like the dachas and manors of our vanished Russian squirearchy, the Slocum House is of wood. I like the look of the veranda; I imagine myself snoozing there through many a summer afternoon. If the cryptic "Cathy" is indeed my small doe-eyed darling, I plan to stay on in Hastings and play with her and poetry. I may even, I think (as a train pulls in and the conductor shouts, "Hastings Haven, Hastings, Nowedonah, and Montauk!"), resume work on my *Oblomoviad*, cantos in praise of doing nothing. These have not been published, even in *samizdat*, but the rumor that I was working on them was enough (I now realize) to prompt the KGB Cultural Section to arrange for my sudden weaning from Mother Russia.

Soviet literary authorities, I reflect while attempting to view the Long Island countryside through train windows opaque with grime, grudgingly acknowledge Goncharov's novel to be a classic. They publish it with a preface pointing out Oblomov's "errors," the evils of absentee landlordship, the "feudal" bond between Ilya Ilyich and his serf and body servant, the devoted but abrasive Zahar; they would burn the book if they dared. It is deeply subversive, not only for Soviet society, but for all societies with a strenuous work ethic. For example: "This is why they say that people were stronger in the old days. Indeed they were; in the old days no one was in a hurry to explain to a child 'the meaning of life' and make him feel that living was a baffling and difficult affair; they did not trouble his mind with books that rouse scores of questions, grinding down one's heart and mind and shortening life."

Woolgathering at Oblomovka, I nearly fail to get off at Hastings, where I shall encounter an upwardly mobile ethos that is the polar opposite of Ilya Ilyich's—and mine.

6

PARAMETERS

Of oral history—M. FAIRCHILD tape—
D. SCOTT tape—The two accounts synthesized—Oral
abused

Oral history is much in vogue in the States at present. When I first heard of it, I thought of those grisly charts of the mandibles and the gray, bite-sized X-ray pictures that dentists delight in showing us. In fact, oral history consists of turning on a machine while others talk. The day Dreda gave me one of her old tape recorders, I became a practitioner.[32]

The social scientist must approach oral with caution.

It is cutting, they say, that makes the movie. A clever film editor can take the dailies, the raw footage delivered to the cutting room, and do as he pleases with the story, turn hero into villain, or ingenue into femme fatale. So it is with oral.

First you tape; then you put the spoken words on paper. In transcribing, you take out all the questions that you, the interviewer, have asked, so that the interviewee's stream of blab seems to burble from a natural source and move in a smooth relentless flow. Of course you delete superfluous words, such as "Well" and "uh" and "Have another beer?" After excising repetitions and all dialogue and detail that fail to interest you, you arrange each section of the interview so that it builds toward the effect you desire, be it climax or cliffhanger.

You can deliver the words of the interviewee as a prolonged artillery barrage; you can break them down into staccato machine gun bursts; you can squeeze off single shots of a sentence or less. The speaker may be made to recite a monologue or to engage in conversational skirmishing with other persons interviewed at another time and place.

To illustrate, I shall present two versions of the same event, a house meeting, first as reported by Moira, then by Dreda. Both interviews will appear here unedited, just as they came off the tape. As a means of emphasizing the raw nature of unedited speech, I shall use no punctuation; pauses will be

---

[32]I should make it clear that all the interviews on which this book is based were taped *after* the commune disbanded.

indicated by paragraphing. (Sometimes half an interview is
pause.) My own questions are included. I shall even attempt
to transliterate my famous "oxsent."

After Moira's and Dreda's uncut interviews, I shall show
various uses to which an editor might put them.

INTERVIEW 1 ▸ *Moira Fairchild*

V.Y.O. ▸ ready moira
M.F. ▸ sure whatll i talk about this time
V.Y.O. ▸ first house mitting be so kind
M.F. ▸ well lets see
that friday we moved in
uh we held the meeting on the back porch
that was to include mort and rick who were cooking steaks on the outdoor grill down on the lawn
it was evening dark almost but clive and i wanted
to have the meeting right away so that we could
lay down ah so we could get general agreement
on a few basic rules i rang the captains bell on
the porch and shouted house meeting and they all
congregated there was some grumbling but basically they all agreed it was necessary clive rapped
on the wicker table for order we all settled down
and everything went smoothly except oh yes stu
and dreda asked who elected clive chairman and
treasurer clive fielded those questions adroitly he
calmed them down by tactfully proposing that they
both be named deputy treasurers
V.Y.O. ▸ that is dreda and stu
M.F. ▸ yes then clive was called to the phone edgway
again so i took the chair and outlined a few parameters no pets no overnight guests no drugs in
the house and how we would rotate on cooking

and cleaning and gardening and id try to find a cleaning consultant to come in a few hours each week and we would all chip in on groceries so they all agreed and that was it

V.Y.O. ► that was all rilly i mean you were deciding how to organize life of commune and it all went so orderly

M.F. ► yes it was a good meeting perfectly orderly stu even volunteered to do the gardening we were all mystified you remember why he wanted to

V.Y.O. ► you bet your swit oss i do

M.F. ► vlady that expression is
it is considered vulgar

V.Y.O. ► sorry moira i frequently hear stu yemploy such terms

M.F. ► of course mort or was it rick got up and made one of their insurance pitches about how all our personal property would be in the house unguarded during the week and how providential has this interesting low cost floater policy so everybody began shouting things like to hell with this lets take our chances and cathy said she was going to be in the house every day all summer to work on her book and mort said but cathy sleeps providential never sleeps

then clive came back from the telephone all excited he said moira mr edgway invited us both for tennis tomorrow at the spindrift club thats whites of course and i said i dont have a white tennis dress dreda lend me your tennis whites and dreda said what whites i always play in my old yale crew shirt and my plaid shorts we all said how preppy can you get then rick announced dinner and the meeting adjourned and despite all the complain-

ing about the steaks they all rushed down to the
grill it was dog eat dog every man
uh
every person for his or her self hows that was it
ok vlady

V.Y.O. ▸ very ok thank you moira

INTERVIEW #2 ▸ *Dreda Scott*

V.Y.O. ▸ so now we talk about first house mitting dreda
D.S. ▸ it was utter chaos moira rang that idiotic bell and
screamed house meeting and i thought what a
drag just like back at andover i mean all my life
ive been going to girl scout meetings sixth grade
meetings meetings of debating clubs dramatic societies field hockey team afro american club the
yale crew squad i was cox and the real purpose of
every meeting is to allow some dingdong to be
chairman
most chairpersons are a lot worse than clive and
moira who are basically i admit pretty good guys
anyway the purpose is to allow these self important overachieving yoyos to demonstrate their quote
natural leadership unquote and bore everybody
out of their skulls by saying the next order of business will be
et cetera

V.Y.O. ▸ so at house mitting what hoppens
D.S. ▸ first chip and cathy and i who are used to quiches
and gazpacho and good old nouvelle we com-
plained about the steaks the degans were grilling
that greasy smoke kept blowing over us all on the
porch it was yucky cathy said ugh charred flesh
im a veggie guys how bout a refund chip said oh

god couldnt we send out for sushi and stu came
out of the house all excited and said cathy i just
called carson city she said why stuey he said capital of nevada i found out who owns that license
number its big hes big mr big

V.Y.O. ▸ yexcuse me dreda
from telephone call stu found out only name lou
gross yes

D.S. ▸ correct but the name lou gross is famous apparently to all who bet stu kept saying hot damn big
lou himself big story clive said stu please i have
called this meeting to order so stu yelled who elected
you chairman and clive smiled this constipated
smile and said i signed the lease then i jumped
up and said mr chairperson are you also mr treasurer and if so why again that sphincterlike smile
and he said ive deposited your checks to my account whereupon stu shouted i nominate me for
treasurer and i hollered no me i pay double
to be honest vlady i was beginning to enjoy myself
stu and i had disrupted many a meeting at andover we were a great team but clive came back
at us gamely with i move that stu and dreda be
named deputy treasurers and stu bellowed seconded frankly i was disappointed in stu i thought
he was playing into clives hands clive said motion
carried and stu heaved himself to his feet saying
the deputy treasurers will now inspect the books
and i realized clive had laid himself wide open the
meeting was ours it was ideal stu and i in a quiet
parliamentary way could now raise holy hell luckily for clive his boss called up just then so he went
inside to take it and moira took over with this no
nonsense look on her face and laid all these house

rules on us stu was no help to me now all he
wanted for some reason was to do the gardening
he said ill garden the living shit out of this sadass
place then mort and rick tried to sell us insurance
but for once we were unanimous thank god and
shouted them down i tell you vlady i was sick of
being pushed around by these clods who were paying half what i was paying

V.Y.O. ▶ i see tell me dreda how did mitting adjourn

D.S. ▶ it disintegrated chip got up and said whoever bought
the groceries i move a vote of censure theres nothing to drink its happy hour i crave my sauterne
spritzer stu produced a bottle saying i got some
vodka thats healthy cathy said what id give for
some nice crisp arugula moira said order order i
said hey these degans arent even using mesquite
thats unheard of and then rick banged his skillet
on the grill and said steaks ready i move we eat
so we formed this chowline it was already dark by
now and you know what happened next
whats so funny

V.Y.O. ▶ i hoppen next

The sociologist Ouspenskiy can use this material in various
ways. You can imagine it in the rough narrative form in which
I have thus far chosen to write this study:

*Night is falling. Fumes of grilling steak waft over
the Slocum property. Moira is on the back porch,
ringing the handsome captain's bell that hangs by
the door. "House meeting!" she calls.*

*Grumbling, our Y-persons assemble. Cathy is upset
over the menu. "Charred flesh? I'm a veggie, guys,
How 'bout a refund?"*

*Dreda's disgruntlement goes deeper. All her life
she has been attending meetings ...*

Or I could choose to blend the two interviews. It is considered
masterly in oral history to have two or more interviewees appear to be talking to each other. Note that in the following
synthesis many phrases, sentences, and paragraphs have been
suppressed.

SYNTHESIS A: ▶ *Interviews 1 & 2 as edited by V.Y.O.*

Moira Fairchild ▶ Clive and I wanted to get general
agreement on a few basic rules. They
all agreed it was necessary. Everything went smoothly.

Dreda Scott ▶ Utter chaos. The purpose is to allow
Clive and Moira, these self-important
overachieving yoyos, to bore everybody
out of their skulls.

Moira Fairchild ▶ It was a good meeting, very orderly.

Dreda Scott ▶ Stu yelled, "Who elected you chairman?" Then I jumped up and said, "Mr.
Chairperson, are you also Mr. Treasurer, and if so, why?"

Moira Fairchild ▶ Clive fielded those questions adroitly.
He calmed them down.

Dreda Scott ▶ Clive had laid himself wide open. The
meeting was ours—it was ideal. Stu
and I in a quiet, parliamentary way
could raise holy hell.

Now let us suppose that for some reason an unscrupulous
oral historian wishes Dreda to appear to be the advocate of
order and Moira to be the disruptive element. He can accom-

plish this without altering or adding words, simply by cutting a good many.

SYNTHESIS B: ▸ *Interviews 1 & 2 re-edited*

Dreda Scott ▸	The meeting was ideal, in a quiet, parliamentary way.
Moira Fairchild ▸	Everybody began shouting things like "To hell with this!"
Dreda Scott ▸	For once we were unanimous, thank God.
Moira Fairchild ▸	It was dog eat dog, every person for his or her self.

Such is the editor's art. But now, if Interview #2 is to be believed, your field researcher is about to "hoppen."

7

NUCLEUS
INVADED

I*nvasion of commune—Attempts to expel foreign body—Strategic withdrawal*

At this point in time I happen, happen along, happen in. Here is how Ouspenskiy happens.

He arrives at the Hastings station at dusk. Everyone there is in a hurry; none has ever heard of the Slocum House. You must imagine the poet asking in his comic accent, "Where is Historic Slocum House, C-wan-seven-six-oh, be so kind?" The benighted Slav has some notion that "c. 1760" is an American rural address. (Yes, reader, I am aware of the convention that the social scientist should keep his own person modestly in the background when reporting on field research; be patient; this is a digression; I shall presently recede into the woodwork.) At last Ouspenskiy finds a young farmer with a pickup truck and a black Labrador[33] who admits to knowing the whereabouts of a Slocum Lane. Thus, after a spine-chilling ride through the twilight, the poet arrives at his destination, filthy, famished, and exhausted.

In the words of Pushkin, *"Dikhovnoi zhazhdoyu tomim', / V'pustinye mrachnoi ya vlachilsya."*[34]

Ouspenskiy cannot be sure as he wanders in this dark wilderness, weary and athirst, that he has found the house on "Cathy's" postcard. Therefore he decides to reconnoiter. Voices are coming from the garden behind the house. He starts toward them. A dog barks thunderously from the porch next door: a large, deep-chested beast by the sound of him. The poet quickens his pace, directed toward the closest tree. A woman's voice calls, "Do hush, Randy! Bad dog, come in here this minute." A rectangle of light slides across the neighbors' porch as the door is opened. Once Randy is inside, Ouspenskiy steals silently

---

[33]All Bonackers, young or old, own pickup trucks, which they drive at unlawful speeds, passing only on curves. It is *de rigueur* to have a black Labrador behind, riding on the truckbed.

[34]*Prophet*, 1–2, of course. The immortal lines lose something in transliteration to the humdrum Roman alphabet.

along a row of privet hedge toward the other voices. The delectable effluvium of steaks grilling over live coals assails his nostrils. The poet salivates. He recalls one of his father's countless stories of the Great Patriotic War, telling of how a starving German, separated from his unit and wandering in snow and bitter cold behind Soviet lines, infiltrated a Red Army mess queue under cover of darkness. It was my father, then on duty in the field kitchen, who spotted him, took him prisoner, and later received a People's Medal of Valor and other suitable rewards for his exploit.

Reader, you have guessed. The next thing Ouspenskiy knows, he is standing in line in the deep shadow of the tall hedge between two total strangers. Huge juicy slabs of steer simmer and crackle on the grill, oozing bubbles of their own grease. All thought of identifying "Cathy" has fled. Here is meat; let the poet feast.

The line moves closer to the grill. Ouspenskiy leans forward, squinting through his granny glasses to determine which piece is largest. The glowing coals light up the shaggy lower third of his face. Swallowing his saliva to keep it from trickling into his beard . . .

. . . he is rudely seized by his auburn locks! Ouspenskiy's head is jerked sharply up and back, his collar grabbed and twisted by the strong hand of a strong man with a strong voice.

"Who the fuck is this bohemian?"

One of the two gargantuan individuals tending the grill trains a flashlight on the poet's face, and a girl's voice cries out, "Vlady!"

Yes: it is "Cathy"; she is indeed the doe-eyed darling. At once she throws her arms around Ouspenskiy.

The man with the strong voice releases him. "You *know* him, for Christ's sake? Who's he dressed up as—Allen Ginsberg or General Grant?" (A fair enough question. My hair is long, my beard full; I am wearing a mélange of 1860s military gear, Union and Confederate, and antique 1960s hippiewear. In Moscow *samizdat* circles, as among the émigré painters and poets of SoHo, none of us, I fear, reads the magazine *New York*.)

"Vladimir Yurevich Ouspenskiy," Cathy announces. "The great Soviet dissident poet. I met him at this reading, and he was so amazing that I asked him—"

"House guest?" A tall, bespectacled youth peers down at me. (I am only five foot four.[35])

A pretty black girl speaks up. "Rule one-oh-eight-nine—"

All stare at the poet as if he were an alien who had just stepped out of his saucer. (Persons affecting counterculture clothing, hairstyles, and facial hair are repugnant to upwardly mobiles. Fortunately they seldom come in contact with them.)

Cathy tucks her arm through the poet's and faces the others. "Vlady's my guest, yes. A dinner guest."

"Refund!" the gargantuan one with the flashlight shouts.

"I don't eat dead animals, why shouldn't I invite Vlady?"

They all begin to talk at once. While debate rages, the poet inches closer to the grill. No one is looking at him. He is of interest to them only because they must determine who is to pay for his feed. A bubble of fat explodes with a succulent pop.

"What's the rule on dinner guests?"

"What if we all started asking—?"

They are all shouting now, except for the second of the gargantuan individuals, who is staring down at the grill. "Hey. There are only six steaks here. Two fell?" He drops to his knees, gropes in the grass. "They didn't *walk* off . . . "

All begin to search. The flashlight beam traces zigzags across the lawn.

"Where's my jug of vodka?" he of the strong voice roars.

"Vlady, Vlady!" Cathy calls. "Honestly, guys! He's terribly sensitive, a true artist. You've frightened him away."

---

[35]163 cm.

The poet V.Y. Ouspenskiy meanwhile is crouched under the back porch, wolfing steaks, swilling down vodka. If this is American hospitality, he thinks, best to sort things out in the morning.

Cathy's voice grows nearer. "I could kill you guys, honestly . . . " She peers under the porch and gives a little gasp. The poet puts a finger to his lips. The doe-eyed one smiles uncertainly, then plants a quick kiss high on his forehead, up where naked scalp is fighting a winning battle against flowing auburn locks.

Her voice moves away from him across the lawn.

"You'll see, guys, you're just going to love Vlady. He's not only my friend, he's a genius."

Cradling the vodka bottle in my arms, I close my eyes. Like a corpse in the desert I lie. Or, as Pushkin put it (I admit) more gracefully: *"Kak trup v' pustinye ya lezhal."*[36]

---

[36]*Prophet, op. cit.* 25.

8

INTERPERSONAL
RELATIONSHIPS

A word on material in this chapter—I.R. #1:
C. WHEELWRIGHT, M. FAIRCHILD—I.R. #2: C. BU-
FORD, D. SCOTT—I.R. #3: S. STUART, C. FAIR-
CHILD

Some believe that Y-persons are too self-centered to bother
with sex. This is nonsense. No one would buy all those manuals
for the style. They copulate like the rest of us, when they have
time. Sex to them is *interpersonal relationship*, often abbre-
viated to *relationship* or *I.R.*

In this chapterlet we shall observe three I.R.'s. No, reader,
I did not crawl out from under the back porch and find a ladder.
Most sociological researchers would be unable to induce interviewees to provide such detailed information on I.R., but Ouspenskiy is no ordinary sociologue. It is surprising what women
will tell you if you keep nodding and stroking your beard and
making sympathetic clucks of the tongue.

The third of these I.R.'s involves a person who (the reader
will have guessed) has since become dear to me. It pains me
to report on her doings with another partner, but in the interest
of social science, I shall be coldly objective.

I.R. #1

Too sleepy to read, Moira turns off her bedside light. At this
signal, Clive marks his place in Mrs. Slocum's bird manual,
puts down the book, removes his glasses, sets them carefully
in their case on his night table, takes a clean towel from a
nearby chair and spreads it in the center of the bed. He helps
Moira pull the nightie over her head, tucks it under her pillow,
switches off his light, kisses her neck, her shoulders, runs his
hands over her breasts. Before long, his face is against her
thighs. He works his way slowly up along her body and enters
her gently but with sureness. Moira moans, then wonders if
she has been heard in the next room.

Sensing the break in her rhythm, Clive is patient. She loves
him for caring. Together they rise to climax. He stays within
her, kissing her face, her eyes. Her man is good at love, she
thinks, just as he is good at law, sailing, running, skiing, back-

gammon. She wraps her arms around his neck, loving him, squeezing tight, hoping to stifle the words she knows are coming, but there is no stopping him.

"Was it nice for you, darling?"

I.R. #2

For Dreda, the sky outside her bedroom window is a midnight-blue screen; the constellations have become squared-off digits skimming across it. The screens she lives with at work and at play won't leave her, let her sleep. She sees another window, the window arbitrageurs watch for: the quote on gold is one-quarter point higher in Amsterdam than in Paris. Her fingers tense, ready to tap out an order, but in the second that she hesitates, the discrepancy is gone, the window closed.

Insane, she thinks, reading the word in computer characters. She stands up, shucks off the Brooks Brothers man's shirt that serves as her nightdress, lifts the sheet on the other twin bed, slides in next to Chip, kisses the nape of his neck. He doesn't stir. She bites his shoulder. He rolls over on his back, making sleepy noises. Her hands race over his body, now touching lightly, now more insistent. He is slow to come to arousal. She wants him. The tip of her tongue tickles his ear. He groans happily. Dreda kneels, takes his tool in her hand, straddles him, lets herself sink upon him. Chip is smiling, but his eyes are still closed. Is he awake? Her haunches move, slowly at first, then faster. He is there, deep inside her, flat on his back, contributing next to nothing. Dreda is infuriated: the man is an underachiever. Her tempo quickens. She throws herself back, digs her nails into his thighs. He makes an upward thrust, his first. They both come. He opens his eyes at last, clamps his arms around her. She lies panting, her face against his chest.

He smiles languidly. "Well, well."

"Well what?"

"Well, the twin beds. You had me worried."

"Oh, that."

"And in front of all the others."

"My dominance thing."

He closes his eyes again. "Dominance I'm used to. But your manners."

What a preppy thing to say, she thinks, lying imprisoned in his arms, listening to his maddeningly regular breathing. The squared-off digits begin to skim across the blackness of his chest.

I.R. #3

Cathy sits propped up in bed, trying, as she has tried for years, to read *Finnegan's Wake*. Beside her is Stu, his Walkman over his ears, eyes closed, probably asleep. A while back, he talked to her, but between bafflement over Joyce and worry over Vlady, she can't remember whether he was telling her about a Mr. Big from Las Vegas or a Mr. Gross from Atlantic City.

She imagines a book jacket, *Halcyon Nights* by Catherine Fairchild. When Halcyon and Stefan smoke grass and make love, should she try a Joycean flourish? "Marry, wanna? Oi weh Maria grassia plena roaming cathylick Stefan diddle us . . . " She gives up, snaps off the light, snuggles down against her Stuey, puts a hand on his furry chest. He rolls her way, throws one leg over her hip, crushes her. She hangs on, trying to breathe. Walkman onus earwickers, Stu pendous Stu Deus outagin inagin finickin's wick agin. Stefan oh 'tis climb Max or gas Mick. When I was a vlad I surgedasperm. He rolls away from her. The Walkman still hides his ears. Cathy thinks of removing it, sees he looks happy, lets him be. Salaam balm thank imam. Post go eatem Tristan. A time to re-joyce?

9

FITNESS: COMMUNAL AND OTHER

Of fitness—*ExerCycling—Heavy gardening —A kitchen whodunit—Brush with a rival commune—A four-footed recruit—Workplay on the beach—Return to locus—A vegetarian breakfast— Procurement of workplay material—Workplay on the court—Account of R. Degan's attempted I.R.—Club life—Confrontation of two commune members—The reckoning*

SATURDAY, MAY 29

The reader will infer from the chapter heading that this portion of our study will deal with strenuous sports and calisthenics as practiced by American Young Upwardly Mobile Professionals, to be observed, the reader assumes, by the researcher last seen lying with vodka bottle amid leaf mold and mouse turds under Mrs. Slocum's back porch, a person who, in the reader's mind, is uniquely unqualified to report on such matters, being neither particularly young nor upwardly mobile nor professional, a person, furthermore, who by the very fact of being a poet, is almost certainly unathletic, having been, the reader generalizes, the sort of puny, pasty-faced child who is always in the library, never on the soccer field, or else in the school infirmary in quest of an excuse, never at the swimming test or the gymnastics competition. Little does the reader reckon with the fact that it is exactly such a bookish and uncoordinated lad who, when not racing through Lermontov or Dumas or Jack London, is avidly reading and committing to memory the names, weights, heights, and scoring records of such stalwarts as, e.g., Dynamo of Moscow, worshipping from afar these heroes of the stadium.

As to the rest of the reader's snide assumptions, it is true of course that the field researcher is not an American, but he is still Young (mid-thirtyesque), Upwardly Mobile and Professional (professing, as he proudly does, the profession of poet). Nor is there reason for the reader to leap to the conclusion that the upward impulse is lacking either in the author's Soviet and socialist homeland or, for that matter, in the family Ouspenskiy. Of this clan's rise from serfdom; of the poet's grandmother, born emancipated but condemned by circumstance, like her mother before her, to life as a scullery maid in the manor of a

Prince Menshikov; of the tradition that the blood of this noble (or ennobled) family courses in the poet's veins; of the peregrinations and persecution of his alternative paternal grandfather, a former second footman, in the time of the October Revolution, the Civil War, NEP, and the Stalinist purges; of the honorable service of the bard's father on the Leningrad front in the Great Patriotic War; of the father's promotion from kitchen orderly to mess sergeant after his capture of a German infiltrator; of his postwar enrollment, through the good offices of his colonel, in the Hotel Management Institute at Sochi; of his appointment as assistant manager (later manager) of the Hotel Ritz-Engels in Novosibirsk; of his courtship of the poet's mother, a Tatar hatcheck girl; of the birth of their son, Vladimir Yurevich; of the family's move to Moscow, where Ouspenskiy *père* became director-general of student mess facilities at the University; of the son's matriculation at the prestigious Graduate School of Ethnology, thanks in part to certain services rendered by his mother to the eminent rector of that school; of young Vladimir's subsequent transfer to the Institute of Linguistics, where he could better indulge his addiction to the word; of his decision to request leave of absence from the Institute on the eve of presentation of his thesis; of his parents' lack of empathy and comprehension when confronted with this career move; of his word-driven agon with the naked Muse of Poesy; of his menial and temporary employment in snow removal and earth displacement units of the Moscow park system; of his unauthorized poetry readings to unresponsive audiences in locker rooms and union meetings in the park department; of later readings in bookstores and so-called "literary" cafés, frequented largely by American lady students of Slavonic languages; of his life of creating and dreaming by day and making love to minor female poets by night in the meager space allotted him in a shared basement apartment, twelve square meters walled in by cartons full of books; of the ridicule heaped upon him by the bootlicking "poets" of the Writers Union; of his gradual emergence as cult hero in the city's grimy bohemia; of the *succès de scandale* of his verse polemics in scorn of such establishment poetasters as Yevtushenko and Vosnesensky; of the unprecedented sales of his work in *samizdat*, wretchedly proofread, polycopied, and pirated as it was; of his threatened arrest after KGB classified him as a social parasite (*tuneyadyetz*); of his banishment to a distant continent—of these matters the reader knows nothing. Nor need he. Our present topic is fitness.

The Y's equivalent of *Liberté, Égalité, Fraternité* is Fitness, Image, Career. Fitness of course contributes to Image, which can be key to Career. Indeed it may be more important in the Y ethos to look (or "come on") healthy than to feel or *be* healthy.

The poet wakes at dawn Saturday in the dark and womblike underporch with the aftertaste of vodka in his mouth and an all-too-familiar afterthrob in his head. These are city sensations, common to Moscow and Manhattan, but there are country sounds and scents as well: the fresh smell of earth, the honkings of a flight of Canada geese overhead, the raucous cry of a jay. A column of ants is taking a shortcut through the bard's beard. There is also a sound he cannot identify: a regular whirring and creaking from some point fifteen or twenty feet[37] above his head.

He will later learn that this is the wheeze of the ExerCycle, installed between bed and window in the southeast corner bedroom. Clive pumps away, strengthening his calves while reading up on trust law. Suddenly he stops pedaling, stares out the window for a moment and turns to Moira, who is sitting up in bed with her stress vitamins and a glass of Evian.

---

[37]Henceforth, let us use the idiosyncratic Anglo-American system of weights and measures.

"My God. I misjudged him. He's serious about this gardening gig."

Down on the lawn is Stu, an even earlier bird than Clive, pushing a wheelbarrow full of tools. As he rounds the corner of the back porch, he trips on something; from his window, Clive can't see what, but cursing is heard in AmerEng and a melodious foreign tongue.

S. Stuart has stumbled on a leg sticking out from under the porch. He grasps an ankle, pulls. The body of the poet appears, in a moist and much-soiled uniform of the Fifth Massachusetts Rifles, c. 1864. He hauls me roughly to my feet and points to the wheelbarrow.

"Push! *Raspoutine, tu pousses ça. ¿Comprende? Puschen.* Ugh. Push."

I get between the shafts like a patient burro and follow him across the grass. If the loud-voiced one chooses to think I speak no English, well and good: I am content to play the dumb brute.

On coming downstairs to get his raisin yogurt, Clive finds chaos. The door of the fridge has been left wide open. Eggshells, orange peels, milk containers, bacon wrappings, empty beer cans are strewn all over the counterspace and floor. He and Moira, on dish duty last night, left the kitchen spotless. Clive looks into the fridge and gasps.

A moment later, he is on the back porch, shouting. "Stu! Did you trash the kitchen?"

"Haven't been near it—never eat breakfast!" Stu sees that Clive is peering suspiciously at me. "The Bolshie's innocent. Just woke up." He turns back to me, points to the ground around the copper beech sapling, thrusts a gardening implement into my hands and says slowly, loudly, "Dig—like in salt mine. Dig, *capisce?*"

Clive hurries back inside, goes to the front hall, shouts up the stairs.

"Who trashed the kitchen? Also, *who put my Chateau Margaux in the fridge?*"

Sleepy voices answer him. "Shut up!" "It's only seven, for Christ's sake!" "Order, order!"

"It's that dirty Commie!" Mort yells from his room. "Kick his ass out!"

Cathy appears at the head of the stairs, wearing a mininightie imprinted with marigolds. "If it was Vlady, okay, he's my guest, I'll pay, I'll get you all breakfast, and please, guys, try to be a little cooler about things." She glares down at Clive. "Clive-o, I am talking to *you.*"

He is speechless.

Using muscles threatened with atrophy since I resigned my post with the Moscow park service, I have begun to dig a hole around the little tree. He of the loud voice lolls nearby, proffering advice in polyglot pidgin. My nominal hostess, Cathy, comes out of the house, bringing me yogurt, a mango, and unidentifiable roughage. I smile and thank her.

"*Spasibo.*" The doe-eyed one looks vague; I am mildly astonished. "*Govoritye po-russki?*"

She shakes her head. "But I *love* going to Russian poetry readings. It's like opera, you don't have to know a word."

Young people are meanwhile pouring out of the house, all dressed in sweatshirts and running shorts. I recognize the two gargantuan individuals, the tall bespectacled man and the pretty black girl of last night's 'round-the-grill gathering; in addition there is a girl, equally tall and bespectacled, and a youth, equally pretty and black. It occurs to me that all eight of these persons are living in the Historic Slocum House. My interest is aroused. Given the disparity of pigmentation, they cannot be members of a single family. The social scientist within Ouspenskiy stirs after a ten-year sleep.

They do exercises on the lawn. Some trot in place; others do knee bends; others perform a rite that consists of bending over and jiggling up and down slightly, letting the head and arms hang, just hang. I look over at the loud-voiced man, who has made no move to join them. He taps his forehead.

"*Sie sind Yuppen, versteh'n? Das ist Yuppensport.*"[38]

A Chevy pickup truck drives at five miles per hour along Slocum Lane. In the back is a black Labrador; at the wheel, an elderly, red-faced man, staring at us all. He turns in at the next driveway.

Cathy comes up to me, touches my hand. She is so different from the strapping Russian poetesses with whom I usually consort: so delicate, fine-boned, slender, so fair, so clean. Talking slowly, with precise enunciation, she looks with her enormous eyes deep into mine, begging me to receive her message.

"Vlady, we're just getting organized here. Please understand, the guys say we're just not ready for house guests. You're welcome to share the weekend with us, but there's really no room in the house, you'll have to find a room in the area or something. You must think I'm awfully rude."

"*Da.*" It suits me for the moment to go on with my idiot-immigrant role.

"Then you do understand?"

"*Nichevo.*"

"I'm sorry, Vlady, but I'm a grouper, and groupers have to obey the house rules."

Grouper? *Grouper!* It is the first time I have heard this baffling and beautiful word.

"Raskolnikov *non capisce,*" the loud one yells. "Eat up your organics, *tovarishch,* and let's get on with this hole."

Cathy looks at the six sweatshirted housemates, who have finished their limbering up and are falling into a rough double file in the driveway, shaking their wrists, jogging in place.

---

[38]The exception proves the rule! I observed only one other instance all summer of a Y-person pronouncing the tabooed word (See chapter 11). Note that S. Stuart had the delicacy to speak in a foreign tongue.

"Go with them!" she says to me suddenly. "Run with them, then they'll get used to you. Isn't that a fabulous idea?"

"*Nyet*," the poet says with conviction.

"Please go, they'll love you once they get to know you. They're just going to the beach, they say it's an eleven-minute walk, it can't be more than three minutes running."

I hesitate, then gallantly offer her my arm, moving my feet up and down in a jogger's tap dance.

"I can't jog today, Vlady, I'm on breakfast duty. Stuey, go with him, please, for me, just to see he's all right."

No man, not even the loud-voiced Stuey, could resist her voice, her eyes. He heaves himself up from his lolling place.

"*Vamos, Kamerad.*"

Noisy Stuey and I jog down the drive in pursuit of the others, who have just turned into Slocum Lane. No sooner have we caught up with the platoon than he says, "Can't run in these, going back to get my Reeboks. I'll catch up. *A tout à l'heure, alligateur.*"

He executes a U-turn and trots back toward the Slocum House. The poet valiantly clomps along behind the others. We shall see no more of stentorian Stuey until our return.

At the head of the platoon, Clive is setting a moderate pace. The others, he thinks, are somewhat out of condition; it won't do to overdo. After studying the map, he has planned an easy three-mile run leading by a roundabout route to the ocean. Down Slocum Lane he takes us, then left into Horsetrade Road and left again after a few hundred yards into Aunt Emily's Way. Clive is running relaxed, filling his lungs with the cool morning air, an improvement upon that of Central Park. Pursuing his resolve to bone up on natural history, he tries to match birds on the wing with those on the pages of Mrs. Slocum's bird manual. He spots one cardinal (*Cardinal cardinalis*) for sure, some sort of sparrow (family *Fringillidae*), and a probable variety of thrush (*turdus*).

Ouspenskiy is in pain. His lungs, coated with the residue of twenty years of smoking *papirosi* and hash, wheeze their protest against the sudden intake of country air. Moira, the fair-haired girl running alongside him, is winded too. She gives him a smile of encouragement; he tries to smile back; a macabre rictus results. Through granny glasses streaked with sweat, an enormous field planted with potatoes is seen reeling blurrily past; then another field, planted in sorghum, a red barn, a farmyard cluttered with agricultural machinery from every decade of our century, a paddock where a mare suckles her foal. The leather of my Russian boots, made for café and disco wear, not running, scrapes skin from the top of my ankle, the base of my toes. These young Americans are mad, I realize. Unless the poet drops out now and walks slowly home, he will be mourned, like Byron and Pushkin, for his early death. He thinks of his putative ancestor, the upwardly mobile first Prince of the line. If Menshikov had faltered at Poltava, he tells himself, slab-faced Swedes would be munching smorgasbord in the Kremlin today, and their hideous language would have supplanted the noble and mellifluous *russki yazik*. Ouspenskiy thunders gamely on.

The black couple is on the heels of our bespectacled leader, running with the ease and grace popularly attributed to their race. My sweat-soaked Union tunic prickles and chafes. The two gargantuans ahead of me, streaming wet, exude a miasma reminiscent of basketball in the ill-ventilated gym of the Novosibirsk lyceum. The landscape is changing. What few barns I see have been converted into residences. Newly built houses stagger by, some offensively modern, others showily rustic. Lawns; hedges; pools. My lungs scream. We cross a bridge spanning a narrow arm of a pond or estuary. I take heart; the beach cannot be far.

Through the blood pounding in my eardrums, I hear a sound like a cavalry charge coming up behind us. We are passed as if standing still by another platoon of joggers, all in matching yellow sweatshirts, yet not sweating, running with military precision. Lurching ahead on what feel like stumps, I pray that the bespectacled one will not see fit to race them.

Up front, Clive glances over his shoulder at the rival joggers. Their leader, a tanned and splendidly fit girl of twenty-five, is almost abreast of him. Behind her lopes a big, fluffy, taffy-colored dog of indeterminate breed, followed by a red-faced, bullet-headed man in his middle forties, who is calling cadence. Eight awesomely muscled men and women jog behind him. Most humiliating of all, every one of them except the tanned girl looks to be over forty.

The girl has moved ahead of Clive; the bullet-headed man is running even with him. A Parisian string shopping bag hangs from his belt; in it is a ball, thumping rhythmically against his thigh.

"Hup-two-three-four. Hup!" He gives Clive a pitying look and says, "So long, slacker."

"My group's out of shape. By July we'll whip you."

"Put a hundred dollars on that?"

Clive looks back. The Slocum House joggers are far behind. Pretending not to have heard the challenge, he spurts and catches up with the girl.

"Hi."

She is brown: brown hair, soft brown eyes, brown face, brown forearms where she has pushed back the sleeves of her sweat-shirt, long, smooth, brown calf muscles. When she smiles, her teeth are a blinding white against her heavy tan.

"Hi, slowpoke."

"Name's Clive." He moves slightly into the lead, to show he can do it.

"Patsy Magee." She lengthens her stride to run in step with him.

"Patsy, may I ask who these flying geriatrics are?"

"City people. Groupers. Grouper house over on Butternut

Lane. Been out here every weekend since Easter. Call themselves the Sodas."

"Sodas?"

"Success-Oriented Divorced Adults. Cy made it up."

"Cy?"

"Cy who counts to four. Cy who hired me to coach them." She tosses her head to indicate the forty-five-year-old Tarzan running just behind them.

"Cy picked a good coach." Clive means it: Patsy is a natural runner. It is a joy to watch her move.

"What's your group called? The Slowpokes?"

He forces a smile. "We're in the Slocum House. Call us the Slokes."

There seems to be nothing more to say. Clive slows down, lets the "Sodas" pass him, then jogs in place until the "Slokes" catch up. He sees that they are all huffing and wheezing, particularly the little Russian. Moira moves up to his side, panting. She is a fierce competitor, strong in racquet games, but no runner.

"Who's your friend?"

Clive thinks she means Patsy until he sees her looking down. The fluffy dog is at his heels, its round dark eyes rolled up toward him.

"Patsy!" he shouts. "Call your dog!"

She is far ahead, out of earshot. The dog rubs a cool muzzle against the back of Clive's knee as he runs. Moira sneezes. It is true, Clive thinks, about her allergy.

The dunes loom ahead of us. *Thalatta! Thalatta!* Ouspenskiy's spirit cries. The Slokes break into a final sprint.

"Come on, Macho!" the larger of the gargantuas shouts to the dog, who has stopped to sniff the dunegrass. "Let's go, Macho boy!"

We race across the sand, shedding clothes as we run. The dog—henceforth known as Macho—bounds behind us as we hurl ourselves into the Atlantic.

The Slokes shout, gasp, shriek. Long Island waters at the end of May still remember winter. Most of the groupmates run straight back to the beach, but Clive, a Maine man, has to show his hardihood. So does Ouspenskiy, last of the Menshikovs, child of the frozen steppes. I swim a few strokes, reliving in memory a plunge on a drunken evening of my twentieth year into the partly ice-covered Moskva. Clive is knifing through the water ahead of me; Macho paddles behind him. When they turn back toward shore, I gratefully follow. The pretty black girl is wading toward us, gritting her teeth to keep them from chattering. Not far away, the bullet-headed leader of the rival joggers is standing in waist-deep water, tossing an oblate ball back and forth with a short, incredibly hairy man.

Dreda has reached us. She nods toward the two men. "Like wow. That is Cy Herkimer. I am in the same ocean with Cy Herkimer."

"Who's Cy Herkimer?" Clive asks. "Does he walk on water?"

"To us arbitrageurs, he's the cutting edge. Since the crash, others firms have been laying people off; Herkimer & Co. is still hiring. Cy Herkimer is the biggest arb on the Street."

"If he's that big, he could rent Long Island. What's he doing in a grouper house?"

"Arbitrage is watching the nickels and dimes. The guy is a state-of-the-art cheapskate." There is awe in her voice.

We watch the fabled Herkimer and his hairy groupmate ride in to the beach on a wave. Clive looks at Dreda.

"Let's go."

"Go where?"

"Don't you want to meet him?"

Dreda's expression changes. Even to Ouspenskiy, who has known her so briefly, she looks un-Dreda-like, suddenly shy. Clive signals "Follow me," catches the next wave, rides it all the way. Dreda and Macho ride with him. The poet, having no prior experience in surf, is tumbled, rolled, mashed into the sand. When he catches up to the others, they are heading toward Cy Herkimer, who is organizing his group for a game with the oblate ball. The formerly fluffy dog now looks like a wet mop.

"Mr. Herkimer?" Clive waits until the bullet head turns toward him. "I'm Clive Wheelwright, Mr. Herkimer, and this is Dreda Scott." He fails to present the poet.

"Call me Cy." The words are friendly, his eyes wary.

"Dreda's in arbitrage too."

She moves closer to Herkimer. "I'm with AstroSums."

Cy is not interested; he turns back toward his groupmates, shouts, "Coming at you, Gerda!" and tosses the ball to a woman with great Wagnerian thighs.

Clive gives it another try. "Mind if we join your game?"

Herkimer glances at him, half frowning. "We've been playing together for years. Afraid you'd be out of your depth. Sorry."

Rebuffed, we start back toward our own group. The poet sees that Clive is in a controlled boil.

"Out of my depth—letterman three years in a row at Dartmouth!" He glances at the tanned girl, who seems to be defending an improvised goal, two sticks upright in the sand. Curtly, he says, "Call your dog."

"He's not mine, never saw him before, we were running and he just suddenly materialized."

"You must know *where* he materialized; you could drop him off on your way back."

"Deertrack Lane, but you drop him off." She flashes a wicked smile. "He seems happier with the slow group."

The ball sails toward her. She catches it and is off and running. Clive watches her evade the opposing tacklers, pass to the thick-thighed Gerda. "She's good," he says, then looks at fluffy Macho. "Down, boy. Sit. Good boy. Stay."

The dog stays, both round, liquid eyes yearning toward Clive as he walks away. Ouspenskiy takes pity, snaps his fingers. The dog bounds past him, racing toward its newfound master. Dreda, who has seen, gives me a smile of complicity.

When Clive reaches his group, Macho is at his heels. Moira
sneezes. Clive moves away, picks up a piece of driftwood and
throws it for the dog, who bounces happily after it, retrieves
and trots back with the stick in its mouth. Man and dog play
with the stick until the man's bad humor has passed.

"Here they come back. Six of 'em, Earl—no, seven. Plus that
little tiny girl who just popped out of Lavinia's kitchen, and
the boy with the football who's shouting 'Suckers!' at the jogging ones."
"Nine?"
"Nine and a dog. Did they have a dog before? I'm going to
call Lavinia in Denver."
"Waste a call if you do. She only left yesterday."
"Two colored ones and the dirty little beatnik one. Look, the
football one's taking him back to that poor tree. What right
have they got to dig up Lavinia's copper beech?"
"Take 'em all summer if they don't use proper tools. That
thing they got is a coal shovel."
"Where you going?"
"Out. Lend 'em a spade. Or we might just yank 'er with
m'stump puller."
"You'll do no such thing. When Lavinia sues those groupers,
you want to be named as an accomplice?"
"There goes Randy to pay a call on their dog."
"Go shout to him, Earl. I don't want that mongrel's fleas in
my house."

Standing in the hole at the base of the little tree, the poet
sees the powerful black Labrador lunge joyfully, knock Macho
over, and try to mount the fluffy dog once it is back on its feet.
Macho, evidently a canine Clark Kent, snaps at the Lab, then
stands snarling, keeping him at bay.
"Good boy, Macho!" the lesser gargantua (whom I now know
as Rick) shouts from the back porch. "Mort," he says to the

larger one, "you really named him. Macho's scared the shit out
of that black monster."

The red-faced neighbor comes bumbling across the Slocum
lawn, collars the Labrador and glares at the poet in the hole.
"Vicious dog you got there. I'll keep mine where he belongs.
See you do the same."

"*Nye ponimayu.*"

"Christ, another Polack."[39]

He goes back to his house, leading Randy. Macho dashes up
on the back porch to join Clive, who is about to go in by the
kitchen door.

"No, boy, no," Clive says, not at all sternly. Then he shouts
to the others, who are engaged in what the poet presumes to
be *un*limbering exercises. "Don't let that dog in the house!" He
points to me. "Him either!"

Cathy bursts out of the door, brushes past Clive and hurries
toward the poet, who is still in his hole, reflecting upon the
nonergonomic design of the American entrenching tool.

"Oh, Vlady, I just hope you didn't understand that. Clive-o
doesn't mean to be mean. It's sweet of you to help out in the
garden. I'm afraid I won't be able to be much of a hostess for
a while, so can you just sort of hang out with the guys until I
get my twelve hundred done? Actually it's twenty-four hundred
today, yesterday I goofed off. You'll be okay?"

"*Ochen trudno.*" I show her the blisters rising on my palms.

"Oh, honestly . . . Stuey!" At her call, Stu stops kicking his
ball and comes over to us. "Stuey, you're working poor Vlady
to death."

"*Basta*, Ivan. *Sehr gut, le trou.* Now let's yank the bastard."

As Cathy goes back to the house, Stu grips the sapling by
the trunk and pulls. I shove the blade of my garden tool under
the roots and apply leverage. The little tree won't budge.

---

[39]Since the early 1900s, Polish farmers have been buying out and working East
End farms formerly owned by Bonackers. Their success is resented.

"You pull. *Tire ça.*"

I pull; Stu snips roots with shears. At last the little tree is uprooted.

"Christ, here comes Den Mother. *Schnell!*"

I stare at him blankly; this time I have really not understood. Stu tosses the sapling into the wheelbarrow, strips off his shirt and throws it over the mutilated roots, just as the girl called Moira reaches us.

"Transplanting," he says. "Had to get it out of midfield." Moira looks dubious. "Don't worry, we'll put it back when the season's over." She is frowning. "Moira, you don't want me hurt again, do you?"

Disarmed, she gives him a smile. We follow her into the garden, where she picks a spot for the temporary replanting. When she has left us, Stu again thrusts the long-handled implement at me. I dig. Oblomovka! I would have been better off in Levin's hayfields.

This phase of the landscaping bores Stu. When the new hole is scarcely half as deep as the old, he says "*Ça suffit,*" shoves the sapling into it and kicks some earth upon what remains of the roots. We then return to the lawn, cut squares of turf from an area near the hedge, go to the old hole, refill it and cover the bare earth with newly cut sod. To my surprise, Stu does the resodding himself, and with great care. Finally he leads me back to the bare spot where we dug the turf.

"Needs grass. *Herbe.*" He points to a two-wheeled vehicle parked in the drive. "Take trailbike—putt-puttski. Go to Hastingsgrad." Stu pulls money from the pocket of his cut-off jeans and puts it in my hand. "Buy grass seed. Sow grass." Again he gestures toward the bare spot. "Grass, *wakarimaska?*"

"*Da.*"

"*Ah so desuka.*" He heads for the house.

The poet pockets the money. From another pocket he draws a pouch, then kneels, shakes out some dried vegetable matter on the blade of the bizarre tool and begins sifting through it, to separate the wheat from the chaff, so to speak.

The vegetarian breakfast prepared by Cathy consists of shredded carrots, diced apples, radishes. It has little success.

"Rabbit food." Rick pushes his plate away.

Clive, usually courteous,[40] is squinting at his celery. "Mine's got a worm in it."

Dreda looks at Cathy. "Refund on grocery money."

"Don't be so menu-driven, guys. It's pure, it's organic, great action on the grazing."

"Organic!" Mort stands up. "You mean they grow this stuff in cowshit?" He leaves, making retching noises.

"Clive-o," Cathy says, "we've got to clarify this house guest thing."

Moira shakes her head. "The rule is no house guests. No room."

"But Vlady is *here*, guys, it's embarrassing. Couldn't we make an exception, this once?"

"Then everyone will want an exception," Dreda says. "If Cathy chooses to feed him, fine. But at her expense—and outdoors."

Cathy stands by the kitchen window, fighting tears. Her eye falls on the poet Ouspenskiy, who is sowing seed on a bare patch near the hedge.

"Look at him, guys, he's *un*believably visual. The timeless gesture of the Russian *muzhik*. Remember in *Easy Rider*, the scene where the commune people sow their crops and then ask the Supreme Being to bless their labors? Oh, I could . . ."

She could die.

By mid-morning, Stu and Rick are practicing chip shots on the lawn, having drafted the complaisant Ouspenskiy to re-

---

[40]Except to "dissident" poets.

trieve their golf balls and replace divots. Once again, as in a rewound videotape, Clive comes loping up the drive with Macho galumphing at his heels.

"Where you been?" Stu shouts.

"Over to Deertrack Lane. Only a mile, not worth driving. Four houses on Deertrack; I tried them all; nobody's ever seen Macho before."

Clive enters the house by the kitchen door, which he shuts in the dog's face. Macho trots out on the lawn and takes over the poet's retrieval duties. In a couple of minutes, Clive comes out of the house, dressed in white from head to toe and carrying two tennis racquets. He puts these in the Subaru, looks at his Rolex, toots the horn for Moira.

Stu drops his golf stick and joins Clive in the driveway. "What's up? Big day at the Spindrift Club? What's the scoop on this club? Pretty exclusive?"

Clive is shouting toward the house: "Moira! It's ten thirty-five! Got to be on the court at eleven!" While his back is to the car, fluffy Macho leaps through the open door and settles down in the back seat.

"This club got a golf course? Private beach? How many tennis courts? Any of 'em grass? How many years on the waiting list?"

"*At last!*"

Moira has just emerged from the house, still in her jogging clothes. She and Clive jump in the car and are gone, dog and all, leaving Stu's questions unanswered.

The noisy one has lost interest in chip shots. "Club," he keeps saying. "How do you like that? Clubbable Clive. Club-a-dub." After a while, he says, "Let's go, Ricardo," and gets into the Skylark. Rick joins him. As he switches on the ignition, Stu looks at me. He is big-hearted, for all his noise, and cannot imagine that anyone could look forward to being alone. "You too, Czarevitch!" The poet gets into the back seat, his dream of a pleasant snooze on the cool veranda abandoned.

We speed down the back roads and turn at the light into

Main Street, where Stu spots the Subaru parked in front of a shop called Sportsgear Unlimited. It takes him some time to find a parking space; competition is fierce on Saturday mornings. I trail along the sidewalk behind Stu and Rick. By the time we reach the door of the shop, Moira is coming out, wearing one new white tennis dress and—world-class shopper that she is—carrying two more in a clear plastic bag.

Stu whistles. "Great dress, Moira. Great legs." Indeed she looks extraordinarily pretty in white.

Clive is already behind the wheel. "Six minutes!" But Moira is studying a painting in the window of Galerie Nadya next door. He blows his horn, races the engine. She gets into the car and instantly sneezes. Macho thumps his tail in the back seat. From their expressions, observant Ouspenskiy can tell that until now they had no idea the dog was aboard. Stu and Rick have entered Sportsgear, but I am still lingering in the doorway when Clive starts to back out of his space.

Moira gives a little shriek. "My card!"

"Damn." Clive stops the car. She goes running into the shop, the poet in her wake. Stu is looking at an underwater watch. Moira finds her credit card on the counter near the cash register, waves it at the clerk to show she has it, and dashes back out.

"Win, Moira! Win big!" Stu shouts in his loudest voice, as if to make sure the salesclerk knows they are friends. Now he sets down the underwater watch and moves over to a display of windsurfers.

"What are we looking for, Stu-babe?" Rick asks.

"Browsing. Think I'll buy myself some whites, go stand in Main Street, see if I can get invited to a club." Ouspenskiy observes that sporting goods excite him. Just as people like Cathy or the poet himself cannot pass a bookstore without buying half a dozen paperbacks and a couple of hardcovers, Stu has no resistance to sports equipment. He runs his hand along the smooth plastic edge of a windsurfer.

The salesclerk moves toward him. "This model's a good value. They're very popular."

"Yeah? Got something more upscale?"

The clerk shows him a real beauty. "Here's the Grand Master. Comes with light-air, moderate, and stiff-breeze sails."

"I'll take two Grand Masters," Stu says instantly. "Each with suit of sails."

The salesman is delighted. "Will that be all, sir?"

"Yes. No. Water's still cold. Got a Thinsulated wet suit?"

Ten minutes later, Stu is equipped to windsurf or scuba dive in any season in any latitude. The poet has never seen spending on such a grand-seigneurial scale.

"Cash or card, sir?"

Stu looks around and sees that Rick is at the other end of the store, fondling footballs. Close by is Ouspenskiy, but Ouspenskiy doesn't count; Ouspenskiy is a known non-Anglophone. Even so, Stu drops his voice to answer.

"I'll be around all summer. Might as well open an account."

The clerk bites his lip. Clearly, he doesn't want to lose this tremendous order. "In what name, sir?"

For Stu, this is the exciting part. I can almost hear the quickened beat of his heart, sense the adrenalin pumping. His eyes dart toward Rick, still out of earshot.

"Slocum House Associates, Slocum Lane." The look on the salesman's face tells him this isn't good enough. Stu takes the plunge. "Moira Fairchild and Clive Wheelwright, co-chairpersons and treasurers. I'm Sturgis Stuart, deputy treasurer."

The clerk looks relieved. "No problem, Mr. Stuart. I've just seen Miss Fairchild's Gold Card."

As easy as that. Stu is so exhilarated that he buys Rick the football he has been feeling up. For this, he pays cash.

S. Stuart's behavior here is both typical and atypical of the Y-person. Typical: his compulsion to purchase nonessential wares, his use of credit. Atypical: his use of another person's credit. Y's are acutely aware of their own credit ratings; hence they respect others' credit. The archaic code of honor is replaced in their microcosmos by a code of credit.

It is no match: the Edgways are twice the age of their opponents. The senior partner, Moira concedes, has a certain cunning; one must watch out for his backhand cut and his crosscourt lob. His wife Leila, a weatherbeaten pioneer preppy, has nothing, except a trick of barking "Out!" or "Close—nice try!" when the shot is on the line.

Moira is in great form. Her last three serves have been aces. The Edgways are growing edgy. Clive comes over to her, bringing balls for her next serve.

"Downscale."

"What?"

"Play worse. He's my boss."

Moira double-faults.

Ouspenskiy watches as Stu and Rick, girt in wet suits, fuss over their windsurfers at the water's edge. It is a day for light-air sails, but they are having trouble rigging them.

"Prick of a salesman," Stu says. "He could have thrown in an instruction booklet."

"He's not such a prick, he let you charge. You want to see a real prick, you ought to see this prick of a bartender Mort and me met last night."

"Yeah? Where was that?" Stu, none too pleased that Rick noticed he charged, steers him toward another topic.

"Well, after the cookout, the two of us go and check out this disco, and there's a broad at the bar, not a hooker exactly—semi-pro—with knockers as big as your head. We're kidding around, I start to feel her up—hell, we've had a few brews, smoked some shit—and she up and tells me I better cool it, she's waiting for Big Lou."

Stu, fitting the luff of his sail into a groove on the mast, is almost too casual. "Huh. What Big Lou was that?"

"This guy named Big Lou she's waiting for. I pay no attention, I'm too busy gazing down her awesome cleavage. I maybe pat her ass, she complains to the bartender, and that prick of a bartender tells me if Big Lou walks in, I'm dead. So Mort and I want to punch him up—shit, we're both pissed—and the bartender and the waiters and the disc jockey start crowding us, saying how Big Lou's coming, he comes in every night at this time with his walkaround, Schlitz, or Schrunz. So I haul off and belt that prick of a bartender, and they all jump us, and next thing we know, Mort and me are on our asses out in the street."

Both sails are rigged at last. Stu and Rick carry their boards into the sea, leaving Ouspenskiy beached.

"So you never saw this Big Lou Whadjasayhisnamewas?"

"Didn't see him, didn't say his name."

"Could have been Gross?"

"Could've. You know him?"

"No, but I will."

They lie on their boards, paddling in the shallows.

"Prick of a bartender made it sound as if this Big Lou owned the place."

"Maybe he does. What's it called?"

"The Slipped Disco."

Stu whistles. "Like the one in Reno!"

"I wouldn't know. Never been to Reno."

"And there's one in Ventnor, near Atlantic City. Probably one in Vegas. It figures: a chain. Slipped Discos in all the betting areas, and Big Lou owns them. So what's he doing with a disco in sleepy, God-fearing Hastings-by-the-Sea, Ell Eye?"

Rick is standing on his board, ready to go. "Not in Hastings. East on the Highway, beyond Nowedonah, going toward Montauk."

Stu stands too. He happens to look my way. "Hey, Boris, want a ride?" As I wade toward him, he begins to heave his sail out of the water. "All very interesting," he says to Rick. "I don't see why. In insurance you meet pricks every day." Stu helps the poet clamber up on the back of the board. "Shall we motor?" He raises sail. "What would you sportsmen say to a little club life?"

Flushed with victory, Edgway leads partner and opponents to a table in a decked and awninged area where members can drink, eat, and contemplate the ocean.

"You two had us worried in the first set, didn't they, Leila? Better luck next time." He grips Clive's arm. "Ever set up a trust, Clive?"

"No. Never."

"Do it. Best way to learn. Wetlands Trust will be your baby."

While the men talk law, Leila Edgway holds forth to Moira on her favorite topic, membership. "They're summer members," she says, nodding toward a group at another table. "You have to be summer for three years before you apply for permanent. We're permanent, of course." She glances at a woman coming from the buffet. "That person is a *guest* of a summer member. I must say, she doesn't look like member material."

Not far from the nonmaterial woman's table is a noisy group of children in tennis clothes. Sitting with them, Moira sees, is the overtanned jogger Clive seems to fancy. The two girls exchange waves. Clive turns his head while Edgway is ordering drinks, recognizes her too and calls over, "Patsy, I've got him in the car. They never heard of him on Deertrack Lane. You'd better phone the SPCA."

"We call it the ARF out here," Patsy says, spooning ice cream into the nearest child. "Look it up in the book."

"You *know* Patsy Magee?" Leila Edgway asks Clive.

"Not really. Who is she?"

"She gives tennis and sailing lessons to members' children. Teaches public school here in winter. Strictly a local. Not a member, of course."

Moira sees that Clive, who hardly ever takes a drink, is downing his daiquiri with relish. Club life: he thrives on it. She has been around clubs all her life; in her part of New Jersey, to be without a country club is unthinkable.[41] Clive grew up as a headmaster's son, the poor but bright boy in a school for the rich and dim, the boys who couldn't get into a better one. Obviously he had to hear a lot from his affluent classmates about club life in places like Newport and Hobe Sound and Hastings. Today he is overcompensating.

Clive, finishing his daiquiri, scans the scene. Lunching at nearby tables are men he recognizes, men his friends and classmates work for: partners in Merrill Lynch or Morgan Stanley, or in large law firms like Cravath Swaine or Debevoise & Plimpton or Shearman & Sterling.[42] The Secretary of Defense is standing at the buffet with his shirttail halfway out of his lime-green golf slacks. On top of everything, Nicholas Edgway is saying he should go ahead and draft the trust instrument for Wetlands on his own. The senior partner has faith in him; Clive is under his wing. He tastes his second daiquiri and thinks, welcome to the club.

Edgway is signaling to a tall man who has just come out of the clubhouse. "Brooksy, here we are."

The man approaches their table. He is about sixty, tanned and bland, in blazer and Nantucket reds.

"Mr. Brooks—Miss Fairchild, Mr. Wheelwright. Brooksy is our club secretary."

After they have all shaken hands, Brooksy reaches in his

---

[41]Joining a country club is not comparable to joining, say, a chess club in the Soviet Union. The new member is admitted solely on the basis of his social acceptability. He need not be skilled in golf, tennis, or any country pursuit.

[42]Again, names meaningful to Clive, not to me.

pocket, brings out a blue-and-white card, hands it to Clive. "Little surprise for you, young man. Arranged by our friend Nick, of course."

Clive reads the card and looks stunned.

"Summer member? Me?"

Leila claps her hands. "Nicky, what a lovely idea." She kisses Clive, then Moira. "I'm so happy for you both. There's no guest fee, you know, for bona fide fiancées."

Brooksy and Edgway slap and thump Clive by way of congratulation. He thanks them both. Then the club secretary gives him an envelope.

"Another surprise. Your first club bill."

Moira stares into her Diet 7-Up, thinking: down payment on apartment, mortgage points, reception, Sri Lanka.

Brooksy is patting Clive's shoulder. "Don't worry, summer members under thirty get bargain rates. You'll also have privileges at Spindrift Yacht, our annex over in Squaw Harbor. Nick tells me you're quite a sailor."

Suddenly a raucous whooping and hallooing is heard from down on the beach. Every head at every table turns to look. Two young men in wet suits yowl happily as they ride a lazy breaker in to shore. On the back of one of the boards crouches a terrified, near-naked and frozen gnome. Stu and Rick beach their craft and start walking up toward the club. The shaken poet follows.

Leila Edgway is aghast. *"But they're not members!"*

Clive stirs uneasily, speaks in his lawyer voice. "Beachfront is public land, of course, up to the highwater mark."

Edgway corrects him. *"Mean* highwater mark. They're close to it now."

As the three approach the Spindrift's rows of blue-and-white umbrellas, the club's lifeguard hops down from his perch and starts toward them. Ouspenskiy is perhaps the most conspicuous of the trio, both for the ivory pallor of his torso and for the Soviet version of the Jockey short, which is his only garment.

Brooksy is pleased. "Watch. Leon will give them their come-uppance."

The lifeguard addresses Stu, who gesticulates with abandon. He looks up toward the clubhouse, finds a familiar face, waves.

"Yo, Clive! Come down and represent me with this asshole!"

All members at all tables turn to stare at the newest summer member.

"Friends of yours, Clive?" Edgway sounds testy. "If so, go down and help Leon explain to them the laws of tidelands—and of common courtesy."

Clive looks at Moira. Her face tells him nothing. This one she wants him to work out for himself. He gets to his feet. As he walks to the steps leading down to the beach, he can feel her eyes boring into his back.

Stu is bellowing at the lifeguard. Rick stands a few feet away, looking embarrassed. Ouspenskiy's back is turned on Stu's *nyekulturniy*—indeed, barbaric—behavior; he chooses to con-template a fishing boat on the horizon. The people under the umbrellas—mothers, nannies, children, couples playing backgammon—have their eyes on Stu and Leon.

"Here's my lawyer! He'll take you and this rinky-dink club to the Supreme Court!"

Clive puts his hand on Stu's arm. "Calm down. You're above the highwater mark, you're on private property."

"Yeah? Who's going to kick my ass off? You?"

"I'm with my boss. He asked me to speak to you. Stu, please don't make this difficult for me."

"You're a member of this Spinshit Club?"

"Summer member. I'll invite you for lunch tomorrow. We'll play tennis, golf, windsurf, you can write your own ticket."

"What about today? I'm not good enough for your Spinshiting fellow members today?" He is shouting at the top of his lungs. Some of the younger men have left their backgammon boards to stand, arms folded, around Stu and the lifeguard.

"Want us to throw him in the ocean, Leon?"

"*Try it!*" Stu's fists are up.

Rick Degan makes his move. He comes over, grasps Stu by the forearms, forces his fists down. "Let's go. Clive's with his boss. You understand about bosses."

"Sure I do." Stu is glaring into Clive's eyes. " 'Shit,' said the king, and thirty thousand loyal subjects squatted and strained."

He turns and strides toward the beached windsurfers. As Rick goes to follow him, Clive gives him a grateful salute. The bearded manikin in wet, see-through Jockey shorts is standing in knee-deep water. When he climbs up on the back of Stu's board, he tries to look as though he were hitching a ride with a total stranger.

Clive walks back up the steps to the club. Facing Stu has been bad enough. Now for Moira.

Going down to the Spindrift parking lot, Moira is thinking of all she wants to say about social cowardice and loyalty to friends and getting priorities straight. What finally comes out is, "You don't seem to realize that Stu is a very sensitive person."

Clive does not feel up to discussing Stu's sensitivity. In his hand is the club bill. To create a distraction, he opens it.

Moira stands by the door of the Subaru, her eyes on him. "How bad?"

"Dues, fifteen hundred."

She tries to keep her voice calm. "Clive. Do we have to accept? *Must* we gentrify at this moment?"

"You know the answer to that."

He opens the car door. Macho leaps out and rejoices all over him. Clive takes one look at Moira's face and leads the dog away. Among the Porsches and Mercedes in the club lot is an old Ford station wagon with the license plate P MAGEE. He opens the back door of Patsy's car and shoves Macho in. Walking back toward the Subaru, he can hear the dog whimpering, scratching at the windows.

Moira looks somewhat mollified. Not much.

10

COMMUNAL

HYPOSYNERGY

N*arrative method vs. scholarly convention—*
Of Y's, non-Y's, Y-oids, sub-Y's, pseudo-Y's—Of
hyposynergy—Gadgetplay—An outage—Electroplay
—Another outage—MDRQ

Cathy, who has read my text to here, accuses me of writing not a socio-scientific study but a story, using a device much favored by nineteenth-century writers, the Omniscient Author. A quibble. Need Freud hang his head because his case studies are superb short stories? Need Proust blush because his enormous novel is first-rate sociology?

Omniscient I am. Have I not lived through a whole summer with Moira, Clive, and Dreda, near-perfect specimens of the Y? As for the others: Stu is Y-oid in that he owns the appropriate garb and gadgetry of the subcaste, but departs from Y norms in his cavalier attitude toward money. The Degans are sub-Y because insurance-oriented; Chip Buford is non-Y because lacking in ambition; Cathy is pseudo-Y because, while fiercely ambitious, destined by her artistry for things surpassing Y-dom.[43]

We shall see that our newborn commune is sadly deficient in the spirit of give-and-take (or "synergy," to use a word often on Y lips), which is essential to community life. This deficiency I shall call *hyposynergy*. One factor contributing to hyposynergy is the Y's preoccupation with gadgets, of which they have brought a surprising number to this weekend house.

Exercise: Count gadgets in chapter. Note truly astonishing fact that only one groupmate has brought along her TV. Remember as you read that the Y's favorite word is "sharing."

Mindful of the bespectacled Clive's instructions that I, like the dog, am not to be allowed in the house, the poet has maintained a low profile. Since returning from his brush with club life, he has lain on the porch swing, dozing and observing. The others come and go, laden with golf bags, racquets, skateboards, beach gear, groceries, and newly purchased summerwear from the brimming boutiques of Hastings, tromping across the ver-

---

[43]So thought I when I wrote this chapter. Today, as I revise, I wonder. See chapter 21, C. FAIRCHILD interview. O my doe-eyed Y—*why?*

anda, banging the screen door, sometimes saying things like "Still here, Borschtface?" or "What a couch potato!" or "Time to purge the Red." Clark Kent does not deign to reply. They seem to suffer my presence as they do the fluffy dog's; perhaps better, for the fluffy dog has disappeared.

Now, as evening falls, I lie musing upon the work ethic, curse of both socialist and capitalist society. It strikes me that in the year 1857, when Ivan Aleksandrovich Goncharov was completing his sublime *Oblomov*, the wretched Marx was sitting down to write his *Zur Kritik der Politische Oekonomie*. There springs full-blown into the poet's head the first septet of what is to become Canto IX of his *Oblomoviad*:

> *Didactic Karl with leaden pen indites,*
> *"An object's value is derived from labor ..."*
> *While lyric, languid Ivan sings,*
> *"The cows at Oblomovka moo the softest ..."*
> *Ah, History, History, what a trick you played*
> *By heeding not the inspired Slav*
> *But that dull Kraut.*[44]

The flavor of my verse, depending as it does on subliminal wordplay, contrapuntal puns, internal assonance, and mnemonic rhymes, is untranslatable, even by me. Let the reader learn Russian.

Like Coleridge, who lost the thread of *Xanadu* when the infamous "person from Porlock" rang the bell, Ouspenskiy is interrupted in the fine-tuning of the nascent canto by the sound of televised baseball coming from inside the house and the

---

[44]V.Y. Ouspenskiy, *Oblomoviad*, New York: USSUCRI, 36 pp. Unfortunately the first edition of this work was sold out; subsequent editions are unauthorized and of inferior quality. The author will be glad to provide Xerox copies of the first edition to those desiring them. Please send $24.95 by certified check or money order to Ouspenskiy, Box 101, Hastings.

thumping and cursing occasioned by Stu's lugging his trail bike up the steps to the veranda. He wheels it to the living room window, so as to be able to watch the Mets game on the TV inside while working on his carburetor. This day, Ouspenskiy will write no more. What follows may be taken as a typical half-hour in the life of the commune.

Sprawled in an armchair, Mort watches the ball game while leafing through *Penthouse*. Moira, wearing a leotard, comes down the stairs, spreads a straw mat in front of the television, inserts a cassette, presses a button. An aerobics exercise presented by a person named Fonda appears on the screen. Stu and Mort shout, "Hey, Moira! The Mets!" Flat on her back, following the exercise, Moira says crisply, "It's my tube. And my VCR."

A station wagon pulls into the driveway with Patsy at the wheel. The reaction next door is instantaneous: Judy Jessup speeds to the phone.

"Chief? FIVE cars over there now!"

A fluffy dog is released from the station wagon. Macho races up on the veranda, sniffs Stu, leaps onto the swing and curls up beside me, as Patsy drives away.

"Hold on. Chief, forget it. Only four."

A sound of hammering above us makes Macho bark.

Upstairs, Cathy rushes out of her room into the hall and sees Chip standing on a ladder, pounding nails into the molding. Dreda is beside her, holding coils of wire.

"Give me a break, guys, how can I write my big love scene with all this racket?"

Chip gestures toward Dreda. "It's for her speakers."

"Speakers! God!"

Dreda stands on her dignity. "I've noticed this about you Anglos. No feeling for music."

"*That* is what I call a racist remark!" Cathy goes back into her room and slams the door. Plaster falls.

Chip says "All systems go," and Dreda steps into her room to plug the cord into a socket. Deafening atonal music, a Schönberg piece, blasts from speakers in the room, the hall, and other strategic points throughout the house.

Down on the veranda, the dog begins to sing along with Schönberg.

Upstairs, an incoherent cry comes from behind the closed door of the room where Clive is drafting his first trust instrument. Dreda has just sat down at her computer when Cathy rushes in, pink with rage.

"Honestly! Didn't you ever hear of a Walkman?"

Dreda smiles sweetly and with a graceful gesture touches both her ears. "Ever hear of *cotton?*"

Cathy squeals, kneels, and tries to rip the plug out of the socket. The entire socket comes out of the wall. The music stops. So does every appliance in the house. Macho stops yowling. Shouts and groans are heard from downstairs.

Dreda stares at her darkened screen. "Hey, you may have lost me some memory."

"Good!" Cathy flounces out of the room into the hall, nearly colliding with Rick, who has emerged from the bathroom, wet, soapy, naked but for a towel.

"My shower! What the hell?"

Heading down the hall, Dreda says, "We've got our own well and electric pump here. No juice, no water, you yo-yo." Chip follows her downstairs. Cathy returns to her room, sits down, touches the keyboard of her electric Olivetti,[45] and realizes that of course it has gone dead too.

"Oh, God, it's not *fair.*"

At the Jessups', Judy is saying, "Where you going now?"

---

[45]It may astonish the reader that Cathy uses a typewriter, albeit electric, rather than a word processor. This lapse is similar to that of Clive, who still owns a Subaru, the Y-car of two years ago, rather than a Saab. No Y can do it all.

"Over to Lavinia's. Lights gone out. Thought I'd take m'tools and—"

"Sit down. Stay put. That goes for you too, Randy."

"Jude, what's the harm in—?"

"We don't know what's the harm. For all we know, they're a cult or something."

Down in the Slocum cellar, by candlelight, Dreda and Chip study an ancient fuse-box.

"It's more than fuses, Chipper. We've got to rewire." She yanks several wires out of the box. "Interface this with that. Then correlate this dingus with that doodad."

Cathy has come down to the porch, where she joins me on the swing. Both of us play with Macho. When my hand touches hers in the taffy-colored fluff of the dog's belly, I shudder with joy. The plumed tail waves a blessing on us both.

"This carburetor," Stu announces, "is a piece of shit."

In the shadowy living room, Mort has moved close to the window, the better to see the crotches in *Penthouse*. Rick, still wearing his towel, is disconsolately bouncing a tennis ball off the wall. Moira lies on her mat, trying to continue her exercises before the blank screen. "It's not the same without Jane," she says with a sigh. Then she sits up. "Rick! Mrs. Slocum's wall!" She stands, goes to the wall, spits daintily on a Kleenex, and tries to rub off the tennis ball smudges.

Stu pokes his head through the open window. "Hand me that phone, Mort."

"Hand him that notepad too," Moira says drily.

"Max?" Stu bellows into the phone. "Stu here. No, no bet today. Research. Fill me in on Big Lou Gross." He listens, whistles sharply, and jots a note on the pad that Mort has just passed to him. "Yeah? What about The Slipped Discos?" Another note. "And the one out here? Just opened? Got it. Thanks, Max." He sets down the phone on the windowsill and tears a sheet of notes from the pad.

"Stu," Moira says, "that's our telephone log. I counted ten digits. Write it down."

"Christ, Moira."

Suddenly the lights come on, Fonda is again onscreen, Schönberg blares forth, the dog resumes its yowling, and running water is heard from upstairs. All cheer.

"Good girl, Dreed!" Stu yells.

Dreda enters from the cellar stairs, triumphant. Chip follows her, grimy, cobweb-covered, carrying his tools. All applaud her, but ignore him.

Cathy leaps up from the swing and heads for the front door. "Back to my big naughty scene!"

My love has left me. Dully, I watch Stu try to start his reassembled motor. No go. I rise, take a hammer from his kit, and rap sharply, once, on the carburetor. Stu again tries the motor. It starts. He claps me on the back, leaving a greasy handprint on my Fifth Massachusetts sergeant's blouse, and vaults through the window into the living room.

Clive comes down the stairs, goes straight to Stu, looks him in the eye, offers him his hand.

"Stu, I'm ashamed about that business at the club."

"Yeah? Well, to thine own self be true, man." Stu, unaccustomed to being on the receiving end of apologies, is uncomfortable. They shake. Clive's hand is now grease-stained too.

At the sound of Clive's voice, the dog has rushed to the window, whining. Now it scrambles up on the sill, leaps into the living room, and slobbers all over Clive, who pats it with his greasy right hand. Greasy Macho jumps into a chintz-covered armchair. Clive drags the dog off the greasy chintz. Moira looks at them both, then at the door. Clive expels Macho from the house. Moira watches. Seeing her back turned, Mort winks at Stu and reaches toward the VCR, to recover the Mets. As he touches the button, by some freak of Dreda's rewiring, the screen goes black, Schönberg stops, all lights go out, and running water is heard no more. All groan.

"Honestly!" Cathy cries from upstairs.

Stu takes command. "To hell with electricity. Fix it tomorrow. Group, be my guest. Big night on the town. Cocktails at The Pub, pig out at the Pot, dance and romance at The Slipped Disco. Wining, dining, and mainlining, courtesy of Stu Stuart."

"There's got to be a better disco," Mort says ungraciously.

Rick agrees. "Right on!"

"Stu," Moira says, "that is truly generous."

Clive squints at his Rolex in the twilight. "What about reservations? It's Saturday night."

"No sweat. I got high MDRQ. Maitre D' Recognition Quotient." Stu sees the forlorn face of the poet at the window. "Cheer up, Gorby, you're invited too."

Water drips on them from the living room ceiling, the overflow from the shower left running in the interlude when the lights went on again. All turn to Rick and tell him he'll pay for the damage. Towel flapping, he bolts up the stairs.

11

COMMUNAL
SYNERGY
ENGENDERED

T*he author as listening device—Persons with-out past?—Celebplay—All about "Them"—The se-cret of C. WHEELWRIGHT—Secret of the sisters FAIRCHILD—Secret of D. SCOTT?—M. FAIR-CHILD's manifesto—Credit code breached again*

That night my research began in earnest: I was earwitness to a conversation involving all eight Y-persons, their first but for the house meeting. Not one word was addressed to me; Ouspenskiy listened. As they talked, I was able to observe the genesis of an embryonic communal synergy.

It is noteworthy that this was the only time I heard my young friends mention their parents. I am still surprised that they did. Anyone entering their rooms at the Slocum House (as I later had frequent occasion to do) would have assumed they were all orphans. On every bureau, stuck in every mirror, were photographs of the room's occupants and no one else. It was as if they had had no parents, brothers, sisters, lovers, dogs. Except for Clive, who displayed snapshots of various boats he had sailed at various ages, they gave no evidence of having a past.

A Y delusion: *I have invented myself.*

At The Village Pub, where Stu has taken us for the refreshments he archaically calls "cocktails," there is no question of conversation. People are standing four deep at the bar and shouting. Nobody asks me what I wish to drink; why ask, Ouspenskiy is Russian, let him drink vodka. I am given three shots in rapid succession. Many persons at the bar, my Y's included, are playing a popular Hastings game, the object of which is to identify the celebrities present. The names, the faces, say nothing to me; I observe that these "celebrities" speak only to fellow "celebrities." My bewitching Cathy makes a spectacle of herself by throwing herself at a certain distinguished Book-of-the-Month-Club judge. I am glad to get out of the place.

Before we do, Stu calls for the bill for all nine of us. I notice that he uses neither card nor cash; he signs. For someone with so short a name, he takes rather a long time signing.

The Lobster Pot is one of those places where they tie a bib around your neck and encourage you to wallow in butter. After

The Pub, it is a haven of refuge. By feigning ignorance of lobster lore, I am able to attract the attention of my hitherto neglectful hostess. Cathy cracks claws for me, extracts morsels, feeds them to me on the end of a delicate, forking instrument. Apparently helpless and hard of hearing, Ouspenskiy makes mental tapes.

Stu sits at the head of the table, shouting. "What drives me crazy about Them is The War." He snaps a large claw in his bare hands. "When my old man says 'The War,' it's not 'Nam and it's not Korea, though he was in both of those; you can bet your buns he means Doubleyou-Doubleyou Two. Got into it at the very end, nineteen years old, tank commander, joyride in Germany, down the old Autobahn with Gretchen's ersatz silk panties flying from the antenna. He keeps saying The War was different, They had a cause, and our generation—he calls us 'You People'—can't possibly understand."

Moira nods. "My Dad's like that too. He was with the Marines on Iwo Jima."

"*With* them?" Cathy's enormous eyes widen in mock surprise. "Big sister, are you sure? I thought he took Iwo singlehanded."

Clive, the lobster expert from Down East, draws a tiny tidbit from a pincer. "My father was on a destroyer, but The War ended before he saw action. Tragedy of his life, apparently."

"Mine parachuted into Normandy six weeks before D-Day." All turn to look at Dreda. They are impressed. They are also surprised.

"Hey, Dreed, did he have any camouflage problems?

"Stu-*ee!*"

"No, dear, he just happens to look very French. He was good at blowing up railroads or something. They gave him a *Croix de Guerre.*"

Mort and Rick's father dropped bombs on Germany; Chip's was a sergeant in the Medical Corps somewhere in Texas. The poet says nothing about how his father fought from Leningrad to Berlin, rising to the rank of mess sergeant.

"It's not just the old man," Stu yells. "Mother's worse." He goes into a falsetto. " 'Too bad we can't have a war like The War for You People. Your father's generation had to learn what Discipline is!' "

"And Sacrifice!" Cathy cries.

"And Teamwork!"

"And Hardship!"

"And Writing Letters!" Moira mimics her mother's voice: " 'You People don't know what it is to write a letter.' Apparently they all wrote each other all the time on something called V-mail, a kind of toilet paper for writing."

Cathy picks a few grains of butter-soaked roe out of my beard, then bathes her fingers in a plastic bowl decorated with a cartoon lobster wearing a top hat. "What'd They get out of all that Sacrifice and Discipline? They're just as materialistic as anyone else."

"They blame that on Postwar. The Eisenhower years."

"Ike grinned and grinned. No one saw fit to complain."

"About the grin?"

"About anything."

"So They went to college on the GI Bill."

"Got married young."

"Gave you the Baby Boom."

"Honestly, guys, They must have had some kind of rule that everybody had to have four children!"

"Yeah, and spend the next thirty years complaining about tuition."

They compare notes. Moira and Cathy have an older brother and a younger one. The Degans are the two boys in a family of six children. Chip has two sisters; Stu, three brothers. Alone among them, Dreda is an only child.[46]

"Did your parents plan it that way?" Moira asks her.

"They did something amazingly ahead of their time, waited

[46.]So am I, Ouspenskiy. But never mind.

until their middle thirties, when their incomes perked up, before they had me." Dreda turns to Clive, who has not been heard from. "What about you? Siblings?"

"One sister, one brother, both older. Sister's in Chicago, works for a museum, been living eight years with the same guy. They're the tail end of the generation that didn't see any point in getting married." The others nod. "My brother Henry . . ." Clive hesitates, makes a face, goes on. "Henry's different, he's a lot older, sort of a relic of the hippie era." Everybody stops dissecting lobster. "He . . . went to Canada during Vietnam and stayed." Ouspenskiy can see that this is torture for Clive. "Has a Ph.D. in philosophy, University of British Columbia. Lives in a mobile home. Looks like an Orthodox priest. Picks apples for a living."

They are uncomfortable. None of them can look at Clive. No one looks at Ouspenskiy either, garbed and coiffed as I am. For these young people the hippies, flower children, student protesters and draft resisters of the Vietnam years are legendary beings, half a generation older, heroic because of their principles, loathsome, like cockroaches, because of their sloppiness, uselessness, lack of purpose.

Dreda announces the result of her latest mental arithmetic. "Our families averaged three-point-five children. Procreation-driven. Why?"

"The Pope," Rick suggests.

"Pre-Pill," Cathy says.

"Masochism!" Stu shouts. "Whole goddamn generation is hooked on nonleisure spending. They loved having kid after kid, just the way they loved their mortgages, tuition loans, installment buying—anything to spend money as long as it was *no fun!*"

Everyone seems to agree but Clive. "My father's never made money, never had debts either. All my life he's been headmaster of the Academy, which ranks as, well, frankly, maybe the eighth-best prep school in Maine. Pitiful salary, but he's got an old ketch and a shotgun and a setter. No credit card, doesn't believe in them. Still has a black-and-white thirteen-inch TV. Never travels except to raise funds from the alumni. Hasn't bought a new sports jacket in twenty years. Just keeps adding leather at the elbows. And he's a happy man."

They are appalled. This is worse than the hippie brother.

"What about your mother?" Dreda asks him, to break the silence.

"When Mother wants a real toot, she'll pile into a station wagon with six faculty wives and drive to Boston—ten hours, round trip—for the Symphony. In summer she goes out to Monhegan Island and paints birds."

Moira smiles at him. "Now we know why you're so big on natural history. My mother never goes into New York, and it's only twenty-two miles. She's too busy with her charities, the Bloodmobile, the UJA. Her favorite saying is, 'I'm exhausted.' "

"Which suits Daddy," Cathy says. "When he gets home from the refinery, all he wants is to look at the sports news and have three bourbons and talk all through dinner about his pension plan and IRA and whether to live in Colorado Springs or Virgin Gorda after he's sixty-five."

"Excuse me," Dreda says to Moira. "Did you say UJA?"

"United Jewish Appeal. Mummy helps them raise money."

"She's Jewish?"

"No. We're Presbyterians. Daddy's parents were Jewish."

Cathy catches her breath. "*What?*"

"Of course they were. Daddy switched over to marry Mummy. Didn't you know?"

"But . . . but . . . *Fairchild!*"

"Used to be Feuerkind. I can't believe they never told you."

"I knew we had cousins named Feuerkind. Aunt Beth said they were Pennsylvania Dutch."

"Jewish. Now you know. Mummy and Daddy were a pioneer interfaith marriage. What did you think UJA was?"

"I don't know, just initials. United Joiners Association? Moira, actually this is *great.* It explains why we're both so artistic."

"Racist, racist!" Stu shouts.

Cathy turns to Clive. "Did *you* know?"

"Sure. Moira told me long ago." Clive looks pleased with himself, every inch the liberal Wasp.

"I still can't believe it. How could they not tell me?"

"Probably forgot," Moira says, "which goes to prove how assimilated we all are. Even the people at UJA don't know Daddy used to be Jewish. They just think Mummy's a little crazy."

"Assimilated," Cathy says. "I'm . . . assimilated?"

"You know what it means, don't you?"

"Yes," Dreda says.

Mort wipes his mouth daintily on his bib. "Blond Jews, live and learn. I figured you were all Wasps, except me and Rick and . . ." His voice trails off. He looks down at his gutted lobster, rather than at Dreda and Chip.

"Hey, guys," Cathy says. "I'm Jewish. Are you upset, Stuey?"

"Nah. What's the difference? Been some great Jewish-Americans—Sid Luckman, Hank Greenberg, Barry Goldwater. Better not tell Beef Stroganoff here. Russians are anti-Semitic."

Ouspenskiy's adoring look tells the doe-eyed semi-Semite not to believe a word of it.

From Jews, the conversation turns to Celts. Stu tells the Degans that the Irish are less pure Celts than the Scots. Soon he is boasting about Clan Stuart. It appears he is descended from James I, and if a Stuart restoration occurs, we'll all be invited to the coronation of Sturgis I. Only his father stands between him and the throne.

". . . and the old man's sure to abdicate in my favor. He got out after Grenada, Major General, USA, retired, lives near West Point, goes to the football games, bangs the junior officers' wives, writes articles about Leadership nobody ever reads. What good's the throne to him? He's happy as a pig in shit. Mother gave up and took off with some old fart of an Ordnance colonel, lives in La Jolla, plays five sets of tennis a day and mails her printouts."

"What kind of printouts?"

"They all begin with 'Dear ExFam.' She's gone ape on the extended family concept. Two of my brothers have kids, and one of their wives has more kids from another litter, and her ex has new kids who are half-siblings of some of her kids, and the colonel has grown-up daughters, who have husbands and/or lovers plus exes and kids, and his wimp of a son lives with this humongous fag in River Oaks, Houston, so my mother wants us all to 'feel close to each other.' "

Rick reaches out with his lobster fork to spear bits the rest of us have left on our plates. "I'd say ours is just a normal American family, wouldn't you, Mort? Dad and our uncles run this insurance agency their dad started in Newton. Mom keeps busy going around to stay with whichever of our sisters has a baby in the works. They're not exactly rolling in money, but Dad drives an El Dorado and he just bought a new one exactly like it for Mom."

"Do they have HIS and HERS on the plates?"

"They wanted to, but those were taken. You must be psychic, Dreda."

"My father's chief of neurosurgery at Detroit General," Chip says, dumbfounding them all. "Mother doesn't really do anything; she doesn't have to. They've got this live-in Swedish couple."

Cathy looks over at Dreda. "Isn't your father a career diplomat? Ambassador somewhere?"

"Well, he managed to retire with the rank of ambassador. Lives in Washington, does consultant work now." The ever-cool Dreda seems flustered. Sharp-witted Ouspenskiy leaps to the conclusion that her father, he who parachuted into Normandy, has spent his life scaling the echelons of CIA. To confirm his suspicions, Dreda has changed the subject. "I seem to be the only one whose *mother* has had a career. Lived all over the world, wherever Daddy was posted, and wrote books on African cuisine, Brazilian, French, Italian. In between tours, it was

Washington. She was the first black housewife in no less than three previously lily-white neighborhoods. Got a book out of that called *Breaking New Ground*. Now she's this tweedy lady of sixty with a new career as a decorator, specializing in re-gentrification of ex-ghetto tenements."

"Did you notice?" Moira says. "We all described our fathers first. Are our families male-dominated?"

"Ours is," Mort says, at the same time that Rick is saying, "Not ours." Nobody else answers.

Cathy unties my bib and folds it neatly. "Hey, guys, ever wonder what Their sex life was like?"

"Not *was, is*," Clive corrects her. "There *is* sex after fifty. Few years ago, my mother almost ran off with one of the younger masters at the Academy." We are all obliged to scrap the mental picture we have formed of Mrs. Wheelwright as a prim, bird-watching, concert-going New England matron. "But then the guy got offered the headmastership of a school in New Hampshire, and Mother said she couldn't go through *that* again."

"When I met your parents," Moira says, "I thought they had a real relationship."

Clive makes a face. "Modus vivendi. My mother is a selfish bitch; my father just keeps puttering around with his dog and his boat and his school and pretending not to notice."

"Remember when Daddy and Mummy had the trial separation, Cathy? You were pretty young."

"Sure. I had two of everything. Two dollhouses, two kitties, two stereos. Then they went and decided they couldn't afford it."

Moira is a sociologue *manquée*. "Six sets of parents, one divorce, two separations patched up, three marriages apparently okay. Are these figures significant?" Nobody knows. "And why is it that none of us do what our parents did—except for Rick and Mort?"

"Yuh, but Rick and me left the Hub for the Apple, where it's at. Key career move."

Moira turns to Chip. "A lot of doctors' sons become doctors. Did you ever consider it?"

"No. I'm creative."

She looks blank.

"He's an AE in an AA," Dreda says. "Account executive in ad agency."

"People describe us as career-driven," Moira says, "but our parents must have had their eyes on the top of the ladder once. Now they all seem to have opted for security."

"Tell my father that," Chip says, "and he'll beat your ear for an hour about malpractice insurance."

"Insurance *is* security!"

All but Rick tell Mort to shut up.

Moira persists. "Look, are we really as success-oriented as *New York* and *W* tell us we are? And if so, why? None of our parents is in the poorhouse. They like to say they've worked and saved and slaved to give all of us a better life. What are we working for? Our eventual children?"

"Big sister, we're none of us thirty yet. A person's not even meant to think about her biological clock until she's thirty-five."

"And then?"

"Then I become a Jewish mama!"

"If we're in no rush to childbear," Moira says, "it's maybe because we're all a bit leery of a 'The War' of our own."

All stir uneasily. The subject is not a popular one.

"At the age of precisely thirty-five," Dreda says, "you and I and Cathy will get to work on producing families averaging one-point-zero-zero children apiece."

"Maybe that's it," Clive says to Moira. "I'm working for our one hypothetical kid. I don't really think I'm success-driven, résumé-driven, money-driven, thing-driven. All I want is to prove one thing to myself and that kid—that I can make it big in a big firm in the big city." He leans back in his chair and smiles at his own earnestness. "With no leather elbows. Ever."

"For me, Clive-o, it's glory. If I do my twelve hundred a day all summer and Dreda doesn't make me short out again in the middle of a Halcyon orgasm, in a year I'll be famous."

"You guys are as full of shit as a Christmas goose with bulemia!" Stu roars. "Your priorities suck. I'll never be rich. If I get it, I spend it. If I don't, I spend it anyway. Sportswriters die poor and leave their livers to science. But sportswriting is fun—Christ, it's fun!"

Most at the table are embarrassed for Stu. What kind of motivation is that?

Only Dreda sees his point. "Money is numbers. Playing with numbers is fun. The bigger the numbers, the more fun. But could I do it all day, all year, if the numbers weren't money?"

"For me," Moira says, "it's not exactly the money . . ."

"Then what is it, big sister?"

"I don't know. Other things."

"Things is right," Cathy says. "It's things, it's clothes, it's eating the best, it's going everywhere, it's shopping."

Moira bristles. "You make me sound like a real airhead."

"I didn't say that. I'm saying you want it all and you want it now. In other words, you're a typical yu—"

Again, all squirm. Cathy has almost said the unsayable. Moira's fair skin turns shocking pink. Worse is to come.

"Are you calling me . . . ?"

"Yes, I'm calling you—"

"What the hell is wrong with *being a yuppie?*" The word has burst out of Moira. "What's so terrible about being young and upwardly mobile and professional? Why the stigma? Sure, you can say I'm thingy. You can also say I'm trying to fulfill my parents' dream, their *American* dream, by having a better life than they did." She thumps her glass on the table. "Fear not, Daddy and Mummy, I'll yup through. I'm damn well going to lead a fuller, richer life than you!"

For a second or two, the others are speechless. The young

and the upwardly at neighboring tables turn and gawk, appalled by Moira's impropriety. It is as if she had stripped naked before them. Then her groupmates all begin talking at once, and it is small talk, directed at Moira, about how to get to the disco, who should follow whose car. They are covering up for her, closing ranks, rallying round.

Ouspenskiy thinks of Moscow's dirt-poor counter-élite, of the fierce friendships forged in the face of all odds, and senses the spirit of solidarity suddenly flowering in his companions' hardscrabble Y souls. Moira belongs to them; she can do no wrong; they won't let her.

When the waiter brings Stu the bill, he turns away from us all to sign it. But Ouspenskiy, presumed literate only in Cyrillic characters, is able to read:

Slocum House Associates,
Slocum Lane, Hastings
per
S. Stuart, deputy treas.

They are all standing now, gathering up their things, ready for the move to The Slipped Disco. The poet sees the groupers as a group, all much the same, each sure that he/she is different. Each secretly admires Moira's courage in defending their lifestyle; each knows in his/her heart that however Y all the others may be, he/she, him/herself, isn't.

12

WORKPLAY AFTER HOURS: THE COMMUNE DANCES

An oversight of K. Marx's—Workplay of C. FAIRCHILD—Of D. SCOTT—Dance of C. WHEEL-WRIGHT and a non-Y—Dream-life of the brothers DEGAN—Workplay of S. STUART—The communal locus penetrated by two outcasts

For the émigré Ouspenskiy, force-fed all his life on Marx and Lenin, so frank a discussion of money, profit, and personal advantage is heady stuff. "From each according to his ability, to each according to his needs" sounds fair enough. "I want it all and I want it now" sounds unfair, but expresses a basic aspiration ever-present not only in the Y, not only in the capitalist, but in us all.[47] The ablest in any society, the Nick Edgways, the Cy Herkimers, the Lou Grosses, the Clives, Dredas, and Moiras take what they need, which is only (according to K. Marx himself) fair. *But the ablest need it all.*

Having caught old Karl in error, Ouspenskiy decides to celebrate. At The Slipped Disco, a converted potato barn, the diminutive poet-sociologue slithers through the crowds of drinkers and dancers like a fish through water. Whenever he is spotted by one of the Slocum House males, he is treated to a vodka. When Ouspenskiy encounters a female Sloke, he bids her dance. Drunk on vodka, hard rock, and strobe lights, he stomps around the floor, cutting down couple after couple with his version of the Cossack sword dance. He is too much for Moira, too much for Dreda. Clive helps him up off the floor and he looks around for the enchanting Cathy.

"Ekaterina?" I inquire of Clive. *"Ekaterina!"* I bellow.

The good young Wheelwright leads me to a far corner of the vast room, where Cathy is deep in conversation with a toadlike, hairy individual of forty. So engrossed is she that she fails to notice the arrival of the great dissident poet.

". . . highly desirable to be on the spring list," the hairy one is telling her. Ouspenskiy finds his hairiness familiar; it conjures up a vision of an oblate ball. "So be sure, doll, your draft is in by September First." *Doll!* By what right does he call my

---

[47]Even Ouspenskiy, apparently so self-effacing, who lives on offal and dresses in rags, yearns to be recognized as a genius. Is this not to want it all?

doe-eyed one "doll"? "I'll do what I can for the book, but our budget for first novels is worm turds."

"Vlady, Clive, hi, this is Jim Stubbs. Jim does PR for Duff/ Lorenz. Isn't that an awesome coincidence?"

Clive shakes the odious Stubbs's hand. "I know you. You're a Soda."

"You group with this guy? Doll, he don't know doodley-shit about running." Stubbs idly strokes her bare arm. "By the way, what's the book about?"

"Well, the heroine's this Sarah Lawrence girl who *doesn't* want to spend her junior year in Paris. But she keeps having this recurring dream concerning Prince Andrew—the Brit one, not the Tolstoy one . . . Clive-o, don't go."

She removes her arm from Stubbs's strokings and tucks it firmly through Clive's. Hating the hairy one, jealous of C. Wheelwright because she wants him by her side, I flow off through an eddy in the crowd and swirl up to the bar, where Dreda is chatting with a bullet-headed, hard-eyed man also linked in my increasingly vodka-sodden subconscious with an oblate spheroid. On her other side, bored and ignored, lurks Chip, who promptly orders me a vodka.

Dreda stands close to the hard-eyed one, head tilted back, chattering upward toward his raised and rectilinear chin. ". . . So on my very first day as a trainee, the boss went out to take a wizz and, all of a sudden, there on the screen was this fantastic window. I thought for half a second, then I bet the whole wad on the riyal. By the time he came out of the loo, Mr. Herkimer, we were back in D-marks and I'd made two and a quarter for the firm."

He is amused. "So that was you. I'd heard that story. Smart girl. 'Call me Cy,' I told you this morning. Your name again?"

"Scott, with two *t*'s. First name, Dreda. That's D-R-E-D-A."

"As in Dred? Funny. I wouldn't have thought he'd be a hero to . . ."

"Dred tried. He almost made it. I try. And I've got it made."

Left out of their conversation, Chip has slipped his hand down to Dreda's superb buttock, only to find that the hand of Herkimer has beaten him to it. Impish Ouspenskiy takes the one hand and places it in the other. Both men withdraw their hands as if they had touched jellyfish. In gratitude, Dreda pats the poet's head.

My vodka downed, I reel along the edge of the dance floor. Stu is dancing with Moira, but his eye is on the door. Two cube-shaped men in dark city suits enter. Abruptly, Stu ditches his partner.

"Going to work. Thanks a bunch."

Moira, who is without her glasses, peers around her, looking for Clive. Ouspenskiy sweeps her into his arms.

This time it is a slow number. I try to rest my head in the shaded vale between her breasts. She fends nimbly. Clive appears beside us, dancing with the tanned jogger-girl.

". . . and you know, Macho somehow found his way back from your house to mine. Doglike devotion."

Patsy seems to be laughing to herself. "Really."

"Wonder why he keeps following me?"

"It's called love, ever hear of it?"

Clive moves closer to her; they dance cheek to cheek. Do I feel Moira's body grow taut, or is she simply trying to keep me on my feet?

"Who brought you here—Cy?" Clive asks.

"I came on my own. Cy pursued me. He's got this idea in his head, wants me to marry him. No way!"

"Because of his age?"

"His values. Hi, Cy."

She smiles her blinding smile at Herkimer, who has just cut in. Clive cuts in on us, puts his arm around Moira and leads her to the bar, whither Ouspenskiy eventually finds his way. The brothers Degan look down at me from their barstools and absentmindedly order me a vodka, as if throwing crumbs to a pigeon. Their attention is focused on the big, sloppy breasts of the woman sitting next to Mort.

"Hey, man, suppose she was choking. How'd you like to give her the old Heimlich maneuver?"

They both guffaw. Mort lowers his face to his beer glass and squints through it at the enormous dug.

Rick pokes him. "Go on, I dare you to bite it."

They howl, punching one another on the arms and thighs. The bartender moves toward them, sets both his fists on the bar.

"Familiar faces."

"Shit, me and Mort's on our best behavior tonight. Don't tell me this broad is Big Lou's too?"

The barman nods toward the bar's far end. "Cool it, wise-ass. Big Lou's on the premises."

I finish my vodka and turn away, to behold my alluring hostess dancing with the *nyekulturniy* Stubbs, who is wrapped around her like a boa.

". . . and guess what, Jim, I just found out I'm Jewish. Maybe Halcyon is, too?"

"Moot question, doll. A few years back, Jewish-American lit was big, very big. Today . . . let me trance on it, I'll get back to you on that one. Like I say, I'll push hard for your book."

She tries to back off from him. "You *do* push hard."

Gallant Ouspenskiy lurches up to cut in, but his beloved shakes her head at him. *Werkspiel über alles.*

The aggrieved poet turns away and stumbles along the length of the bar. He sees Stu, who has just slid into the vicinity of the two cubes in dark suits.

"Great place you got here, Mr. Gross."

The large cube turns his impressively padded torso away from Stu and nudges the smaller one.

"Take it from the Prince of Wales, Schulzie."

The barman hands Stu a bill four pages long. He puts it on the shoulder of the besotted poet, to steady it as he signs, but finds himself eyeball to eyeball with Moira and Clive. Feigning myopia, he holds the bill close to his nose and scrawls on it. Meanwhile (the addled but observant Ouspenskiy notices) he is monitoring the conversation going on behind him.

"So how's your health, Lou?"

"I saw Doc Hop today."

"Yeah? Did Doc Hop give you any medical advice?"

"Belladonna first, Schulzie."

"Noted."

Noted also by Stu Stuart, ace sports reporter.

I fall upon the porch swing. Macho cuddles against me. The others are by now used to seeing us there. Assimilation progresses. But May nights can be chilly. After a couple of hours we decide to move. The poet's stomach stirs queasily as he totters to the front door, opens it. The communal locus is penetrated at last. I follow Macho up the stairs, along the dark hall. The dog lies down next to a door, surely Clive's. The poet sees another door standing open. He rolls through it, hoping to find a bed, but there is no bed. To the floor he sinks and is soon asleep, dreaming a poet's dream of the melodious, mysterious word "groupers."

13

THE COMMUNE'S
SABBATH

For the Y-person, Sunday is "something else." Both Saturday and Sunday are considered a time to "unwind," but a Y may permit himself to workplay or even work on Saturday, to catch up on the week past or prepare for the "upcoming" one. On Sunday, unless the Y is "on the God squad" (as two of our specimens prove to be), work and workplay are theoretically "out." (Singing hymns is workplay—ingratiating oneself with a Higher Boss.) Unwinding is recognized as conducive to Fitness; Fitness is better than Godliness.

On Sunday a Y may sleep late. He need not jog. It is obligatory to begin the morning with coffee, croissants, and the Sunday *Times*. In the city this breakfast is often followed, oddly enough, by "brunch," at which either Bloody Marys or mimosas must be drunk; in Hastings the Y must "hit the beach" before midday, to "catch some rays" or "bronze the bod." Whether on beach or in urban apartment, it is permissible to lie around, even "rack up a few Z's." (In autumn all male Y's must watch professional football on TV on Sunday afternoon; female Y's must also be present, if not attentive, foregoing the museums they visit in other seasons.) Y's in Hastings or any other resort will spend the latter part of Sunday afternoon in a state of masochistic apprehension as they plan and prepare for the Long Haul, the ritual drive on traffic-choked highways back to the city.[48]

Since Monday was to be a holiday, this sabbatine worry was absent on Sunday, May 30th. Perhaps for this reason, our spec-

---

[48.]Riddles heard at The Pub, Hastings:

a. What would you call a parking lot a hundred miles long?
b. If you put all the cars in New York City end to end, what would you have?
c. Give an example of an oxymoron.

If you answered "Long Island Expressway" to all three questions, score yourself 100.

imen Y's neglected to unwind and proceeded with workplay as usual. The brothers Degan of course tried to sell insurance. C. Wheelwright jogged, but planned to unwind; the senior partner had other plans. S. Stuart, M. Fairchild, D. Scott, and C. Fairchild workplayed. Only C. Buford managed to observe the traditional Y sabbath. He racked up fully as many Z's as Ouspenskiy.

In the first light of dawn, Mort pitches through the screen door of the kitchen, stoned out of his mind. Rick is there ahead of him, hauling food and beer out of the fridge. He takes the soggy joint from his own lips and pastes it on his brother's.

Mort fills his lungs. "Man, this shit really does it to me. I mean, y'know, like my min' was in orbit, looking down on my body . . ."

Rick slaps bacon into the skillet. "Yuh. Y'see yourself, like from an ascetic distance." He picks up a futuristic kitchen gadget and diddles it. "Got to get ourselves one of these high-tech whatever-it-izzes."

"I feel no longer earthbound. Metaphizzy. Good karma. *Shantih, shantih, shantih*." Mort passes back the joint, looks at the gadget in Rick's hand. "Egg clipper, y'dumb asshole. Costs fourteen bucks."

Rick snips the top off six or eight eggs and begins dropping yolks into the pan. Mort is gazing out the window.

"Rosy-fingered dawn steals into the mysterious east. In my skull, man, the music of the spheres. Remember Eng Po 1 ? Old T. S. ? And J. Alfred? 'I have heard the sirens wailing, each to each.' "

Rick peels off his tee shirt, drops it on the floor and moves it around with his foot on top of several yolks that have somehow missed the pan. Mort looks at his brother's biceps, his pecs, the beads of sweat glistening on his big freckled shoulders. Again he is moved to poetry; a verse of Herrick's surfaces. " 'Whenas in silks my Julia goes/Then, then methinks how sweetly flows/The liquefaction of—' "

". . . my nose!"

They yowl and cuff each other. A beer, a milk carton, and a can of orange juice are knocked off the counter and roll about on the floor. The grandfather clock in the next room strikes six.

"No more grass, time for mass."

"Bet your ass."

Mort follows his brother out through the living room and up the stairs. On the way up, Rick turns and glowers at him.

"What's this *shantih* shit? You know goddamn well we're lace curtain."

Coming downstairs to let out the dog, Clive lets out a roar of rage instead. Macho has reached the kitchen before him and is busy lapping up raw egg from the floor. Near the dog lies a tee shirt, soiled, sweaty, yolky, beery, milky, juicy. Bacon, burned to a crisp, sizzles in grease, along with a cigarette butt or roach. Eggshells and beer cans litter the counterspace. Clive grasps Macho by the collar, pushes the dog out the back door, and rushes up the stairs.

He pounds down the hall, waving the B.C.A.A. shirt.

"Mort, Rick, damn it—"

The brothers, freshly shaved, showered, and apple-cheeked, emerge from their room. They are in blazers and flannels. Each carries a missal.

"Yuh, yuh. We'll clean up after mass."

The bathroom door is ajar. Clive throws it open. "Just look at this! Drain clogged. Water-Pik left running. Sink full of whiskers and Barbasol. Dirty towels and washrags all over this sopping wet floor!"

Clive gives a vicious kick to what appears to be a pile of blue towels. Instead of being towels, it is the poet Ouspenskiy, who rolls over and smiles sleepily up at him.

"*Dobroye utro.*"

Clive leans against the doorjamb, all passion spent. The Degans go down the hall, bound for the Church of the Holy Innocents. Cathy is calling in piping tones from her bed.

"Clive-o? Please, Clive-o, your sense of order happens to be symmetrical. Did it ever occur to you, ours may be *a*-symmetrical?"

Order in the kitchen has been restored. Cathy is preparing an *omelette basquaise*. Stu stands by the telephone, leafing through the yellow pages of the local directory and cursing. Mort, Dreda, and Chip sit around reading the Sunday *Times*: sports, business, and social sections, respectively. Moira is planning menus on an electronic calorie counter. Still in his Sunday best, Rick approaches her.

"Moira, me and Mort been talking. Lots of upscale antiques in this house, lots of us. We might get careless. Now if we had coverage on Mrs. Slocum's valuables—"

"No. We voted."

Mort looks up from the box scores. "There's a fire hazard, what with Dreda's rewiring—"

"No!"

"Knock it off!"

"It's Sunday, for Christ's sake!"

The beeper beeps on Cathy's Swatch. Her omelet is done. She dumps it onto a plate. Moira watches her in wonder.

"Some vegetarian. Eggs are animal matter; there've got to be eight of them in that."

"Must be the sea air. I'm famished." When Moira goes back to counting calories, Cathy passes the plate out the window to the starving Ouspenskiy, who, banned once more from the house by symmetrophile Clive, has been lurking on the back porch.

"*Spasibo*." I fend off Macho, also hungry, and make short work of the eggs.

Through the window I see Dreda standing behind Chip and languidly massaging the nape of his neck. "Does this turn you on? If you were Japanese, you'd be mad with desire."

Chip swats at her hand with the *Times* society section. "Dreda,
I'm trying to read the ladies' sports page. Guy I knew at Groton
got married—"

Dreda swings away from him. "Take the day off."

On her way out of the kitchen, she passes Clive, who has
just come downstairs dressed in a yellow oilskin jacket, khaki
shorts, floppy white hat, and Topsiders; in his hand is a ditty
bag. He goes straight to Moira.

"I still think you're making a mistake. Beautiful fifty-foot
yawl. Sure you won't change your mind?"

She kisses him. "No thanks. Not if anyone named Edgway
is aboard."

Clive opens his ditty bag, pulls out another pair of shoes, sits
down, and begins to unlace the topsiders.

"What on earth are you doing?"

"If you're not coming, might as well jog to Squaw Harbor.
Can't run in Sperrys, need the Adidas." He knots the laces,
stands, nuzzles her neck. "See you at the gallery after five."

Coming out on the back porch, Clive frowns through his pre-
scription Polaroid sunglasses at dog and poet.

"Do me a favor, will you, uh, Vlady? Hold Macho so he doesn't
follow me."

"*Konechno.*"

Clive jogs out the drive into Slocum Lane. We have both made
errors of protocol. He has addressed me in a normal voice,
rather than shouting in pidgin English. I have answered as
though I understood him.

The poet sits on the steps, holding the dog, who whimpers,
pining for the vanished Clive. From inside I can hear Stu,
roaring into the telephone.

"Got any listings, new listings, summer listings in the name
of Hopkins? . . . Hopkinson? . . . Hopfman? Anything beginning
with H-O-P? . . . Operator, that strains my credulity!" He slams
down the phone. "Cath, come along, help me. Could be a big
story."

Standing, the poet sees through the window that his doe-eyed darling is at the kitchen table, reading the *Times* book section.

"I can't, Stuey, I've got to create and create from now till Labor Day." She taps her finger on the book section. "Or else I won't be in my eleventh week on the List this time next year."

Stu turns impatiently to Moira. "Big sis, want to go? Might need a girl on this."

"Sure, why not?"

When Stu and Moira come out the back door, Macho greets them with effusion. Moira reaches for her Kleenex.

"Control the allergy." Stu looks at Macho. "May also need a dog on the case. C'mon, boy."

Macho happily follows them toward the Skylark. Lucky dog, I think, as I head for the swing on the veranda. Lucky because needed.

At the Café Olé, a popular coffee shop in the village, it is easy enough to tell the summer folk from the locals. Stu walks the length of the counter, selects a seat next to two big old Bonacker farmers, orders coffee. Moira sits down and is about to say something when he signals her to hush. He is tuned in on the farmers' conversation.

One of them points to an article on the sports page of the *News*. "See as how the Jets picked up this guy Hunsicker."

Stu swings his stool toward him and says loudly, "Hunsicker sucks. He can't play worth a fairy's fart. Why do you think Dallas got rid of him?"

The younger farmer looks Stu up and down with cold blue eyes. "What the fuck do you know?"

"Ever read *Sports Illustrated*? I'm Stu Stuart. Last time I interviewed the Dallas front four, they . . ."

While Stu talks Cowboys to the farmers, Moira reads the art news in the *Times*. "This is work?" she says sotto voce, half to herself, half to Stu. When the farmers get up to go, they still seem unconvinced that Hunsicker sucks.

"Nice talking to you," Stu says. "Say, you guys live around here?"

The blue-eyed farmer sets his mouth in a tight smile. "On'y 'bout sixty years."

"Know a good vet for my dog?"

"There's Doc Browne, there's Doc Stark. . . ."

Casually, Stu asks, "What about Doc Hop?"

"Hopper? He's no use to you."

"Why not?"

The older farmer rubs the stubble on his chin. "Hopper's semi-retired, though he's a young fella. Travels a lot, drives his Bentley, sits around in that big house over on Beachplum Lane."

"Try Doc Browne," the other says. "He's the best."

"I will. Thanks a lot."

As soon as they are gone, Stu slides off his stool, slaps a tip on the counter.

"Moira, baby, let's haul ass. I learned a lot."

Mystified, she follows him out.

Stu drives to the end of Beachplum Lane and stops in front of a driveway marked simply "H."[49] A big silver-gray Bentley is parked at the foot of the steps leading to the house on the dune above them. Moira is more baffled than ever.

---

[49] There is a subtle point of local class distinction here. In Hastings every driveway is marked in some fashion. The lower orders favor signs shaped like whales or Canada geese, with such legends as LIZ & HAL or POP 'N' DOT. Locals and the more fastidious of the summer and year-round residents from other parts have their last names on their mailboxes, e.g., SLOCUM, JONES, WOOD. Those who fancy that they are sufficiently rich or prominent to be of interest to burglars mark their drives with a single initial. Nicholas Edgway's sign, Clive tells me, says E.

"I thought we'd be going to Dr. Browne's."

"You got to be kidding. All I want you to do is walk up those steps, calling, 'Here, Macho, here, boy!' If anyone stops you, say you're looking for your dog, not trespassing. Engage them in conversation until I get there. Got it?"

"Why don't you do it?"

"Easier for a girl."

"Not this girl."

"Moira, you said you'd help me. Investigative journalism."

Dragging her feet, she gets out of the Skylark and walks up toward the house, calling, "Here, Macho!" She can hear the dog whining inside the car. Then Stu's voice: "Shut the fuck up."

Moira has reached the top of the steps. Avoiding the front door, she walks around the corner of the house, out of Stu's sight, calling forlornly for Macho, feeling more and more the intruder, the idiot.

On the side facing the beach is a broad wooden deck. A smooth, sleek man in his late thirties is spread-eagled on a chaise longue, soaking up sun. He is wearing a minimal Italian bikini, pastel apricot. His slender tanned body has been freshly oiled. Beside him are a newspaper and an old leatherbound book. Moira calls for Macho again, louder. The man removes his green plastic eye shields and gets to his feet, frowning. When he sees that the trespasser is a pretty girl, the frown is gone.

"Can I help you?" His accent is Mitteleuropa crossed with Middle America, something between a Kissinger and a Reagan.

"Excuse me, I'm looking for my dog. He's sort of a . . . ?"

"Come on up here, great view of the beach. If he's anywhere on it, you'll see him. Let me build you a drink. Just built myself a Bloody Mary."

She goes onto the deck. The man's eyes, dark and deep under outsize, unkempt eyebrows, make her uneasy. "Not a sign of him," she says, pretending to scan the beach. "I'll have a Virgin Mary, please."

"You mean a Bloody Shame." He chuckles at his own wit.

"I'm Enos Hopper. Everybody calls me Doc Hop."

"Moira Fairchild." Having said her name, she panics. Did Stu wish her to conceal her identity?

Doc Hop hands her a tomato juice. "Sit down, tell me all about Macho." He sinks onto the chaise longue and pats a cushion beside him.

Moira hesitates, wondering how to play it. She hates Stu Stuart.

"Found him, Moira!" a loud voice bellows.

Relief: she loves Stu Stuart. The frown is back on Doc Hop's face. Stu and Macho appear at the corner of the house and come up on the deck, uninvited.

"Hi, nice place you got here." When his greeting is not acknowledged, Stu looks around, sees a long fishing rod leaning against a doorjamb and goes toward it. "You're a surf caster? How're they running?"

"How's what running?" Doc Hop's voice is icy.

"Whatever you fish for." Giving up on the topic, Stu leads Macho toward the vet. "Don't know what's wrong with this dog. Won't eat."

As they draw near the heavy-browed man, Macho hangs back and moans.

In a professional voice, Doc Hop says, "Let's have a look." He goes to Macho, who cowers and snarls. "Macho, eh? Funny name for this one." The vet clamps both hands on the dog's muzzle and stares down with deepset, tired eyes. Macho stops growling, relaxes, wags a fluffy tail. When Doc Hop releases his grip, the dog gives his hand a lick.

Stu has just enough time for a quick sideways peek at the folded newspaper and the old book lying on the chaise longue before Doc Hop turns back to him.

"Seems healthy enough to me, but large animals are my gig, strictly consultant basis. See Dr. Browne."

"I'll do that. Thanks, Doc, sorry to bust in on you."

"Doctor, thank you for the drink."

As they walk down to the Skylark, Moira can see that Stu is delighted with the progress of his investigation.

Clive cannot believe that the New York Yacht Club membership committee was properly informed on Nicholas Edgway's helmsmanship: he is having trouble tacking his lovely yawl *Equity* out of the harbor. After failing for the second time to fetch the nun buoy off the breakwater, the senior partner turns to him.

"Like to take her?"

Eagerly, Clive gets behind the wheel. He trims the main a bit, eases the mizzen. The yawl begins to point better. Sam, the paid hand, comes up from below, bringing them Gibsons.[50] He has felt the boat pick up speed. Now he looks at Clive with approval.

Ahead is a ketch of about *Equity's* size. Determined to overtake her, Clive works his way upwind, succeeds in getting above her. He is straining every nerve to inch ahead when Edgway spoils it all.

"Let Sam take over. We'll go below and have a look at your draft of the trust instrument. Bring your drink."

Commiseration is in every wrinkle of Sam's weatherworn face as he watches Clive follow their boss down the companionway.

The Skylark is caught in the Saturday morning traffic jam on Main Street, which is not only the social and commercial center of Hastings but also a part of the Highway to Montauk. Moira is still trying to make sense out of their intrusion on Doc Hop.

"What a creepy man. Did you notice his eyes?"

"I notice everything. Goddamn traffic. I'm going to miss post time."

---

[50]Clive, as remarked earlier, is no drinker. But he is a Y-person, it's Sunday, and it is in his interest to be convivial with Mr. Edgway.

"Mind telling me what all this proves?"

"Nothing yet. Last night I happened to overhear this conversation at the disco: Lou Gross, big in Vegas, big in Atlantic City, telling a guy named Schulzie about somebody he calls 'Doc Hop,' whose 'medical advice' is 'Belladonna, first.' But there's no vet named Hopkins or Hoppenstrudel listed in the local directory. I knew he'd be a vet."

"How?"

Stu stares at her as if she were retarded. " 'Belladonna, first!' So my investigative reporting this morning turns up a vet named Hopper, semi-retired, travels a lot, has Bentley and million-dollar beachfront house with unlisted number. Pretty good large-animal practice! By the way, you seen any large animals around here?"

"A few horses. There are livery stables—"

"No cows. Now, the *Sporting News* on the Doc's chaise lounge happens to be folded to the chart for Belmont."

"And that old book?"

"Title, *Animal Magnetism*. Must be a vet text. Couldn't read the author's name upside down, but it began with an M." He pounds on the steering wheel and yells, "Christ, this traffic!"

All forward movement on Main Street has ground to a halt. Stu flings open his door, leaps out, sprints to a sidewalk phone.

Above the honking in the traffic jam, Moira can hear him shouting into the instrument. "Max? Stu . . . Belladonna in the first at Belmont. To win. One hundred bucks." He hangs up, runs back to the car, grins at Moira. "I put my money where my mouth is."

She is thoughtful. "Stu, you meant it last night. You really love your work, don't you?"

"Doesn't everybody?" His surprise is real. "Doesn't Clive love the law? Don't you love art dealing?"

It is a moment or two before Moira answers.

"Define 'love.' "

* * *

The poet lies on the porch swing, watching Cathy and Dreda, both in bikinis, hard at work upon the lawn. Do not imagine they are gardening. The electric typewriter of the one and the computer of the other are linked by a long string of extension cords to the house. So are the stereo speakers, tuned today to moderate volume, playing Afghan shepherd's-pipe airs. The two girls are sitting on beach towels, leaning forward over their keyboards, thus affording Ouspenskiy a view of Dreda's full breasts brimming from her bikini top and of Cathy's legs, crossed before her as she writes, the fair skin beginning to turn an auroral pink, the slender thighs showing a womanly swell.

Is there any greater pleasure than to loll in idleness, watching others work? The poet is reminded of a favorite passage in *Oblomov*, when Ilya Ilyich sits on a kitchen chair, admiring the erotic motion of the plump elbows of his landlady, Agafya Matveyevna, as she kneads the dough for his dumplings. Who has time for a woman's elbows today? I do. I look at Cathy's. Far from being plump, they are finely turned and roseate, with dimples in the crook.

I think again of my canto about Marx and Goncharov. Ivan Aleksandrovich was, it appears, a colorless fellow, almost as correct and boring as the sainted Karl. Like Chaucer, like Trollope, he was a civil servant, first in the finance ministry, later, when Nicholas I wished to give the impression that he was liberalizing the censorship, a censor. He followed the path of least resistance all his life. His one adventure was a voyage to the East. "Having casually expressed the wish to go to the Far East as secretary to a mission to Japan, he was taken at his word, and only when it was too late, he realized that he was obliged to go, at the risk of appearing ridiculous."[51] How Oblomovian!

Besides Ilya Ilyich, there are two other important male char-

---

[51]D. S. Mirsky, *A History of Russian Literature*. Edited by Francis J. Whitfield. London: Routledge, Kegan & Paul, 1968.

acters in the novel. One is Zahar, his irascible serf and valet, whom Soviet critics see as a victim of the exploiting class. They miss the point: Zahar is as lazy as his master, and, for all his grumbling, happy in his sloth. The other major male character is Oblomov's energetic friend Stolz, half German (Goncharov couldn't imagine an efficient Russian), an entrepreneur, full of idealistic projects that invariably make money. Critics see Stolz as hopelessly tedious, a failure of characterization. Wrong again. Just as Oblomov is an example of the *lishniy chelovek*, the Superfluous Man, who keeps turning up in our literature from Onegin to Uncle Vanya, Stolz is a caricature of the New Man, who in the 1850s was preparing to remake society, whether capitalist or socialist, in his own image. *Stolz is Marx.* He is also John D. Rockefeller.

Do I regret that the Stolzes won and the Oblomovs lost? Am I nostalgic for the late-feudal Russia of the last century? Must a man answer his own rhetorical questions? It is not easy to emulate Oblomov in Russia or America today, but one must try.

Time, the poet thinks, to steal another look at Cathy's elbows. They have stopped moving; she is having trouble concentrating. Dreda on the other hand is computing a mile a minute. Cathy watches her with envy.

"Dreda . . . please tell me what you're doing."

"Correlating data on recent fluctuations of the foreign currency market." Her eyes are still on the screen, her fingers flying over the keys. "Got to stay ahead of those big Koreans."

"What are those lines moving up and down?"

"Graphics. Sometimes they surprise you, like the ocean; sometimes they're predictable, like Bach. I'm trying to identify a pattern whereby a 'window' could be forecast in, e.g., the Swiss franc-Dutch guilder or the yen-peso rate."

"That's arbitrage?" Cathy is limp with admiration. "I'm not even computer-literate."

"And I'm not lit-literate." Dreda stops computing, looks over at her. "How come you're a writer? You don't look bohemian."

"It's a long story, really gross. Shall we take a break?"

Both girls rise and walk through the privet arch into the garden, taking their beach towels with them. It might be time (the gardener's aide Ouspenskiy thinks) to do some discreet weeding. He is restrained by the thought that it might be an even better time to raid the fridge. Cathy has neglected to bring his lunch.

In a remote corner of the garden, screened by the privet from prying eyes, Cathy and Dreda spread their towels, take off their bikini tops and apply suntan oil.[52] Cathy has begun telling her long and gross story.

"... then you go to college and get A-minuses in freshman English, and some wimp of a section man tells you how talented you are, so you major in Creative, and you sign up for a summer writing workshop in Vermont or somewhere ..."

Meanwhile, Earl Jessup happens to be up in his attic, rummaging about.[53] Through the dormer window he sees his Lab Randy heading toward the Slocum garden. A splash of pink, a flash of brown catch his eye. He rubs the dust from the pane, looks again, then rushes to the head of the attic stairs.

"Judy! Judy! Come bring m' field glasses. Randy is pointing some birds!"

She calls up to him from the kitchen. "Earl, I just dropped 'em off at the optician's. Needed cleaning!"

Cursing, Earl clatters down the steps.

The girls are lying on their towels, sunning their backs.

" ... and finally you go on a hike to the top of some dumb mountain with the youngest, least nerdish writer-in-residence,

---

[52]This, I swear, comes not from personal observation, but from notes on subsequent conversations with C. Fairchild and D. Scott.

[53]I have E. Jessup's remarkably frank account of this incident on tape. (The researcher Ouspenskiy supplied bourbon.)

and he says he'll send one of your stories to the *Oberlin Review*, so you naturally have to let him—"

"Skip that part."

"Then you get published in a couple of lit mags, and some airhead from the *Paris Review* introduces you to an agent, and after four martinis the agent invites you for D & D, that's Dinner and 'Dynasty . . .' "

Earl is feverishly looking through his gun collection, which is housed in a cabinet in the sunroom. He finds a German sniper rifle and races for the stairs.

". . . and the agent gets you asked to a power brunch with some big horny editor from Duff/Lorenz—go away, dog—and after six margaritas you manage to say 'Advance?' But what he really wants is to advance his knee into your lap."

Dreda looks at Cathy as if she had never seen her before. "I didn't know writing was so fast-lane. You've got to be tough."

"I *am* tough."

Cathy's Swatch and Dreda's Seiko beep simultaneously. Both girls sit up.

Earl huffs and puffs his way up from the second floor to the attic. He goes to the window, opens it, takes careful aim.

The cross hairs of his powerful telescopic sight are trained first on Dreda, then on Cathy. Both have just turned over to lie on their backs. From the waist up, they are hidden by Mrs. Slocum's rosebushes.

"Goddamn shameless hoors . . ."

Down in the cabin, Clive can feel *Equity* lift and glide as Sam guides her through heavy swell. He is impatient to go topside and take the wheel, but Edgway is still reading through his draft of the trust instrument. At last he sets it down, takes off his glasses, rubs his eyes.

"Yes . . . but there's no reason to mention the Hemisphere Foundation."

"Why not, since they're funding Wetlands?"

"Wetlands is a New York State trust. Beneficiary, the people of this state. Hemisphere, a Bahamas nonprofit organization, happens to be the first donor. There will be other donors." Edgway replaces his glasses, draws a line across the page with a gold pencil. "Strike Hemisphere."

"What exactly is the Hemisphere Foundation?"

"Consortium of private benefactors from the US, Canada, and various Latin American countries, concerned about the environment in this hemisphere. I've got a full list at the office. Ready for another trick at the wheel?"

Clive springs to his feet. "Yes, *sir!*"

"Nick. We're on a Clive-Nick basis. Good job you've done here. Keep it up and we'll make you *sole* trustee."

Clive is dazzled.

The poet, having pillaged the fridge with more subtlety than the brothers Degan, decides it would be politic to ingratiate himself with the groupmates by doing some further gardening. He finds fertilizer in a toolshed, piles a couple of sacks on the wheelbarrow and pushes it across the lawn.

Moira, spraying the roses, wears some sort of surgical mask over nose and mouth.[54] Macho is nipping at Randy's hocks, chasing him back to the Jessup house. Australian aborigine chants are now coming from the stereo speakers. Returning from the garden, the two sunbathers pass Ouspenskiy and his barrow.

"I'd love to be like Vlady," Cathy tells Dreda. "He says that all you have to do to be a poet is to live like one."[55]

"You don't have to work?"

---

[54] Y-persons are deathly afraid of chemical products that may affect themselves or the environment. Many would prefer to be bled white by mosquitoes or see their roses eaten by Japanese beetles, rather than use a spray.

[55] Cathy has apparently read the English text of my *Zhizn' Poeta*, a Xeroxed handout at my USSUCRI readings.

"*Nyet.*"

The two of them settle down by their machines. During their sunbath they have come to know each other. Time now to work.

"You know, Dreda, Jim Stubbs doesn't think the market is right for 'another Jewish novel,' but he told me I'd sell fifty percent more copies if I found some other way to 'broaden the ethnic base' of my book. I may throw in a black girl as Halcyon's best friend."

"Call her Mandy."

Dreda touches the switch on her computer; the screen glows. Cathy turns on her typewriter; it hums. Both are poised to hit the keyboard when Moira plugs an electric hedge clipper into the string of cords.

A crack, a spark, and everything shorts out.

Dreda rises. "*More* rewiring."

Stu comes running out of the house. "Moira! I won! Belladonna won and paid $28.20! I've made thirteen hundred bucks!"

"That's nice, Stuey." Cathy's tiny voice sounds a bit dry. "Now you can pay me back my share of the rent refund."

"Not the point. Big Lou consults vet; vet picks winners. I'm on to a real story here. I can smell it!"

Nearby, the organics freak Ouspenskiy is putting manure on the newly seeded bare patch.

Clive arrives at the club dock in *Equity's* tender, piloted by Sam, and is greeted with a wave by Patsy, who has just given a sailing class to ten-year-olds in twelve-foot dinghies. She has been hauling the little boats up onto the float, but there are still two in the water.

"Want to race?"

He jumps from the tender directly into one of the dinghies and hoists the sail. Patsy, sitting in the other, points across the harbor.

"Race you to those pilings off the boatyard."

"You're on."

And they're off. Clive moves ahead of Patsy and backwinds her. He is close to the pilings when he hits a sand bar. Hard aground, he has to get out of the boat to pull himself off. Patsy laughs at him as she passes.

"No fair!" he shouts. "Local knowledge!"

"Race you back!"

But Clive has seen something that interests him ashore. He wades toward the boatyard, dragging the dinghy behind him.

When Patsy joins him a minute or two later, he is standing in shallow water, staring at the skeleton of a small boat propped on a cradle twenty feet away.

"She's lovely," he whispers. "I didn't know anyone still bothered to build boats out of wood."

Patsy wonders why he is whispering until she sees the old man in dungarees sitting on an upturned crate at some distance from the skeletal boat, staring at her with an expression as rapt as Clive's.

"Keelson, strakes." Clive speaks as though reciting a litany. "Sternpost, clinker-built . . ."

"You're into boatbuilding?"

"Making ship models used to be my hobby."

"Used to?"

"A hobby's what you do in your spare time. I haven't had any in seven years."

"You kidding?" Patsy sees he is not. "Would you like to meet the builder? Rufe Hawkins, right over there."

Clive hesitates, then shakes his head. "He's thinking about her, not about anything else. I'll meet him another day."

"Seven years from now?"

He smiles absentmindedly. Like Rufe, he has eyes only for the boat.

Chip, who has had the good sense to take his afternoon snooze on the beach, is absent when Dreda needs him. She recruits

Ouspenskiy to help her out in the cellar. By crossing wires at random, then banging the box with a lug wrench, I get the lights back on. As a reward, Dreda allows me to accompany her to the opening at Galerie Nadya, on which Moira has told her she would like to have a lay opinion. Thus I am treated to my first ride in a BMW.

Having attended the openings of émigré acquaintances in New York who fancy themselves painters, I am not surprised by the scene at the gallery. The people are in sports clothes, but the faces are the same as you would see at an opening in SoHo or on Fifty-seventh Street. There is the same miserable white wine in plastic cups. Nobody looks at the paintings. Conversation is chiefly about traffic.

Moira, who arrived before us in the Subaru, is talking with the gallery owner, one Nadya, a squat, fiftyish woman with short gray hair, rough-knit gray sweater, charcoal-gray jeans.[56] I hover near them.

". . . and I'm with Art Futures on Fifty-seventh."

Nadya waves a hand toward the paintings. "What do you think?"

"Plasticity." Moira's voice is guarded, neutral. "Varietal. Tending toward the Kandinski-esque?"

"Dear, you must meet the artist. Elowyn's a darling."

She leads Moira to the painter Elowyn, who looks like Nadya, but worse. On my way to refill my cup with the dreadful plonk, I pass Dreda, who is moving at a glacial pace from one painting to the next. To me they all seem alike, although variations may be detected if one cares enough to look for them. They are apparently abstract, abstract in a way that makes a man nostalgic for socialist realism. I watch Dreda. First she reads the title; then she steps back a few feet and studies the whole picture; finally she moves in until her nose is scraping canvas

---

[56]Nadya, Moira informs me, was the woman described by Leila Edgway as "not member material."

and scans it inch by inch. What (the esthete Ouspenskiy wonders) can she see in them?

I drift over to Moira, now talking with Nadya and Elowyn, and getting thoroughly patted, petted, and palped by both.

"Some people even describe my work as abstract expressionist," Elowyn says, sneering the last two words.

Moira is crisp, professional. "Which of course it's not."

"No. It's satellitic photo-realism."

"Sat . . . ?"

". . . ellitic. I used to be an analyst for the National Weather Service. My paintings are based on satellite photos."

To escape the pawings of the two women, Moira goes to the nearest picture. "This one . . . homage to Frankenthaler?"

Nadya gives Moira's waist a joyful squeeze. "She understands!"

Dreda joins them. "I'm intrigued by the titles," she says to Elowyn. "This one, for instance: 'Storm Suite 38.' What does it mean?"

"They're all storm patterns, based on satellite and other data on tropical storms that have hit the Northeast in the past fifty years."

With her forefinger, Dreda traces a curved line running down the middle of the painting. "The Atlantic coast?"

"Yes, a recurring theme. This one's the most dramatic—the Great Hurricane of '38, which simply ravaged this area. No satellites then, of course; I had to extrapolate from weather records." She gestures toward other canvases. "Hurricane Dora, '54 . . . the one in '63 . . . '75 . . . Gloria, '85 . . ."

"Riveting."

Ouspenskiy can't think why. Moira and Nadya are standing apart from the other two, talking prices. I begin to wonder how long Dreda plans to stay. Is it worth waiting around for a second ride in the BMW? Dare I walk?

Clive, still in his sailing clothes, has just entered the gallery.

Although he has jogged all the way from Squaw Harbor, he is neither perspiring nor out of breath. After a brisk trot around the room, during which he squints incredulously at each painting, he ends up near me.

"What do you think, Vlady?"

"*Skuchno.*"

"Yep. Crap."[57]

Moira is still talking earnestly with Nadya. Clive catches her eye, sends a message by body language.[58] She disengages and joins him at the door. I loiter near them. If Dreda remains riveted, Ouspenskiy will ride in the Subaru.

"I'm grossed out," Clive says in a mumble.

Moira answers, fast and low. "It's not Elowyn's art I'm big on, it's her prices. You know I've got that C.D. coming due. After paying you back on the rent, I could use the rest of it and some of my discretionary income to buy a few Elowyns." Clive's face is a storm pattern; she hurries on. "Then I persuade my boss to give her a one-person on Fifty-seventh, I network with every critic I know, make sure she gets the reviews. In a year, hopefully, she moves to a better gallery, her prices triple, and I make a bundle."

Clive is stunned. He has seen a new Moira.

"Is that ethical?"

She smiles, not her usual smile, a smart Manhattan smile.

"My therapist always says, 'If you want ethical, you got no business in art business.' "

Stunned again. "You're seeing a therapist?"

Moira is stunned in her turn.

"Aren't you?"

---

[57] I stated earlier that Y-persons use obscenities freely. Clive is an exception. "Crap" is strong language for him.

[58] A thoroughly American gesture: he holds his hand palm down at the level of the bridge of his nose, to tell her, "I have had it to here."

14

RITUALS:

A) CONTEST WITH

PEER GROUP;

B) DISPERSAL

Competition: lifeblood of the Y—A challenge —The commune measures itself against a peer commune—Presence of the author authorized—Police intervention—Power of the word "traffic"—The Long Haul for almost all

Competition is the mainspring of ambition. A noncompetitive person is a non-Y. The Y is driven to test his skills against those of his peers not only in the workplace but at all times and places. If a Y prepares a meal, he is competing as a cook with all his Y-peers *and* with all professional chefs; if he orders a bottle of wine, it must be more "suitable," if not more expensive, than the bottle a peer might order. Y's take eagerly to games, all games.

Here our specimen group of upwardlies engages a peer group[59] in a popular word game. Possibly some of them have never played this game before. No matter. In the marketplace, they play all day with words, with numbers. They are instant experts in any game. It is imperative for them to compete, to win, to give proof of skill and cool and keenness—imperative in terms of Image, imperative for the joy of overcoming a peer or peers. Y-manship is itself a game. The rule is: *Win*.

That Sunday night, what few Z's Ouspenskiy managed to rack up were uneasy Z's indeed. I was feeling increasingly insecure about my status in the Historic Slocum House. Although permitted to eat dinner at the table on the back porch with the groupmates (squid, shrimp, and unidentifiable *japonaiseries* ordered up on the telephone by Chip, supposedly on cuisine duty), I was asked by Clive if I needed a ride back to town. I could reply only with *"Po-russki, pozhaluista."* Monday would mark the end of the long weekend. Was it possible that these rude young Americans considered me merely a weekend guest?

After supper, Cathy was no help. She disappeared before the

---

[59]Although the Sodas are older and better paid, the Slokes consider them peers in "career potential."

table was cleared, saying "Halcyon calls." For fear of being thought pushy, I bedded down on the porch swing. Macho, for much the same reasons, slept beside me in a fluffy ball.

Early next morning the dog leaps out of my arms with a cry of joy to greet Clive, who is hanging out the American flag. Monday, the Memorial Day holiday, has dawned rainy and gray. After caressing dog and ignoring poet, Clive goes back inside the house. From the swing, I hear his voice as he shouts up the stairs.

"Everybody up for jogging!" Dead silence. He shouts again. "Happy Memorial Day! Who's for jogging?"

More silence, broken by the telephone ringing. Clive takes it. "Yes? . . . Oh, hello, Cy . . . Yes, the weather sucks . . . Sure, great . . . Here, we'll play here . . . At ten? Fine. See you." A click. He again shouts upstairs. "Everybody up! The Sodas have challenged us to any indoor game we name! Up and at 'em!"

Groans from above, but the spirit of competition routs them from their beds.

"Chief? This time we got 'em. Guess how many cars in Lavinia's driveway? Nine, count 'em, *nine!*"

In the brouhaha over the joust with the peer group, the guest Ouspenskiy has been forgotten. Cathy has again failed him. Not a drop of coffee, not a crumb of croissant has been offered to the poet, who sits damp and forlorn upon the swing with Macho, listening to the rain pelting on the veranda roof and the snarls of the adversaries in the living room.

The game is team Scrabble. It begins with Cy Herkimer demanding, "What are the stakes?" None of the Slocum House players has ever heard of Scrabble for money. "We play as two teams," Cy explains. "Losing team's score subtracted from winner's; losers pay, say, ten dollars a point."

"There's a lot of luck in Scrabble," Clive says. "If ours is bad, it could cost us a thousand dollars."

"So what? There are eight of you."

"Take the bet, Clive baby, we'll wipe our asses on 'em."

Sporting Stu and cautious Clive confer. To Cy's disappointment, stakes are set at five dollars a point.

The Slokes and Sodas stand, sit, or kneel around the Duncan Phyfe coffee table, playing at great speed. They shout advice at teammates, taunts at the opposition.

It so happens that in ignoring their guest, the Slokes have deprived themselves of a priceless asset. Ouspenskiy has never played Scrabble, but anagrams of course exist in Russian, and he is one of the world's great anagrammarians. The poet consoles himself by playing with the names of the groupmates.

The name Clive Wheelwright yields CHEW WRIT, GIVE HELL, not bad for a lawyer. Moira Fairchild breaks down into the appropriate RICH AM I, OR FAIL'D. Cathy Fairchild is good for HIT FAR, CHIC LADY, a reference to her commercio-literary ambitions. Sturgis Stuart makes TRUST US, GRATIS (ha). Dreda Scott, TRACED DOTS—and what else has she ever done with that computer? Rick Degan is GIN-RACKED; Mort Degan, DR. MONTAGE. For Chip Buford, the best I can do is DIP FOR CHUB; how I wish this freshwater fish were of the grouper family! Vladimir Ouspenskiy, DEVIL SKIMS YOUR PAIN.

Moira leaves the game and goes to a table near the window to make a telephone call. I catch her eye; she smiles but doesn't invite me in.

Patsy is playing her letters. "J, A, blank, Z, Y—JAZZY. The Z on a triple letter score!"

"Well played." Cy pats her sun-browned thigh.

I can tell by Clive's face that he has seen this and doesn't like it. No more does Dreda.

Stu pounces on the board and lays down all his letters through a T rashly played in the row nearest the edge of the board.

"Read 'em and weep, scumbags! QUIXOTIC—through two triple word scores! X on a double letter! Greatest play in history! Thirty-four times six—"

"Two hundred four points!" Dreda cries.

"No!" the legalistic Clive shouts. "The *first* triple word gets tripled! Multiply 34 by *nine!* That's—" He looks at Dreda.

"Three hundred six."

"Holy shit, I've just earned us fifteen hundred bucks!"

"Fifteen thirty," Dreda says primly.

"QUIXOTIC is capitalized," Cy announces, "hence doesn't count. You wouldn't write 'Don Quixote' with a small Q."

Everybody shouts. They don't hear the police car in the drive. Only Macho and the poet are aware of the tall young policeman pounding on the front door. When he pushes it open and enters, the two of us, cold, wet, and bedraggled, scurry in behind him.

All fall silent as Officer Breitschwanz strides into the room. Macho goes to Clive, I to Cathy.

"Sorry, folks, it's the nine cars. May I see the lease?"

Clive goes to get it. I huddle on the floor next to Cathy's loveable knees. She dries me with the only thing handy, an Alençon lace table mat. Breitschwanz stands over us, leaning forward to look at the game.

"HONOUR with O-U-R?" he says.

Stu jumps up, pointing his finger at the loathsome Stubbs. "I told you! Only Limeys put a U in HONOR! Way to go, Officer, lay down the law!"

Clive returns and hands the lease to Breitschwanz, who scans it.

"You're Clive Wheelwright? . . . This here clause, Mr. Wheelwright, about the anti-group-rental ordinances of the Town of Hastings—"

"I am the tenant of record. My friends here are guests and

house guests. Paragraph Eleven specifically authorizes me to invite 'house guests in reasonable number.' What, Officer, would you consider a reasonable number for a house with three double and two twin beds?"

The young cop tugs at his ear. "Got to phone in to the Chief."

Moira, who has been making one call after another, surrenders the telephone to him.

"Cop car's there. Finally going to get some law and order around here. They'll all be out on their ears."

"I'll miss 'em, Jude. Gotten kind of fond of 'em. And it was nice for Randy."

"I don't know which is worse, you or that dog."

Returning to the game, Moira sees that the drenched Macho has climbed up on the couch beside Clive. Her nose wrinkles prettily.

"That dog reeks."

Clive hugs the wad of moist fluff beside him. "Best smell in the world—wet dog. If I could find a way to bottle it, I'd make millions."

"You've simply got to phone the Animal Rescue Fund about him. The lease says—"

"Macho can live outdoors. Cathy's here all week, she'll look after him."

"Clive-o, please. No responsibilities. I'm much too busy with my magnum opus."

Macho thumps a plumy tail and gazes up at Moira, imploring. Clive tries another tack. "Can't the cleaning person look after him?"

"I still haven't found one. I've phoned and phoned."

The game has meanwhile continued; it is Cathy's turn. She tilts her stick toward me to show me her letters: O T S B R H C. Quickly she arranges them to form HOT, then ROBS, SHOT,

BOTH, BROTHS, BOTCH. The wordsman Ouspenskiy takes the stick from her hands. In a trice he sees that he can play without revealing his mastery of English. He lays down: BORSCHT.

"Another fifty-pointer!" Cathy hugs me. "And it's all thanks to our resident dissident Soviet genius!"

Cy Herkimer has noticed me for the first time. His finger points at me, trembling an inch from my nose. "What is *this*? Is *he* playing?"

Moira gives a delighted cry. "Vlady! Vlady can be the cleaning person!"

"*And* kennel person!" Clive shouts.

"Work in the garden!"

"Run errands on the trail bike!"

"Sleep in the attic!"

Cathy hugs me again. The rest all congratulate me. Am I a *grouper* now?

"If we can get back to the game," Cy says, "BORSCHT is a foreign word."

"Foreign! *You* played PASTA!" The words are out of her before Dreda realizes she is screaming and pointing at Cy Herkimer, her *beau idéal*. In a softer voice she says, "Really, Cy, pasta *is* kind of Italian . . ."

Officer Breitschwanz hangs up, clears his throat.

"Your attention, folks. The Chief says, next time please come on bikes or maybe park your cars in the neighbors' drives, anything so people don't call us on these anti-grouper laws. We're overworked as it is. Like right now, the Chief wants me out on the Highway. Account of the rain, he says, the traffic's fierce already."

At the word "traffic," all panic. The game, the stakes are forgotten. Everyone is on his feet, ready to pack and go.

"Traffic—Christ, let's split!"

"Try the Sunrise?"

"Yeah, and cross to Northern State on the Sagtikos."

"Stay off the L.I.E."

"L.I.E. to 57, and then—"

"Let's go, Mort. We'll pick up a twelve-pack for roadies."

Like all summer weekenders in Hastings and the East End, our Y's live for the Long Haul. At the proper moment, the drive can be done in an hour and a half. Today they could wait and drive in after nine or ten in the evening or get up at six tomorrow and be in town in time for work. But the Haul offers them a masochistic pleasure; it is the stuff of legend, the stories they will dine out on until Friday: "Four hours on the L.I.E., bumper-to-bumper from Grace's Franks to the Tunnel."

To each his joys.

Stu's Skylark, Dreda's BMW, Clive's Subaru, and the Degans' Volkswagen are all in the hundred-mile traffic jam on the Expressway. Rain streams down. They inch forward. At times the Skylark and the BMW are parallel to the others, moving at five miles per hour; at other times the VW and the Subaru are ahead.

"Clive, is it really worth it?"

"Well, everyone who can do it does it."

Dreda calls over to them. "People like us are expected to do it."

"It was fun, sort of." Chip sounds dubious.

"Was it?"

"Was it really?"

"High-prestige area." Mort is trying to think upwardly mobile. "Consider the networking."

Rick agrees. "Contacts. Interface potential."

"A must," Clive says firmly.

"Yes," Moira says. "A must . . ."

Stu's car crawls up parallel to Clive's. He shouts to Moira.

"Can't wait to get back out there! Going to be one hell of a story! Hey, is there a Pulitzer Prize, do you know, for investigative sports reporting?"

V. Y. Ouspenskiy does not participate in the weekly evacuation ritual. Nor does his charming hostess. They are alone for the next four days, alone with Macho in the Historic Slocum House, c. 1760. But the personal experiences of a field researcher, his joys, his sorrows, have no place in a work of social science.

GLORIOUS III FOURTH

15

AMERICANISM

Fourth of July, the Glorious Fourth, Independence Day. Hastings has kept enough of its small-town tradition to stage an annual parade on the holiday, but since Main Street coincides with the Highway, which has enough traffic problems already, the Legionnaires, the band, the scouts, the volunteer fire company, and the church societies now march from the firehouse on School Street to the war memorial on Sea Street via back roads.

It is a Bonacker celebration. Summer visitors do not attend; if they do, it is because they have small children whom they wish to expose to this relic of the pageantry of an earlier America. City folk feel it their patriotic duty to spend the Fourth on the beach; our eight Y's (Chip Buford has disappeared, but a replacement is on hand) are no exception. Another duty for both city slicker and rustic is to watch fireworks in the evening. In Hastings, this is far from easy. The fireworks displays are arranged by the community and by certain private organizations which have secured the appropriate license. Pyrotechnics are shot off from the beach to land in the ocean, to a chorus of patriotic *ooh's* and *ahh's*. These occasions attract large numbers of people; traffic jams and parking nightmares result. Many estivants and locals believe they have a third patriotic duty to perform on the Fourth: to get drunk.

The Y's, for all their surface sophistication, are as American as the next person. Struggling all year to pilot the frail craft *Career* through the maelstrom of the marketplace, they pride themselves on being good capitalists, consumers, competitors. No cataclysm in Wall Street can shake their faith. In a way that no Soviet, no European can fully understand, capitalism *is* America. Moira, Stu, and the Degan brothers are avowed Republicans; Clive, Dreda, and Cathy call themselves neo-liberals, or even Democrats; on tax policy, the two camps are indistinguishable. The Y's profess traditional American values; lower taxes are not the least of these.

The massive Soviet propaganda apparatus, devoted to convincing every Soviet child, adult, and dotard that the socialist state is an earthly paradise, has produced a nation of cynics. Most American propagandists are not conscious of being propagandists. The belief in capitalism, the "free society," the "magic of the marketplace," is simply *there*, in the grade-school history class, the jingoistic film, the TV commercial. Result: a nation of true believers. People like Clive's brother Henry, the dropouts and draft-card burners of the Vietnam period, are the exception; Rambo is the rule.

To the sociologue Ouspenskiy, the annual celebration of the Glorious October Revolution in Moscow has always seemed a good day to stay in bed. Hence he is astonished by the fervor that grips his groupmates as they make their plans to hit the beach early and *en masse*, to lay in quantities of gourmet foodstuffs for a beach picnic, to view the fireworks from an optimal vantage point. These tense young Americans feel obliged on the Fourth to relax, unwind, enjoy. They approach this problem energetically. The very fact that they see it as a problem arouses the poet's compassion. In the five weekends passed with them since Memorial Day, he has grown fond of them. (Yes, reader, I know that compassion and fondness are unscientific.) These are not bad people: the earnest young lawyer, the ambitious gallery assistant, the ever-inquiring reporter, the aspiring novelist, the computer virtuoso, the plodding but good-hearted insurance salesmen. On the Fourth they all want to have a good time. Sadly, they don't know how.

The day might be spent in idling, but idling is unproductive. Idling on the beach is not considered unproductive, because all Y-persons must have a morocco-leather tan by the end of the weekend of the Fourth. To this rule, there are no exceptions. Even more productive, to Ouspenskiy's way of thinking, would be a day spent idling on the beach and wondering what the Virginia planters, the Massachusetts lawyer, and the Philadelphia inventor-printer-platitudinist who declared independence would think if they arrived by time machine in present-day Manhattan or Disney World or Hastings-by-the-Sea. Alas, our Y's are ahistorical as well as apolitical. What, as I have earlier asked, is the use of questioning the status quo when nuclear fireworks are just around the corner, unless meltdown, dying seas, polluted air, and/or overpopulation beat them to the punch? Materialism, consumerist or dialectical, is a present-tense system of values and therefore dominates a world that has forgotten its past and doesn't seem to have much of a future.

Of course, materialism is apathy. An equally apathetic but far more enjoyable response to today's deplorable world does exist, but I can't seem to get anyone to take it seriously.

If our young American over-achievers would read *Oblomov*, they would at least know how to idle their way through a fine, hot summer day.

Early on the morning of Sunday the Fourth, Ouspenskiy is out on the shaggy lawn, harvesting his crop. Clive, even before ExerCycling, has come down to hang out the flag. He is about to go back in the house when the Skylark pulls into the drive, and Stu, haggard and unshaven, steps out.

"Hi, welcome back," Clive calls. "Where've you been all these weeks?" Stu has not been out for the weekend since mid-June.

"Fuckin' Rockies, doing a story on madmen who go down rivers on rafts. What's new?"

"Mail, maybe? We forgot to look yesterday." Clive goes inside. Ouspenskiy watches Stu walk to the mailbox, a sort of tin dachschund kennel nailed to a post. He pulls out some letters, shuffles through them, takes out three or four envelopes, stuffs them in a back pocket and heads for the kitchen door. When he sees I am following him, he touches the pocket, tucks the envelopes well in. To distract my attention, he points to the bushel basket I am carrying.

"Don't throw those weeds away, Igor. Moira will want them for her goddamn compost."

"*Konechno.*" I set down the basket on the back porch and go through the door behind him.

Everyone shouts "Stu!" as he enters. He throws the presorted mail on the table, rubs his two-day beard (to my fury) against the soft skin of Cathy's neck, kisses Moira's cheek, thumps Rick's shoulder, punches Mort's biceps, squeezes Dreda's bottom and eyes her latest acquisition, a handsome but jaded young Frenchman who has politely stood up and is waiting to be presented.

"Stu," Dreda says, "this is Baudouin, a.k.a. Le Vicomte du Boisdormant. Baudouin's doing *un stage à* Citibank, but they tell me he's not productive, just a suit. *Rien qu'un costume.*"

"*Enchanté.*" Stu clicks his heels, bows to Baudouin, gulps down a mug of coffee.

"Stuey, guess what? I may turn Halcyon into a Jap."

"That's nice." He slaps down his mug. "Where's my bike? Traffic's hell. Got to get back to my story." He hurries out, slamming the back door.

Traffic! On weekends there is often a wait to get into beachside parking lots; today, the Fourth, it will be worse than ever. By common accord (for once), the groupmates decide to jog to the beach. Ouspenskiy wants to point out that walking to the beach would solve the traffic problem just as well, but in the interests of social science I am still playing dumb. To my relief, the others agree that in order to maximize tanning time, we will jog directly to the beach, rather than follow one of Clive's scenic routes.

There are delays. Moira goes upstairs to put on an ochre sweatsuit over her designer tank suit. Cathy elects to run in her tennis dress; Dreda chooses a pink button-down and plaid shorts—the Scott tartan, of course. Clive wears his safari suit, the Degans their B.C.A.A. gear, Ouspenskiy his War Between the States uniform. Baudouin appears in a red-and-white striped Breton fisherman's shirt with boat neck, and a flesh-tint jock-

strap from *La Boutique In* at Saint Tropez. He is full of enthusiasm for this holiday comemmorating the war won for the
thirteen colonies by Lafayette, De Grasse, Rochambeau, and
Louis XVI, but disappointed when Dreda hands him the keys
of her BMW.

"Vicomte, you're not in good enough shape *pour jogger avec
le reste* of us; bring the picnic, beach chairs, tote bags, and
umbrella in the Beamers." She answers Baudouin's protests
about *les embouteillages* by telling him to pretend he is in the
Place de la Concorde.

We assemble on the lawn for our warming-up drill: the running in place, the flapping of wrists, the hugging of knees. Clive
does not join us in the ritual, but wanders about, calling for
Macho.

"He really needs the run, he's getting fat and lazy. Spent all
day yesterday sleeping in my closet."

When Moira points out that dogs aren't allowed on the beach
during high season, Clive mumbles something about unenforceable laws and continues calling. He enjoys running with
Macho bounding beside him, adoring eyes upturned, now and
then moving in to give him a playful nip on the ankle. Today
only the neighbors' black Lab answers the blasts of his ultra-
sonic whistle. After shooing Randy home, Clive leads us out of
the driveway. Hot on his heels pound the Degans; Dreda is
next; bringing up the rear are the enchantingly unathletic Cathy,
the fitness-driven but shortwinded Moira, and the fledgling
groupjogger Ouspenskiy. Clive scans the roadside as he runs,
trying to identify birds, trees, and flowers; the others talk.

"What's the story on fireworks tonight?"

"The village has fireworks, down on Town Beach."

"They say it's a mess. Traffic, no place to park, drunken
drivers, the cops . . ."

"Some of the clubs do fireworks."

"We've got a clubman in the house."

As he turns into Dunegrass Lane, Clive sees Patsy, Cy, and the other Sodas running just ahead. He looks over his shoulder at us. Moira, Cathy, and I get the message; we begin to close the gap between rear guard and main body. Clive steps up the tempo. We other six labor mightily with hearts, minds, lungs, and legs to match his pace. Gradually we draw abreast of the Sodas. Clive looks over at Cy with a malevolent smile.

"Told you we'd whip you by the Fourth."

"You haven't yet."

"Still want to put a hundred on it?"

Cy turns his head and sees we are neck and neck with the Sodas.

"Another day, when there's less traffic."

A feeble excuse. There is indeed traffic on Dunegrass Lane, but it is stopped dead, a long line of cars waiting to get into the parking lot.

"*Arrivederci*, Sodas!" Clive begins to sprint. Inch by agonizing inch, we draw ahead. The red-faced Cy is scowling; Patsy is shouting encouragement to her charges; the odious Stubbs is wheezing as he runs; the thick-thighed Gerda is streaming sweat. Moira and I, laggards of our platoon, are abreast of Cy and Patsy now. An incredible triumph is within our grasp.

At this point Stu roars past us on his trail bike, clutching a long rod and other angling gear. He salutes us with the maneuver known as a "wheelie." His exhaust makes us cough.

Although it is only a little after nine, the great beach is already cluttered with umbrellas, ice chests, folding chairs, towels, carryalls, and sand pails. Through the shining air sail kites and balls. The sociologist Ouspenskiy has decided to extend his field research by finding out what S. Stuart is up to. He leaves the others and walks half a mile or so along the beach until he comes upon two surf fishermen, standing about twenty yards apart. One of them is Stu; the other is unknown to me. Although the ocean is warm now, Stu, the sporting goods collector, is dressed in olive-green waders; the other man, clearly an expert caster, wears only a skimpy bathing suit. I stand and watch them long enough to notice that Stu is more interested in his fellow fisherman, to whom he is gradually edging closer, than in catching fish.

Suddenly I am distracted by a piteous squawk. Not far from me at the water's edge is a gull with a broken wing. I go to it; the bird tries to flutter away, fails ignominiously, is picked up by the compassionate ornithophile. The gull screams, beats its wings, empties its intestinal tract on Ouspenskiy. I stroke it to calm it. Clive and Patsy, who have had a long swim parallel to the beach, are walking toward me, deep in conversation.

I go to them, show them the bird, say "*Chaika*." Apparently they miss the allusion to Chekhov.

Clive squints myopically at the gull. "Either a Glaucous Gull, *Larus hyperboreus*, or an Iceland Gull, *Larus glaucoides*. Difficult to distinguish. Adult Glaucous has a red ring around eye, but the book says it's hard to see. Really hard to see on this one. Glaucous."

"There's that friend of yours." Patsy gestures toward the surf fishermen. "The one who doesn't believe in running."

Stu makes a "Don't bother me, I'm busy" signal. Clive and Patsy walk on, heading back toward the others, with Ouspenskiy and gull following at a discreet distance.

"Sand's hot already," Patsy says.

"Walk below the highwater mark. Cooler." Clive smiles. "And sure to be legal."

"The law's never far from your mind, is it, Clive? Do you like being a lawyer?"

He thinks for a second before answering. "Corporate law doesn't sing to me. Lately I've been working on something that does. Do you know a place called Indian Marsh?"

"I know it, I love it."

"I'm working to make it a nature preserve."

"That's terrific. Don't you find that rewarding?"

"Very. I've set up this trust, and Nick Edgway tells me our client, Hemisphere, has agreed to accept me as sole trustee."

"Good for you. I see him sometimes at the Spindrift. Mrs. Edgway I can't stand; Mister has one of those faces that never show anything. What's he like?"

"Fine lawyer. Drives subordinates hard. Sharp mind."

"Is he kind?"

"Is he what?"

"Kind. Is he a kind person?"

"Sorry. I don't hear that word often. In the circles I move in, people ask, is a person smart, is he productive? Funny, nobody ever asks, is he kind?"

"Funny circles." She picks up a smooth pebble and skims it out over the ocean. It skips many times.

"Eleven! Patsy, that's a virtuoso feat."

"Well, is he?"

"Kind? The word doesn't apply. It doesn't apply to the people I meet—clients, lawyers, the persons I group with. Are teachers kind?"

"We try. It's the way to get results. Sometimes it's hard to be kind to the parents."

"My father's a headmaster; he has a sort of professional benevolence. But if you can even think of being kind to parents, you're way ahead of him."

She looks at him. "You're kind."

"What makes you think so?"

"That day at the yard, when Rufe was studying his boat, you didn't want to break in on him. That's kind."

"Only normal."

"Yes, Clive. Being kind *is* normal."

He looks dubious. Walking behind them, kindly Ouspenskiy aches for him and all his peers.

"Is teaching rewarding?"

"I love it—and the younger the kids, the better."

"Don't you miss the city? The cultural things?"

"I've never lived in a city. I'm a true native. College at Stony Brook—commuting distance. Born here, happy here." She picks up a pale blue shell. "Look, a limpet."

"How do you know?"

"How do I know what a cow is? I've always known limpets."

Clive seems impressed; Ouspenskiy surmises that he hasn't begun on shells yet.

"What about financially rewarding? They say teaching isn't."

"They're right. That's why I do summer jobs. But this is the last time I take on Success-Oriented Divorced Adults and the kids at the Spindrift. Next summer Hastings High is starting a program for adult illiterates. I want to teach in that."

"Pro bono." Clive appears to be wondering if she isn't too good to be true. "Your career path, Patsy, where does it lead? High school principal?"

"I might end up as principal, but that means losing contact with the children. Anyway, when I meet Joe Perfect, I'll quit and get married and raise my own."

Clive is startled. "You don't think child-rearing and a career can be combined?"

"Maybe, after the child is eight or ten."

He has never heard such heresy. "I mean, what are your goals? Your ambitions?"

"I never thought about it. Guess I haven't any."

His face shows disbelief. Is she pulling his leg? Even Ouspenskiy can't be certain. They walk for a while in silence.

"Clive?" She waits until he looks at her. "Down at the boatyard, I thought I saw something you may have forgotten."

"What's that?"

"The real Clive."

To hell with the toasting hordes on the beach, to hell with his bright-eyed Soviet shadow: when a girl says that to him, a man must seize her, kiss her. Not Clive. He ducks his head, reaches for a pebble, skims it out over the sea. It skips but four or five times, then sinks to the bottom.

Stu has worked his way over to the other surfcaster. Doc Hop recognizes him.

"How's Macho? And that pretty girl?"

"Dog getting fat. Girl still highly visual."

"I admire that fancy new equipment." Doc Hop seems amused by Stu's ineptitude as a caster. "Mind if I give you a few pointers?"

"Go ahead."

The vet shows him the right way to grip the rod, how to give his wrist the proper flick. He makes a demonstration cast himself. "When it lands, twitch it. Let the spinner mesmerize the fish. Here we go!" He hauls in a fine striper, nets it neatly.

"You're good, Doc. Learn all this since you moved here?"

Hopper's eyes flash from under overweening brows. "What makes you think I didn't grow up out here?"

Stu has made an error, but quickly recoups. "You don't talk like a Bonacker."

"Actually, I'm a Californian. Grew up in Point Reyes. Used to surfcast with my dad, from the time I was big enough to lift a rod."

This, Stu knows, is fabrication. He has looked up Enos Hopper, V.M.D., in a veterinary directory and knows he was born in Austria, a country with no seacoast, and emigrated at fourteen to Kentucky, a landlocked state. He took his B.S. at the University of Kentucky at Lexington—horse country!—and his V.M.D. at Cornell. Apparently he has always practiced on a consultant basis. The million-dollar house on Beachplum Lane was bought only two years ago. Exhilarated at having caught the vet in a lie, Stu casts and promptly gets a strike. Under Doc Hop's coaching, he soon has the fish in his net.

"Good work. Ever tried deep sea fishing?"

"No, but I'd like to."

"So happens I'm going out this afternoon with a friend of mine who just brought his boat up from Atlantic City. Care to join us? Maybe that smashing girl would like to come too?"

It is not easy for Stu to affect nonchalance. "Thanks, Doc. I'll try to make the time."

Bearing the bird, Ouspenskiy marches on, planting his feet now in Clive's footprints, now in Patsy's, in the squish of tide-lapped sand. He cuts a striking if diminutive figure, with his blue Union trousers rolled to the knee, his bare and shining white torso, his smooth-muscled arms and shoulders, his hirsute chest, his breeze-rippled beard, his noble poet's head. Adults point him out to each other; children stare at him in awe.

We come upon Cy Herkimer and his crew, playing their violent and puerile game. The ball pops out of a promiscuously interlocked mass of bodies. In a flash Clive scoops it up and races through the startled Sodas, until only their captain is between him and the goal. As Cy closes in for the tackle, Clive drop-kicks the ball over his head. It sails high over the goalposts—two pieces of driftwood stuck in the sand—for a score.

Disloyal to her employers, Patsy cheers.

Cy claps Clive on the shoulder and speaks to him in what even Ouspenskiy can identify as an exaggeratedly British accent. "I say, Wheelwright, you're jolly good at rugger."

"Played at Dartmouth. You've played too."

Cy's voice grows increasingly "U." "I was a Rheaudes Scholar. Played a bit at Auksfud." He sees Clive's expression and lapses back to AmerEng. "Sorry. Oxford. When I get near a rugger ball, I start talking Brit."

Both men laugh. Clive retrieves the ball, tosses it to Cy. "Let's have a real game some time."

"Ripping. Might put a few quid on it?"

Reader, how could any of us have guessed on that steamy

Fourth that by stormy Labor Day our two grouperhouses would be locked in struggle for a sum considerably larger than a few quid?

We are not far from the Sloke umbrella. Most of the groupmates are flat on their backs, soaking up sun. The painter Elowyn is spreading her towel next to Moira as we approach; Dreda is playing with an electronic backgammon set which beeps every time a move is made; Mort is sitting up, eyeing the Sodas' game with disapproval.

"Why would anyone want to play rugby, when there's football?"

"Yuh," Rick says, "it's so *foreign*. And on the Fourth of July, too."

Baudouin rubs oil on his hairless but perfectly bronzed chest. "*Le rugby m'emmerde; c'est tellement prolo.*"

"Think upwardly mobile," Cathy says. "If it's foreign, it's got to be better."

Dreda taps on her backgammon gadget. "Like this is from Korea . . ." The machine emits a series of angry beeps; she grins broadly. "Gotcha, you little slope. Gammoned!" She stands up and looks Clive directly in the eye. "We've got the solution on the fireworks. It's your club."

He looks uneasy. "Not sure about the guest rules. I'll have to ask."

"Do that." Dreda turns from him and goes over to talk to Patsy.

Ouspenskiy is kneeling on the sand beside Cathy, showing her the gull. She caresses it with her exquisite hand, then takes it and cuddles it against her breast, perhaps forgetting it is not a mammal.

"There, there, seagull. I'm going to call you J. Livingston . . ."[60]

---

[60]The reference is to *Jonathan Livingston Seagull*, a book popular some years ago. C. Fairchild is of course a student of best sellers.

Moira opens one eye and sees that Elowyn has settled herself beside her. "Oh. Hi. Did Nadya tell you? I called her last night to say I'd decided to buy six of your paintings."

"*Six!*" Elowyn is overjoyed.

"I'll drop off a check at the gallery this afternoon."

Clive has reached them in time to overhear. He stands over Moira, frowning slightly. His shadow falls across her face; this time she opens both eyes.

"I've been so busy on Indian Marsh that I've never been there," he says. "Thought I might go now. Want to come?"

Moira again shuts her eyes; the eyelids are tanning beautifully. "Beach day for me. Would you mind moving out of my sun?"

Ouspenskiy is delighted. Surely Moira has forgotten (or never learned) that Diogenes, living in his barrel at Corinth, made the same remark to Alexander the Great. I tune in on another conversation:

". . . certainly not mine," Patsy is saying to Dreda, "all yours if you want him. By the way, he's been divorced three times."

The poet is not the only eavesdropper. Baudouin is watching Dreda with unhappy eyes; Clive, too, has cocked an ear.

"Why do you think that is?" Dreda asks.

"My experience, thank God, is limited, but I'd say it's because he's a pouncer. Wants instant love, like instant coffee."

"Forgivable. He's a busy man. I'm busy too. Thanks, Patsy." Dreda starts back toward her towel.

Clive, who has been waiting his turn to talk to her, approaches Patsy almost bashfully. "I'm going over to Indian Marsh. Interested?"

She is tempted. "It's a magic place . . . but I've got this sailing class at two."

"We'll be back. Only thing is the traffic. Is there a back road?"

Patsy gives him one of her luminous smiles.

"I know a way . . ."

16

ENVIRONMENT

Document #1: C. WHEELWRIGHT memo on
local Environment—No rest from workplay—A Y-
person inspects some Environment—Investigative
reporting as usual—Commercio-literary concerns—
Manual idyll—Law and journalism: ships that pass
—Finance on the beach—The investigator investi-
gated — An expert on Wasps—Document #2: S. STUART
notes re L. Gross—Veterinary fantasies—A strike—Two
victims of Y-fatigue—The fisherman gaffed

"Environment" is key to Y thinking. I am fortunate to be able to present a document written on this subject by one of our specimen Y's. C. Wheelwright composed the following as a personal memo on that very Fourth of July, after visiting Indian Marsh. His purpose in writing it was to remind himself of the high responsibility he had assumed in accepting the pro bono, nonremunerative post of sole trustee.

DOCUMENT #1 ▸ *C. WHEELWRIGHT MEMO*

To: Self
Re: L. I. (S. Fork) Environment
Long Island's problem: people pollution.
Island is Ice Age debris: a long, thin strip of sand and gravel scraped off what is now Connecticut and dumped like snow in front of plow into the Atlantic.
Hence, Long Island Sound. Hence, sandy soil, Hastings loam, etc. (As New Englander, am always amazed by scarcity of rocks. When locals find a nice boulder, they lug it home and set it up on lawn as decoration!)
Geologically, Island is youngest land mass in US. Also our largest island.
On map, L. I. looks like large fish[61] about to swallow a smaller fish, Manhattan. The contrary is the case!
From head of fish (Brooklyn, Queens) to about the gills (Exit 62 on L.I.E.?), Island is chiefly bedroom suburb. (Exit 62 beyond range of most crazed commuter?)
Farther east, fish's tail forks. The two forks enclose Peconic Bay.
North Fork still mostly farmland, with villages. Has charm, but no ocean beach.
South Fork (Shinnecock Canal to Montauk Point) only 15 years ago probably much like North Fork today. Real estate

---

[61]A grouper? —V.Y.O.

boom: good-bye to all that. *Urgent need* to save what remains of Environment!

Going east from Canal on S. Fork: Hastings Haven (not a real port, too silted up), Hastings, Nowedonah. Former farm hamlets, now resort towns: boutiques, health food shops, antique shops; high rents; creeping condominiums.

S. Fork bisected by Highway. Two mini-worlds: "South of the Highway" and "North of the Highway."

South of Highway considered more desirable because closer to ocean. Most potato fields sold off to developers. Expensive and bizarre houses loom over coastal flatlands, waiting for trees to grow. Much-favored style: serrated roof, making house look like wooden mock-up of Sydney Opera House. Pockets of older settlement South of Highway where farmers still farm, or converted farmhouses (e.g. Slocum House) where tall trees and hedges screen out newer excrescences.

North of Highway, some exurban sprawl, creeping north from Hastings or south from Squaw (only good harbor in area, once a whaling port, now full of marinas; opens on Bay). Still plenty of fields, real farmhouses, ponds, woods. For how long?

Charm of South Fork landscape worth preserving. To outsider's eye, land is flat. Stay here a while, subtleties of gentle crests and troughs in swell of land become apparent. Enormous sky. Clear light. Cloudscapes. Moira tells me light has attracted many painters: Porter, Pollock, De Kooning, Lichtenstein, Chemiakin, Leigh-Hunt, Adler, Wood.

I like it here.

East of Nowedonah landscape changes. First, stretch of about ten miles of woodland, mostly state park. Second, Montauk, fishing village turned tourist trap. Third, more parkland, meadows, and woods.[62] Last, Montauk Light, built during second

---

[62]It was here that S. Stuart rode with C. Fairchild and saw the Cadillac. — V.Y.O.

Washington Administration, perched on fast-eroding sand bluffs. (Symbolic?)

Bois de Boulogne and Bois de Vincennes said to be *les poumons de Paris.* Comparable with state and county parks east of Nowedonah and the very few remaining large tracts of woods and wetlands west of there—these allow the South Fork to breathe.

Largest of such tracts is Indian Marsh, on the Bay, northeast of Squaw Harbor. In saving Indian Marsh from development, Wetlands Trust will be performing valuable public service, etc. A magic place!

These notes show Clive's careful mind at work. He begins by considering all of Long Island; then a smaller piece of it, the South Fork; then a tiny piece, Indian Marsh. There is poetry in his fish metaphor and a certain wistful idealism in his entire concept. In writing "A magic place!" he is echoing Patsy; he is also under the spell of his first visit to the Marsh, of which more shortly.

Note his phrase, *"Urgent need* to save what remains of Environment!" Note the italics, the capital E, the exclamation point. Note above all his use of the word "Environment." He uses it to mean "nature," or else what was there before the recent boom. This misusage is characteristic of Y-persons. In fact, environment is whatever happens to surround us. The condominiums (condominia?) at Hastings Haven, the shopping mall at Hastings Haven, the gas stations and gay bars and discos on the Highway are just as much environment as the odd marsh or potato field.

All our Y's try to spend the Fourth, a day of rest and national self-congratulation, in the Environment.[63] Wetlands are En-

---

[63] I shall use the capital E to denote Environment as the Y's conceive it, the minuscule for environment in its proper sense.

vironment; Clive is drawn there, but later finds himself talking law with the senior partner. Ocean is Environment; Stu goes to sea, where he workplays hard on his hypothetical Big Story. Beach is Environment; the others propose to spend the day there, complaining that the Environment has too many people on it. We shall see Cathy driven back to her meager typescript, Dreda working to get a job with Herkimer & Co., Moira doing research on the painter whose work she has acquired in her first independent venture as an entrepreneur. Before the day is out, the Degans will try once again to sell insurance. Even the poet Ouspenskiy will compose in his head the opening lines of what is to become the most delicate canto of his verse cycle. Only Baudouin does nothing. He has no need to; being an aristocrat is something no big Korean can take away from him.

The others put me in mind of Blake's pitiless lines, which I once heard Clive sing in the shower: "I will not cease from mental fight/Nor shall my Sword sleep in my hand/Till we have built Jerusalem . . ."

The Y's Jerusalem, as Dreda commented while Clive soaped and sang, is a megabuck career.

O upwardlies, I weep for you!

A white-tailed deer is grazing. Young raccoons crouch in the summer foliage. Down in the reeds, a great blue heron watches for fish.

A canoe comes around the end of the point. The fair young man, the bronzed girl paddle slowly and in perfect time. As they glide along the shoreline of Indian Marsh, Clive thinks he is seeing the Island as the Montauks and the Shinnecocks knew it, before the first white settlers came down from New England in the 1640s. He remembers his summer with the Penobscots, indulges in an aboriginal fantasy, but the coppery shoulders of the girl in the bow are lovelier in his eyes than any Maine squaw's. They rest their paddles on the gunwales and drift. Patsy points to the sky. An osprey is coasting in toward her nest, a fish clutched in her talons.

Clive turns his head to watch the mother bird feed her young. He feels the canoe give a sudden bobble, hears a splash, looks around to see Patsy in the water, swimming away from him in a fast and flawless crawl. His eyes follow the smooth motion of her arms. Behind her tanned shoulders, a gleam—a round-ness, a whiteness—breaks the surface and is gone. Clive is surprised to see that Patsy's bathing suit is lying on the bow thwart.

It takes him less than a minute to beach the canoe, strip off his own trunks, race through the shallows and strike out after her. She is in the middle of the cove now, floating on her back, her brown hair streaming out around her. When Clive is within ten yards, he surface-dives and strokes toward her underwater. Her buttocks twinkle above him, startlingly white against the deep tan of back and legs. For one split second, as he swims up toward her, Clive knows joy. In the next split second she has flipped over and is churning her feet in his face.

He breaks surface and flails after her, but Patsy is a stronger swimmer: his boyhood was spent *on* Maine's icy water, not in it. Laughing at him, she easily pulls away. When she reaches the canoe, Clive, lengths behind, has one glimpse of white breasts, white belly, dark triangle of hair, glistening wet; then she is back in her bathing suit. He stands up in the shallows, but instantly, instinctively sits again, cursing himself for a child, a fool. Was that, he asks himself, the reaction of a grown man? What is more natural than an erection? He starts to straighten up again. With another laugh, this time short and sharp, Patsy tosses him his trunks.

Now what? he thinks, crouching in thigh-deep water and clumsily shoving one leg into his suit. He imagines tipping her out of the canoe, tussling in marsh grass, burying his head in whiteness of breasts, easing himself into glistening darkness of triangle. But where would it lead? Patsy knows he is about to marry Moira. She has been taunting him, flirting, teasing in the way any girl—any of these local girls at least—might tease any man while skinnydipping. Probably the great local sport. A headmaster's son, he was born to be teased by the townies.

He wades toward her. Patsy is looking not at him but at her watch: the sailing class. As Clive shoves off the canoe, the great blue heron, which has been fishing calmly through all the commotion, spreads his wings, takes to the air, sails off and away. "Beautiful," Patsy says, and he echoes her, "Beautiful." Beautiful the flight of the heron, beautiful the roll of her smooth brown shoulders as they take up the stroke. More than he has ever wanted anything, he wants to drop his paddle, kiss the back of her neck, rub his face against her shining shoulders.

Think, he tells himself, think of staying in stroke, think of, ah, Environment. Stroke, feather, recover. I, Clive Wheelwright, sole trustee of Wetlands Trust, am simply, stroke, feather, a friend of Patsy Magee's. We're friends, stroke, feather, we've had a friendly dip, a good healthy romp in the Environment.

Stu putts down the hellishly clogged Main Street of Hastings on his trail bike. He spots Doc Hop's silver-gray Bentley double-parked outside a travel agency and dismounts to investigate.

A sign on the door says, FOR YOUR CONVENIENCE, WILF'S TRAVEL IS OPEN JULY 4TH. Through the plate-glass window, Stu sees the travel agent handing an airline ticket to the vet. When Doc Hop is about to leave, Stu goes in. He greets him fortissimo—his old trick—to make sure the agent overhears.

"Doc, we meet again. Two-thirty at the marina?"

"Two-thirty, Stuart. Don't forget to bring your friend. Thanks, Wilf."

The agent Wilf, a delicate young man done up in Pucci and Gucci wares, taps his Bic on a memo pad. "Thank *you*," he says archly.

"Hi," Stu roars at Wilf as soon as the vet is gone. "Got any cut-rate ski excursions to the Chilean Andes around August one?"

"That's a tough one. Let me punch it out on my computer."

While Wilf computes, Stu roams the office, pretending to study the travel posters.

"I see you deal with my buddy Doc Hop."

"One of my best customers. Flies two or three times a week."

"That's Doc—restless. Where's he off to now?"

Wilf is concentrating on his display screen. "Atlantic City tomorrow. Yesterday it was Baltimore."

Moving close to Wilf's desk, Stu tries to read a scribble on the memo pad. It says "LAU—", but there is an envelope lying across the rest of the note.

"Here's one." Wilf reads from the screen, "JFK to Santiago, two weeks in Class-A ski lodge, Portillo, all meals, eleven-twenty. Departs August 2nd. Space available."

"See if you can do better. Call me—here's my number."

Stu swoops on the memo pad, picks it up and reads:

LAU—5 NO TRUMP

He scrawls his name and number on the pad, hands it to Wilf.

"I'll get back to you"—the agent looks at the pad—"Stu. I'm Wilf Huggins, by the way."

"Wilf, it's been real. Let's get together some time?"

"I'd love it."

He means it. Wilf adores the virile type.

Stu finds a sidewalk phone two doors down, dials, shouts.

"Max? Stu here . . . A hundred on No Trump in the fifth at Laurel. To win . . . and Max? Make that two hundred!"

* * *

Elbows ceaselessly moving
Pounding sugar and cinnamon
The arcs of two circling elbows
Make my head spin

Shall I steal up behind you
Agafya Matveyevna
Seize your roseate elbows
Kiss the back of your neck
While you stand there straight and still
Like a horse when his collar is put on
Or shall I continue sitting
In this extraordinarily well-made chair
In love with your circling elbows?

The poet lies upon hot sand, enjoying warmth of sun on milky skin, happy, half-dozing, while his great brain composes one of his finest works. Stretched out beside him is Cathy, chatting away in her breathless voice with Dreda, who lies on her other side.

". . . and Duff/Lorenz is being hostile-takeovered by this conglomerate, Megatronix. They make nuclear subs, no-cal sausages, stuff like that, so Halcyon can't be a veggie or a pacifist any more. My problem now is, what else can she be? I could make her a Jap, but if I make her a Jap, I'll never make my deadline. What do I know about Japs, really? I'd have to do research on them. And if Halcy's a Jap, it complicates her relationship with Vyacheslav, my Russian sculptor . . ."

The idea of a Japanese named Halcyon shatters the poet's reverie.

". . . because they say, scratch a Slav, find an anti-Semite. Honestly, Dreda, it's driving me *meshugeh* . . ."

Not until some time later does Ouspenskiy realize that *Jap* is the acronym for Jewish American Princess. By then, Cathy has decided that by reason of her deadline, Halcyon must remain a Wasp.

Dreda, bored with the subject, introduces a new one. "You're creative, you can help me. If my Herkimer caper doesn't work, there are other firms—there's Stein, Vandenhoek, there's Polyarb, there's Morve and Oxblood. Can you write me a really creative résumé?"

"For a price . . ."

I doze off. When I wake, Cathy is gone. Sitting up, I see her standing breast-deep in the ocean, waiting for a wave. A large one heaves toward her. She rides it in—to wash up on the sand at the feet of the unspeakable Stubbs, who has been watching her, waiting. On the pretext of bringing her a towel, Ouspenskiy hastens toward them.

The PR man is helping her to her feet. "How's the book, doll? Got a title yet?"

"I make lists of them." Cathy takes the towel from my hand without looking at me. "How about *Turn Off the Stars?*"

"*Turn Off the Stars.* Tee Oh Tee Ess. TOTS? Well, it's not Gee Doubleyou Tee Doubleyou, but . . . how many words?"

"Four."

"Not the title, the book."

"Oh. My contract calls for a novel of at least a hundred thousand words."

Stubbs purses his hideous lips, rubs his obscenely hairy belly. "Make it two, three times that. Six hundred pages, nine hundred. That's what sells."

"Jim, there's just not that much story. Everything happens in Halcyon's head."

"Look, Halcyon's got a family, hasn't she? Start a couple of generations back. Family saga, that'll sell. I see it as a miniseries . . . where you going, doll?"

"Back to the old typewriter."

Stubbs calls after her as she marches toward the Sloke umbrella, "Three generations, start in 1900, and remember—spring list. Get it in by September First!"

Cathy picks up the beach basket containing the stricken gull and hands it to her serf, Ouspenskiy. A few feet away, Stu, who has just arrived, is shouting at the prostrate Moira.

"You *can't* not come. Doc Hop specifically invited you."

"And I specifically regret. I'm working."

By this Moira means that she has been talking to Elowyn, hoping to learn some of the theory of satellitic photo-realism for use as an eventual sales pitch. All she has picked up so far are a few phrases such as "Canadian high," "jetstream," and "Alberta clipper."

"But Moira, investigative journalism—"

"Not today."

Stu gives up, looks at me.

"Busy this afternoon, Zhivago?"

While Patsy sails around the harbor, calling instructions to her class, Clive is at the yard, helping Rufe on a new dinghy.

The boatbuilder stands back, holds up his right thumb at arm's length and squints over it, inspecting the sheer of the hull.

"Ever work from a plan, Rufe?"

He gives a scornful snort. "Got a thumb, got an eye. What good is a plan? Been doin' this all my life."

"I could do it the rest of mine."

With a stroke or two of his adz, Rufe removes some invisible imperfection. Clive follows up, smoothing with a plane.

A boat's foghorn squawks twice. Clive looks out over the harbor. *Equity* is at her mooring, dressed in all her pennants for the Fourth. Edgway is waving to him from the cockpit. Sam is already in the tender, heading toward the yard.

Clive sets down his tools.

"Rufe, duty calls."

"Come back any time, Clyde."

"I will."

Today there is no question of sailing. Clive sits in the cockpit, nursing his spritzer and listening to Edgway talk.

". . . Next step, of course, is for Wetlands Trust—which by the way, congratulations, you've set up in record time—to purchase Indian Marsh from present owner, Hatch Estate. Funds to be forthcoming from the Hemisphere Foundation. Now, as sole trustee . . ."

A horn sounds close by. Both men turn.

An enormous powerboat, elaborately fitted out for deep sea fishing, wallows past them, heading out. Clive is surprised to see Stu aboard, plus another familiar face. The three other faces he has seen before, but can't place at the moment. The chunky man on the flying bridge waves.

"Hi, Nick."

"Hope they're biting, Lou."

On the stern of the powerboat are the words:

HI-ROLLER
ATLANTIC CITY, N.J.

Clive asks a question considered normal, not impertinent, among yachtsmen, "Whose boat is that?"

"Louis Somebody's. Nodding acquaintance. Sat next to him Friday on Long Island Air. Now, as sole trustee, Clive, it will be your responsibility to contact the executor of the Estate of Ralph Hatch. Wetlands' initial bid should be in the neighborhood of . . ."

He names a figure that makes Clive's hair curl.

The poet feels unwanted. Perched on the lid of a reeking bait box, he huddles into himself, tries to be invisible. He knows he has been brought along simply because Stu hates to go any-

where alone. Two of the men aboard he recognizes from the
night at the disco; the third is the surfcaster of this morning;
all three are out of sorts. Apparently the surf fisherman promised the others his guest would be accompanied by a dazzling
blonde. When Stu appeared on the dock with an émigré poet
in tow, his words, "Moira couldn't come, so I brought Vlady
instead," were ill-received.

Stu is pretending that the foul humor of the three does not
exist. He stands at the rail, hands cupped before his mouth,
and bellows back at the yawl, "Eat your heart out, Clive baby!"
Then he looks up at the heavyset man on the flying bridge, a
granite slab against the sky. "Hey, Lou, whose boat is that?"
Like all good reporters, he has learned that one way to find
things out is to ask questions to which he already knows the
answer.

Lou Gross's head tilts slightly downward. Reflected on the
silvered lenses of his sunglasses are two tiny, distorted images
of Stu's upturned face. He removes the cigar from his lips and
with a flick of blunt forefinger against stumpy thumb sends
the butt sailing past Stu's head, over the rail.

"Mr. Schulz." He rasps out the words; the henchman's head
pops out of the cabin. "Our guest Prince Charles has a question."

Mr. Schulz moves carefully around the unwelcome poet, as
if to avoid stepping on a beached stingray. Iron fingers close
around Stu's biceps. Under the long bill of his swordfisherman's
cap, Schulzie's face is gray as lead. The third man, whom the
others call Doc Hop, moves away from them and lies down to
sun himself in the stern.

"Question?"

"I just asked whose boat that was."

"With what exactly in mind?"

"A guy I know is aboard it."

"Do tell." The fingers tighten. Ouspenskiy sees Stu wince;
Schulzie has found a nerve.

"So naturally I wondered who owned the boat."

"Such matters are no fuckin' business of yours. Do we understand each other?"

"Loud and clear, Schulzie."

The grip is relaxed. "You are Doc Hop's guest. Any friend of the Doc's is a friend of me and Lou's. Sit down, pop a beer, get y'self a suntan. Lou don't take shit from nobody. Bonn voyodge. Enjoy y'self."

"I will, Schulzie, I will."

While Baudouin models a turret of his sand chateau, Dreda studies the *Times* financial section, making heavy checkmarks with her lipstick next to certain listings. Out of the corner of her eye, she watches Cy Herkimer, who is walking on his hands twenty yards downwind. She knew before Patsy told her of the three wives; Cy's biography in *Who's Who* is graven in her heart. Born in South Dakota farm country; B.S. from MIT at nineteen; Rhodes Scholar; graduate degrees at Cal Tech; four years with IBM, during which he published several articles with titles such as *Computer Entropy*; founded Herkimer & Co. in 1972; lived happily ever after but for his marriages, the average length of which was 1.1 years.

Dreda pulls a page out of her paper, stands, holds the sheet of newsprint in the wind, and lets go. Her aim is perfect: the page ends up plastered against Cy's face. He straightens up, glances at the paper, then walks toward her.

"This is yours?"

She takes the financial page from him. "Thanks."

"Couldn't help noticing those bond listings you'd checked. Interesting choice."

Dreda drops a pretty curtsy. "Praise from Caesar."

"How are you going to play those City of Clevelands? Up or down?"

She teases him with a smile. "That'd be telling."

Cy turns impatiently away, hesitates, looks back at her. "Care for a swim?"

Dreda takes his arm, walks with him toward the ocean. "If'n you promise to stay real close, Mistuh Man. When Ah was a bitty pickaninny, white folks done kep' me out o' dem public swimmumpools."

With a swipe of the hand, Baudouin razes the Chateau du Boisdormant.

Hi-Roller ploughs through heavy seas. Stu has not spoken or stirred from his seat since his talk with Schulzie. I see that Doc Hop has roused himself from his sunbath and is coming toward me, tapping the blade of a long knife against the palm of his hand. I scramble out of his way. He kneels beside the bait box, opens it, looks at me with a twitchy smile.

"*Vui—ribak?*"

"*Nyet,*" I say, startled.

"*Kak zhalko.*"

"You are most fluent," I tell him, speaking loudly, slowly, and insincerely in my mother tongue. His Russian is rudimentary, his accent atrocious. "Where did you learn?"

"In Hungary, as a boy."

"You are Hungarian?"

"No. I was born in Austria."

Stu has been leaning forward, hoping to catch a word. When Doc Hop says "*Avstria,*" he looks relieved. "*Sprechen wir deutsch, Herr Doktor,*" he says in his army-brat German.

"Speak American," Lou commands from the bridge.

"Sure thing, Lou," Stu says quickly.

Doc Hop glares at him from under his heavy brows. "What was all that business between you and Schulzie?"

"Nothing. A misunderstanding."

The Doc's voice grows harsh, Germanic. Viciously, he slices a whitefish. "There is nothing to understand, therefore nothing to *mis*understand. Lou is a good guy. He just happens to be very cautious."

"That's it, cautious." Stu is trying hard to be ingratiating. Beads of sweat glisten on his face.

"Lou is a prince among men. A real fun person when you get to know him."

"I'm sure he is, Doc."

"Lou just wants to make sure you're having a nice time."

"I am, I am."

Stu's eyes dart this way and that; anything is better than facing Doc Hop's heavy-lidded stare. He glances up at the bridge, as do I. Lou has put the boat on automatic pilot. Standing by the wheel, he trains a long black pair of binoculars toward shore. Abeam are sand bluffs and the white shaft of Montauk Light. Feet braced wide apart, elbows of half-raised arms clamped to massive rib cage, face stony, Lou looks as solidly planted as the lighthouse, oblivious to pitch and roll.

Stu speaks to Doc Hop in an undertone. "What's he see over there, a school of fish?"

"*You!*" Lou roars, not removing the binoculars from his eyes. "You—Prince Chazz! You have a question?"

"Wondering if you saw any fish . . ."

Lou slowly lowers the glasses and points a bejewelled finger at Stu.

"Strap His Highness to the chair."

Dreda, exulting, drives Baudouin, sulking, along Dunegrass Lane toward home.

"*Merde et re-merde*, you throw yourself at this man. He is old, he is *moche*, he is the contrary of sexy."

"Baudouin, you can't possibly understand the charm of the White Anglo-Saxon Prot. In a Wasp way, Cy simply *exudes* charm."

"You joke. He is a puritan."

"That's what's so sexy. He sublimates. All my life I have studied Wasps—Andover, Yale, the B School. Once I even spent a month in Maine. Maine is Wasp heaven."

A thin smile flutters to Baudouin's lips. *"Ma chère Dreda, you will never be a Wasp."*

"Can't join 'em, I'll lick 'em. Sublimation's their secret: they think about *other stuff* all the time."

"Other . . . ?"

"Look, if you're black or French or Jewish or Catholic, it's think, think about sex, sex. But for Clive, it's law, law; for Stu, the Cowboys, the Cowboys—"

"And Cy thinks . . . ?"

"Numbers, beautiful numbers. I try to, too."

"Tiens, you think all the time numbers? Dreda, you are sure you are not being . . . co-opted into the elite?"

"Baby, *l'élite, c'est moi!"*

They overtake a lone jogger, Cy himself. Dreda slows down, waves to him. He points to a number on a mailbox by the side of the road.

"Look at that, 4-0-1-5. Factors out to 55 times 73!"

Dreda, coasting beside him, has an instant reply. "Or 11 times 365—exact number of days in eleven years."

Cy turns into a side road, looks back with a snide smile. "Provided none are leap years!" He jogs off.

"You see, Baudouin? Sexy."

He replies with Gallic body language: a classic shrug.

DOCUMENT #2 ▸ *From S. STUART'S notebook, research data on L. GROSS*

RECAP, Info on L.G.:

—Real name, Luigi Grosso—*not* Italian, *SWISS*

—Parents from Lugano—L.G. spks. Ital. w/Swiss accent(!)

—Born L.A., 1928
—To Vegas, '44—busboy, Desert Inn
—Croupier school, '50
—Bought into slot-machine concession Vegas airport, '52—
since then, has never looked back
—Owns 2 casino-hotels in L.V. (Miramar, Caravan), pieces
of 2 more in Atl. City (Fortuna, Beachcomber)
—Married, 2 dgtrs.
—No dir. Mafia connection estab.—considered *LONER*
—No crim. record
—Pd. $2.3 mil. Fed. inc. tax last yr.
—Keeps suite in Sheraton, Albany—*Why?*
—Freq. trips Lugano—Swiss bank acct?—*Find out—How?*
—Since '80, investments blue-chip stocks & legit. biz. (laun-
dromats, pizzerias, r. estate, Slipped Discos, etc.)
—Big contrib. to charities—R. Cross, Am. Cancer Soc., etc.
WHAT ELSE???—FIND OUT!!
(*Note*: L.G. v. careful—plays it safe & sane—prob. never get
real story on Lou—*but* STORY IS DOC HOP—what is Lou/
Hop linkage??—*FIND!*)

Strapped into the swiveled fishing chair, holding the butt of
the rod tight against the socket between his legs, eyes fixed on
his line astern, Stu is doing everything Doc Hop told him. He
has been silent and motionless for some minutes.

"You're certainly on your best behavior, Stuart."

"Easy enough to behave, Doc, when the alternative's a pair
of concrete shoes."

The vet translates for me and explains that the reference is
to a way of providing certain persons with a watery grave.

Ignoring Lou's patriotic injunction against conversing in foreign tongues on the Fourth, I ask, "How did you learn such
beautiful Russian in Hungary?"

"Not just in Hungary. As a boy, I traveled all over eastern

Europe—Hungary, Czechoslovakia, Bulgaria, Rumania.
Everywhere Russian was the lingua franca. We had to learn."

"You are from a diplomatic family?" (Like all Soviet émigrés,
I suffer from KGB phobia. The purpose of this question is to
ascertain whether his parents were spies.)

He smiles his disturbing smile. "No, no, I wasn't with my
family. I was with another family. My father was a biologist
at the University of Vienna. He had many laboratory animals.
I have always empathized with animals; that is why I am in
veterinary medicine today. One fine day I released all the dogs
and rabbits and guinea pigs. My father punished me severely.
I ran away, I joined a Hungarian circus that had been performing in Vienna, I became for two years a member of a circus
family."

Obviously he is making up this romantic nonsense, pulling
the leg of a poor dumb immigrant. But since I know that Stu
is in pursuit of a story, and that the story somehow involves
the three men on this boat, I decide to feed Doc Hop questions,
in the hope that he may let slip something that can be of use
to my friend S. Stuart.

"A family of acrobats?"

"No, no, this family rode and trained the performing horses."

"Hungarians are splendid horsemen," I say, trying to lead
him on.

"These were gypsies, actually."

Worse and worse! His fantasies are getting out of hand. I see
that our sotto voce Russian is driving Stu mad.

"Gypsies?"

"Delightful people. I spent two happy years with them before
my family found me, brought me back to Vienna and sent me
to live with an uncle in the States, fearing I might run away
to the gypsies again." He taps my leg with his slender hand,
lets his fingertips rest there. "Gypsy years—glorious years. I
slept in the straw with the horses, galloped them at dawn,

learned to deliver a foal." Aha, Ouspenskiy thinks, a *veterinary* fantasy. "Our horses danced on two legs, danced backwards, leaped over six or eight barrels in a line. One would jump through a burning hoop—and I trained him."

The hot sun, the pitch and roll of the powerboat are making me drowsy. I am bored with the vet's fictions. "How did you do that?" I ask with a yawn.

He lifts his hand from my leg, lays it on my bared forearm. His eyes stare out at me from under the deep shade of the brows. "It is not difficult. One must reason with the horse, one must persuade him."

"Whisper to him?" I suggest. Somewhere I have read that gypsies have a way of calming horses by whispering in their ears, blowing gently up their nostrils, something of the sort. Doc Hop seems not to have heard my question. I rephrase it. "Gypsy whispering?"

"What lovely words." He repeats them in Russian, then in English. " 'Gypsy Whispering' would be a fine name for a horse."

He removes his hand from my arm, rises, goes to join Schulzie at the rail. Why has he fashioned this romanesque past for my benefit? Perhaps it is all one to Doc Hop that I am not a dazzling blonde. He is surely, as the French say, *bon pour la voile et la vapeur*: in AmerEng, *AC/DC*. (Ouspenskiy, while not conventionally handsome, is irresistible to one and all.)

Reader, had I been ready to believe him, had I been willing then to reveal to S. Stuart that I could—after a fashion—*spikka da Eng*, he might have broken his Big Story months earlier. But how was I to know, rolling that day aboard *Hi-Roller*, that the Vienna part—at least—of the Doc's improbable tale checked out with what Stu had read in the veterinary directory?

Doc Hop and Schulzie are talking at the rail. Slowly, so that his chair won't squeak, Stu swivels round to hear them.

"So what's the good word, Doc?" Schulzie asks.

"Bagpipe in the fourth at . . ." Without turning to look, the vet seems to sense Stu's sonar scanning him. Eyes still on the

sea, he says, "Hang in there, Stuart, I'd like to see your first
time out be a big success."

"It is already."

A success (I shall later learn) because Stu already knows
from Wilf that Doc Hop is flying to Atlantic City tomorrow,
July Fifth. Bagpipe, he reasons, must be running the following
day, July Sixth. Just to make sure, Stu thinks, he will pick up
a *Sporting News* on his way back to—

Doinnnng! Rod nearly wrenched from hands, line whirring,
strike, a big one, a monster—

"Out! Out!" Lou thunders from the bridge. "Out, Chazz, more!
Basta! In, in, you dumb fuck, play him—"

Clive arrives at the house and goes up to his room, eager to
put on paper his memo to Self re. Environment, several felic-
itous phrases of which have formed in his head on the jog home
from Squaw. He finds Moira lying on the bed, naked but for
her glasses, examining her tan.

"Oh, Clive, I'll never be as brown as Patsy."

"What's that meant to mean?"

"Nothing. Should it?"

He tells himself his guilt feeling is irrational. Patsy and he
are friends; why can't friends go for a swim? Big deal. Remembering Macho, Clive goes to the window and blows his ultra-
sonic whistle. The neighbors' big black Lab comes bounding
across the lawn.

"You might kiss me."

He sits down on the edge of the bed, kisses her on the mouth.
She enfolds him in her arms. Her body is warm against his,
moving against his . . .

Moira lets go, turns her face away.

"I'm sorry. It's just . . . oh, this house is such a mess, and
you ought to see the phone bill. We'll have to call a meeting."

"Today? But it's the Fourth." A meeting will leave him no
time to draft his memo.

"Today. We all go back tomorrow. Clive, don't look so worried. I still love you."

"And I love you."

"You're as wound up as I am. Share it with me."

"Macho, for one thing. Haven't seen him all day."

"Probably there's a female in the area. Does it really matter?"

"Of course it matters. Usually when I come home, big brown eyes, tail going like crazy, paws on my chest, pink sloppy tongue . . ."

"I've never understood the charm of dogs."

"Companionship."

"I'm not companionship?"

"Sure you are, but you don't lie at my feet and lick my toes when I sit up nights working."

"You'd like me to."

"I like you like this." He touches her breast.

"Clive, I'm going to ask you something. Promise me you'll do it?"

"You know I will." Memo postponed, for how long?

"Take off your clothes. Get in bed. Hold me. Just hold me. And we'll both go to sleep. A nap, a nap is what we need. You promised."

At last the fish is aboard: a young swordfish, a real beauty, a six-footer. Stu stands gasping and sweating by the swivel seat, rubbing his blistered palms, feeling the ache in his calves and thighs. Doc Hop and Schulzie are congratulating him, pounding his back; the poet is bringing him a beer. He looks up at the flying bridge. The great stone face of Lou Gross is crumbling, cracking into a smile.

"Chazz, you done good."

"Thanks, Lou."

"Come up here."

Stu scrambles up the ladder to the bridge.

"Take the wheel, Chazz. Watch the lobster pots, head for the Point."

While Stu steers, Lou walks with heavy steps behind him.

"You're a reporter, Chazz."

"Sports reporter. I'm with—"

"*Sports Illustrated.*" Lou has done his homework too. "So what's the story now, Chazz?"

Stu talks fast. "Plan to do a story on sportfishing off L.I. People think you have to go to Key West or Baja to—"

"Yeah?"

Silence, but for the measured tread of Lou's heavy feet on the decking. Stu turns to speak to him. Sun refracts, blazing, from the silvered lenses.

"Eyes ahead! Lobster pot to port. Hold your course."

Stu holds it. Lou stops pacing to light a fresh cigar.

"Seen you before, Chazz. Three times back in May. The Pub. Out riding. The disco. Each time you showed a certain interest in my activities. You were already planning this fish story?"

"That's right, Lou."

"You knew I had the boat?"

"It's my business to know things."

"Your business. Funny thing is, I just bought this boat last week. Maybe you got ESP, like Doc Hop?"

"I'll level with you, Lou. What I really had in mind was a casino story."

"Funny thing number two, Chazz: your magazine ran a Monte Carlo story couple months ago. Pretty soon, isn't it, for another casino piece?" Further silence. Smoke billows around Stu's head. "How'd you meet Doc Hop?"

"Looking for a lost dog."

"A dog lover. Sure. So you saw the vet. When did you next see him?"

"This morning, on the beach, surfcasting."

"Quite the angler, aren't you, Stu?" It is the first time he has called him Stu. The metronome beat of his pacing moves to starboard, to port, back to starboard. "Stu Stuart. I've read your stuff. On football, you're good, you're good."

Stu is about to turn to thank him, but remembers: eyes ahead. "Means a lot to me, Lou."

"And you done good with that swordfish. First time out?"

"First time."

"You played him good. You're strong. You learn quick."

Stu breathes easier. He and Lou are going to be friends.

"Only one thing, Stu." The grating voice has sunk to a whisper.

"Yes, Lou?"

"That stuff you write. You're full of shit about the Cowboys." This is too much. "I am fuckin'-A right about the Cowboys!"

"Dallas won't win ten games this year."

Stu whirls on him, snarling. *"Bet you on that!"*

Lou releases smoke into his face. "Sure. How much?"

"Anything you want, you cheap two-bit asshole."

Fear grips Stu's gut. What he has just said to Lou Gross is so preposterous that he can do only one thing: laugh. Lou's large but sloping shoulders are heaving with laughter too. He thumps Stu's back with one hand, grasps the wheel with the other.

"Stu-ball, you are okay, you're a fighter. Run down, get us a couple brews."

"Aye-aye, Lou." He starts for the ladder, but the harsh voice stops him in his tracks.

"Another thing wrong."

"Yes, Lou?" Sweat runs cold in Stu's armpits.

The voice rasps like an emery wheel:

"You ask too fuckin' many questions."

Stu hurtles down the ladder. He has asked exactly two questions since coming aboard.

17
BREACH OF THE
COVENANT

T he communal covenant—Document #3: M.
FAIRCHILD'S minutes of house meeting—Of telephone, pets, cleanliness—A grave breach—A heated
debate—Proposal and counter-proposal—Of club life,
discrimination, pyrotechnics—Truce called—A happy
resolution

In any community there is a social contract: members must
not step on others' toes. Until the national holiday, our Y-
persons cohabited without excessive friction. They learned to
compromise between an exclusively protein and carbohydrate
diet (the Degans) and organically grown roughage (Cathy); between twenty-four-hour stereo concerts (Dreda) and monastic
silence conducive to concentration (Cathy again); between a
selfish, penny-pinching hostility to outsiders (all but Cathy)
and a warmhearted welcome to those less fortunate (once more,
my darling Cathy). Indeed it was she (Cathy) who discovered
on Independence Day a grave breach of the covenant on the
part of one of its members.

The bone of contention was of course money, and money it
was that resolved the matter. (Reader, you have guessed: it
involved S. Stuart.) As already stated (*supra, passim*), money
is the be-all and end-all for Y's, to an even greater extent than
for the society as a whole. In this crisis we shall see our upwardlies at their worst, yet also at their best, for in the end
they agree to forgive and forget. (Yes, I am aware that "best"
and "worst" are subjective concepts.)

Again I am able to present a documentary source. The following draft minutes of the meeting were jotted down by Chairperson M. Fairchild immediately after its adjournment:

DOCUMENT #3 ▸ *M. FAIRCHILD's minutes of July 4 house meeting*

H. MTG. 7/4—6:30 PM
1. Call to ord., all pres., mins. prev. mtg. disp. w/, etc.
2. Phone bill—div by 7
3. Pets—
    a. dog
        i. where?
        ii. *fat*
        iii. fleas?

     b. cats (!)

     c. bird—X

4. Ins.—NO

5. C. beech dead—S.S. to pay & replt.

6. Gen. cl'liness—rug—Cath.

7. *STU—*

     a. Gen. fury

     b. Mot'n to expel

     c. ETC.

As to what this document may mean, the reader is obliged to rely on the account of honorary grouper V.Y. Ouspenskiy.

We assemble in the living room. Moira stands before the portrait of Cap'n Caleb Slocum, her mien austere as his. All are present, including the non-shareholders V.Y. Ouspenskiy and Baudouin, Vicomte du Boisdormant. A proposal to dispense with the reading of the minutes of the previous meeting is carried by acclaim. The chairperson's motion for a vote of thanks to S. Stuart for providing us with swordfish is carried by raucous acclaim, which Stu appears not to hear. He is lying on the floor with his head (I tremble with rage as I report this) resting in the lap of C. Fairchild. The Walkman is over his ears; his eyes are closed; he looks blissful.

The first order of business is the telephone bill. It amounts to over four hundred dollars. No one knows anything about a call to Los Angeles, a call to Paris, an eighteen-minuter to Wenatchie, WA.

"On these unclaimed calls," Moira says, "we all pay pro rata. I'll divide by seven."

"Why not by eight?" Rick asks. "Dreda's got a double share in the rent. She ought to pay twice."

Dreda's rebuttal is so vehement that it is agreed to divide by seven.

There have been three hundred and sixty-eight calls to Area Code 212, Borough of Manhattan. After much debate, the housemates vote to treat them as local calls, to be divided by seven. Fortunately there have been no calls to Moscow.

"Rochester, New York," Moira reads from the bill. "Nine minutes, June Eighteenth, $5.25." Silence. "Who knows somebody in Rochester?"

Nobody knows anybody in Rochester.

"Dallas, twenty-one minutes, June Nineteenth, $16.75."

"Dallas! Guess who?"

"That's a no-brainer!"

"Somebody advising Tom Landry!"

Stu lifts an earpiece of his Walkman to hear them. "June Nineteen I was in the fuckin' Rockies."

"Dallas pro rata." Moira puts down the bill. "That's all the calls. I'll ask Co-Deputy Treasurer Dreda to compute what each of us owes. Next order of business? Clive?"

"Where's Macho? I can't find him."

"I've found his fleas," Dreda says, "and I hereby move that Clive be deputized to contact, contract with, and pay the exterminator."

Clive shows us a new piece of gadgetry for the Y-dog. "I bought him this Micro-Tech collar today. It emits a low-frequency sound that repels fleas. Seventy dollars, plus tax."

"Repels fleas off dogs, onto people."

"And furniture!"

Two young cats scamper across the room.

"Where the hell do they come from?"

"What about the no-pets rule? Whose—?"

"They are mine," Baudouin says with dignity. "You could not expect me to leave Minou et Tonton in New York?"

Moira purses her lips. "Baudouin, we have a rule—"

"Save your breath," Dreda interrupts. "The Vicomte's a footnote. Soon he'll be history."

Baudouin stares at her; this is news to him.

Rick gets to his feet. "Re. pets, I'd like to bring it to the attention of this meeting, there's catshit all over the cellar."

"*Pas possible!* Minou *et* Tonton never—"

"Come look."

Baudouin follows Rick to the door giving onto the cellar stairs. When they open it, the seagull flutters out and hobbles about the room, leaving a trail of droppings on the Erevan carpet. Cathy chases the bird, mopping up with Kleenex as she goes. It is Ouspenskiy who catches him, holds him in his arms, soothes him with melodious Russian baby-talk.

Moira looks at her sister with exasperation. "*Really*, Cath . . ."

"What were we meant to do, guys, leave J. Livingston to die on the beach?"

"Ever hear of a C-A-G-E?" Dreda asks.[64]

"He's got to exercise, poor thing." Cathy kisses the bird in my hands. I tremble with desire. "Oh, Vlady, the splint! Look, guys, Vlady has made the *dearest* little splint for J. Livingston's poor wing. . . ."

Mort stands up. "The soiling of the carpet underlines the need for insuring the contents of this house. Is Mrs. Slocum's personal property insured? I move we call her in Denver and find out. The Fire Department should inspect Dreda's re-wiring—"

"No!"

"Sit down!"

"Screw that!"

Mort sinks back into his chair, which creaks loudly.

"I invoke the Hepplewhite rule!" Clive shouts.

Reluctantly, Mort heaves himself up.

"Next matter, the grounds." Moira frowns down at the recumbent Stu. "That little copper beech you transplanted is dead . . . Stu? Stu?"

"Okay, okay," he says, removing the apparatus from his ears. "I'll buy a new one when the season's over."

---

[64]It is the curious custom of certain Y's to spell out simple words.

Cathy picks up the Walkman, listens for a moment, looks surprised. "What *is* this?" She ejects the cassette, reads the title aloud. " 'Super Bowl VI. Dallas Cowboys 24, Miami Dolphins 3 . . . Stu—eee!"

Catcalls from all. Moira raps for order.

"Next, general cleanliness. It's not just the seagull. Look at the slipcovers, the curtains. We have a responsibility to Mrs. Slocum. I move we get everything cleaned . . . Rick?"

"May I amend that motion? I move we get everything cleaned, but not until just before Labor Day. It'll only get dirty again."

There is mumbled assent. Cathy stands up.

"Sister Moira is right. I may not be the world's most orderly person myself, but we've got to clean as we go, not let things get out of hand. So, to set a good example, guys, I'll pay for having J. Livingston's doodoo cleaned off the rug. Might cost thirty, thirty-five dollars? I'll get my money and put thirty-five into the kitty right now." She heads toward the stairs.

Stu calls after her, "Dangerous precedent, Cath!"

Dangerous indeed for him. The breach of the covenant is about to come to light.

Cathy goes up to their room and rummages through the mess on her desk. Stubb's suggestion to turn TOTS into a family saga has resulted in an afternoon of feverish longhand scribblings, most of which have been crumpled and discarded. Money, she is sure, is somewhere under all the paper. In searching for it, she inadvertently knocks her billfold off the desk and into the wastebasket. She pulls it out, along with several envelopes, unopened but torn in two. They are addressed to "Slocum House Associates." She pieces together the contents of one of them and gives a little cry.

"Honestly!"

"Earl, look at that! Suitcase lying on Lavinia's lawn—girl throwing things out the window!"

"God almighty . . ."

"Golf clubs! Another suitcase—racquets—clothes—riding boots—"

"Girl's gone crazy. Where are the others, inside?"

"Must be. All four cars here. They probably don't even know."

"I'm going over to warn them."

"No, you're not. Not unless she throws out one of Lavinia's antiques."

"Ah, Jude . . ."

In the living room, we can hear Cathy thumping about upstairs, emitting cries of rage. Stu jumps to his feet, starts for the front door, but Cathy comes rushing down, squeaking at him.

"Honestly, Stu, honestly!" She waves the tattered envelopes in his face. Unable to express her fury, she turns to the rest of us. "Honestly, guys, I'm sorry, but I can't stand it another minute. He can get out, he can move, he can go, well, to hell, even—"

Here, reader, I must confess to an ignoble emotion. I sense that this is the end of S. Stuart as *amant en titre* of my doe-eyed one; my heart sings.

Cathy is sobbing. Moira encircles her with a sisterly arm, beating out the solicitous Ouspenskiy by inches.

"Please, Cathy, tell us . . ." She sees that Stu is again making for the door. "Stu!"

He stops. "Can't a guy go wee-wee?"

"Oh no, you don't, Stu Stuart! Look at this!" Cathy flies at him, brandishing the envelopes. "Village Pub! Sportsgear Unlimited! Slipped Disco! Lobster Pot!" Tears stream down her face. "Hundreds and hundreds and hundreds of dollars! All billed to Slocum House Associates! *Us!* And oh, Stu, we all thought you were so *generous*—"

She collapses against Moira, clings to her shoulder, shudders, sobs. Dreda goes to her and takes the bills from her hand.

In a few seconds she announces, "Comes to $3,491.53 in all."

General uproar.

"I move," Cathy cries, "that Stu Stuart pay every single cent, and I further move he be expelled from this house!"

Many a voice yells, "Seconded!"

Stu gets up on a chair to address the meeting.

"Not the Hepplewhite!" Clive shouts.

"Fuck the Hepplewhite. Fellow Slokes, lend me your ears—"

Cathy shrieks, "That's Stu Stuart—always wanting to borrow something!"

Further hubbub. Moira finds a hammer on the windowsill[65] and raps it on the tabletop.

"Order, order! Give him a chance to explain."

Somehow the meeting quiets down. Stu bows to Moira.

"Thank you, Ms. Chairperson, and may I point out, firstly, you have dented the Queen Anne tabletop. Secondly, you all elected me co-deputy treasurer of this house. Surely a deputy treasurer has certain discretionary powers—"

All shout at once. Cathy is sputtering incoherently. Ouspenskiy moves in, slips an arm around her waist, places his steel-woolly jowl against her deliciously fevered cheek.

To the surprise of all, Moira stands up on another Hepplewhite to speak in Stu's defense.

"I've got some points to make. We've all used the windsurfers and scuba gear Stu bought—"

"All but me! I've been in the fuckin' Rockies!"

"They've been shared, they've been treated as common property. And when Stu took us all to The Pub, the Lobster Pot, and the disco, it proved productive, we talked, we got to know each other, it made us synergetic. Therefore"—Moira has to raise her voice to be heard above the general outcry—"therefore I move we effect a compromise. To wit, that Stu pay fifty percent

---

[65]Where handyman Ouspenskiy left it after repairing the carburetor in May!

of these bills, and that we all share the rest." Ignoring new shouts of protest, she nods toward Clive, whose hand is up. "The chair recognizes Clive Wheelwright."

Clive mounts yet another Hepplewhite and looks down at us over the top of his glasses. "In a court of law, I would not find myself unable to defend the actions of Stu Stuart." We are caught by surprise; we had expected an attack on Moira's proposal. "It is true, as Stu himself has pointed out, that we elected him co-deputy treasurer. It is also true that we failed to define the powers of that office. *Lapsus legis*—a legal oversight, a loophole. On the other hand, Stu had a duty to report his expenditures to the other deputy treasurer, Dreda Scott, and to the co-treasurers, Moira Fairchild and myself. He has been less than forthright in allowing us to believe that we were borrowing property belonging to him when we used the scuba and windsurfing equipment, and that he was treating us to drinks, lobster, and dancing on that Saturday night in May." We are all restless; Clive hastens to his peroration. "Fault lies with us in not defining Stu's powers, and with Stu in not disclosing commitments made in the name of us all. Therefore, compromise is indicated." Cathy, Dreda, Mort, and Rick cry, "No! Sit down!" Clive ignores them. "I am willing to vote for Moira's compromise, provided that all present agree to pay for one-half of my summer membership in the—" Surprised by the shouting, Clive loses his lawyerly aplomb. "Look—I've taken you all to the Spindrift, haven't I? For lunch, tennis, swimming—"

"Not me." Dreda looks up into Clive's eyes. "Your club has not yet felt the need of a token spade."

Clive cannot face her. He crumples completely, stands down, sits down. One leg of the Hepplewhite buckles ominously, but holds.

"About that club," Mort says, "I move that Clive invite us all, regardless of race or creed, to their fireworks party tonight."

"Second the motion!"

"Why not, Clive?"

"Ashamed of us or something?"

Clive looks miserable. "I checked the rules, and I'm allowed to invite two guests. There are nine of us."

Snarls of disbelief. Moira thumps the hammer. "My motion for a compromise is still before this house. Do I hear a second?"

"Seconded!" Stu says. "I further move we adjourn for five minutes, so that I can go piss and the rest of you can discuss Moira's proposal."

Motion carried by acclaim.

Stu goes straight to the library. Impelled by a purely scientific curiosity, Ouspenskiy follows.

"Max?" Stu shouts into the phone. "Max, got some numbers for me?" He listens, incredulous, then whistles. "Three-six-four-oh . . . dollars? . . . Listen, Max, Bagpipe in the fourth at Atlantic City day after tomorrow, July Six. Five hundred bucks, that's five-oh-oh, on the nose. Over and out!"

He strides triumphantly back to the living room.

"You miserly sleazebags, hand over those bills! Who said I couldn't pay? Rick, get the grill going! Mort, clean that fish! It's swordfish steak tonight, group, thanks to Deep Sea Stu, the sportsman!"

18

COMMUNAL
FIREWORKS
RITE

T*he rite discussed—A sisterly confrontation—
Search for Y-dog—Pyrotechnics procured—An inter-
Y-personal quarrel—Rite prematurely celebrated—
Emergency procedures—A non-Y to the rescue—Y-
dog found—The arm of the law—Another non-Y to
the rescue—Changes of quarters—The morning after: communal resolutions—Aid from an unexpected
source*

Since the Chinese invented fireworks, the more advanced nations have used them for celebrations. Less advanced peoples have similar rites involving bonfires. Fireworks are beautiful (a nonscientific concept) and theoretically harmless substitutes for the thunder and lightning of war. I reject out of hand the analogy to the sexual act that certain colleagues see in the pyrotechnic rocket's gratifying rise, glorious burst, and dying fall. Nonsense: no one enjoys fireworks more than children; yet children have no means of drawing the sexual parallel.[66]

Y-persons are akin to children. Childlike, they enjoy putting on costumes for, e.g., skiing, sailing, tennis, office, night on town, seduction, bed. Childlike, their minds dwell on food ("cuisine"). Childlike, they cherish their toys—home computers, VCRs, stereos, BMWs, trail bikes, Walkmans, electronic calorie counters or backgammon sets, egg clippers, Skee-Trax, ExerCycles, Micro-Tech flea collars. Childlike, they vie for the attention and approval of their elders—the employer, *in loco parentis*. What, after all, is more childlike than to want it all, and want it now?

Deprivation of the fireworks rite on a day of national rejoicing is intolerable to our Y's, even though the deprivation is caused by their own pathological aversion to parking problems (in comparison they almost enjoy traffic) and by Clive's uncharacteristic reluctance to find a loophole in the bylaws of his club. In their frustration, they attempt to organize their own pyrotechnic rite—with foreseeable consequences.

Moira is at the grill in the garden, raking the coals, now almost ready for the swordfish. It is growing dark. Baudouin uncorks a bottle of wine from the Squaw Harbor Winery, tastes, expectorates, says *"Imbuvable."* Mort and Rick sit on the back steps, halfway through a twelve-pack of Bud. Dreda sips her

---

[66]It is true that interpersonal interface (sex) bulks almost as large in this section of our study as the fireworks rite. I deem this coincidental.

margarita and walks slowly through the garden, her beautiful eyes upon the sky.

Cathy brings a fresh supply of mesquite chips to the grill. Her tear-streaked face, her sniffly nose tell Moira it is a time for sisterly advice.

"You're being too hard on him, Cath. You and Stu had a really synergetic relationship, and so much in common. You're both in the writing industry and—"

"And? Go on, big sister."

"And you're both quite messy, and—"

"Oh, you're such an order freak!" As soon as the words are out of her, Cathy is sorry she said them. Moira's face seems to have fallen apart. "My God, what did I say?"

"Just what my shrink says—I'm too 'order-oriented.' " Moira forces a smile. "Apparently it's because Mummy put me on the potty too early."

"That's really weird. If it's true, why am I so messy?"

"Probably by the time you came along, Mummy could afford a lifetime supply of Huggies."

Cathy looks at the glow of light reflected against the sky by the Highway to the north. The predicted traffic jam has materialized: horns can be heard from here. "Which is why I should give Stu Stuart another chance—because we're both slobs?"

Moira pokes at the coals with a pair of tongs. "There's more to it than that. Stu is a truly awesome person. Greathearted, great fun, bubbling over with ideas and energy." Her voice is tender. "He's a bear. You want to hug him, but he might cuff you—"

She stops, aware of her sister's stare.

"Ms. Chairperson," Cathy says in a dry voice, weighing her words. "To gratify your mania for order, let me make it clear that Stu and I are history. This is a quitclaim. The way is clear for a leveraged takeover."

Moira feels her face flush and is glad it's twilight. She answers coldly, very much on her dignity. "Save your imagination for that novel of yours. I *like* Stu. Clive, I love. Clive is an orderly person; so am I. We are getting married in an orderly manner on Saturday, October Second." She adds, in quite another voice, "Cathy, I want you to be maid of honor."

Both sisters burst into tears, hug, snuffle.

From the back steps, Dreda, Baudouin, Mort, and Rick are looking at the fireworks that have begun to light up the sky to the south, over the ocean.

"Oh. Wah."

"Wow."

Mort is moved to misquote Keats. " 'Then felt I like old Cortez in the skies/When some stout planet swum within his ken . . .' "[67]

Clive comes through the privet arch, forlornly calling, "Macho!"

"Swimming within our ken at this point in time," Dreda says, "is Upwardly Mobile, whose C-L-U-B is shooting those things off. We peons must admire from afar."

"Hey, Clubman," Rick calls out, "how come you're not down at the club?"

"Anybody seen my dog?"

Nobody has.

Where, you have doubtless been wondering, is the egregiously observant Ouspenskiy? Down in the cellar, reader, bending over the workbench, upon which lie a packet of cigarette paper and several trays of dried weeds. The poet's granny glasses gleam as he works, preparing for his American friends his own contribution to their day of chauvinistic revelry. Upon his shoulder perches the gull, J. Livingston.

Feeling highly unpopular, worried about his dog, Clive comes down the outdoor cellar steps. He is too preoccupied to wonder what Ouspenskiy's nimble fingers are up to.

---

[67]Correct version cited on an early page of this work. It was Mort's taped account of this incident that drove me into first looking into Keat's sonnet. Lovely, but his enthusiasm baffles me. Have you, reader, ever looked into *Chapman's* Homer?

"Vlady, have you seen Macho?"

"*Nyet.*"

Clive goes up the indoor stairs, emerges in the front hall and calls for Macho. Seeing that the door of the hall closet has been left open, he goes to it and peers in, looking for the dog. A bulky package wrapped in brown paper is on the floor of the closet, propped against a wall. He glances at the label:

From: *Galerie Nadya*

To: *Moira Fairchild*
   Slocum House
   Slocum Lane
   Hastings

Clive pulls the package halfway out, rips a corner of the brown paper and counts the paintings inside. Not six, but eight. In dropping off her check at the gallery, Moira has been unable to resist upping her investment by 33⅓ percent.

He goes out the front door, letting the screen bang. It is now over twenty-four hours since he has seen the dog. Clive imagines a grisly death on the Highway, the fluffy body mangled by the pitiless stream of cars. It occurs to him that Macho might, on the other hand, have been kidnapped. The dog is adorable: who could resist?

He goes down the front steps to the lawn, peers under the veranda, calls "Macho!" The putt-putt of the trail bike makes him look up. Stu swings into the driveway with Patsy on the seat behind him and a large cardboard box balanced on the handlebars.

"Found this madwoman jogging."

Patsy dismounts. She has been in Clive's mind every second since Indian Marsh. His eyes try to tell her so. "Only way to go to the fireworks is on foot," she says. He wants to convince himself that her smile is for him, a loving message from—his friend. "Nowhere to park," she goes on in a perfectly flat, mat-ter-of-fact East-End-of-the-Island voice. "But I was late, so Stu . . ."

". . . made her a better offer. To help eat my swordfish and view our private pyromaniac show later. Get a load of this!" He holds out the cardboard box to Clive, who peers into it. "Pinwheels, Roman candles, star clusters, you name it. My pal Schulzie got 'em for me."

"We can't shoot them off here."

"Of course not," Patsy says, "but down on the beach after midnight, when the crowds and the cops are gone . . ."

A solution to the Spindrift problem. "Sure," Clive says, "why not?" In his mind's eye is the beach, silvery in moonlight, the sea black but for the creamy foam of the rollers. While others watch fireworks, two naked figures go racing into the surf; the girl's bottom, white as a rabbit's scut, winks at the young man as they throw themselves into a wave.

Carrying the box, Stu walks around to the back of the house, toward the garden. "Look what I got!" he calls to the groupers at the grill.

Clive puts a hand on his arm. "Not near the coals—leave them here."

Stu sets down the box next to a rose bush, well away from the grill. Baudouin, Dreda, and the Degans walk across the grass to have a look at the supply of fireworks. The public benefactor Ouspenskiy comes up the outdoor stairs from the cellar, ceremoniously bearing a silver cigarette box presented to Lavinia Slocum and her late husband Harold on their fortieth wedding anniversary. It contains a number of freshly rolled, home-grown joints, the harvest of my May sowing. They are gratefully accepted by most of my housemates, but alas, my offering is not destined to provide these overwrought young persons with the evening of Oblomovian oblivion I have naively imagined.

Patsy takes a joint; Clive, however, shakes his head. "No thanks, Vlady, never use 'em."

"Go on," she says, alert to my disappointment. "Take one, be polite."

Clive selects a joint, holds it as though it might explode, thanks me, tucks it behind his ear. Aware that Moira is eyeing him from her post behind the grill, he walks over to her.

She greets him with, "Whose idea was Patsy Magee?"

"Stu asked her." Clive hastens to change the subject. "You heard the news? Thanks to Stu, we've solved the fireworks."

"I heard, and I think it's crazy. It's also illegal."

"Moira, the beach won't burn. Neither will the ocean. We're all responsible adults. Stu's worked with explosives at West Point; I've shot off flares at sea. Extenuating circumstances."

Busy marinating the swordfish steaks, she gives him a tight smile. "Oh, the legal mind. Remember when you thought up your famous distinction between groupers and house guests?"

An edge comes into Clive's voice. "Leave law to me. I don't sound off to you about art. By the way, how much did those eight alleged paintings cost?"

Moira stops marinating. "This is not sounding off on art?"

"Elowyn's things are art?"

"Your fireworks are legal?" They stare at each other across the coals. "I say you are flouting the law."

Her remark so disturbs him that Clive takes the joint from behind his ear and sticks it in his mouth. Moira can't believe it. *"Flouting!"*

Of course he has no matches.[68] He gropes about the grill, but the kitchen matches are out making the rounds, lighting up

---

[68]Y's shun tobacco. Some carry lighters for use on joints, or to light cigars or cigarettes for persons of higher rank at the office, or for persons of opposite sex met in bars.

the joints of others. Finally he picks up the tongs, lifts a live coal from the grill, and coolly lights up.

"Oh, Clive, why do we have to get into these confrontational situations? I do wish you'd reconsider about seeing—"

He takes an inexpert drag and blows a cloud of smoke into her face.

"No, Moira, I will not reconsider. I have no intention of accompanying you to your analyst for premarital counseling."

To mark his point, Clive swings the tongs and hurls the coal far into the darkness.

Reader, again you have guessed. It scores a direct hit on the fireworks box.

Seconds later, pyrotechnic devices are flying every whichway.

All of us shout and scream. Clive pulls Moira's head down and screens her with his body from the flying fireworks. She sobs against his chest. Ouspenskiy looks around wildly for Cathy, sees her dashing for cover in the house. Crossing the back porch, she knocks over a can of lighter fluid, carelessly left there without its top. Foreseeing the disaster, the poet rips off his Union blouse and rushes forward to throw it on top of the puddle of fluid now spreading across the porch.

Too late. A Roman candle lands in the puddle. Flash and glare force me back.

For a moment, we all stare dumbly at the blaze; then everyone begins to shout orders to everyone else.

A dazzling fireworks display lights up the picture window of the Jessup sunroom. Judy is on the telephone.

"Chief, they're shooting off illegal fireworks in a residential—" She stares out the window in disbelief. "Fire! *Fire*! FIRE! *FIRE!*"

Earl springs up from his Barca-lounger and rushes to the door.

* * *

Clive has turned on the outdoor tap; Stu is hauling in hose from the farther reaches of the garden. We all yell. The back porch is on fire, the house is in danger—

Cathy! Inside! No way to get through the flames to the kitchen door—I am running around the house to the front, racing through it, shouting her name. I find her in the kitchen, at the telephone.

"Fire company doesn't answer, Vlady—" She screams; a curtain in an open window has caught fire. *"My manuscript!"*

Cathy bolts for the stairs. I intercept her, sweep her up in my arms, and run to the front door; she clings to me, crying "Halcyon!" A joyous moment for intrepid Ouspenskiy. We hurry back around the house to the blaze. Stu has trained his hose on the flaming curtain.

"The shingles!" Mort bellows. Stu hoses down the burning shingles in the siding.

Dreda screams, "My wiring! Stu—that wire near the drainpipe!"

But the wiring has already caught fire. Every light in the Slocum House goes out; the stream from the hose turns to a dribble; the blaze on the back porch spreads.

Stu throws down the hose. "Goddamn electric pump. Kiss that house good-bye."

"Yextinguishcher!" I shout, thus revealing that I know at least one four-syllable English word. The cellar—I have seen an extinguisher there. I dash to the cellar steps.

Coming toward me across the Slocum lawn is an elderly man in a leisure suit, dragging a long hose.

Yes, reader, it is Earl Jessup to the rescue. He strides through us, pushes us aside, levels his hose toward the flames, sprays them with water from his own well. Judy arrives, dithering.

"Do be careful, Earl—"

The black Labrador is barking wildly, trying to get close to the burning porch. His mistress seizes him by the collar, raps him on the snout.

We all cheer as Earl puts out the last of the blaze. Then everyone crowds around the Jessups, thanking them, offering drinks, inviting them to stay for swordfish. Earl looks at Judy, who smiles shyly and accepts.

The Lab is still barking, straining toward the porch. Clive takes a flashlight from the grill, drops down on all fours and looks under the decking.

"Macho! He's crying! Macho, come out, boy, come on out, it's all over!" Suddenly he pulls his head out from under, turns toward us with a stunned smile. "A medical miracle. Macho has produced a litter of puppies."[69]

"Some Macho!" Dreda cries. "Call her Masha!"

The tension is broken. We laugh, we cry. A police car pulls into the driveway, siren screaming. Officer Breitschwanz comes hurrying toward us.

Clive goes to meet him. "We put it out, Officer."

"Good thing. Fire company's down at the beach." The young cop's face looks mournful. "Sorry, Mr. Wheelwright, I'm going to have to arrest every one of you for illegal possession and use of fireworks."

Judy Jessup begins screaming in his face. "It was an accident! They're just kids—*good* kids! *Who asked you to butt in?*"

Breitschwanz looks at Earl. "Control her, Mr. Jessup. Please?"

Earl leads Judy and the Labrador back toward their house. Ouspenskiy is searching in the grass for Mrs. Slocum's silver cigarette box. Breitschwanz turns back to Clive.

"Also, Mr. Wheelwright, sorry about this, illegal possession of . . ."

He takes from Clive's lips the still-lighted joint that has hung

---

[69]How, the reader may ask, could these intelligent young persons have failed to notice the sex of a bitch, even an exceedingly fluffy one, during the last five weeks of her pregnancy? If you have read this work with care, you know the answer: the attention of the Y's is focused only on themselves. What, you ask, of Ouspenskiy? Ha. Ouspenskiy knew it all along.

there forgotten throughout the fire. The Slokes shout incoherently in protest.

"*Vot kak!*" Ouspenskiy has found the silver box. He leaps to his feet. The lid swings open. Several joints spill out, right at the feet of Officer Breitschwanz.

There is nothing to do but be polite. I hold the box out toward him, as if offering a cigarette.

"*Papiros?*"

Breitschwanz seizes the box from my hand, sniffs one of the joints. "Confiscated." He raises his voice. "Your attention, please. Line up here. Hands on the porch rail. I'm calling in for the wagon."

We line up, feet in the flower bed, hands raised to grip the railing. The red flasher light on top of the police car swings over us. None of us can believe what is happening.

"I'll be disbarred . . ."

"We get one call—I'm calling Lou Gross. Big Lou will make these goddamn pigs shit blood!"

"The house, we've ruined the house." Moira is close to hysteria. "Oh, Clive, *why* did you have to . . . ?"

"An accident, for God's sake. The odds were ten thousand to one against that coal hitting the box."

Ouspenskiy is sure they will take away his green card.

"I hate to be preachy, but if we'd taken out insurance . . ." All are too dispirited to tell Mort to shut up.

A second police car arrives, drives straight across the lawn, stops beside us at the porch rail. Chief Sweeney steps out.

"Possession, Chief. Ten of 'em."

"Nice work, Breitschwanz. Biggest drug bust in town history." The Chief struts up and down, looking over our sorry line-up. When he reaches Patsy, he stops. "Miss Magee. Well, well. Fancy meeting you here."

"Hi, Uncle Kevin. You're just the man to tell us what to do about this swordfish." She takes his arm, leads him toward the grill.

The Slokes utter groans of relief. But for Officer Breit-schwanz, all illusion about law and order in Hastings has fled.

Swordfish eaten, Chief and Breitschwanz escorted to their cars, damage inspected by flashlight. It looks bad. The ex-hausted Slokes agree to go to bed and deal with it in the morn-ing. Stu is the last to mount the stairs. He stands in darkness outside Cathy's door, wondering whether to knock, barge in, or forget it.

From Clive and Moira's room, he can hear voices raised in argument. Suddenly the door bursts open and Clive comes out, wearing only boxer shorts. In his hands are a pillow, a sleep mask, and a light blanket. He passes Stu without a word and goes up the stairs to the attic.

Stu knocks softly on Cathy's door. He waits, knocks again.

The door is opened by the poet, naked but for the seagull, with which he modestly conceals the crown jewels of Russia.

Ouspenskiy is grave and apologetic. "Cathy fock me now."

Stu wheels away, heads for the attic stairs. As he starts up them, Clive comes down again.

By the dim moonlight shining through the dormer window, Stu sees Baudouin asleep on the attic couch. The cats Minou and Tonton sprawl beside him on the pillow.

Stu goes back down to the second floor, opens Dreda's door without knocking. He finds her in one of the twin beds, Clive and his sleep mask in the other. The solution, he decides, is to lift the sheet on Dreda's bed, slide under it with her and take the consequences. In a moment he has stripped off his shirt, dropped his slacks and boxers. He flexes his shoulder muscles, pats his hairy chest. If this were a pornographic work, you, reader, would be in a lather.

Dreda opens her eyes, looks at him, points to the floor be-tween the two beds, throws down a pillow and quilt for him.

Stu collapses on them.

MONDAY, JULY 5

In the light of cold, gray dawn we stand on the back porch and survey the damage.

Clive ticks off various items in a tired voice. "Porch flooring badly scorched. Door and window trim scorched. Shingles in siding burned, must be replaced. Extensive water damage in kitchen."

"The whole electrical system," Dreda says, "needs rewiring."

Stu pounds his fist against his palm. "It'll cost us a goddamn fortune."

"Not if she was insured."

Dreda's eyes sear Rick Degan. "If we contact Mrs. Slocum, you nerd, she'll throw us out."

"And we'd miss the rest of the season," Cathy moans.

"Which," Stu says, "is fuckin' unthinkable."

Moira takes charge. "Here's what we'll do. We'll work on the house every weekend. We'll repaint, reshingle, rewire. We'll do it all ourselves. We'll all take the last two weeks in August off, to make sure the house is in tip-top shape by Labor Day."

The Slokes stand in stunned silence. What a summer! They nod grimly. They try to look resolute.

Only the sharp-eyed Ouspenskiy has noticed that Earl Jessup has come up behind us to reclaim his hose.

"If that's what you're going to do, Miss, I'm a neighbor, I'm pretty good with m'hands, I'll help you out. If that's what we're going to do, let's get going!"

WEEKEND
BEFORE
LABOR
DAY

IV

19

COMMUNAL
OUTREACH

FRIDAY, AUGUST 27

*C*ommunal synergy attained—Refurbishment of locus—Communal feast planned—A trial
separation—An alliance for journalistic research—
Computer-graphicizing—A literary critique—Further graphics—A curious introduction—Workplay
of D. SCOTT: colloquy with the brothers DEGAN—
An offer of employment—Fruits of S. STUART'S research disclosed—The fruitful research of M. FAIR-
CHILD

Challenge and response: communal synergy is achieved at last. Instead of pulling apart, the commune members pull together. For seven weekends plus a week of "vacation," the citified hands of the Y's, mightily abetted by the strong country hands of the two non-Y neighbors,[70] hammer, saw, nail shingles, scrape and apply paint, rewire, sew new curtains, wax furniture and floors. Their goal, the repair and refurbishment of the locus, is triumphantly attained, a full week ahead of schedule. A celebration is planned. The same synergy is applied to preparations for the celebratory feast, an apparent effort to reach out to the world beyond the communal microcosm. But on the great night itself, each of our Y-persons resumes his/her pursuit of upward mobility. The result is of their own making.

The house looks beautiful.

We have finished the finishing touches. All of us stand on the lawn, admiring our handiwork: Clive, Moira, Cathy, Stu, Dreda, Rick, Mort, Earl and Judy Jessup, V.Y. Ouspenskiy.[71] We are gathered around the new copper beech sapling that Stu and I have just planted.[72] Masha, the former Macho, romps with her eight-week-old puppies on the grass. J. Livingston is practicing takeoffs on his newly healed wing. We are happy.

"Great job," Moira says.

Clive throws himself on the grass to cuddle a puppy. "The best is being finished a week early. We can relax."

"Let's celebrate." Stu drop-kicks his football over the privet arch. "Keg of beer—"

"Gourmet brunch," Cathy says.

---

[70]And the equally willing hands of the poet. (I got blisters.)

[71]Baudouin has long since joined his predecessor Chip in limbo, taking Minou and Tonton with him.

[72]Hole by Ouspenskiy, advice by S. Stuart.

Moira takes command. "Dinner party. Candles, crystal decanters, Mrs. Slocum's best silver, long dresses, the works. Just us." She looks at Judy and Earl. "And the two of you, of course."

The Jessups beam. Judy says, "What will I wear?"

Clive sets down the puppy and stands up. "We really ought to invite Patsy. She saved our necks the night of the fire."

"If you ask Patsy, I'm asking Cy."

"And I'll invite Jim Stubbs. I'm so far behind on my book, I've just got to make a clean breast of it to him."

"*Vot kak!* Breast is boobs, no?"

Cathy strokes my arm. "Career first, Vlady. Sex is nothing. *Nichevo!*"

"I'll run by the gallery to invite Elowyn and Nadya."

"Yeah, and there's Wilf, the travel dude; I owe him. And there's Lou Gross and Schulzie and Doc Hop."

"Hey, Stu, think you could line up a couple of big-ass broads for me and Mort?"

"For sure. Tonight I go on pussy patrol."

SATURDAY, AUGUST 28

After a day and a half of fevered shopping, the wardrobes of Stu and the Sloke ladies have been appropriately replenished. Somehow the raging passions as to choice of gourmet dishes have been appeased, *crus* chosen, guests convoked. Cuisine is a-cooking, white wine chilling, red breathing, night (as foreseen) falling.

Clive is in the attic, dressed in his seersucker suit, working out on the ExerCycle, which was moved upstairs in early July. The lectern on the handlebars holds a legal document. Now that Wetlands Trust's purchase of Indian Marsh from the Hatch

Estate has been wrapped up, Clive is back on LBO's. He pedals, reads, and ties his bow tie, green for Dartmouth. The attic couch is neatly made up as a bed. His clothes, Skee-Trax, typewriter, law books, and papers are close at hand. Masha and her pups are asleep in an enormous wicker dog basket, $99.95 at Pampered Pet.

Moira comes up the attic stairs, wearing a long dress purchased this very day at Saks, Hastings Haven. In her hand are carnations. She pins one in Clive's lapel, adjusts his tie, lightly kisses the top of his head.

"Thank you. *Dianthus Caryophyllus*. Moira, you look beautiful."

"And you, resplendent. Where'd you disappear to today? I was worried."

"I worked with Rufe at the yard. Then Patsy and I had a run."

"Good, you needed to unwind. Was it nice?"

"I guess so. Moira?" He has stopped pedaling. She looks at him. "How long is this trial separation going to go on?"

"As far as I'm concerned, it's over."

"You mean—" He starts to dismount.

"I mean we're history."

He sinks back on the seat and begins to pedal slowly, as if pumping up a long hill.

"We'll always be friends, Clive."

"The best."

She smiles. "No palimony. You can tear up that pre-nup thing."

A silence. He again stops pedaling.

"Somebody else?"

"I'm not sure."

"Stu?"

"What an idea." She heads for the stairs.

Clive pedals furiously.

* * *

The gourmet dinner party is to be on the veranda. Mrs. Slocum's Sheraton dining table has been moved outside; with all its leaves in, it is barely long enough. The tablecloth is a Slocum heirloom. Upon it, candles, crystal, and flowers have been lavishly deployed. Stu, in new blazer, dazzling white ducks from Dudewear, and his Dallas Cowboys tie, is decanting the Sancerre. Moira comes out the front door and pins a carnation on him.

"There! Gorgeous. . . . Tell me, whatever happened to your big story?"

"I still believe in it. Went to Albany to research it; missed a Landry press conference. Gave up covering the Cowboys-Seahawks pre-seasoner tomorrow to be here with Big Lou tonight. It's Doc who's got me stymied. Doc Hop is key."

"But you've been seeing a lot of him."

"I have. I've established the gambling linkage, got a source who feeds me tips. Not Doc, a source fed by Doc. The Doc's horses win, damn near always win. Doc and I are buddies. We fish, we shoot pool, he even took me to Belmont once. Of course I couldn't go into the stables with him. All I got out of it was a telescopic shot, Doc Hop patting some horse's face. Horse won next day, paid $11.40. He's doping them silly, but how do I prove it? Steal his black bag?"

"Did you look up that old book of his—*Animal Magnetism?*"

"Blind alley. Not even about animals."

Moira pours herself a Sancerre kir. "In my business, they tell us to look for the collector's weak point."

"Schulzie!" Stu snaps his fingers. "Not weak, he's tough, but he's got shit for brains. Moira, do me a favor tonight. Cultivate Schulzie."

"Really, Stu. It was bad enough when you made me cultivate Doc Hop."

"Forget Doc Hop. It's Schulzie who requires cultivation."

"I'll try." Moira is smiling but earnest. "My shrink says I should open myself to nonmainstream experience."

Cathy and Dreda come out on the veranda, bringing two ice buckets and a trayload of glasses for the bar. Stu takes one look at the deep *décolleté* of Dreda's dress and gives forth with a piercing whistle.

"Yo, Dreed! Dressed nonprep for once!"

"It's lovely," Moira says. "Whose?"

"Bill Blass, how can you ask? From Beautique in Nowedonah. Tonight I make my big play for the big job with the biggest arb. To get to yes, I'll go all out." She glances down at her startling neckline. "I'll even pull 'em out."

Cathy takes the glass from her sister's hand and sips at it. "How's my hair, guys? Am I nervous! I gave Jim Stubbs my typescript to read. It's only a hundred and three pages, but I lied and said I was still polishing the other four hundred."

"He'll love it," Moira says. "Shall we go in and be creative with the hors d'oeuvres?"

"Yeah," Stu says, "I want to see Vladski in the new outfit I bought him."[73]

Cathy and Stu follow Moira into the house. Dreda picks up the decanter of Sancerre.

A car arrives and parks in the drive. The painter Elowyn comes toward the front steps, carrying a canvas.

"Dreda, I know I'm early. I wanted to show Moira my latest." She holds up the picture for Dreda to admire. "I'm so excited, I've been painting like a mad thing. It's another storm pattern."

"I can see. When was this?"

"Today. Today's satellite weather photo. I dashed it off this afternoon. Like it?"

Dreda studies the painting closely.

"Let's compare it with the others, Elowyn."

---

[73]The cleverest ploy of Y women has been to convince Y males that men are more gifted as cooks. Ouspenskiy, unconvinced, has been dragooned by Cathy. At this point in time, granny glasses opaque with steam, he is stirring the gourmet cuisine.

"Good. Let's!"

The brown paper package has spent eight weeks in the hall closet. Dreda lugs it up the stairs; Elowyn follows with the new acrylic.

In Dreda's room they unwrap the brown paper. Elowyn is all a-twitter. She is surprised when Dreda sits down at her computer with one of the paintings propped before her and begins translating art into computer graphics.

About half of the fifteen "outside" guests have arrived. They more or less mingle on the veranda. Earl and Judy greet each new arrival; they feel they are part of the family now. He is arrayed in white tuxedo jacket and maroon bow tie; she has chosen to appear in a 1950s bridesmaid's gown. Tied to Randy's collar is a bow to match his master's.

Patsy comes up the front steps. Clive is not at all pleased to see that Cy is behind her. Have they arrived in the same car? Patsy and Clive have seen each other every day; they have run, swum, and sailed together, but are still—infuriatingly—friends, nothing more. She, the tease, the townie, has drawn a line he cannot cross. They seem to be standing waving to each other across a canyon. Locals and summerfolk: never the twain?

Tonight Patsy's tan is perfectly set off by a long white dress with ochre sash. Shooing away Masha, who wants to jump up and paw her, she goes over to Clive.

"You didn't tell me, I had to hear it from Dan, my cousin down at Town Hall. He says Wetlands Trust has bought Indian Marsh right out from under the noses of the developers."

"Yes, we closed Thursday." Clive wonders if she is sending him a signal by bringing up Indian Marsh, the erotic high point of their summer.

"You know something, Clive? You have done a great and good thing for the whole South Fork." She kisses him, a fast and friendly brush of the cheek.

What he wants to tell her is that he and Moira are for the

archives, that he is free to move from friendship to relationship, but with Cy still lurking at her elbow, he must stick to small talk. "Patsy, could you use a puppy? Could any of your relatives? Could Cousin Dan? Uncle Kevin? Could you, Cy?"

"Puppy, what in hell for?" Herkimer is impatiently scanning the other guests. "Where's Dreda Scott? Thought she was meant to be here."

Over at the bar, Stu is shouting at Mort and Rick, "Wait'll you see the great snatch I lined up for you guys!"

The brothers snicker and punch each other.

The travel agent Wilf, in chartreuse ruffled dress shirt, is having a lively conversation with the gallery owner Nadya, in gray knit turtleneck and matching denim slacks. Earl Jessup, standing nearby, draws Judy's attention to them.

"Wonder how they do it?"

Nadya says to Wilf, "Have you seen my friend Elowyn? I can't think where she is. She told me she'd be here early. You don't think she's been in an accident?"

"Yexcuse me, I overhear," says a short but distinguished bearded gentleman in the full-dress uniform of a US brigadier general of the Mexican War period, plus an apron lettered CHEFS DO IT TASTEFULLY. "I see this Yelowyn go op with Dreda to her room."

"How could she?" Nadya is so distraught that she fails to notice the silver box Ouspenskiy is politely offering her.

The poet-chef is even more distraught than she when he sees Cathy hurrying to greet Jim Stubbs, who has the typescript of *Turn Off the Stars* in his hand.

"Did you read it?"

The hairy humanoid looks deep into her doe eyes.

"Yes, and it's beautiful." Even the jealous Ouspenskiy has to concede the sincerity in his face, his words. "Catherine Fairchild, you are a great writer."

Almost inaudibly, Cathy says, "I am?"

He presses the typescript to his heart. "I thought of Virginia

Woolf, of Djuna Barnes. A major new voice. You made me cry,
you made me laugh"—he speaks throatily—"you made me love
you."

Ouspenskiy forces his way into the narrowing gap between
their bodies on the pretext of offering the silver box. Neither
of them seems to notice.

"Another thing, Catherine. The book is finished."

"It *is?*"

"Don't change a comma, don't write another word. It's perfect
as it is. Those other four hundred pages you mentioned, stick
them in a drawer, some day you'll use the material. Can I get
you a drink, doll?"

"Champagne!"

Several paintings are propped along the base of a wall. Dreda
keeps glancing at them as she computes. Elowyn goes to the
one empty chair and daintily removes a jockstrap before sitting
down.

"Throw it on the far bed." Dreda's fingers fly over the keys
like will-o'-the-wisps. "He lives in that half; I'm here. We don't
interface."

Her half of the room is orderly, Stu's an unbelievable mess.

"Today's picture, here." Dreda points to a spot on the lower
right corner of the newest painting. "Tropical Storm Irving?"

"That's Irv. They say he's blowing harmlessly out to sea off
Cuba."

"Do they now?" She correlates data at blinding speed. "Elowyn,
did you ever know the Weather Service to be wrong?"

The painter giggles. "Did I!"

Two real floozies, Annie and Jinx, are what Stu has produced
for Rick and Mort. Ouspenskiy recognizes Annie as the woman
with large breasts the Degans admired at the disco. Stu hovers
proudly around the girls; Mort appears dumbstruck; Rick gamely
makes conversation.

". . . so there I am at the Steelers' camp, and first thing I know, the old groin muscle starts acting up . . ."

Jinx and Annie go into hysterics. Stu mumbles into Mort's ear, "Great twat, what? Floppy disk!"

He leaves them, goes to the front steps to welcome Doc Hop. Dreda and Elowyn have just come down to join the party. Nadya greets Elowyn with *"Well!* Where on earth *were* you?" Cy sees Dreda coming toward him and breaks into a smile. She brushes past him, says "Later," and interrupts Rick's faltering conversation.

"Hardly the moment, I realize, but it's business. May I borrow a Degan brother?"

"Sure," Mort and Rick say in chorus.

Both follow Dreda to a far corner of the veranda, ditching their dates. She talks gravely with the hulking brothers. Earl takes two steps in the direction of Annie and Jinx before Judy hauls him back. Doc Hop leaves Stu to join the ladies. Ouspenskiy approaches the three of them with the seagull perched on his shoulder.

The vet shakes his head.

"Sorry, I'm in large animals."

"Pozhaluista." The hospitable poet offers the silver box. Jinx and Annie decide to share a joint. The vet takes one for himself, not looking at me. He seems to have forgotten how fascinating he found me that day aboard *Hi-Roller;* tonight he is DC only, high voltage, looking for a female receptacle.

The Edgways have arrived. Clive fusses over them, brings them drinks, asks if they would like to have a puppy. Leila seems not to have heard him. She has smelled the burning cannabis, is wrinkling her nose. When she glances behind her, she sees smoke rising from Annie and Jinx, by no stretch of the imagination member material.

Stu pushes past them, hurries down the front steps and all but prostrates himself before the black Cadillac limousine.

"Gourmet munchies, Doctor?"

Doc Hop accepts an hors d'oeuvre from Moira's platter. "Hi, lost-dog girl. How's Macho? How many pups?"

"Six. You mean you *knew?*"

"Young lady, are you questioning my professional competence?"

"Thanks a bunch for telling us." She moves off.

Stu comes up the steps, escorting Lou Gross and Schulzie. He immediately presents them to Clive and the Edgways.

"Mr. and Mrs. Edgway, Clive Wheelwright—my friends Mr. Gross and Mr. Schulz."

They all shake hands. Clive observes the meeting of Gross and Edgway.

"Glad to meet you, Mr. Gross."

"The pleasure's all mine, Mr. Edgway."

Clive tries to catch Stu's eye, but for once the investigative reporter has missed a trick: he is busy quizzing Leila Edgway on sporting amenities at the Spindrift Club. Impatiently, Clive awaits his chance to take him aside and find out what he knows about Lou Gross.

Not far away, Nadya and Elowyn are quarreling in undertones. Beyond them is Dreda, still talking with the Degan brothers.

Moira approaches Schulzie with the hors d'oeuvres: carrot scrapings, cauliflower shreds, bits of Brie on bits of Zwieback. Nothing so crass as a Triscuit is in evidence. Schulzie hesitates; he is unused to such gracious living.

"I've heard so much about you, Mr. Schulz."

"Nothing good, I trust."

"Can I get you a drink?"

"If you permit me to escort you."

The two of them stroll toward the bar, talking. Stu catches Moira's eye and makes a thumbs-up sign.

Near me, Dreda is shaking hands with the Degans in a brisk, businesslike way.

"You won't tell the others?"

"Why not?"

"It's such a crazy long shot." She smiles. "Got to safeguard my Wizardess-of-Wall-Street image."

Dreda leaves them and starts toward the bar, where Cy Herkimer stands alone. Her way is blocked by Nadya and Elowyn, still locked in sotto voce quarrel. Cy sees her, waves, then bulls his way straight through the two women to join her. Delighted that he has sought her out, she gives him her warmest smile. He salutes her by raising his glass, bringing it not to his own lips but to hers. Dreda gulps down a minimal dose of Glenlivet on the rocks—dreadful stuff, the sort of thing her father would drink—and realizes with shock that this hard-eyed man is almost a generation older than she. He can probably remember the end of The War!

"Not a bad house. Got a view of the ocean?"

"From the other side. Want to scope it out?"

"Lead on, we've got a thing or two to talk about."

Dreda takes his hand, guides him down the steps to the lawn and around the house to the privet arch. The gibbous moon has laid a shimmering track along the horizon. Perfection, she thinks, and in that instant Cy's free hand slides into her plunging neckline and gives her left breast one quick, excruciating squeeze. Is this, Dreda wonders, a job offer? Remembering Kimmie, the tall Korean girl at AstroSums, she returns Cy's kiss. He presses his iron forearm against her spine and drives his tongue and torso into her, forcing her to lean back, back, back, like the heroine in a Ramon Novarro movie. His mouth tastes of Glenlivet and Listerine. Just as she decides to take a pratfall rather than break in two, Cy withdraws his tongue, pastes it momentarily against her throat, then slides it rapidly down her Bill Blass vee. He bites her right and unsqueezed nipple. His erection prods her, rides up along her thigh. It is time, she realizes, for a line lifted from one of those Novarro flicks.

"Cy, this is so sudden."

It works. He raises his face, beaded with sweat, and rubs it against her bare shoulder. "Dreda, oh God, Dreda, *now* . . ."

"Not now," she says, in command again. "Tonight, later." She brushes aside his pawings and clawings, adjusts her dress.

"I, God, I . . . I wanted to . . . talk . . ."

"Let's do that, Cy." She pats down rumpled hair on his bullet head. "Let's hold hands and talk. What about?"

"I wanted, that is, intended, to talk business." The last word brings him back to earth as if by magic. He releases the hand she has just placed in his, puts on an executive expression, speaks in a strong but butter-smooth Wall Street voice. "Dreda, I'll come right to the point. My shop's in deep trouble. Conceivably you can help us." She smiles to encourage him; this is far closer to the way she imagined the evening. "We're under fire from the Equal Opportunities people because we're all—except for the secretarial personnel, of course—Caucasian males. Now, if we took you aboard, we'd be killing two birds with one stone. What do you say?"

Determined to maintain her cool, Dreda stares at the moon-track on the ocean. She counts to infinity before answering.

"Ask Frank Perdue. He'll tell you that two birds are twice the price of one."

She smiles her B School smile, turns from him, and walks smartly back to the party.

Poor D. Scott, the poet thinks, reading her face as she crosses the veranda to take a joint from him. Poor misguided upwardly.

Poor C. Wheelwright, I am soon to add. He has at last managed to get Stu away from the others. I move toward them, to catch their words as they stand talking on the front steps.

"Tell me about Lou Gross."

"What for?"

"The day you were aboard his God-awful ostentatious stink-pot, he and Edgway knew each other, remember? 'Nick' and 'Lou' then; 'Mr. Edgway' and 'Mr. Gross' now. What do you know about Gross?"

"Plenty. Owns a big piece of the action in Vegas and Atlantic

City. Lately he's been doing some fancy lobbying in Albany to get casino gambling legalized here."

"What kind of lobbying?"

"All Lou has on his menu is new legislation on gambling, a lease on some state land on the bluffs at Montauk, and a license to open a casino-hotel there. In return, big-hearted Lou will deed to the state some crummy swamp."

Clive looks as though he had taken a punch in the solar plexus.

"Ever hear of Wetlands Trust?"

For once, he has caught Stu by surprise. "That's it! The goddamn swamp!"

"And the Hemisphere Foundation?"

Stu whistles; all other conversation on the veranda stops.

"Money laundry in the Bahamas," he says, so low that Ouspenskiy can hardly hear him. "One hundred percent owned and operated by Big Lou Gross." He sees Clive's expression. "Anything the matter?"

Clive thrusts out his chin, stands tall.

"I have been used. And I am *not* user-friendly."

He strides up onto the veranda and goes straight to Edgway, who is talking with his wife and Cy Herkimer. Clive stands beside him, near the boiling point, waiting for his chance to confront the senior partner in private.

I move down toward the other end of the veranda, where Moira and Schulzie are sitting on my beloved swing. He is smoking. She has just identified what she has been smelling, coming from Doc Hop, Jinx, Annie, Dreda, Ouspenskiy, and her present companion.

"Mr. Schulz, I'm sorry, but . . . that *is* cannabis? We've been in trouble over it before, and I'm afraid . . ."

Schulzie takes a deep drag. "Just lemme finish it. Stu's little Polack, the guy with bird-doo in his beard, gimme this. Y'know, it's the first time I ever smoked this substance."

"Really? I'd have thought—"

"Pot is for kids. I go for the adults-only stuff." He pulls smoke deep into his lungs, holds his breath, slowly expels it, snuffs out the joint. "It don't do nothing to me."

This is obviously untrue. Perhaps it is the cannabis, perhaps the novel experience of sitting on a porch swing with a pretty, well-mannered, well-educated young lady: for whatever reason, Schulzie is high as a kite. He rocks the swing, he snuggles in the cushions, he lolls toward Moira—and he talks, he blabs, he sings like a bird.

"You like horses, kiddo?"

"Yes!" Moira is keen, alert.

"The horse I happen to like is Al Fresco in the fourth at Saratoga tomorrow. Little tip, between you and me." He lays his heavy white hand on her knee. "You won't tell nobody?"

"I promise. Thank you for the tip. Do you . . . go to the races often?"

"Never. Don't have to. I got a foolproof system."

"A system . . . for getting foolproof tips?" She is tempted to bat eyelashes. "How clever of you, Mr. Schulz."

"You see that guy over there?" He raises his hand from her thigh, points a finger at Doc Hop. The vet is leaning over, beckoning to Masha, who cringes away from him. "That guy over there is my system."

"I see him." Moira can't believe it is going to be this easy. When she catches Ouspenskiy's eye, the sharp-witted Slav understands what she wants. I go to the swing, take the lighted joint from my own lips and put it between Schulzie's.

"That guy over there who's my system just happens to be the greatest vet in the long history of the turf. A genius. Flies to the track the day before a race, talks to a horse, just talks to him, and the horse wins."

Moira phrases her next question with care. "He talks to the horse while giving it . . . some form of medication?"

"Nah!" Schulzie's hand seeks out a pressure point in her thigh. His voice drops to a whisper. "He hypnotizes 'em." The disbelief in her face makes him laugh aloud: one short, harsh bark. "I swear to God, he's a horse hypnotist. It's not even illegal. A genius. Hey, promise me, bright eyes, you won't tell a single soul?"

Moira can't wait to tell Stu, but Cathy is ringing the captain's bell to announce dinner.

20

COMMUNAL
FEAST

R aison d'être *of the feast—The social event
as workplay—Inevitability of disaster—Document #4:
M. FAIRCHILD'S plan—Workplay conversations—
M. FAIRCHILD at career fork, S. STUART at same
—A new I.R.?—C. WHEELWRIGHT'S career forked—
A near-I.R. of M. DEGAN'S—A Y-person derailed
—Violence as catharsis—The day of reckoning—The
author's challenge*

O perspicacious reader, you are right once more: the communal feast will be a fiasco. This is so evident that it is scarcely worth my while to describe the Y-persons' gourmet dinner and its consequences. Note, however, that disaster is inherent in the guest list. Of the fifteen outside guests, no fewer than ten (66.6 percent) were invited to further the professional interests of various Y's. The Edgways have been included for career reasons of Clive's; Elowyn and Nadya because Moira hopes to be able to continue to exploit the satellitic photo-realism of the one and the low prices of the other; Lou Gross, Schulzie, Wilf, and Doc Hop because each has something to contribute to the Big Story that is to catapult Stu to fame and fortune; the appalling Stubbs because he is key to the marketing of Cathy's novel; Cy Herkimer because Dreda is in search of more lucrative employment. The others are present for what we may term normal social reasons: Jinx and Annie as sex objects; Patsy, Earl, and Judy as persons for whom the Y's feel affection—in short (although this may appear to run counter to my thesis), as friends. By and large, our upwardlies are indulging in workplay masquerading as hospitality. In inviting these fifteen outsiders, they have invited the catastrophes that are to befall them that night and the agon of the following weekend as well.

So why describe these disasters? Yes: I shall move directly to my concluding chapters of socio-scientific analysis, leaving the communal feast and its dreary aftermath to my readers' fertile imaginations.

But first it would be well to present Document #4. I have before me Moira's holograph seating plan for the dinner, together with her guest list and notes. After we have examined Document #4, I shall conclude with several chapters of solid expository prose, page after unparagraphed page of monolithic scientific analysis, the natural element of the sociologue.

Narrative mode, adieu.

DOCUMENT #4 ▸ *M. FAIRCHILD'S guest list, notes, and seating plan*

US

Me (at head) R—Mr. E (Clive
insists)
L—Lou G (Stu
insists)

Stu—wants Schulz
next (!) + —?
Clive (other head—R—Mrs. E
L—?

Cathy—wants J. Stubbs

Dreda—wants Cy H
(3)

Rick—betw. Annie + Jinx
Mort—Jinx + —?
(Vlady)—Cath. + Patsy?
(spks. Russ.?)
(5)

THEM

L Edgway—betw. Clive
+ Cy (?)
Nadya—Mr. E + —?
Elowyn—Clive? (he'll get
used to?)
+ —?
Judy J—(anywh.)
Patsy—Dr. Hop + —?

Jinx—betw. Rick + Mort
Annie—Rick + —?

N Edgway—*Me* + (Nadya?)

L Gross—*Me* + —?
Schulz—Stu + —?

Dr. Hop—(pr. girls)
—Dreda
—Patsy ??
J. Stubbs—Cath. + (Dreda?)
Cy H—Dreda + Mrs. E (?)
Earl J—(anywh.)
Wilf—betw. 2 men? (OK, acc.
Stu)

(7)
——
10 W

(8)
——
13 M

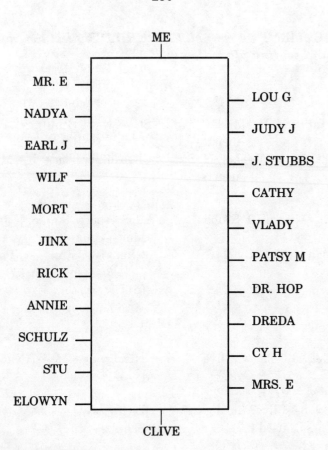

ME

MR. E

NADYA

EARL J

WILF

MORT

JINX

RICK

ANNIE

SCHULZ

STU

ELOWYN

LOU G

JUDY J

J. STUBBS

CATHY

VLADY

PATSY M

DR. HOP

DREDA

CY H

MRS. E

CLIVE

Analysis of Document #4

Before proceeding to the closely reasoned exposition of Y-person behavior patterns which will form the bulk of the strictly sociological chapters that are to follow, let us pause to analyze Document #4. Moira's method is to list all members of the house, then all outsiders, dividing each group into a left (female) and a right (male) column. It is perhaps a clue to her inner feelings that she places Stu at the head of her list of males, but Clive at the head of the table. She then notes the seating preferences of each of her housemates. Clive naturally wants Mrs. Edgway on his right and Nicholas Edgway on Moira's; Cathy wishes to be seated next to J. Stubbs; Dreda to Cy. Mort and Rick (for non-career-related reasons) have targeted Annie and Jinx. Stu has invited four guests; he chooses to sit next to Schulzie, whom he considers the weakest link in the L. Gross chain. As yet unaware that Moira has cracked the case, the investigative reporter has decided that Dr. Hopper is unlikely to tell him anything; he is perhaps afraid of Lou, for whom he requests a seat of honor on Moira's left. The travel agent Wilf he sees daily; Stu considers that he will be happiest "betw. 2 men." Moira puts Nadya near her; she is cultivating the gallery owner in the hope that she will find other saleable painters. Note that as friends and non-Y's, the Jessups may be put "anywh." The non-Y Patsy Magee is next to Doc Hop simply because he is thought to have a pre-dilection for "pr. girls." (It is of interest that Moira has put Dreda in the "pr. girl" category without a question mark; to Patsy, she has awarded two.) Patsy is given the poet on her other side because she supposedly "spks. Russ." Elowyn, potentially a source of great profit to Moira, is in a seat of honor next to Clive, who in fact (although this has not been noted on Moira's list) asked for Patsy. I cannot explain the parentheses around the name (Vlady). Having assessed her parameters, Moira drew her seating plan with great sureness; she did not have to erase or cross out a single name. One may predict success for her: here is a person who knows how to make a plan. Like many of the best-laid, however, this one is fated to gang agley.

Analysis of failure of theory underlying Document #4 when put into practice

Curbing the impatience of the author and his readers to get to the chapters of scientific analysis that are to crown this work, let us examine the reasons for the failure of the theoretically flawless plan of M. Fairchild. Clive later told me that the entire meal passed for him in a haze of righteous wrath; he could hardly wait to get N. Edgway alone. He says he made some effort to converse on art with Elowyn, the lady on his left; he recalls telling her that his favorite paintings were the sailing scenes done by Winslow Homer at Prout's Neck, Maine. When she appeared to disparage his taste, he conceded that Dufy had done "some pretty good boat stuff," but added that Van Gogh's beached dories struck him as unseaworthy. He also offered her a puppy, without success. Clive made no effort to talk to Leila Edgway, perhaps foreseeing that his future dealings with her husband were destined to be of brief duration. She in any case gave her full attention to her other dinner partner, Cy Herkimer, in whom she saw a potential Spindrift member. Cy agreed. Dreda, sitting at Cy's right, was thus left to mull over his racist-chauvinist job offer. Dr. Hopper, on her other side, indeed found her a "pr. girl," but antagonized her while recounting his recent experiences on a photo-safari in Kenya by referring once too often to "the natives," "the bearers," "the boys." On his right was Patsy; the vet, however, thanks perhaps to the ESP with which L. Gross once credited him, sensed that Patsy's sensors were beamed Cliveward. P. Magee's "Russ." (two years at Hastings High) did not get her beyond a few *zdravtvuitye*'s and *kak pozhivaetye*'s with (Vlady). The attention of (Vlady) was focused upon Cathy, who, high on champagne and critical kudos, would speak to no one but the lamentable Stubbs. Their conversation, however, proved *Disappointing* (see below). Judy Jessup, seated between the PR man and Lou Gross, talked little to either. She was obsessively interested in the table manners of her husband Earl, to whom she kept signaling "wrong fork" or "wrong topic." L. Gross, surprisingly, talked with animation to Nadya of Galerie Nadya, seated across the table from him. This conversation was, from a Y point of view, *Stimulating* (again, *vide infra*). Moira, like Clive, was in a haze. Eager to tell Stu of Schulzie's astonishing indiscretions, she barely listened to what N. Edgway had to say about Clive's promising future; he went so far as to declare,

"That boy is like a son to me." Earl Jessup, on Nadya's right, was furious because he had been placed (as he would later phrase it to me) "between a dyke and a fruitcake." His conversation was *Terse* (as we shall soon see). The travel agent Wilf was too engrossed by his duologue with Mort Degan to notice that Earl kept his back turned to him throughout dinner. Mort described horseplay and towel fights in the B.C. locker room in the good old days; Wilf hung upon his words. Rick was busy playing kneesie and footsie with Annie and Jinx. On Annie's right, Schulzie sat stoned, saying little to Stu, who was trying to pick that befuddled brain. Seated between discouraged Stu and smoldering Clive, Elowyn had a dull time of it.

Reader, we have made the round of the twenty-three *convives*. Let us now classify the conversations. Most were *Desultory*, e.g., that of Clive and Elowyn. This type is so common, alas, in the lives of us all that it suffices to label it Type A and discuss it no further. The remaining conversations fell into three categories: Types B, C, and D.

Example of conversation, Type B, Stimulating

Stu has signaled Moira (by pointing at L. Gross with his forefinger and making a flatulent sound with his lips) that it is time for her to pay attention to the gentleman on her left. When she tunes in on Lou and realizes that he is about to offer Nadya a dream job, she emerges from her haze.

". . . in Lugano, that's where my folks came from, I often go back, there's this retired industrialist, he just died, and it seems the guy collected modern Swiss masters, Paul Klee,[74] Jean[75] Arp, you name it, his heirs have to sell and they've offered me the whole can of worms. My financial advisers tell me nothing is more blue chip than art, I been thinking of moving into art

---

[74]L. Gross pronounces "Klee" to rhyme with "flea."
[75]Rhymes with "bean."

for years. What I need is an art consultant. First thing he'd do for me is fly over to Switzerland now, tomorrow, and appraise the stuff. Later, who knows, there might be the Gross Collection, the Gross Blue Chip Art Fund, maybe the Gross Culture Foundation. Can you recommend anybody?"

Nadya pretends to reflect. "Well . . . I studied at the Kunstinstitut in Zurich, I do know a thing or two about the Swiss expressionists. I spent a year in Florence; *parlo italiano*. The gallery here is closed in winter. I could always find time for a quick trip to—"

"Lou," Moira says, "I'd love to do it."

Gross turns politely toward her. She tells him of her studies at Barnard and the Rhode Island School of Design, her summer in Europe, "all museums, no beaches"; she even hears herself talking about "my projected book on Arp" (in fact, a term paper that never got finished). Lou finds her charming. Nadya seethes.

Example of conversation, Type C, Disappointing

During dinner, Cathy wishes to talk of nothing but *Turn Off the Stars*; she hopes to induce J. Stubbs to repeat his rave.

". . . so Halcyon's still a Wasp, but maybe if you played up my ethnic background in the publicity, it would help on the reviews. What do you think?"

"Don't worry about the reviews. They'll be laudatory."

"You're sure of that, Jim?"

"Sure, but not positive. I'm no critic, doll, just a PR man. All I know for positive is whether a book will sell. Yours won't."

"It won't?" Cathy says in a small voice.

"Didn't I tell you? It's delicate, it's subtle, it's literate. We'll be lucky if we sell two thou."

"But you said I was great. Like Virginia Woolf—"

He shrugs. "Not great like Michener. Not great like Judith Krantz."

"*Jim . . .*"

"I can't help you. Some things are beyond PR. You could write twenty novels, you'd still starve."

"What am I going to *do?*"

"Marry somebody rich. Or teach. All writers do one or the other. When you're fifty, you'll be trending to be a cult figure, and when you're sixty, the lit world, meaning those three dozen readers who actually read, will hail you as a genius."

"I'll settle for that." Her voice is very small indeed.

Helping out with the serving, Ouspenskiy[76] reaches them just as Cathy bursts into tears. I see Stubbs lean toward her with repellent sham-gentleness and plant his blubbery lips upon her cheek. Jealousy so far overcomes me that I deliberately spill gourmet borscht over his white linen suit.

Two examples of conversation, Type D, Terse

Example 1

E. Jessup has been seeking a way to indicate to his hostess Moira his displeasure over being placed next to the epicene Wilf.

"Earl, would you care for some fruit? It's at the other end."

"No, he's at our end."

Example 2

D. Scott has been sitting throughout the meal staring at C. Herkimer's back. Cy is apparently fascinated by Leila Edgway's chatter about "membership." When she can stand it no longer, Dreda leans across him and addresses Leila.

"Mrs. Edgway, *à propos* of your club, how should I go about applying for summer membership next year?"

Leila shrivels.

Everyone is relieved when Moira rises from the table and the gourmet dinner is done.

---

[76]The poet has found that he is expected to be not only the cleaning person, the kennel person, the gardening person, and the gourmet chef person, but also the waiting person. Yes, I have experienced capitalist exploitation.

Schema

Reader, we are approaching the final movement of this work. Already, hundred-word sentences, ten-thousand-word paragraphs, festivals of footnotes, parades of parentheses, symphonies of socio-prose are thundering in my head. But my present schema requires me to conclude this chapter with 1) two examples of that *rara avis*, Y altruism; 2) an account of an I.R. differing in kind from the Interpersonal Relationships described *supra*; 3) an example of violence as catharsis—a truly sociological concept; and 4) a study of challenge and response (even more so). After which, *floreat Sociologia!*

Y ALTRUISM, EXAMPLE 1 ▸ *Sacrifice at career-fork, Emotive*

M. Fairchild is on the back porch, alone with S. Stuart at last, transmitting to him the information gleaned from Schulzie.

"... he hypnotizes them! Schulzie swears he hypnotizes them."

Stu's whistle threatens to break every pane in the house. His mind whirs.

"Yes! It checks out. That book of Doc Hop's—*Animal Magnetism* by Dr. Friedrich Anton Mesmer, first published, Vienna, 1766. Mesmer as in mesmerize!" He lets out a war whoop. "What a story! Big—much bigger than doping! Way to go, Moira!" Stu throws an arm around her, gives her a rib-cracking squeeze. "I'll be famous, a legend in my time!" Somehow sensing that her mood is not in sync with his, he releases her. "Problems with that?"

Moira puts both hands on his shoulders, looks directly into his golden eyes. She can't believe she is going to be this selfish. "I want you," she hears herself saying, "to understand this, to share it with me. Stu, Stu dearest, I am at a career-fork." Did she really call him *dearest?* Moira hurries on. "Tonight Lou Gross asked me to fly to Switzerland to appraise an art collection. It could lead to something really awesome. I might end up as curator of an important art foundation."

"Great, go for it, grab it." He smacks her butt. "Jesus, what a night for us both!"

His high nervous pitch, his physical nearness are making her groggy. "Do you mean that, Stu? Consider carefully." She holds up her hand, ticks off points on her fingers—like a drunk trying to reason, she thinks. "Lou Gross knows we're friends. Doc Hop even thinks I'm your live-in. Now if your story breaks, they'll be out to get you any way they can. You see how that affects me?" She has said her piece; she is ashamed of herself.

"Sure. Guilt by association—good-bye, art foundation." Stu pats her reassuringly. His face for once is touchingly serious, sincere. "Don't worry, I'll kill the story."

"You can't!" Moira barely recognizes her own voice; she has wailed the words. "It's your big break," she says, modulating the volume, trying to sound her usual level-headed self. "Oh, Stu, I *can't* be that selfish." It's true, she sees; she can't. More than she wants career advancement, she wants to make an offering to this man, this vital, noisy, outrageous, thoroughly screwed up but nonetheless great-hearted man who is willing to forego his own big chance to give her hers. "*You* go for it, Stu. I'll have other opportunities."

Does he understand her sacrifice? He clears his throat—not the way anyone else would, but with a loud hawking noise, like a boy preparing to go for a spitting record. "Look, I've got my own reasons for not filing this story." Stu looks embarrassed. "Here's the bad news—if I file, I'll be famous, but I won't be rich anymore."

"You're rich now?"

"Only since July Four, haven't you noticed? I get Doc Hop's tips through Wilf, my favorite travel agent, and I'm rolling in discretionary income. Am I going to give that up for one crummy story? You want me to go back to poverty level?"

Moira, having made up her mind to sacrifice herself at the fork for his sake, is not to be bilked of that pleasure now. She puts on her noblest face.

"Stu. In this case, money is not priorital. The story is key for your career path. Think of your duty to your readers, to the racing public, to the sport itself, to the best that is in Stu Stuart."

Suddenly Stu goes completely out of character: he looks bashful. "The best that is in Stu Stuart . . . I go for that."

Softly she says, "So do I."

"Okay, you win, I'll file."

"Stu, I'm so proud of you!"

Impulsively, she throws her arms around him, kisses him. It is more of a kiss than either has bargained for. On and on it goes, until Moira's jaw is sore, her ribs aching, her lungs so squashed she can't draw breath. Just as she begins to wonder if she is a consenting victim of rape, Stu breaks out of the clinch.

"What horse, what race?"

"What?"

"Schulzie's tip. What horse, what race, what track?"

"I have no idea."

"No idea! What the hell—?"

"I was concentrating on working the conversation around to Doc Hop. That was my assignment. Stu, you didn't say anything about memorizing tips."

"Kee-rist," Stu says, then snaps his fingers. "Wilf will know. I saw him go out. Where is he?"

"But you promised me—"

"I promise I'll file, but first I'll make one last big killing." He starts down the back steps. "*Wilf!*"

Moira watches him disappear into the garden, calling for Wilf; she remains standing at the top of the steps, alone.

Smiling to herself, she remembers her therapist and murmurs the words:

"*Nonmainstream . . .*"

Y ALTRUISM, EXAMPLE 2 ▸ *Sacrifice at career-fork, Pro bono*

Clive has brought Nicholas Edgway into the library on a pretext. While the senior partner takes his time clipping the end of a cigar and lighting it, Clive stands waiting, thinking of Patsy in her white evening dress saying, "A great and good thing for the whole South Fork," thinking also for some reason of his brother Henry, war resister, man of principle.

"You wanted to show me that deed?"

"No." Clive is calm but firm. "I want to talk about your 'nodding acquaintance,' Lou Gross."

Edgway settles himself in the Chippendale armchair. "What about him?"

"You were on Moira's right, Gross on her left. I noticed you two didn't say a word to each other."

"That so?" Edgway allows himself a slight smile. "I don't think Mr. Gross and I have much in common."

"You accepted that cigar from him after dinner, also without a word."

"I smiled at him; we were both polite. Excellent cigar, by the way. Havana, panatela. What would we have talked about?"

Clive feels completely in control, as if he had just put a rival boat in his wind-shadow.

"His Hemisphere Foundation, for example."

Edgway's face shows nothing. "Foundation's our client, not Louis Gross."

"It's Gross's laundry!" Composure suddenly gone, Clive is shouting like a Stu. " 'Private benefactors'! Wetlands! 'Pro bono'! You're not out to save the Environment, you're out to wreck it! Casino at Montauk—equals motels, busload after busload of tourists, eight-lane highway, monster jetport—might as well pave everything east of the Shinnecock Canal! 'Sole trustee'! You think I'm a goddamned fool!"

Nicholas Edgway has watched Clive impassively throughout this outburst. Now he draws on his cigar.

"Clive, you understand about confidentiality; I'll confide in you. Louis Gross is my client, yes. Not the firm's, mine. Good client, too. A bit *arriviste*, but clean as a hound's tooth. Never the slightest problem with the federal authorities, IRS, anybody. Now, you are a young man of great promise." He observes Clive's impatient movement, raises the hand that holds the cigar. "Hear me out. In a year or two, I see you making partner—unusually young. Consider that prospect before you give way to these idealistic shouting fits. Consider also that it is quite legal to operate casinos in Nevada and New Jersey. Consider that it is not unethical to seek tax shelters. Nor is there anything reprehensible in pressing for new legislation in Albany. Every citizen has the right to do so. That, Clive, is the way our great republic works."

Having heard him out, Clive takes Nicholas Edgway's panatela from his hand and rams it down his throat.

I.R. #4[77]

Stu is in the garden, looking for Wilf. Suddenly he sees him, lounging in the hammock with Mort Degan. The two are deep in conversation.

"Funny thing, Wilf. I like girls, but I have trouble getting to yes with them."

Wilf pats Mort's thigh. "There are times, Mortie, when we fellows simply have to help each other out."

Stu can't believe it. The two figures in the hammock seem to have become one.

Rick Degan comes strolling by with one hand fondling Annie, the other caressing Jinx. He calls out cheerfully to Stu, "Seen Mort? I got more than I can handle here."

---

[77]Compare this I.R., aberrant but abortive, with I.R.'s described in chapter 8.

Stu points to the hammock. "Mortie's busy handling Wilfie."

"Are you calling my brother a fag?" Rick unhands the girls and looms over him.

"Don't put words in my mouth, Ricardo." Stu moves backward a few steps.

"Mort, this little turd says you're light on your feet!"

With a shout of rage, Mort leaps from the hammock. The hulking brothers converge on Stu, who bolts through the privet hedge. The Degans come crashing behind him. Wilf follows, wringing his hands.

"Now, fellows—"

Example of violence as catharsis

Clive's juices course furiously. He watches from the library window as the taillights of the Mercedes disappear down the drive. A cool nose nudges his hand. Masha has sought out her master in his hour of need.

"I saw the Edgways blast off. Clive, what happened?"

Patsy is present for the same reason as Masha.

"I've quit. Or been fired. We didn't discuss details." He groans; he just can't believe it. "I am off the fast track."

"Oh, Clive." She moves close to him, slips an arm through his. "What are you going to do?"

"Build boats, I guess." He thinks for a second. "Build boats and fight the Montauk casino."

"Montauk casino!" She stares at him, her brown eyes wide. "What casino?"

"A project of Gross's—and Edgway's. I'm going to fight it."

"You've got to. But how?"

He gives a great groan, lowers his head, rests it against her cool and nut-brown shoulder. "I don't know."

A sudden commotion in the next room makes them turn toward the door. Masha rushes out, barking wildly. Hand in hand, they follow her. All summer long, Clive thinks, his brain too sore to focus on anything else, all summer long I have known this girl and tonight we are holding hands.

The Degan brothers have cornered Stu in the living room.

"Nobody can call my brother a 'mo!"

Rick swings on Stu, who ducks and tackles him. While Mort is trying to pry the two apart, Wilf hurries in.

"Fellows, be reasonable—"

Stu, Mort, and Rick roll about on the floor, punching each other. Everyone comes crowding into the room. While the men try to break up the fight, the women shriek.[78]

The anti-sodomist Earl Jessup knees Wilf in the groin. Wilf floors him with a karate chop. Then the travel agent, evidently a Black Belt, begins throwing people around the room. Ouspenskiy takes advantage of the brouhaha to seek out Stubbs and punch him black and blue. Tensions have been building all evening, all summer: here is catharsis. Clive, to vent his fury at Edgway, throws a punch at Cy. When Cy swings back, Masha sinks her teeth into his ankle. Dreda screams and pulls the snarling dog off him, then wonders if she has acted because love-driven or career-driven. Annie and Jinx have playfully wrestled Doc Hop to the floor; he is caught in a vise between their massive bosoms. Nadya and Elowyn attempt to settle their lovers' spat by pulling out each other's hair. Finding herself near Moira, Nadya takes time out from the main event to spit in her face. Stubbs is on top of Ouspenskiy now, banging the poet's noble head against the floor. Sobbing, my doe-eyed Cathy tries to claw him off me.

Catharsis is costly. The Queen Anne table comes down with a crash. A Hepplewhite chair breaks, then the Adam sewing stand, another Hepplewhite, the Duncan Phyfe coffee table, the coromandel screen . . .

Lou Gross and Schulzie appear in the doorway. With an enraged yell, Clive hurls himself toward the good client of the man

---

[78]Stereotypical gender roles, but true. Ouspenskiy was there.

who duped him. Schulzie whips out a handgun, fires a warning shot in the air. The bullet hits a brass picture-hanger in the molding above the mantel and ricochets around the room, screaming. Cap'n Caleb Slocum falls to the floor. Everybody stops fighting.

SUNDAY, AUGUST 29

EXAMPLE OF CHALLENGE AND RESPONSE ▸
Challenge: the craftsman's response

It is another cold, gray dawn. Stu, Clive, and Dreda stand in the living room, looking at the wreckage of Mrs. Slocum's priceless furniture. With them is Rufe, down on hands and knees, carefully examining each fragment.

"Boatbuilder?" Dreda whispers.

"Rufe does cabinetwork in winter." Clive raises his voice. "How long will it take, Rufe?"

"Need two weeks, Clyde. No way I can work faster."

"Our lease is up in just over a week. Day after Labor Day."

"Still need two weeks. But I'll give you a break on the price. Eight thousand, even."

EXAMPLE OF CHALLENGE AND RESPONSE ▸
Response: the poet's challenge

Dreda, Stu, and Clive walk slowly down Slocum Lane. Behind them trail Masha and Ouspenskiy.

"She'll let us have it an extra week," Clive says. "It'll cost two thousand."

"Eight for Rufe, two for the old bag. Ten."

"Stu, don't look at me. I am unemployed, as of last night."

They both turn toward Dreda.

"Sorry. My gentrified loft is going co-op."

"Moira," Clive says, "sank her C.D. into buying Elowyn's stuff."

"Cathy," Dreda says, "is afraid they'll make her pay back her advance."

"Mort and Rick," Clive says, "live on commissions. Trouble is, they never sell any insurance."

"It would appear," Dreda says, "that everyone's broke but Stu."

"Wilf never gave me that tip last night. He's pissed off at me; he never will."

Clive explodes. "Come off it—you've won thousands!"

"Blown. Don't ask me how."

"Groupmates," Dreda says, "we have had it; this is the pits. *Nous l'avons eu; ce sont les puits.*"

A drumroll of running feet comes up behind us—Cy, Patsy, Stubbs, Gerda, and the other Sodas, familiar but nameless. Cy has the rugby ball tucked under his arm.

The genius Ouspenskiy is inspired. In an instant, he doffs the double-breasted of mild-mannered Clark Kent and reveals himself at long last in the blue, red, and gold raiment of the Man of Steel. He dashes out in front of Cy Herkimer and screams:

"*You pipples ron like old pipples fock!*"

The Soda chief stops dead in mid-jog.

"What's he want? A race?"

I pound my fist on the rugby ball. "No, no. Balls game!"

Cy makes a smooth transition into his Oxford accent. "Rugger? Right-o. We'll take you on any time."

I leap up and down before him, screaming. The spindrift of a genius's sputum sprays Cy Herkimer's face.

"Laboring Day! You bet, we bet! Ten thousand fockin' box!"

Clive, Dreda, and Stu stare at each other. There is hope; not much hope, but a straw to clutch.

Cy's hard eyes drill into Clive's.

"Labor Day, ten thousand dollars. You're on."

V

LABOR
DAY

21

THE COMMUNE AGONISTES

MONDAY, SEPTEMBER 6

The poet on rugby—The Big Story—Storm warnings—Seven tapes from seven Slokes—A moral victory?

Attend me, Muse, I sing of Slokes, of heroes. I sing of Clive, the fleet of foot, of Stuart, terrible in wrath, of Dreda, sage in council. I sing of fair-hair'd Moira and of doe-eyed Cathy, of hammer-handed Rick, of tow'ring Mort, and last, not least among the Slokian host, I sing of Vlad, ferocious in the scrum.

Without the walls of Slokedom gird for battle the bloody-minded Sodas, fearsome foes. I sing of Cy, rock-muscled Sodian chief, of bronzèd Patsy, she of wingèd foot, of Gorgon-headed Stubbs, of ham-thigh'd Gerda. I sing their cohorts, faceless and unknown to fame, but strong of arm and sharp of tooth and nail, who gouge and goose and knee in close-lock't scrum, then hail the ref and cite the loathèd rulebook.

O Slokes, O Sodas, all one bruising week your hosts have practiced plays, have passed and kicked and run in ruthless scrimmage. Ye gird not for a game, but for an agon. At night your rival armies practice on, the greensward lit by headlights of your chariots. Yea, after midnight, e'en, the wily Clive sits in his tent to memorize the rules by light of flick'ring taper. By day the lynx-eyed Stuart, Slokian scout, has crept within the Sodian lines, espied their practice. Returning to his comrades, Stu reports the Sodian host looks pretty goddamn good.

Both sides, O Muse, thirst mightily for glory, the victor's wreath and, yea, ten thousand dollars. The Sodas, black of heart, the noble Slokes, are out, O Muse, for blood.

Labor Day, day of the big game, dawns (as it must in song and story) bright and clear.

By the light of rosy-fingered Eos, the epic bard Ouspenskiy is limbering up on the Slocum lawn by tossing the rugger ball back and forth with his boon companions Rick and Mort. Sneer not, O reader. In a week of nigh-ceaseless workouts on the playing fields of Hastings, Ouspenskiy has become the closest friend and confidant of both the hulking brothers. Indeed he is their communications link. Since Mort's frolic in the hammock, Rick, who so fiercely defended the family honor that

night, has refused to speak to him. He has moved out of their
double-bedded room and now sleeps chastely in the twin bed
in Dreda's room vacated by Stu (the latter and M. Fairchild
having become "an item"). All inter-Degan dialogue passes
through the poet. Thus the message, "Tell Mort to get his fat
ass onside," might be delivered, "Mort, your brother say, be so
kind, get onside your oss."

Ouspenskiy has undergone a sea change. Gone is the whey-
faced intellectual. A week of calisthenics, aerobics, running,
tackling, and close combat in the scrum has tautened his muscles, tanned his hide. As a boy in Novosibirsk, he was exposed
minimally[79] to soccer. Rugby is soccer gone crazy. The coarse
camaraderie of the rugby field has filled him with roistering
high spirits. Like the others, he has trained on red meat and
beer. Sore in back and hip and rib and thigh, he rolls into bed
at night with the bone-tired Cathy, perchance to screw, more
often to lie cheerily, beerily in dreamless sleep, naked in her
arms. In the morning he springs from bed, earliest of all, crying,
"Op and at 'em, Slokies! Fock the Sodas!" Ouspenskiy has become a jock.

Hence he is at home in the locker room ethos of the brothers
Degan. He has had long talks with Rick, an idealist who yearns
"to find a nice R.C. girl like one of my sisters so I can settle
down and stop beating my meat." With the disgraced Mort, the
poet talks poetry. The former B.C. great once took a course in
Eng Po recommended by his coach as a "gut." Dozens of graceful
classic lines live on, in garbled form, in his gridiron-groggy
head. "At heart, Vlady, I am a fuckin' esthete."

On Labor Day at dawn, then, behold jocks three—Morton,
Richard, and Vladimir Yurevich—heaving rugger ball with joy-
ous cries. Near us Cathy jogs in place, lifting dimpled knees.
Clive is on the veranda, performing his holiday duty of hanging

---

[79]Minimally by choice. Young Vladimir became adept at writing excuses in his
father's, mother's, and doctor's hand.

out the flag. The five of us are witness to an awesome and amazing sight: into the driveway swings Stu. *Déjà vu*, think you, O reader; he arrived by battered Skylark while Clive was unfurling Old Glory on the Fourth. Ha. This time, O smart-ass reader, S. Stuart is jogging. Leaner, harder, fitter than a week ago, he has jogged two miles into Hastings, bought a magazine, and jogged back. He trots up the front steps, flashes at us the magazine cover—a picture of a man communing with a horse—and disappears into the house.

In the living room, Rufe is already hard at work. He has turned the beautiful room into a furniture repair shop: workbench, pots of glue, vises, clamps, tools, dripcloths. His work is about half done, but no single piece of furniture has yet been completely restored. Such is Rufe's method.

Stu jogs through, waves the cover of *Sports Illustrated* at him and heads for the kitchen.

Moira is in her leotard, doing knee-bends by the microwave. Dreda is watching the weather on the TV, which has been moved in from the living room. Stu dashes in and shows them the magazine cover, a photo of Doc Hop staring deep into a horse's eyes, with a face-shot of Lou Gross, inset, and the legend:

"DOC HOP"—RACETRACK SVENGALI
THE VET WITH THE VEGAS CONNECTION
An Exclusive, Explosive Story
by
STU STUART

"Name on the cover! Giving me everything I asked for! Big raise—and I get to cover all Cowboys games, home and away! Write my own ticket! Story's a sensation, racing commissions meeting all over the country. Doc Hop's already barred from the tracks in New York, New Jersey, Maryland, Delaware—"

Moira hugs him. "Stu, aren't you proud? The best that is in Stu Stuart!"

The phone rings. He springs out of the hug to take it.

"Yeah? . . . Cy? What's up? . . . Hurricane Irving?" He looks at Dreda, who points at the weather map on the TV screen. "Heading out to sea again, isn't it?" Again he looks at Dreda, who nods to confirm. "OK, sure, good idea, see you then. *Ciao.*" Stu hangs up, turns toward the two girls. "Cy says they're predicting heavy rain in P.M., backlash of Irving. Wants to play at nine A.M." He goes out on the back porch and shouts at the rest of us. "Get your asses in gear! Game time in one hour!"

Game time. The home team wears blue-and-silver rugby shirts[80] with the words FIGHTIN' SLOKES across the chest; the equally chic yellow jerseys of the opposition say SODA! The field is the Slocum lawn. The new copper beech sapling has been dug up and sits in a burlap-wrapped ball of earth near the house. Thanks to Ouspenskiy, the hole it came from has again been sodded over. Touchlines have been marked in whitewash. The goalposts are fence rails standing in earth-filled trash cans, with rickety crossbars nailed on.

Glowering at each other across the field, the Slokes and Sodas run through their warm-up exercises. When Earl and Judy Jessup come out of their house, Clive goes to greet them, carrying two spare FIGHTIN' SLOKES jerseys.

"For you. To thank you."

Judy immediately pulls her jersey over her head. "I'll treasure it always."

"Won't put mine on till after the game"—Earl sets his shirt down on the grass and winks at Clive—"seeing as I'm timekeeper."

---

[80]The Cowboys' colors. The shirts were ordered and charged to us by Co-Deputy Treasurer S. Stuart at Sportsgear Unlimited.

Our co-captains, Clive and Stu, meet in midfield with the Soda captain, Cy, and the referee, Officer Breitschwanz.

In his British accent, Cy says, "Officer, what do you know about rugger?"

"Oh, I played a few pickup games at St. John's freshman year before I flunked out." Ignoring Cy's scowl, Breitschwanz waves his rulebook. "Official rules will apply, with the following exceptions, previously agreed to by both sides: No shoes, account of Mrs. Slocum's lawn. Eight players to a side; no side may have more than eight on field at any time. Each side gets one time-out per half. Unlimited substitutions, provided captain or co-captain so informs referee—that's to oblige Captain Herkimer, who's got ten players on his squad, but only four men to Slocum House's five. All players must wear team colors. And no ringers, only honest-to-God residents of each house."

Cy speaks up, his voice clipped and Oxonian. "We intend to play Patsy, although she resides with her parents."

"We accept Patsy," Clive says. "We'll play only bona fide residents."

Breitschwanz flips a coin. Stu calls it, calls wrong. Cy elects to receive. We all line up for the kickoff.

"Hold it!" Cathy cries. "Dreda's still inside, listening to the weather."

"*Weather!*" Stu begins bellowing for her to come out.

Dreda appears and lines up at some position to the rear of my own. She looks unusually subdued. Old Rufe, who has followed her out of the house, is shooed back inside by Clive: there is no time to lose on the furniture. A cloud moves across the face of the sun. Breitschwanz blows his police whistle. Stu kicks off.

Here, reader, I had best confess that I know nothing about rugby. I never even learned the name of my position. With the exception of an unorthodox defensive maneuver invented by Dreda and myself, no plays were built around me. I seldom touched the ball, either in practice or during the agon; when I did, I got rid of it immediately, often with disastrous results. It was in the push, shove, sweat, and blood of the scrum that Ouspenskiy proved his worth, there that I earned the sobriquet Ivan the Terrible.

Rather than attempt to sportswrite, I have asked my teammates to describe the agon. All of the following interviews were taped *almost a year after the game*, as I approached the end of my labors upon this book. There may be discrepancies, lapses of memory. Some of my former groupmates I see often; others, not at all. I enjoyed the reunions. Except for the punctuation, the tapes are unedited. It will be seen that the interviewer Ouspenskiy has made little progress in his spoken AmerEng.

M. FAIRCHILD ▸ *rugby interview, taped early July of following year, ten months after game, in William the Bastard Room, The Village Pub, Hastings*

V.Y.O. ▸ Tell me, please, Moira, what you remember about big rogger game.

M.F. ▸ Very little, I'm afraid, Vlady. I guess I've blocked out those awful last days. I was so upset over what had happened to the house and to that lovely furniture, and I hadn't really gotten over Clive, even though it was obvious he and Patsy—that's terrible, I'm making it sound as if I wasn't in love with Stu then—I was, I am, we empathize—but it was a difficult adjustment. Clive was—is—such a caring, sharing, *responsible* person, and along came Stu, who's anything but responsible. He'd been growing on me all summer, and suddenly, the night of the gourmet dinner, well, I'd really had a ball eliciting all that from Schulzie, and here I had this gift for Stu, this amazing story, and all I wanted was to give it to him, even if it did mean passing up this awesome job opportunity Lou had just dangled before my eyes. I mean, there we were, both at career-forks, and I wanted, really wanted, to sacrifice my big chance for his, so it had to be love, didn't it?

V.Y.O. ▸ I guess so. And the rogby, Moira?

M.F. ▸ I *did* make a sacrifice. Nadya is now pulling down eighty-five thou plus perks. She's chairperson of something called Gross Masterworks.

V.Y.O. ▸ And the game?

M.F. ▸ The game . . . Well, all that week I'd been simply overpowered by Stu, he *is* overpowering, he yelled at me constantly on the field, he overwhelmed me in bed, he was on a terrific high, he was so proud of that story, which he dashed off in about three minutes between rugger practices, and he was happy, he was proud of me, he used to sort of strut around with me—that part was embarrassing, with Cathy, my own sister, right there. Don't look that way, Vlady, Cathy adores you, you know she does. Anyway, at the game, there was Stu, our co-captain, our best kicker, runner, tackler, and there I was, I've always hated contact sports, field hockey, basketball, even, and he kept yelling at me, telling me to mark Cy or to beat Patsy, and I couldn't do any of that, I didn't even know what he meant. Most of the time I was thinking about my lungs, I was sure they were going to burst. Vlady, I just didn't feel *worthy* of him.

V.Y.O. ▸ Let's take game from start. Stu kicks off and . . . ?

M.F. ▸ It was a beautiful kick, remember? Cy caught it and started running, he was their best player, best man—person!—on the field, unless Stu was, and here he came, charging straight at me. I had to at least try to tackle him, I was petrified. Luckily he passed to that awful Gerda, and Mort knocked the ball out of Gerda's hand—well, all I really remember is that from then on we were passing, running, heaving, shoving, cursing, tripping, biting, spitting, it was horrible! I knew from that first run of Cy's they were better, I knew we didn't have a chance. Is that enough, Vlady?

V.Y.O. ▸ One more thing, be so kind. What do you remember of scoring plays?

M.F. ▸ There was that time Cy ran right through poor Dreda for a . . . a touchdown, is it?

V.Y.O. ▸ They say, *try.*

M.F. ▸ That's it, a try. Four points for a try, two for a conversion. Cy scored their first try and kicked the conversion, they were six points ahead, and then Stu got the ball, he made this wonderful run, he dodged, he jinked or whatever, they couldn't lay a hand on him, and he looked so happy! That's the way I like to think of him, that look on his face, pure bliss and you know, he was shouting to himself, Vlady, shouting himself on. He was shouting —let's see if I can do his voice—he was shouting, "It's Tony Dorsett exploding through the Bears' line, shaking off tacklers as he goes!" Stu's fantasies! Have I ever seen him that happy since? In New York now, he just mopes around our living area at Central Park West—you know I bought out Clive's share of the apartment?—and feels guilty about the book. You do know about the book? Well, after he broke the Doc Hop story, Stu was a nine-day wonder, so he went to Cathy's publisher and talked up this idea of his and got an enormous advance, but of course the money was gone in about two days. He claims he's taken leave of absence from the magazine; more likely he quit—and he hasn't written a word, and of course he keeps brooding about last fall, the Cowboys had their worst season ever, didn't even make the playoffs. He keeps wondering if Big Lou didn't bribe people to throw games, just to get revenge on him; he's underachieving like mad, and to add to his guilt trip, I'm on a roll career-wise. You know I sold those Elowyns at a 450 percent profit, and next month I'm going to open my own gallery in NoHo. You'll get an invitation, Vlady.

V.Y.O. ▸ Congratulations. So Stu is ronning toward Soda goal . . .

M.F. ▸ Running, he's running brilliantly, he's happy, he's shouting, "There's no stopping Dorsett!" and Jim Stubbs trips him. So we all scream and argue, Stu keeps calling the ref a mega-wimp, I try to make him stop, we can't afford a penalty—a nightmare! The whole game was a nightmare. It was all so brutal, and we were losing, and those Sodas such rotten sports, always claiming our dogs had gotten in the way or bitten them or something when they were about to score, and that sinking feeling about the money, the ten thou going, going, gone, and the other ten thou, for Mrs. Slocum and for Rufe— and the weather! All that wind and rain in the second half, though at least we scored, and Stu kicked the conversion perfectly, I remember that, and of course I remember that unbelievable last minute, but the one really vivid picture is of Stu running and happy, running and thinking he's Tony Dorsett, invincible, unstoppable. Vlady, I'm just not the sports reporter of the family. I'm sorry. Can I stop?

V.Y.O. ▸ Of course. All very yenlightening. Thank you, Moira.

R. DEGAN ▸ *rugby interview, taped mid-July, 10½ months after game; interview by telephone: V.Y.O. in Hastings, R.D. in Newton, MA*

V.Y.O. ▸ Hello? Rick?

R.D. ▸ My God, is that you, Vlady? How the hell are you?

V.Y.O. ▸ Okay, thank you. Rick, I tape this. I want you tell me what hoppened in rogby game.

R.D. ▸ Sure, but listen, Vlady, it's got to be quick. In about five minutes, Dad's picking me up, we're going to a bachelor dinner. In honor of me. I'm getting married Saturday.

V.Y.O. ▸ Wonderful, Rick. Who is locky girl?

R.D. ▸ Mary Doyle, she's a registered nurse, Catholic, got four brothers, we all play touch together. Mary's the star, and you never saw such knockers. Best thing I ever did was move back to Newton.

V.Y.O. ▸ I am hoppy for you. If you don't have time now, let me talk to Mort. He is there, naturally?

R.D. ▸ No. Mort is not here.

V.Y.O. ▸ But he comes? He is best man?

R.D. ▸ Vlady, please don't talk to me about Mort. Dad is best man. I couldn't take it about Mort, that's why I left the Apple. You want to talk rugby? Here's how I saw it. Sodas dominated in first half. Cy was half their team, but he'd drilled them in the basics; they were marking our men so closely, we couldn't develop. Stu kicked well, Clive was good in the loose, you were a holy terror in the scrums. Never dreamt it would be that dirty. Sweet Jesus, those Sodas! We've just got time for a scoring summary. Cy scores early, Cy converts. Sodas 6, Slokes nothing. Then Cy gets beaten up at halftime, all that business, but he goes back in and scores another try. Sodas 10, Slokes zilch. Conversion kick blocked by brilliant Dreda-Vlady maneuver, great work! Still 10-oh. Cy is all bent out of shape, zaps Dreda. Stubbs gets hurt—nice work on that too, Vladski—and they call a time-out. Clive talks to this guy on the touchline, gets all steamed up, yells at Patsy in a ruck, necks with her, even, right there on the field of play, and next time he gets his hands on the ball, he scores a try. Sodas 10, Slokes 4. Here comes Dad, got to hurry this, sorry. Stu converts, and it's Sodas 10, Slokes 6, with two minutes left to play. The Sodas play keepaway for a full minute and—well, you remember the rest! Vlady, got to go now, got to get drunk with Dad and my uncles and Mary's brothers and the old gang from B.C. Good-bye, Vlady, duty calls. I'll be puking bile tomorrow!

V.Y.O. ▸ Thank you, Rick, good-bye, love to Mary.

D. SCOTT ▸ *rugby interview, taped one week after R. DEGAN, 10 months and 3 weeks after game, in D.S.'s loft in East Village*

D.S. ▸ Really great to see you, Vlady. How goes it out there?

V.Y.O. ▸ I love it. Mrs. Slocum is kind. I finish my verse cycle. I see Clive and Patsy frequently, bot I am sad that Cathy comes out so very seldom.

D.S. ▸ She's working hard, I hear. I've been so busy I hardly ever see her. You heard I changed jobs?

V.Y.O. ▸ Yes, I read where you work, where you were yeducated and other very yexciting news on ladies' sports page. So! Yeverybody is getting married. I congratulate. Dreda, please, can we talk about rogby?

D.S. ▸ Sure, let's go. Vlady, your English is fabulous! "Ladies' sports page." You've really made strides. The rugby. I'll leave all the technical data, plays, scoring, all that, to Clive and Stu and the Degan Bros.

What you want from me is personal input. Vlady,
I was running scared. Scared about what the weather
was going to do, scared about losing the ten thou,
scared I'd blown my chance to get a job with Cy,
scared of breaking something—a hand, a finger.
Hand in a cast, how could I compute? And while it
healed, those other nerds at AstroSums would get
ahead of me. Thank God I'm out of AstroSums. Morve
& Oxblood is Cy's biggest competitor, in some ways
we're bigger than Herkimer & Co. I'm making twice
what Cy offered me, I'm bossing big Koreans around,
and I met Andy. Where was I? Early in the game,
in that first big pile of bodies—ruck—Cy's squashed
against me and he says—no Brit accent, he's talking business—he says, "Dreda, I've been thinking
about what you said re. the cost of two birds. We're
prepared to make you a very interesting offer. Talk
after the game?" I say, "Fine." Vlady, I am really
excited, big J-O-B with the biggest A-R-B. Next thing
I know, Cy has the ball, he runs right over me,
tramples me. I grab his ankle, I've got him, I can
feel him going down, but he manages to shake loose,
he scores, and it's Sodas 4, us zero. Cathy says,
"Dreda, you had him, you just seemed to let go,"
and I don't know if I let go or not. I'm shaken, I
think, oh God, was it a career move? I play the rest
of the half in a daze, and at halftime there's this
vicious attack on Cy. I go to him, I help him up,
I'm really upset about him, I say, "Cy, I'll call you
an ambulance." He gives me this hateful look and
barks at me, "You'd love that, wouldn't you? You
all would." He insists he can play, and he's right,
he can, because first thing in the second half he
scores, and it's ten-zero. Then—Vlady, you remember the Scott-Ouspenskiy maneuver!

V.Y.O. ▸ Our moment of glory, Dreda.

D.S. ▸ Herkimer swings back his leg to boot the conversion, Ouspenskiy goes into his crouch, D. Scott runs right up his back, jumps from his shoulders, touches the ball. Deflected! No score! Cy is *livid*. Walking back toward midfield, he scowls at me and says, *"There goes your job, Black-Ass."* All I can do is grit my teeth and vow I'll get him somehow.

V.Y.O. ▸ And you did.

D.S. ▸ I did, but only by telephone. Then wind and rain, and Clive scored with two minutes left, Stu converted, we'd narrowed it to 10-6, and that *happening* at the end. Well, it's all for the best. At Herkimer & Co., I'd never have met Andy, and Andy's divine. Andrew Delancey Oxblood Jr., Harvard, Old Philadelphia, his father a name partner of the firm. Andy's father started out as a poet, by the way, but saw the light. Poetry of money. Andrew Sr. is crazy about me, he loves black people in this fuzzy old-fashioned liberal way. Not Weezie, though. Weezie is Andy's mother. She doesn't care that I'm brilliant, and Andover and Yale and the B School, I'm just not good enough for her young Andy. The hell with Weezie. I may break the engagement.

V.Y.O. ▸ Rilly? Why?

D.S. ▸ Baudouin has resurfaced.

V.Y.O. ▸ Dreda, I am flobbergast.

D.S. ▸ Baudouin is a big success story. Got his own company in the Street now—Boisdormant et Cie. They say he's a front man for the Paris Rothschilds. Baudouin drives a Maserati, flies his own jet. And he's obsessed with the idea of taking me away from Andy. Imagine—Dreda, Vicomtesse du Boisdormant.

V.Y.O. ▸ So?

D.S. ▸ Oh, I'm better off with young Andy. I might give Baudouin to Moira. Why not? That chateau—Moira's a born chatelaine. And a foreign husband could be a drag on me when I go into politics. Don't laugh, Vlady, I'm going to make megabucks in the next few years, then get out and run for office. You need megabucks in politics these days. This is a secret, Vlady: I'm a Republican now. Rep. Scott, Republican, New York, and then . . . Stop smiling, I'm a Washington girl, politics is in my blood. You know my father's a retired diplomat?

V.Y.O. ▸ You told us that. Forgive me, Dreda, he is truly CIA?

D.S. ▸ Of course. He'd kill me if he knew I told you, but everyone in Washington knows, and everyone in Moscow. Being CIA probably seems terrible to you, a Russian, but it came naturally to him, he springs from a long line of government employees. His father was a clerk at Interior, his grandfather a janitor at the old State, War and Navy Building. And Daddy wasn't a *spy*, or anything. He was in psych-war, black propaganda—not a pun. They sent him first to Abidjan, but that was hard; Africans aren't crazy about us slave-descended émigrés. So they transferred him to Paris, where they *are* crazy about us, then London, Rio, Rome. He did beautifully until the Agency made him Deputy Director for Culture.

V.Y.O. ▸ We are far from rogger, bot . . . continue, be so kind.

D.S. ▸ You know, CIA funds a number of cultural storefronts, you must have read about it. Pop records in Mexico, comic books in Mali, video in Finland. What got Daddy in trouble was cultdefs.

V.Y.O. ▸ Cultdefs?

D.S. ▸ Cultural defectors. His pet project was this cultural institute with offices in New York and Moscow— what's wrong, Vlady?

V.Y.O. ▸ USSUCRI?

D.S.	►	That's it. You know them?
V.Y.O.	►	They are poblishing my *Oblomoviad*.
D.S.	►	Typical. In Russian?
V.Y.O.	►	Rossian verse on one page, Yenglish translation on facing page. Poblication date, tomorrow. Limited yedition, five hondred copies.
D.S.	►	They'll never learn. USSUCRI was bringing out all these Soviet cultdefs, hoping to use them as culture agents in psych-war, and none of them would play ball, they wanted to make a buck, buy a VCR, eat TV dinners, go bowling, wear leisure suits, be good Americans. And we were spending millions on them, so when the Senate investigated, Daddy came under fire and had to retire with the rank of ambassador. He's fine, though, he's still on a lot of boards, everybody needs that token. There's an idea—Rep. Scott could campaign against tokenism when she runs for higher office. You're smiling again? *Senator* Scott, then—
V.Y.O.	►	Then?
D.S.	►	Who knows? Young Andy may find himself the first First Gentleman. Consort of the first woman President—my God, I forgot—first *black* woman President. Wow. We should have stuck to rugby.
V.Y.O.	►	Fock rogby. I have yenjoyed this, Dreda.

C. FAIRCHILD ► *rugby interview, taped early August, 11 months after game, in Slocum garden, Hastings*

C.F.	►	It seems really weird to be interviewed formally like this, Vlady, after all you and I have been through. But since it's a formal occasion, let me formally congratulate you on the success of *Oblomoviad*. I've never read such reviews! Is it selling?

V.Y.O. ▸ Yes, thank you. All five hondred copies sold out in four days. But *Halcy* too has had yenthusiastic reviews.

C.F. ▸ *Succès d'estime*. It's been out since April, no sale of paperback rights, just 3,419 copies in hardcover sold to date. Jim Stubbs called it about right.

V.Y.O. ▸ Yexcuse me, Stobbs said two thousand, no?

C.F. ▸ He revised his estimate. That's about all I remember of that horrible game—it was absolute mayhem, I was panic-stricken, and how was I ever going to pay my share if we lost? I remember Jim Stubbs sprawled on top of my bod in one of those rucks, and you know what he said? He said, "I been thinking, doll, I may have been a bit harsh on you. The book might sell thirty-five hundred." That's when I began crying, I couldn't stop, and you—

V.Y.O. ▸ Ha. In next scrom, I rip out Stobbs's dentures.

C.F. ▸ You were like a wild animal in that game. I loathed you that day, I loathed you all—Stu, Clive, Cy, Jim, the Degans—you're all animals. I think I'm becoming a feminist, Vlady.

V.Y.O. ▸ Is that why you refuse to shock op with me, why you stay in that shitbox apartment?

C.F. ▸ Shoebox, Vlady. No, that's not it at all. I stay in Brooklyn Heights to work. An artist needs the city. You're an exception. If I'm out here, I write something lyrical, like *Halcy*. My new one, *The Fenwicks*, is anything but lyrical. It's grimy, gritty realism: the Lower East Side, Jersey City, the Jewish immigrant experience—

V.Y.O. ▸ Rilly? Fenwick family is Jew?

C.F. ▸ Of course. I'm exploiting my heritage, Vlady. I spent days in the New York Public Library, researching immigrant history from before the Civil War to the present. Six generations of Feinwerks, Fenwicks.

My agent, who's a goy, by the way, says it's sure to be a blockbuster, and he's only read four hundred pages.

V.Y.O. ▸ Four hondred pages!

C.F. ▸ Out of an eventual thousand. It's going well, I wrote twenty-nine thousand words last week, and I don't even have an advance. When I finish, my agent's going to send it to a bunch of publishers, the biggest spenders, and let them fight over it.

V.Y.O. ▸ No advance? What are you living on?

C.F. ▸ My second career. The résumé I wrote for Dreda was a big success, and other people heard about it and called me, so now I spend two days a week doing creative résumé writing at $150 an hour. That's another reason I can't move out here with you. Don't look so sad, I miss you, I miss J. Livingston, but career first, and anyway, where would I stay? Up there with you in the attic? What would Mrs. Slocum say?

V.Y.O. ▸ Surely she say yes. I am opple of her eye.

C.F. ▸ Of course she's pleased, the place looks lovely. The larkspur, the zinnias, the bee-balm. The garden was the only thing that *did* please her when she came back last fall. No wonder she wanted to hire you. How is she, by the way?

V.Y.O. ▸ She thrive. House and furniture fully restored. Shall we get back to rogby?

C.F. ▸ I don't know anything about rugby. Kiss me, Vlady.

S. STUART ▸ *rugby interview, taped mid-August, 11½ months after game, in bar of St. Règis Hotel*

S.S. ▸ Christ, Vlady, I hardly recognized you in that monkey suit. Turn around. Beard trimmed, hair cut. You look like a Czarist diplomat. Hey, congrats. This is a great occasion.

V.Y.O. ▸ Thank you, Stu. And thank you for coming early so we can talk rogger before Arts of Piss dinner.

S.S. ▸ How much is that award, anyway? Two and a quarter?

V.Y.O. ▸ That is what I read in *Times*, bot Arts of Piss Award Committee inform me check tonight is for two hondred fifty-three thousand seven hondred forty-four dollars and change.

S.S. ▸ Holy shit—and your book is only thirty pages!

V.Y.O. ▸ Thirty-six, actually. Bot only eighteen are poetry. Eighteen other pages are translation, which socks. Shall we talk of rogby?

S.S. ▸ Over here, waiter. Bullshot for me and—vodka?—double vodka on the rocks for Prince Tearhertitsoff. Tell me, Vlady, what is this Arts of Peace Foundation, and why are they showering you with all this money for hardly any pages?

V.Y.O. ▸ You have heard of William Williams, inventor of Little Willy missile? In his will this Williams yestablished Arts of Piss Foundation, to which he leave megabox. His widow Natasha Williams—she is Rossian—will present me with award, of which I am first recipient.

S.S. ▸ An award for what, exactly?

V.Y.O. ▸ For "most distinguished contribution during past twelve months to world literature." I blosh.

S.S. ▸ Jesus, a quarter of a mil. Hey, you think my book will be a best-seller, win prizes? Why not? Irresistible title: *From Glory Unto Glory: The Saga of the Dallas Cowboys.*

V.Y.O. ▸ I am surprised you do not write book about that vet.

S.S. ▸ Vet story's dead. All charges against Doc Hop dropped for lack of evidence. He's out on the Coast now, technical-advising the feature production *Racetrack Svengali.* What are you going to do with your new-found wealth?

V.Y.O. ▶ Buy house. Actually, I find house, small farmhouse, like dacha, shingled, two miles north of Hastings, on three point seven acres, with barn, woodlot, pond. I get cheap. Clive is drawing agreement of sale. I pay cash.

S.S. ▶ Will you have anything left over?

V.Y.O. ▶ Perhaps few thou. I dream that Cathy come live with me. I show you pictures of house, be so kind?

S.S. ▶ Later, Vlady. Thanks, waiter. So—here's to the Arts of Peace Award.

V.Y.O. ▶ Here is to you—and to Moira.

S.S. ▶ Yeah. Looks like Moira's gig as my main squeeze is over.

V.Y.O. ▶ Oh, no!

S.S. ▶ I'm doing it for her. She's not in love with me, she's in love with something called "the best that is in Stu Stuart." Moira's a goddamn nanny, wants to make me over. I'm good to go, I've got to get away, take a swing around the NFL to broaden the database of my book, or slope off to Monte Carlo—Atlantic City and Vegas are out for me, obviously—or go to Scotland, see about regaining my throne, or join the Marines, get some fresh air and exercise even if I have to go to Nicaragua and kick Nic ass to get it. There's no "best" in me; I'm a stone that's got to roll; I am mobile, but not upwardly.

V.Y.O. ▶ One day, Stu, you will do some splendid thing.

S.S. ▶ You've done it already. Quarter of a mil. You are one lucky cultural defector.

V.Y.O. ▶ I am not defector. Also, I am not coltural. I am poet, I am man. *Coltural* is bozzword. I detest. Before I accept award, I ask Clive to investigate thoroughly this Foundation—he is very sensitive on sobject of foundations—and he assures me it has nothing to do with US-Soviet Union Coltural Relations Institute, USSUCRI, on which I spit. Now we talk rogger?

S.S. ► Okay. You want a professional sportscribe's appraisal? Sodas the more experienced and stronger side, better in getting the ball out quickly, beating their men, kicking ahead, dirty playing. Herkimer brilliant at standoff; Patsy Magee a good speedy wing three-quarter; Stubbs their mainstay in the scrum. Rugby supposed to be fast, clean game of constant motion. In Sloke-Soda September classic, perhaps due to players' prior experience in American football, teams piled into one ruck after another. Slokes stronger only in kicking, thanks to educated toe of Stu Stuart, and in scrum. With Mort and Rick Degan as props and Ivan the Terrible at hooker, Slokes dominated grunt-and-groan aspect of play. Clive Wheelwright at fly half was fastest man on field. Stuart outstanding at scrum half; Dreda Scott an alert fullback; Fairchild girls at wing forward and wing three-quarter hopeless; they let down the side. Sodas declare superiority early with Herkimer's try and conversion. Sucking hind tit, Slokes hold on grimly. Six-zip at half. In second half the injured Cy Herkimer—

V.Y.O. ► Be so kind, Stu, tell how Cy get injured.

S.S. ► At halftime, bloodied adversaries cluster around five-gallon jug of Diet Gatorade provided by Sloke rooter Judy Jessup. Stuart, Sloke standout, goes to take piss behind hedge. Ten yards away is Herkimer, doing same. The two exchange glares. Suddenly a couple of pasty-faced creeps in brown suits, black shirts, and white ties pop out of shrubbery and say, "Are you Stu Stuart?" Lightning-witted Sloke co-captain jerks thumb in direction of Soda captain and strolls away. Two hoods jump Herkimer. Teams hear thuds, smacks, ows, pows from behind hedge and hasten to scene. Hoods working Herkimer over, saying "Love from Lou, Stu," and "Kisses from Schulzie, Stu," and "This'll teach you to ruin Lou and Schulzie's hobby, da turf, for 'em." Sodas rush to rescue, Slokes pretend to help. Referee Breitschwanz arrives, blowing police whistle; hoods take off like big-ass birds. Herkimer is really tear-ass. D. Scott of Slokes, with eye on job, helps him get up, all the time telling him to lie down while she calls an ambulance. He tells her to fuck off, he's going to play. Breitschwanz says, "Captain, you're in no shape to play." Bleeding, battered Herkimer walks toward field, forcing self not to limp. "I can play," he says, and a minute later he scores on interception of ill-advised pass from one Fairchild sister to the other. Ten-zip, Sodas. Herkimer's conversion kick blocked by Scott, with assist from Ouspenskiy. Play continues in seesaw fashion. Late in second half, Sodas call time-out to stanch bleeding in mouth of their ace hooker, Stubbs—way to go, Vlady baby! Strong wind blowing by this time, black sky, beginning to rain. Wheelwright has hurried conference on touchline with spectator in yachting cap and returns to game inspired. In next pile-on—

V.Y.O. ▸ Yexplain about man in cap, Stu. I never onderstand what hoppen.

S.S. ▸ There we are, totally demoralized, angry skies, getting wet, ten points behind, four minutes to play, about to lose ten thousand dollars, which will put us twenty in the hole. During Soda time-out, Clive sees Judy Jessup waving to him from touchline and pointing to this little dude in yachting cap standing next to her. It's Sam, the flunky from Edgway's boat, so Clive trots over. I go too; I'm co-captain; I need to know. "Sam," Clive says, "what brings you here? How's the boat?" and Sam says, "Fine, but I got to get back to her before this storm hits," and hands him an envelope. I see it's on Tucker, Edgway stationery and I say, "What's up? What's he say?" and Clive reads me, "Dear Clive, Young men are impetuous, so I've decided to let bygones be bygones. Would you mind signing the enclosed and returning by hand of Sam? I've enjoyed our sailing and wish you luck in whatever you may, blah, blah, et cetera." I say, "What's the enclosed? What's he want?" and Clive looks at a second sheet of that stationery and says, "My resignation as trustee of Wetlands." Sam says, "He said there'd be an answer." Clive says, "There is," and tears both sheets in half and hands them back to Sam, saying "Tell him to—" and I yell, "Tell him to stick it where the moon don't shine!" Then Clive runs back into the game all fired up, and in the next ruck he starts shouting at Patsy Magee, "Patsy, I've got 'em by the short and curlies! As sole trustee of Wetlands—" Magee, who's got her mind on the game, she's been playing one hell of a game, says, "What *are* you talking about?" and Clive shouts, "I'm sole trustee of Wetlands—court-appointed! Won't resign, they'll have to petition the court to remove me, could take years! I can block the transfer of Indian Marsh to the State!" Patsy looks bewildered, we pick ourselves up, pretty soon there's another ruck, and Clive is yelling at Magee again: "I'll save what's left of the Environment out here! With no Indian Marsh, Gross has got no deal, no goddamn casino! I'll fight those assholes, I'll beat the shit out of them! Country lawyer Clive! Pro bono!" Patsy says, "Clive, don't use those words. It's not you. Kiss me." He kisses her. When the ruck unpiles, they're still kissing. Christ, what a kiss. Breitschwanz had to blow his whistle, remember?

V.Y.O. ▶ I do. We were scondalized. Both sides. Fraternization with yenemy.

S.S. ▶ So: ball back in play, Stuart makes awesome pass to Wheelwright, who knifes through Sodas, crosses goal line, cuts over and touches down between posts. Sodas 10, Slokes 4. Sides line up for conversion attempt. Stuart to kick. Twenty-knot gale blowing in his teeth, ball wet and slippery, but barefoot Stuart—

V.Y.O. ▶ Please, Stu, tell about Moira.

S.S. ▶ Moira? Oh, yeah, Moira comes up as we're lining up and kisses the back of my neck and whispers, "The best that is in Stu Stuart." I say, "I'll pretend it's Lou Gross's fat ass." Whereupon majestic kick of barefoot Stuart neatly bisects uprights. Sodas 10, Slokes 6, two minutes left. Sodas try to freeze ball, passing from Stubbs to Cy to Patsy to Cy to Gerda, then kicking forward and piling on. In howling wind, twigs snapping from maples, it looks like curtains for the Fightin' Slokes. With just over a minute left to play, Co-captain Wheelwright gets ball, kicks for touch, calls time out—and speak of the devil, there's the old shyster himself. Look—over by the door, Vlady, near the hatcheck, squinting through his glasses, looking for us. Yo, Clive!

V.Y.O. ▸ Why is Clive here? He is meant to be working on my closing.

S.S. ▸ They're all coming, all except for Mort, who's dropped out of sight, and Rick; he's too tied down up in Newton now that he's married. Hey, Mary's got a bun in the oven already, you heard? Look, Vlady, before Clive gets to the table, can you loan me, say, five biggies, just until payday?

V.Y.O. ▸ Five hondred? Glad to, Stu, bot after award, okay?

S.S. ▸ Thanks, pal. Cathy's coming, of course, and Moira, and Dreda. Dreed is coming with her parents—

V.Y.O. ▸ Her parents, rilly? Why?

S.S. ▸ Didn't you know? Dreda's old man is on the Arts of Peace jury.

V.Y.O. ▸ *Son of a fockin' bitch, I refuse!* They can stick their award where there is no moonshine!

S.S. ▸ Vlady, sit down—

M. DEGAN ▸ *rugby interview, late August, almost one year after game; interview by telephone: V.Y.O. in Hastings, M.D. in N.Y.C.*

V.Y.O. ▸ Hello, Mort? Here is—

M.D. ▸ Vlady! How on earth did you track me down?

V.Y.O. ▸ Stu work all day yesterday to track you down. Today he leave for boot camp.

M.D. ▸ He must look gorgeous in uniform. What can I do for you?

V.Y.O. ▸ Mort, I tape. I want you to talk about rogby game.

M.D. ▸ A pleasure. The game was pure joy for me, Vlady. It brought me to a recognition of my true self.

V.Y.O. ▸ Rilly?

M.D. ▸ Truly. All my life I didn't know who Morton Degan was. I thought Morton Degan was a jock. I went along, I played the football, I chased the girls, but I knew that somewhere there was a finer Morton Degan—a sensitive, artistic Morton. That night in the hammock, nothing really happened, it was much to-do about nothing, Vlady. But there is something about rugby—I began to sense it in practice and it came over me in full flood during the game—how to say this? Rugby is different from football. In football you're encased in this *armor*, you can't really *feel*, although they call it a contact sport. But in rugby it's shorts, a thin jersey, skin to skin, muscle to muscle, body to body—I really adored the scrum—and as we played, I knew in the heat and sweat of contact, wind-raked, rain-scoured, I knew who Morton Degan was. I came back to town next day, quit my job, went out in quest of kindred spirits and I'm free now. I'm happy, Vlady.

V.Y.O. ▸ I share your hoppiness, Morton. You prefer Morton?

M.D. ▸ Indeed I do.

V.Y.O. ▸ Morton, have you memories of any particular plays?

M.D. ▸ None. It was a symphony, flesh singing to flesh, beyond that I remember nothing. I don't even know who won. I'm afraid I've disappointed you, Vlady.

V.Y.O. ▸ Not at all, Morton.

M.D. ▸ I'd love to see you. I'm here in TriBeCa, I'm a partner in a boutique called Hi Fellas, we do avant-garde sportswear. Call me when you come to town. Oh! I was thrilled to read about your award.

V.Y.O. ▸ Thanks. I am not too hoppy about that.

M.D. ▸ Old Vlady. Anyone else would be ecstatic. Promise you'll call?

V.Y.O. ▸ I promise. Thank you, Morton, and good-bye.

M.D. ▸ *Da svidaniya.*

C. WHEELWRIGHT ▸ *rugby interview, taped in early September, one year after game, at Ouspenskiy residence, Hastings*

V.Y.O. ▸ So, Clive, I come last to you. You have heard tapes of others, you see how they all tell me story of their lives. Perhaps you start with that, get it out of way, then we talk rogby.

C.W. ▸ You mean you want a record of what happened to all of us since we broke up—a sort of epilogue?

V.Y.O. ▸ No yepilogue, I detest yepilogues, I never forgive Tolstoy for indulging himself in two yepilogues at yend of otherwise great novel. I am not having yepilogue; I am not writing novel.

C.W. ▸ Okay then, let's get on with the rugby.

V.Y.O. ▸ No, your life first, then rogby, so nothing interrupt game.

C.W. ▸ You've seen me so much, there's nothing to tell. Am I happy? Sure. Once you've spent a fall and a winter and a spring out here, you see that Hastings is really a country town, just as much country as Penobscotport, Maine. City people, summer people, are another crop, like potatoes or Bay scallops, to the locals. I like this place. I hung out my shingle here last fall, I bought the sloop with my first fees, I see Patsy, I go to zoning board meetings and sound off, I write indignant letters to the *Conquest*. Re that sloop, you want to go sailing tomorrow?

V.Y.O. ▸ You bet. Boat is ready now?

C.W. ▸ Yes. Rufe and I have been working on her all summer. She was in sad shape, I bought her for nothing, but now *Pro Bono* is a proud ship. I keep her at the marina, by the way, not the yacht club. We'll all go sailing, the two of us and Patsy and Masha.

V.Y.O. ▸ They are well?

C.W. ▸ Very. They've got a truly synergetic relationship.

V.Y.O. ▸ Tell me about your work, Clive.

C.W. ▸ I take only public interest cases. Environment mostly—it's a litigious matter out here—and I've done some work for the Shinnecock Indians, and your closing, an exception. This house is beautiful, Vlady.

V.Y.O. ▸ It is dream. Of course, J. Livingston has longer commute to ocean. And I have bad conscience about money.

C.W. ▸ Don't. Good thing I arrived at the St. Regis when I did. If you'd walked out and refused the check, we'd have been in deep trouble. You were already committed to a point where they could have sued.

V.Y.O. ▸ I know. You yexplain all this that night.

C.W. ▸ You had no choice. And at least you had the satisfaction of denouncing "official culture," Soviet and American, in your acceptance speech.

V.Y.O. ▸ Nobody onderstand speech because of my oxsent.

C.W. ▸ I did. It was a ringing denunciation. You can stand proud.

V.Y.O. ▸ I am onwitting agent of CIA and KGB.

C.W. ▸ Explain that.

V.Y.O. ▸ CIA is having fifteen thousand copies of *Oblomoviad* printed, Rossian text only, on hand presses, with typographical yerrors on bad-quality paper, to simulate Moscow *samizdat* printing. They distribute in Moscow, Leningrad, the universities. Then they get real Rossian *samizdat* critics—those swine don't care who pays them—to write critiques saying how Ouspenskiy has lyrically and satirically denounced dialectical materialism of socialist state in his hymns to leisure. Psych-war.

C.W. ▸ And we taxpayers foot the bill? I can't believe it. How does KGB come into it?

V.Y.O. ▸ They pay their own *samizdat* critics, who are perhaps same ones, to write how Ouspenskiy has cleverly duped his American hosts by yexposing capitalist and consumerist materialism, while underlining degeneracy of—

C.W. ▸ I get it. You want to sue?

V.Y.O. ▸ No, Clive. You can't fight international psych-war rocket. Rogger now?

C.W. ▸ One more thing. That little barn of yours. Are you interested in renting it?

V.Y.O. ▸ That barn is wreck.

C.W. ▸ I could fix it up, I've learned a lot from Rufe. You charge me a nominal rent, we'll live in the barn, and when we leave, you'll have a guesthouse.

V.Y.O. ▸ We? Patsy has moved in with you?

C.W. ▸ Vlady, I've finally convinced her family that a high Episcopalian is nearly as incense-prone as a Roman Catholic.

V.Y.O. ▸ More wedding bells! Fabulous news, Clive. Naturally you can have barn, and for song.

C.W. ▸ Thanks. Vlady, who'd have thought a year ago that you'd end up a landlord with me as tenant? You're the biggest success story of us all.

V.Y.O. ▸ I am not in competition. I never was.

C.W. ▸ All the more awesome ... I'm really a long way from the old young upwardly mobile now. Country lawyer, engaged to country schoolteacher, renting a ramshackle barn. What would Leila Edgway say?

V.Y.O. ▸ Do you yever see those Yedgways?

C.W. ▸ Hell, no. Edgway and Gross are petitioning the court to have me removed as trustee of Wetlands, but no way they'll succeed, given the fact that Patsy's aunt's sister-in-law is married to the County Supervisor. I've had threatening calls; I tape them; they print them in the *Conquest*. Lou won't dare touch me. I hear he's looking for a new lawyer. I also hear that Schulzie has been scoping out possible casino sites in the Bear Mountain State Park area; easier drive, closer to the city. So the deer and the osprey and the great blue heron still reign supreme at Indian Marsh. Speaking of Edgways, I saw Judy Jessup on Main Street the other day and she asked me for their address.

V.Y.O. ▸ Whatever for?

C.W. ▸ Our famous dinner gave Earl and Judy a taste of high living. They're going to ask Nick Edgway to put them up for the Spindrift.

V.Y.O. ▸ Clive, it is not fonny. They will be hurt when clob turns them down.

C.W. ▸ Then we sue the club for discrimination against locals. Pro bono, class suit. I'll do it for nothing.

V.Y.O. ▸ I love these Jessups. I love Bonackers.

C.W. ▸ Are you and I becoming Bonackers, Vlady?

V.Y.O. ▸ I am hoppy to become Bonacker. If only I can convince Cathy to become same. I miss.

C.W. ▸ I know. I miss Moira.

V.Y.O. ▸ Rilly?

C.W. ▸ I miss—I miss those career objectives we shared. People talk about "nonmonetary satisfactions." I've got those—public interest law, running, sloop, dogs, Patsy. Yet somehow it's easier to count your blessings in dollars and cents.

V.Y.O. ▸ You are incorrigible. Young opwardly-impelled rural person. A Yurp.

C.W. ▸ A Yurp. Maybe you can explain that to Patsy.

V.Y.O. ▸ Can I? Patsy, alone among you all, is mysterious to me.

C.W. ▸ Patsy, woman of mystery?

V.Y.O. ▸ Mysterious because strong. She lives by certain certainties.

C.W. ▸ Yes. And I can never be certain what those certain certainties are.

V.Y.O. ▸ You are from Penobscotport, I from Novosibirsk. That is boonies, no? But we left, we lived in cities, certainty left us. Patsy has never left. Patsy is not "person," she is woman. Patsy knows what she wants. And gets it.

C.W. ▸ Are you referring to me?

V.Y.O. ▸ I talk of Patsy. Patsy and pursuit of hoppiness. One thing about Patsy, she is not mobile.

C.W. ▸ No way. I even had trouble selling her on the concept "wedding trip." Guess where we're going, Vlady? Wilf has found us a cut-rate flight to Vancouver. I want to talk to my brother Henry, the apple picker. Maybe Henry can make sense out of what's happened to me.

V.Y.O. ▸ Does anything make sense? Make sense of that rogger game for me, Clive.

C.W. ▸ Stu's tape is good; he's got it right. From the pure rugger angle, I have nothing to add. The one thing nobody described was our last minute of play.

V.Y.O. ▸ You tell me.

C.W. ▸ After my try and Stu's kick, it's 10-6, Sodas, two minutes left, blowing hard, branches falling, heavy rain, and the ten thousand dollars slipping away from us second by second. With one minute and four seconds to play, I elect to kick for touch and call time-out. I call time-out because I have just seen a dusty Dodge hatchback pull into the driveway and a little old lady step out of it with a big straw basket on her arm. I sprint over to her and I say, "Mrs. Slocum! We didn't expect you for another week." She says, "I know, Mr. Wheelwright, and thank you for the check. Don't worry, I'm going to stay with my nephew. I just stopped by to drop off these." She pulls some bulbs out of her basket. "I dug these up in Colorado," she says. "Would you mind potting them for me?" I take the bulbs and say, "Glad to, Mrs. Slocum," and I politely—hopefully—open the car door for her and ask if there's anything more I can do. She says, "Nothing, thank you, don't let me keep you, I see you're playing a game. Oh, I might just go take a peek at my Montauk daisies." She starts toward the lawn, then stops and says, "My shoes, they're in the car. Oh my goody, does it matter if I get my feet wet?" and trots off to view her daisies, still with that basket on her arm. Moira sees her coming and says in a choked voice, "Mrs. Slocum—welcome home."

V.Y.O. ▶ I remember. We were all fricked out by that.

C.W. ▶ So there's Lavinia Slocum marching along the touchline with Co-captain Wheelwright tagging behind her, the wind howling, the rain pelting down. She says "Chilly!" and hugs her arms, so I pick up Earl's new, unworn FIGHTIN' SLOKES jersey and put it around her shoulders. She sets down her basket and knots the sleeves around her neck and thanks me and suddenly asks, "What's happened to my little copper beech?" I say something stupid, that it died of copper beech blight, and tell her we've replaced it and point to the new copper beech sitting in its burlap near the house. Vlady, did that minute of time-out seem to you the longest minute in history?

V.Y.O. ▶ It did. I am sure that Yearl, our timekeeper, was stretching it out, so you could get back in game.

C.W. ▶ He couldn't stretch it any longer. Breitschwanz blows his whistle; play resumes with a line-out. Mrs. Slocum and I are standing just off the playing field, and I know I've got to stay with her to keep her from poking her nose into the house and seeing the furniture, but it's killing me. Ten thousand dollars, a minute left, the teams locked in a vicious scrum, and she says, "That new copper beech looks sturdier. Let's go over and take a look." So she steps across the touchline to pick up her basket, which is sitting on the ground just inside the field of play—one of those big, sloppy straw baskets with two rope handles, they make them in places like Mexico, it's just flopping there, yawning open—and at that moment the ball bounds out of the scrum, takes a crazy high bounce and drops toward the basket.

V.Y.O. ▶ Tell me how your mind worked then, Clive. As sociologue, I am foscinated by legal mind.

C.W. ▶ My mind was blowing fuses. I thought—I thought of the rules, I thought of how that glowing coal fell into the fireworks box—and I yelled to Breitschwanz, "Slocum for Wheelwright!" and he nodded to acknowledge, just as the ball settled into the basket. It was still in sight—top of the ball poking out of the top of the basket—but Mrs. Slocum just plain didn't notice, she was looking at the copper beech and saying, "I'm mad about that new little tree." So she picked up her basket, ball and all, and trotted off toward the sapling, which was sitting just the other side of the Slokes' goal line. I walked along beside her, taking care to stay *off* the pitch myself and trying to get her to step up the pace. Meanwhile all of you, the Slokes, the Sodas, are running around wildly, looking for the ball—not unusual in rugby. The ball is still perfectly visible, sticking out of the basket. Finally Patsy sees it and realizes Mrs. Slocum is about to score. She races toward her, and Moira, who has also caught on, tries to get in her way, but Patsy moves beautifully, slips by Moira and tackles our landlady from behind, as gently as she can. She even says, "Excuse me, Mrs. Slocum." The rest you remember. Mrs. Slocum has bitten the dust just behind the goal line, and the ball and a few leftover bulbs have spilled out of her basket, so she reaches out to the side for the bulbs—pure reflex, I guess—and happens to touch the ball, touches it *down*—it's a try! Stu begins yelling, "Ten-all! I convert, and it's ten thousand bucks!"

V.Y.O. ► And then all hell broke loose.

C.W. ► It certainly did. But we were right—we had won. Do you want me to go on?

V.Y.O. ► No, thank you, Clive. It is, as they say, all over bot shouting. I can describe shouting.

C.W. ► Good. Vlady, can you use a puppy from Masha's new litter?

V.Y.O. ► Thank you, bot I have decided to buy block Lob, to go with my new pickop. I shall call him Zahar.

Ouspenskiy, scourge of the scrum, resumes the narrative. A miracle! We are tied up, we believe in Stu's educated toe, we know we have won. Stu swings his kicking leg, saying, "Hot damn, ten thou!" as Cy and the Sodas besiege Breitschwanz.

"No score!"

"Hidden ball!"

"Call back the play!"

Clive is in the thick of it, shouting louder than any of them. "The ball was visible at all times! I informed the referee of the substitution and stayed off the field, once she went on! She's a bona fide resident—owns the house! Wearing a Sloke jersey! And no shoes!"

Breitschwanz nods his head at every point Clive makes.

"The jersey," Cy cries in his British accent, "was merely on her shoulders! Bloody outrage!"

"*Basket!*" Stubbs screams.

Stu strides through the angry Sodas. "You guys are piss-poor losers. Show me anything in the rules against baskets!"

"No score!" the Sodas roar.

"Fuck off, scumbags." Stu makes a couple of imaginary kicks. "Let me kick it and win."

Wind and rain lash us all. Breitschwanz blows his whistle.

"Your attention, please. I rule that Slocum has scored a try. Slokes ten, Sodas ten. The Slokes will now attempt to convert. Any time left?" He looks at Earl, who shakes his head.

"After the conversion attempt, the game's over. Play ball."

Cy folds his arms. In his best Oxonian, he announces, "We shan't play."

"Then you forfeit!" Clive shouts. "Forfeit the game, forfeit the ten thou!"

"Furthermore, *we shan't pay.*"

The Sodas cheer their captain and follow him off the field toward their cars.

"Fock the Sodas!" a heavily oxsented voice roars. "*Sukhin sin! Yob tvoyu mat'!*"

Leaves and twigs scud across the lawn. The puppies, Masha and Randy snap at the Sodas' heels.

Stu kicks the ball over the crossbar and says "Fucked."

Mort takes a more sanguine view. "I don't know. We only owe ten thou now, not twenty. A moral victory."

"Vlady," Rick says, "tell him he's got shit for brains."

While I relay the message, the Sloke girls,[81] Patsy and Judy Jessup are at the goal line, helping Mrs. Slocum to her feet.

---

[81]Ever true to their gender roles!

"Are you all right, Lavinia?" Judy asks.

"Fine, just a bit shaken. Let me go into the house and sit down."

The girls exchange glances. Mrs. Slocum must at all costs be kept out of the house, which is now Rufe's Repair Shop.

"There's always danger of shock," Patsy says. "I'll drive you over to the hospital, just to be on the safe side."

"Very well. First let me get my Burberry and wellies out of the hall closet."

She starts toward the back steps, but Patsy grasps her firmly by the arm.

"Later."

Before she can protest, Mrs. Slocum is hustled toward the station wagon with P MAGEE on its plates.

Patsy has done well, but there is no cause to rejoice. The reprieve is momentary. Cathy, Dreda, and Moira look at each other, wondering what comes next, shivering in the wind.

22

AEOLUS EX MACHINA: THE COMMUNE DELIVERED AND DISSOLVED

Gluing—Ruing—Twisterooing—Strewing—Hullabalooing

Why continue? The title of this chapter has already told you, reader, that in some miraculous fashion our Y-persons are delivered from their predicament.

I yearn to go straightway to my socio-scientific coda. Yet conscience tells me there are certain Y behavior patterns as yet unexplored that must be presented to the reader before we move on to the feast of sociological exposition and analysis I have promised. Bear with me yet a little.

Your researcher is with his seven specimen Y-persons in the living room of the commune's locus, Historic Slocum House. Stu, Clive, and Ouspenskiy are gluing bits of furniture together with Krazy Glue, Elmer's, whatever we can find. Everything has been unclamped, ready or not, and pasted together again, however unsteadily. Dreda, Cathy, and Moira are vacuuming and laying rugs. Mort and Rick help Rufe move out his workbench and tools.

The craftsman shakes his head as he leaves. "No way to treat good furniture, Clyde."

Outside, the sky is black, the lawn littered with fallen branches.

Cathy, vacuuming near a window, tries to make light of the storm. "The pathetic fallacy, guys. Fall of the House of Sloke. The wind shrieks through the turrets of the ruined castle . . ."

Both Degans are looking at Dreda. She shrugs. "No big deal. Tube says it's just a spinoff of Hurricane Irving, now a hundred miles off Sandy Hook, heading for Nova Scotia."

Patsy rushes in, soaking wet. Stu is so jumpy that he drops a Hepplewhite shard.

"Christ, is the old bitch *here*?"

"Not quite. She's unhurt, unfortunately. The doctor on emergency happened to be her nephew. He'll drive her back to pick up her car as soon as he gets off duty; that's in about ten minutes." Patsy wrings out her hair. "She says she'll stop in to get her foul-weather gear and 'to say hello to the house.' This place looks awful."

"It does?" Clive has been deluding himself into thinking the reglued furniture looks presentable.

"This screen—it wouldn't fool a blind person." Patsy taps the coromandel.

"Don't!" we all cry.

Too late. The screen has collapsed. Moira sinks into a Hepplewhite.

"It's hopeless. There's no way out."

The chair falls apart, leaving her on the floor. Stu pounds his fist on the mantel. A freshly reglued chunk of gilt drops from Cap'n Caleb's frame. "There's Rufe's bill, plus whatever Pruneface sues us for. Nothing to do now but spread our cheeks."

Suddenly an enormous limb crashes down from a butternut just outside the living room window, cracking a couple of panes. Dreda begins to shriek.

"Irving be praised!" She slaps and punches Mort and Rick. "I *won!* My computer was right! Irving is *here!* A real twisteroo!" She dances wildly around the room. "I collect on my hurricane insurance!"

Clive, Patsy, Stu, Moira, and Cathy are incredulous. Ouspenskiy is baffled, coming as he does from a land where the concept of insurance as speculation is unknown. The Degans, too, are confused: should they be on the side of the underwriters?

"Elowyn's storm pictures! I computed and I won! Bet against the insurance industry and *won!* Ask Rick and Mort! We're insured, house and contents, against wind and water damage up to a hundred K's!"

Another branch crashes against another window; another pane breaks.

"Whooo-eee!" Stu bellows. "Storm damage!" He pulls the entire window frame into the room. Wind and rain blast through the house.

Moira picks up a reglued Hepplewhite. "Order-oriented? *Therapeutic!*" She hurls the chair to the floor.

Yelling like banshees, we all begin strewing furniture about, to unglue it. It is, the sociologue Ouspenskiy reflects, a release from, a revenge upon, the tyranny of material things.

Everybody kisses Dreda. Ouspenskiy kisses Cathy, Stu kisses Moira, Clive kisses Patsy—and Mort, in a fit of passion, kisses brother Rick, who slaps him. When Masha, her pups, and the seagull come piling through the wrecked window to get out of the storm, we kiss them too.

For the last time in our tenancy, the lights wink out. Dreda picks up the telephone. Miraculously, it is still on line.

"Hello, Cy? . . . My, my, still mad?" She waits, smiling, as a spate of abuse pours from the instrument. "That's too bad, Cy. We were going to invite you over for an orgy."

The rain pours in, the hurricane howls, the Slokes yowl for joy. But beneath the rejoicing, the poet senses sadness. The summer commune is no more. Despite the extra week of rental, all but Cathy and Ouspenskiy must be back at work tomorrow, and there is little chance that any of them will come out for a final weekend in the battered house.

For some, there is consolation. The Long Haul to the city in the aftermath of the hurricane, with fallen trees, downed wires, flooded roads, and Labor Day traffic, promises to be a truly awesome experience.

CONCLUSION

Thus we conclude our study.

Where, the reader will ask, are the promised chapters of sociological exposition? I find myself unable to write them. I have grown too close to my seven young upwardly mobile professionals to view them with scientific detachment. I love them.

Ergo, study concluded.

Some may protest that this work is not a study at all, but a narrative. They are wrong. It is the Genesis, the Iliad, of Ouspenskiyan sociology.

The conventional sociologue interviews selected persons and makes notes or tapes of their stories. Although these notes and tapes may later be made into something called a sociological study, the basis is story. However accurate the person interviewed may try to be, what he tells you is not fact, but fact interpreted, hence story. What your father told you about his war or his courtship is clearly story. So is the bill your plumber sends you. So is your income tax return.

A fact is something that indisputably occurred. An eclipse of the moon is fact. The fact of that eclipse as recounted by Mount Wilson's human and electronic watchers of the sky is story. The same eclipse interpreted by a girl sailing with a young man on a sea now moonlit, now black, is another story.

The academic sociologue attempts to turn story into study, and V.Y. Ouspenskiy turns study into story.

But what if there were no study, no notes, no tapes, no file cards? What if the Y-persons Ouspenskiy says he interviewed never existed? What if Ouspenskiy, a known poet, had simply imagined them? What if no Y-person had ever existed? What if there were no Ouspenskiy? What if one or two or even eight Y-persons did indeed exist and Ouspenskiy were the name behind which one of them hides? What if he were the father of one or two or eight of them? What if *she* were their mother? Or a great-grandparent of one of them, writing this study or story as science fiction in 1890? Or the grandchild of one or two of them, writing a historical romance in the middle of the twenty-first century? What if groupers were fish, and only fish? What then?

Would that make it any less true?

V. Y. O.
Oblomovka
Hastings, Long Island